LEGEND OF THE SPIDER-PRINCE

Book One

REBEL

by

MARGO ANDER

Meander
Creek
Books

Meander
Creek
Books

Revised Edition: September 2014

ISBN: 0615835988
ISBN-13: 978-0-615-83598-3

This is a work of fiction. Names, characters, places, and incidents either are the product of the author's imagination or are used fictitiously, and any resemblance to actual persons, living or dead, business establishments, events, or locales is entirely coincidental.

The author does not have any control over—and does not assume any responsibility for—third-party web sites or their content.

DEDICATION

For my husband, Bill, who keeps his priorities straight and his feet on the ground—you're right, I don't know what I'd do without you. Thank you for your daily love and support.

CONTENTS

ACKNOWLEDGMENTS

Generous gifts of time and thoughtful feedback helped improve this book.

My appreciation to the critters at www.critique.org, especially to Felicia Cash, Shellie DuPlain, Alex Lee, Aaron Micheaux, Reid Minnich, the late Peter Morgan, John Pratt, Phil Quayle, Will Rice, John Rodrigues, Tom Tinney, Joe Walker, and Ralph Weimer.

My thanks also to Carolyn Chambers Clark, Ann Dowell, Ravi Mehta, Debi O'Neille, T. E. Shepherd, and Crystal Von Lindenberg, as well as thanks to the more incognito critters at www.critiquecircle.com.

A special thanks to Pamela Milstein (Mom) and Nanette Sasak (sister) for their help with those painful, early drafts, and to my daughters Stephanie and Catharine, for their supportive, helpful suggestions, and willingness to let me pick their brains on a moment's notice.

And, as promised back in May 2011, a BIG thank-you to Michael-Stanley Ridgley, Wyl's very first fan.

Part One

CHAPTER 1

BAD DREAMS

First Day of the Moon of Storms, 113 G.E.
(113 years after the founding of the Gerisari Empire)
Barony of Milkdales
Country of Trascolm

He dreamed of monsters.

He had nightmares, and this one was the worst of them. He couldn't breathe, and his heart wouldn't beat, and as always, it was the same monster, a hulking, dark figure—an indescribable shape emerging from the ground, trying to drag the life out of him as it pulled itself up.

It made closing his eyes hardly worth the effort.

"*Psst*, Wyl!" Lanney's familiar voice with its guttural Dremn accent stood out from the murmur of Tras voices behind them and cut through his fear. "Wyl! Pull yourself together—I think our vanguard's run into trouble."

Wyl twitched awake and jerked upright on his warhorse. He'd gone to sleep with his arms wrapped around him, and when he wrenched them free, his hands came away holding both his throwing knives. His eyes darted around, trying to see everything at once, looking for danger.

Firebrand snorted and danced sideways under him.

He saw nothing except thick, billowing fog with two blurred, familiar figures in it just ahead of him. From behind him came the fog-

1

muffled sounds of the five hundred mounted men of the rebel men-ney. The rebels were twenty-five warbands strong, not counting Calderek's, deployed as their vanguard, or the new warband being used as scouts.

Wyl focused his attention on the warlike pair riding several horse-lengths in front of him on the narrow road undulating through the for-ested dale.

The rebel leader and would-be royenne of Trascolm, Helgurdda, rode with her warleader uncle, Eirgei, beside her. They rode tall, Geri-sari-bred horses, and they had their heads together as they rode. Though Helgurdda and Eirgei spoke in a low murmur, Wyl could hear their words despite the squeak of leather, the clop of hoofs, and the tinkling rustle of bronze mail—during the campaign season, his keen ears made him even more useful as a spy than as one of Helgurdda's bodyguards.

The two leaders discussed what arrangement should be made in the layout of their winter camp to minimize self-inflicted casualties—squabbling warbands of former brigands made up two-thirds of the rebel menney, and they were happy to fight each other if there were no Evroza available.

Whatever had gotten Lanney's attention, the two leaders hadn't no-ticed it.

But Lanney was right—something *was* wrong. Every hair on Wyl's body had risen to stand on end. It had to be magery—but he'd never felt it like this, so strong it made his skin crawl. No wonder, now, that he'd had that awful dream.

Yet, nothing else seemed amiss.

"Easy," Lanney said. "We're good here. I just thought I heard something." The Dremn mercenary riding beside him sat alert, but supple and relaxed in her saddle—not tense from imminent danger. Like their leaders, she wore fine, jegurit-bronze mail in its unpolished brown patina and a red rebel surcoat over it. She was armed with a sa-bre at her shoulder and knives at the small of her back. Little beads of moisture from the fog clung to her short, light brown hair.

Wyl's breath came back, fast and panting, his heart racing double-time, his head spinning with confusion. He seemed to be in the waking world—sometimes, he couldn't be sure. He did his best to look calm, but it took several tries to sheathe his knives under the bronze and leather bracers he wore around his forearms, which protruded from the ragged and stained sleeves of his gray undertunic.

"And anyway," Lanney said, "you were having a bad dream."

So much for hoping the older bodyguard hadn't noticed. Not much got past Wyl's partner.

Awake, Wyl stayed in control of himself and his emotions the way Eirgei had trained him, but nothing worked against his night-terrors when he slept. What else could he expect, given the life he led, the things he did? For what was at stake—the success of Helgurdda's rebellion, even survival itself—he reckoned mere dreams a small price.

He coughed and swiped back his unfortunate hair, a rare blue-black and too striking to go unnoticed even among the black-haired Folk. His hands shook as he rubbed the moisture out of his eyes and off his cheeks.

He'd had that recurring nightmare for as long as he could remember. He always awakened scared spitless, feeling crushed by the weight of something even worse than the fear he'd learned to live with every day, thanks to the hedge-gotten, motherless scoundrels whose company he kept.

That nightmare still echoed in him. His heart pounded hard, but at least he could breathe now. He picked up his slack reins from where he'd looped them over the dirty, dun-colored cloak tied to his saddlebow.

"Are you all right?" Lanney asked.

"Yeah, I'm all right! Do you see me bleeding?" He didn't mean to snap, but sometimes Lanney acted more like *his* bodyguard than Helgurdda's. "I don't need mothering, Lanney."

Lanney rolled her eyes and made an annoyed sound. "Of course, you do, Wyl. A boy your age needs a mother, and if I'm supposed to be your foster-mother, I'm within my rights."

"I'm not a *child*, Lanney, so don't try to treat me like one!" He put a dangerous edge on his words.

"No, you're not." She shook her shaggy head. "More's the pity. What you are is unnatural, boy."

It always annoyed him when she said stuff like that. "It's a good thing. Assassins may get past you, but they don't get past me." He hoped that jab struck home, paying her back for that *unnatural* crack. He took his duty seriously, that was all. There was nothing unnatural about it.

"That was only one of them, *boy*," she growled.

"The Evroza only need one to get past us."

She frowned, but wasn't put off by him bringing up what had happened during the night. "I didn't know you were still having those nightmares even in the daytime. I don't remember them being this bad before you went to Myymor."

"Damn it, Lanney, I'm fine! It's just a dream." This time, he didn't regret the snarl, not with Helgurdda and Eirgei riding within earshot ahead of them. "You wake me for a reason?"

"I was trying to throw you out of that dream of yours before you started screaming," she said, sarcasm in her voice.

"I never!"

She ignored him. "I thought I heard something, but now, I'm not so sure. I don't want to give a false alarm." Though she also rode a tall Gerisari horse, she stood in her stirrups to peer ahead.

Wyl looked into the mist-filled woods on either side of the deeply-rutted road, his senses straining. He didn't know what had caught her attention, but he trusted Lanney, trusted her instincts.

It was her second thoughts he didn't trust.

From some distance to his right, there came a muted, continuous roar. It meant they'd just passed the bend where the road into the northern dales turned west and began its descent to follow the course of the Tor River. The river was less than a quarter-league away, on the other side of the dense wall of trees and brambles lining the road. The broad, impassable Tor crashed through the jagged, jumbled teeth of rock broken off from the Icepeak Mountains that abruptly rose from the other side of the river, forming the border between Trascolm and Dremnar.

Eirgei had driven them hard halfway across the barony of Milkdales to reach this winter sanctuary. Wyl and Lanney, and Helgurdda's personal guard—made up of her warband and Eirgei's—rode in a narrow column behind their leaders, one file in each rut of the road. They had kept pace easily, but the less well-mounted minions among the other warbands straggled behind. With the campaign season over and this part of the barony of Milkdales solidly behind the rebellion, most of the warlords weren't troubling to keep their warbands in proper order.

Wyl caught a whiff of something fearsome, a smell that put him in mind of the foul breeze off a ripening battlefield. *Carrion and death—* that was the smell laced through the fog.

It was the smell from his nightmare.

"Do you smell that?" Had his monster followed him back into the waking world?

"Smell what? I don't smell anything." Lanney cocked her ears towards her side of the forest.

There had to be a connection between the fog, that smell, and that unnerving pressure from magery. Just recognizing that stink from his nightmare put him into a cold sweat. Had he finally lost his grip on the real world?

He closed his eyes and concentrated on feeling the magery pressing against his skin. He was sure that was what he felt, Evroza magery, the gathering of *yyther* that came just before a terrible blast. The pressure seemed to be coming from two different directions, though—one from ahead, where the vanguard ought to be, and the other from the southwest. The western pressure felt stronger, closer, but the magery from the southwest...something about it made his guts twist.

The gut-twisting wasn't new. To his secret shame, he had sensitive guts, though he'd never actually had to puke *during* a fight. He hoped to outgrow it soon, and until then, he struggled to keep it a secret.

"*Ockh*, Wyl," Lanney said, her Dremn accent growing heavier with frustration. "You listen—what can you hear?"

The lingering bits of his nightmare—a sense of the world unraveling around both him and the darkly-looming presence—wafted away, and Lanney's words brought him fully back into the real world.

But the stink didn't go away with the other leftovers from his nightmare. It clearly came from the southwest.

Rebel wolf howls sounded in the distance to the west.

The Wolf of Milkdales—Eirgei had been a living legend for over thirty years—had earned his name because he disguised his command signals as wolf howls rather than sounding them on horns or drums. The night music had phrases, howls with a meaning, and the sound of those commands being relayed through Helgurdda's menney had an eerie effect on an enemy.

Wyl turned to Lanney. "It's Calderek. You're right, the van's been attacked." His voice trailed off on a troubling thought.

Years ago, when Calderek had deserted from the Evroza menney and declared for Helgurdda's side in the blood-feud, he'd brought most of the Evroza's auxiliary menney with him. The royal clan wouldn't forget or forgive that. The fact that Wyl felt any magic at all meant the Evroza had come in force. Yet, the howls were of warning, not howls for help.

Calderek *should* be howling for help.

"That's strange," Wyl said. "The Evroza have their mages here, but if Calderek's *not* seriously outnumbered in this attack—not enough to be howling for reinforcements—then where are the rest of the Evroza? Royenne Sharei never sends so many mages without her whole menney to back them."

He looked to the southwest and wondered why the Evroza royenne would divide her mages.

"Who said anything about mages?"

"*Ockh!* This ambush is some kind of Evroza trick," he said, distracted.

She cocked her head and looked at him with narrowed eyes. "I think spying's made you too suspicious of everything. You're too young for this kind of life. You shouldn't be here, trying to deal with— *no, don't get your back up!* Just listen to me, boy! This is the last place the Evroza would be. We're on our own ground here. Even if we didn't have a score of scouts out, the locals would have warned us as soon as we arrived. I'm thinking Calderek might have flushed some brigands. If he has, he'll deal with them easily enough."

"It's not brigands," Wyl insisted.

He took a deep breath and let it out, striving to look cool and unflappable. He'd never told this secret, not even to Lanney. He didn't want to be mocked. But magery coming from two directions when it shouldn't be coming from any? Lanney had the right of it—they were supposed to be safe here. He couldn't keep his mouth shut, keep his secret, and let Helgurdda ride into an Evroza trap. "There are mages ahead. Lots of them."

Lanney snorted and gave him a sidelong look. She shook her head. "Nonsense, Wyl. This isn't one of your nightmares."

He glared. She knew nothing about what troubled his sleep—he had sense enough not to talk about it. Bad enough to dream of the Evroza, but if anyone knew the whole of his dreams, they'd think he'd cracked, that he *was* too young to hold up under the strain of what he did. Monsters and spiders—they'd be sure he'd gone mad.

"Mages wouldn't be here unless the Evroza were here in force," she said, "which they aren't. We'd know it if they were. And whenever they use mages, the mages always attack first, before we engage. Even with the vanguard a quarter-league away, we'd still hear the crash and boom of their magery. Whatever it was I heard, it wasn't that. There's nothing to worry about."

"Trust me, Lanney! There *are* mages here. I don't know why they haven't attacked us yet."

"How would *you* know?"

He swallowed and let the words rush out. "I—I can *feel* them! I can feel magery. I always know if there are mages nearby or if magic is being used. You have to believe me—you have to get Eirgei to believe me before it's too late!"

"Oh, no!" She gave him a fierce look. "I'm not telling Eirgei that the Evroza are ambushing our vanguard because *you* think you can *feel* magic. You know his views about arcane powers—I'll let you imagine his reaction if you tell him that. Who's ever heard of such a thing?" She narrowed her Folk-dark eyes at him in genuine concern. "Helgurdda is right—go somewhere safe and finish growing up."

"But something's wrong—and whatever it is, we're riding right into it!"

"I said, I thought I heard something. There's a big difference between that and claiming that we're about to run into the entire Evroza menney, along with all their mages, smack in the middle of the northern dales—and without anyone knowing they're here or giving Eirgei warning!"

"Fine. Don't believe me. I'll go see what's happening before we're caught up in it." He started to gather his reins. "Just cover for me if Eirgei notices me missing."

Lanney grabbed Firebrand's left rein and held on. "I'm not going to do that. He's put you on a short tether, remember? You're staying with me. The last time you went looking for trouble—"

"—There *was* trouble," he retorted. "And I handled it! Helgurdda wouldn't still be alive, if I hadn't. I was right then, and I'm right now!"

Lanney scowled and shook her head. Her hair—cropped to jaw-length, the way full-blooded Folk wore theirs—swung against her cheeks. "I was mistaken. It was my imagination. Forget I said anything. Go back to sleep—you're just overtired. There's nothing out there."

"Lanney!" The whine in his voice made him wince. What other reaction could he expect, revealing that he could feel magic?

At least she hadn't laughed at him.

"If there's anything out there, it's just brigands and no challenge for Calderek and his warband," she said.

"I'm *not* overreacting—and Calderek's *not* up against brigands. We need to warn Eirgei that Royenne Sharei's here with the whole Evroza menney, including her mages."

She gave him a hard, assessing look.

He gave her a hard look back and wished he was wrong. "I'm not wrong."

"Sorry, Wyl," Lanney said. "I can't do it. If the Evroza were out there, the scouts wouldn't miss them. Let the scouts do their work. Let it go."

She turned her head away to peer again at the woods beside her.

All Wyl could do now was be ready for when the trouble came.

He groped under his *byrnney's* high leather collar and tugged out a thong with a bit of wax tablet dangling from it. It was as long as his palm and a third as wide, with the broken edges shaved and ground smooth. A hole was bored at one end wide enough for a doubled thong to slide through to hold it flat against his skin. He slid out the narrow throwing knife from under his right bracer to use as a stylus.

Despite his best efforts over the years, he still had only two spitcraft charms that worked, and of the two, only *luck* still worked if he moved.

He hoped *luck* would be enough.

He concentrated hard as he held the broken bit of tablet in his palm and scratched the word into wax that had been softened by the heat of his skin. He cupped the charm in his leather-gauntleted hand and breathed on it, repeating the word under his breath. He did his best to concentrate, but his body didn't start tingling with magic.

Firebrand swiveled one ear back towards him, but she had grown accustomed to his spitcraft experiments. If he got the charm to take hold, the tingle wouldn't alarm her.

He glanced up.

Lanney was staring at him with scowling suspicion.

He quickly closed his fist around the charm.

"*Ockh*, Wyl! Are you trying to do spitcraft?" Lanney let out her breath in an exasperated sigh. "I wish I'd never told you my grand-mother's Folk tales. Dabbling in spitcraft!" She rolled her eyes. "I'm embarrassed to be riding next to you. First, you think you can feel magic, and then you're playing at spitcraft. One moment, you want me to take you seriously, and the next, here you are with this nonsense. Even among the Folk, only *younglings* play pretend with spitcraft."

She was just trying to provoke him, but he couldn't help himself. "I'm not a youngling!"

"Then don't act like you're eight, Wyl. You'll get the wrong kind of attention from Eirgei if he catches you. You know how he feels about real magic, so I'll let you imagine his reaction if he finds out you're playing at make-believe magic. Trust me on this, spitcraft is just coincidence at work. It's not real. Those Folk tales I told you when you were a youngling were just stories."

He set his jaw, and as an answer, dropped the charm back under his collar. "I don't *play!* I'm not a *youngling*, and I'd never make a *game* of anything to do with the Evroza or their mages."

Lanney snorted and went back to scanning the roadside, shaking her head.

He tried to feel warmth from the charm resting at the base of his throat, but he was angry and couldn't get his focus back.

No big loss—there wouldn't have been much *luck* in this charm— he'd obviously botched it, or Lanney wouldn't have caught him making it.

Alright, so, maybe his spitcraft wasn't reliable, especially not as a charm carved into wax. But better a flawed wax charm than nothing at all when they were up against Evroza magery.

"Only a fool fights magery with a sabre," he muttered.

Lanney sighed. "*Heh*, better with a sabre than with superstition. A mage is defenseless against a blade."

Though it was Lanney who had told him all those Folk tales, she was a heretic. She'd given up her mother's people's beliefs after they'd cast her out, when she'd become a hired minion with no birth clan, a mercenary. The only goddess she worshipped was on one side of a de-narrei. Helgurdda's menney was her clan now, just like it was Wyl's.

So, if a *luck* charm worked, it worked; if it didn't, well, there was a reason even hill-Folk called it spitcraft, and why Wyl did his best to hide his spitcrafting from the others.

He looked past Lanney, searching the woods from the west to the southwest for something out of place, something about the Evroza or their mages, anything that might persuade Eirgei to believe his warning even if Lanney didn't.

But he saw nothing except fog and the vague shapes of weedy brush and leafless, fire-scarred trees. Close to the road on either side of him, the skeletal limbs of those trees hung down eerily through the whiteness—like the gibbets awaiting them if Evroza clan had its way.

Wyl had a horror of wasting away in one, hanging from the Traitors' Wall at Crossroads Keep. Just the thought made him shudder. He averted his gaze.

"We're in the middle of the northern dales, leagues and leagues from the nearest Evroza stronghold," Lanney said.

"I thought we were letting it go."

"Don't get snotty with me, boy. I don't know why Eirgei keeps you on bodyguard duty in the first place—it's not like you ever stay where you belong."

"I belong where I'm needed, and so long as we have brigands doing our scouting, that's where I need to be. Helgurdda will still have you, but those scouts can't be trusted once out of our sight. I don't know why Eirgei won't let me keep an eye on them. Does he *want* to be surprised by the Evroza?"

"If he is, the Evroza will regret it—they don't have a warleader who can match him, especially now that you say their new one's little more than a youth."

"Don't underestimate Lord Goffray," Wyl said, with some irritation. "You wouldn't dismiss me because of *my* age, so don't you make that mistake with someone almost twice my age."

"*Heh*, you're a special case, boy. But special case or not, Eirgei doesn't want another scout. Two bodyguards for Helgurdda—you and me. That's what he wants. He doesn't need more outriders. Those new brigands he recruited are locals who know the lay of the land here."

"So do I! I've hunted everywhere in these dales for the last four winters. I know them as well as they do—better! The only reason *they* joined us is because they want to live off us for the winter. You know they can't be trusted, and I wouldn't be surprised if they're still robbing when they're supposed to be scouting. If they were any good as scouts, they'd have already warned Eirgei, even if it *were* only a brigand ambush—which it's not."

"You and your brigands," Lanney scowled at him, then shook her head. "Your hatred of them clouds your judgment. We need them; they're well-over half our menney."

"*They're foresworn hellspawn!* The only thing we can count on from them is to break and run at the worst possible moment. They never do what they're supposed to be doing." He bristled as she laughed; it was deliberate, because she knew how he hated laughter.

"You're one to talk. You obey orders as well as they do," Lanney said.

"That's not true! It's just that sometimes I can't, sometimes there's too much at stake. Name *one* time when I've been wrong! Eirgei *wants* warlords who show initiative."

"Well, you're not one of his warlords. Your job is to keep Helgurdda safe, so just mind what you're supposed to be doing. Right now, you're supposed to be getting some sleep. You had a busy night."

"I *am* trying to keep her safe," he said, from between clenched teeth. He took a breath and tried to sound more reasonable. "There are other ways to keep her alive, better ways than just riding along with her as a bodyguard or lurking in trees in the dark."

Just then, Eirgei straightened, peered ahead, and turned in his saddle to take in his menney strung out along the narrow road rising and falling with the wooded hills. He was just a bit taller than his tall niece, Helgurdda, with a whipcord build, amber eyes capable of boring holes through grown men, gray-streaked brown hair, and a long Tras moustache that fluttered past his jaw. A surprising number of cocky fools thought the gray meant age had undermined his prowess and tried to replace him at Helgurdda's side as her Right Hand; he dueled and killed over-ambitious warlords on a regular basis.

Eirgei turned his horse and howled a command to halt the rebel column.

When Wyl saw the warleader's expression, he grimaced.

Eirgei had to hear the other howls now, but for once, his fabled instincts weren't raising their own alarm. Quite the opposite, by that look on Eirgei's face.

Well, *someone* was going to be taught a lesson here, but this time Wyl didn't think Eirgei was going to be the teacher.

In obedience to the howled command, Wyl drew rein beside Lanney, and the rest of Helgurdda's guardsmen halted as well. Farther back, the warlords of the warbands in the main body of Helgurdda's menney echoed the howls, passing the order back through the fog before halting.

In the momentary quiet around him, Wyl could now pick out distant shouts, but he couldn't quite make out any words. The ringing sound of metal on metal made the road ahead sound like a smith's shop—except nobody died in smiths' shops.

In front of him, Helgurdda and Eirgei took up their shields. Too late now to warn them—Eirgei had already taken the bait. Wyl knew better than to argue Eirgei's orders, especially in front of the whole menney.

Eirgei howled again.

Wyl couldn't hear anything more of the distant ambush. The jingle-jangle of bronze mail links, as Helgurdda's guardsmen behind him responded to Eirgei's howled command, drowned out the other sounds. A few of them joked as they took up their shields and prepared to fight.

The rest of Helgurdda's menney simply prepared to wait. Most of those minions were still too raw to practice advanced tactics that relied on timing.

Given the terrain and the belief that the attackers were nothing more than brigands, Eirgei would want the guard to practice his pincers maneuver.

Wyl suppressed a shiver. He pulled up the twist of rag from where it hung around his neck outside his *byrnney* and used it to hold back some of the hair out of his eyes. He unhooked the Folk helm from behind his saddle. It was made from part of the skull of an aurox, the monstrous, wild forest cattle that Folk hunted as a test of manhood. He had brought down that aurox with an arrow in its eye when he was only ten years old. The thick bone from the top of its skull was proof against anything short of a fine, jegurit-bronze battleaxe. He crammed it onto his head over the twist of rag that also happened to improve the helm's fit. He tied the helm under his chin as Firebrand raised her head and pricked her ears.

Eirgei howled another command.

Wyl was right. It was pincers.

The narrow column of Helgurdda's guard promptly split. Eirgei's warband, the half of her guard riding in the right-side rut in the road, followed Eirgei.

Wyl didn't go with them; he stayed in his bodyguard's position behind Helgurdda at her right flank.

Her own warband, which had been riding in the left rut behind Lanney, slipped into the bare woods on the side of the road. Helgurdda followed them, and he and Lanney followed her.

As simply as that, they were committed to a counterattack—but everyone, even Lanney, thought it was just against brigands, just for practice.

Wyl tensed in nervous anticipation. His guts did their thing, and he tried not to puke.

This deep into their own territory, the rebels depended on the local Folk acting as Eirgei's eyes and ears as much as they did their scouts. Wyl could understand the Evroza getting past the brigand scouts, but not the local sympathizers. How could a major Evroza force be here without *someone* knowing?

It was impossible—but betrayal was not.

Helgurdda's warband moved towards the distant clanging and shouting. They shifted ranks through the fog-shrouded undergrowth, thinner now that they'd left the road, and wove ahead between the trees, taking up their pincers positions, a line of ten guardsmen leading and the other ten behind them to reinforce their line.

With Calderek's stalwart vanguard to act as the anvil, Helgurdda's split guard would pinch the ambushers between them and flatten the attackers against Calderek's warband like twin hammers.

Except, these ambushers were Evrozings, and Eirgei was about to pinch a viper's tail.

Wyl swallowed and nervously flexed his fingers in his bronze-backed gauntlets, smaller versions of those Helgurdda and Eirgei wore.

He wasn't used to this kind of fighting—he was more adept at dropping down on top of an assassin from a tree or sneaking up on one in the dark. He was at a disadvantage in a head-on, toe-to-toe brawl with a fighter who knew his business. He expected fighting on Firebrand would overcome some of those disadvantages—though she was a bit smaller than the average Tras horse, Eirgei had trained her and said she was the best warhorse in Trascolm. On Firebrand, Wyl could hold his own even while sparring against Eirgei—for a while.

He gritted his teeth and kept swallowing. As the youngest of the rebels, he couldn't afford to show weakness.

He had good reason to be afraid—alone of all the rebel minions, he was outfitted in a traditional Folk panoply: his armor was nothing more than a *byrnney*—a half-sleeved, tough, aurox hide tunic overlaid with thick, aurox horn scales. Its only concession to the modern realities of war lay in the high collar stiffened by a few vertical strips of unpolished jegurit-bronze—the modern alloy now used in place of the old jektrar-bronze alloy that struggled to cut through aurox horn. A century ago, before the arrival of Gerisari traders, Wyl's *byrnney* would've been adequate, but not now, with jegurit-bronze weapons plentiful.

"I need a real mail panoply like you and everyone else," he grumbled, not for the first time. The rest of the rebel menney, even the former brigands who made up the majority of it, wore nothing less than sturdy, wholly-bronze mail, no matter that it was in the turquoise-blue patina of unpolished jektrar-bronze, cheaply forged in some obscure Milkdales village. It was still better than a *byrnney*.

"Not going to happen," Lanney said. "Even if we could find some to fit you, you'd probably outgrow it in a moon—you're due for a growth spurt. You've nothing to worry about, so long as you stay in your position. It won't take much to teach these brigands the dales are ours."

"These aren't brigands."

"Then you'll have even less to worry about. Eirgei's right, you know. Between that Folk panoply, your impressive size—" she didn't trouble to hide her amusement, though with her Folk blood, she wasn't much more impressive than he was, "—and your looks, any Evrozing will take you for Folk at first glance, and there shouldn't be time for a second glance to think otherwise, not if you've let one of them get *that* close to Helgurdda. Anyway, you know how the Evroza feel about the Folk. So long as you stay where you belong, at Helgurdda's back and out of the general fighting, that *byrnney's* all the protection you need."

He glowered at her.

The Folk were the original inhabitants of Trascolm, and most Tras harbored an almost superstitious respect for them. They were the favored people of the goddess MiPaatet, distinctively shorter than most Tras and invariably black-haired, dark-eyed, and brown-skinned, with sharp, almost delicate features. The Folk shared Trascolm with the Tras and bowed to the great, landed Tras clans, but they kept to their own customs and ways. They'd discovered the fine art of living in peace, or so people said—Wyl thought it was mostly because the Folk orphaned their violent men, who then took up brigandage and preyed on Tras and Folk alike. Throughout the countries of Trascolm, Dremnar, and Gerisar, the Folk lived humble but protected lives in their own hamlets and villages.

He coughed and disagreed with Lanney. "The Evroza aren't fools. The only kind of Folk they expect to find riding with us are disowned outlaws. All this old-fashioned panoply does is make me look like an easy victory. Any Evrozing fighting his way to Helgurdda will mark me as the weak spot in her defenses and won't hesitate to try to get to her through me!"

"*Ockh*, don't be so worried. You're Eirgei's best pupil. I pity the Evrozing who tries to get past you. You've proven yourself as a good bodyguard, even if there's not much of you to look at."

Few rebels knew him as anything other than Lanney's half-Folk foster-son, who hunted game for Helgurdda's inner circle during the winter. Only Helgurdda's inner circle knew he spied for her during the summer—and none of them knew Wyl helped bodyguard her in the winter; it was Lanney who got credit for his nighttime kills. The fewer people who knew about what he did, the better.

He grimaced at Lanney's backhanded compliment, not nearly so confident about the coming battle. It would take more than a failed *luck* charm to get him through this.

He swallowed.

Eirgei would be mortified if Wyl got himself killed in his first real battle—he'd told everyone Wyl was his best pupil, hoping to spur his new recruits into proving him wrong and mastering the skills he tried to teach them rather than deserting when the training got tough. So far, that tactic had only roused resentment towards Wyl.

Wyl took up his Folk-style shield of aurox hide, boiled and molded over stout wicker, reinforced by a thin, brown, jegurit-bronze rim and boss. Despite those compromises and the constant training, he was still conscious of how the shield weighed down his arm.

Helgurdda's warband threaded between the trees and started to descend on the Evrozings. The fog-dampened leaf litter muffled the sounds of the trotting horses. The fog itself made the faded-red surcoats of the guardsmen ahead of him almost invisible.

In front of him, Helgurdda reached back behind her neck, pulled out a gold hairpin shaped like a flower, and unwound her war-knot. She was a tall woman and fair-haired for a Tras. At thirty-three years old, she was no girl, but she had a trim, warrior's build. She was unscarred and still coolly beautiful, despite the harsh life of an outlaw. With her intense, blue eyes and natural grace, she possessed a charisma worthy of a royenne—or of her determination to be one. No one who'd ever met her was surprised by how staunchly the Traditionalists among the Evroza clan supported her rebellion. There was a kind of purity and a clarity of purpose to her, though those who didn't know her dismissed it, sneering and pointing out that she led far more former brigands than she did noblemen. All that her rebel minions had in common was a desperation to belong to a clan again—and she'd made them into one, though it was an odd sort of clan—all male, except for herself and Lanney.

Her golden hair always held a special fascination for Wyl. He watched her shake it free of its twists and comb it loose with practiced, economical passes of her fingers. The metallic sheen of her long fall of hair was still untouched by gray despite thirteen years of blood-feud and hard living as an outlaw. She wore it braided away from her face, and now it fell loose to billow free behind her like a royal cloak. All she lacked was a royenne's crown.

Wyl disapproved of the display. Her hair was too dramatic. It stood out, even in the chaos of combat. She delighted in using it as a goad for her enemies whenever she could. The sight of it enraged Evrozings, like she dared them to come for her—and she did.

Letting her hair down also meant she didn't expect to do any fighting herself, not against common brigands. She just liked to take every opportunity to defy Royenne Sharei and flaunt her royally-long hair, even if only to impress her followers. It was as much a symbol of her rebellion as her troth-ring.

Whenever Wyl went spying in Myymor, the Evroza's old frontier clanhold, leaving only Lanney as Helgurdda's last line of defense, he always worried that one day too many Evrozings would take up her challenge and successfully carve their way through her guardsmen and Lanney to get to her.

He hoped this wouldn't be that day.

What truly lay ahead was much more than a skirmish. Helgurdda didn't know the Evroza had laid a trap, that she and Eirgei were *not* sweeping down on a paltry warband of half-starved brigands accustomed to terrorizing the local Tras and Folk.

Wyl wished he could offer some explanation for how Royenne Sharei could've brought the entire Evroza menney into the dales without a rebel sympathizer, Tras or Folk, informing Eirgei about it—if this was betrayal, it was on an unbelievable scale.

Over the years, the blood-feud had become like a dance, both sides knowing their part and perfectly in step.

Until today.

For the first time, no matter that the winter snows would begin soon, the Evroza hadn't gone back to Crossroads Keep to lick their wounds, count their dead, and plot for the coming spring. For that, he blamed Lord Goffray, the new Evroza warleader. He was too young, too unpredictable.

And now, it was too late.

Helgurdda showed no sign that she shared Wyl's unspoken concern. Without interference from a properly-working *luck* charm, Wyl could feel the distinctive throb of artisanry—the unique craftsman's magic of Gerisar—against his skin as she unsheathed her Gerisari sabre of golden, brightly-polished jegurit-bronze and let it rest against the well-darned surcoat covering the dull-brown, jegurit-bronze mail visible at her shoulder.

Wyl heard another wolf howl above the din to the north—Eirgei's signal that he was in position. Helgurdda answered with a howl of her own.

Wyl reached over his left shoulder to flick free the wrist strap that kept his sabre sheathed on his back, slid his hand through it, and drew his blade.

His sabre lacked the artisanry that kept Helgurdda's and Lanney's blades unnaturally sharp, but unlike his panoply, there was nothing old-fashioned or rustic about it. The fine, Gerisari-made sabre had been painstakingly hand-picked for him by Eirgei back when he was ten years old. Then, it had been too much sword for him, but now it precisely suited him, its balance perfect, its edge kept meticulously honed into a bright, golden ribbon against the brown patina of its forte.

He hoped he'd live to outgrow it.

CHAPTER 2

EIRGEI STRIKES BACK

Wyl's palms had already started to sweat inside his gauntlets in dread of what was to come. He didn't like fighting, though it was the one constant in his life, a necessary evil. But this would be his first time drawing his sabre in a battle against the Evroza, and only he knew it.

His sabre trembled in his hand, so he copied Helgurdda, resting the blade against his shoulder, and tried to ignore his sick anticipation.

Despite the fog, they rode at a fast trot through the woods towards the sounds of battle on the road. The fog itself felt weird—hot and clammy, like wet smoke.

A faint stench still clung to it, giving him an evil foreboding. His throat tightened against the strength of the magery in the air. Ordinarily, sensing magery was unpleasant enough, but it had never affected him like this before.

The ground sloped abruptly downward. The fog had thinned enough for him to make out the river road below and the shapes of horsemen. Enough red showed for his mind's eye to fill in the details of their distinctive Evroza clan surcoats—shimmering Gerisari silk in brilliant scarlet, with the black outline of the evening rose that gave the clan its name. All he could actually see through the fog were flashes of scarlet and the fainter green of the fancy leather barding protecting their Gerisari horses.

Calderek's deserters were mounted on smaller, native Tras steeds like Firebrand with only their winter coats to protect them. Thanks to

18

the overlay of fog, Wyl couldn't easily distinguish the rebels from the Evrozings—even on a clear day, the rebels' surcoats were outrageously similar to those of the Evroza, except there was no rose device, and their surcoats were of a coarser cloth that quickly faded to a color more pink than red. Calderek's renegades were all wearing riveted, conical helms and mail of jegurit-bronze burnished to the golden sheen favored by the nobility, making it even harder to distinguish them from the Evroza at a distance.

Calderek's vanguard made such a ruckus with their fighting that the Evrozings didn't realize Helgurdda's warband had descended on them—Calderek had ridden with Eirgei too many years not to know what was coming, even if he couldn't hear their howls for the din around him.

Helgurdda yipped to start their charge.

The guardsmen broke into a gallop, and Helgurdda, Lanney, and Wyl followed.

With his reins clenched in his right hand, Wyl planted his knuckles hard against the bright, copper-colored crest of Firebrand's neck to hold her back. The mare wanted to run, and he had to fight her to stay back with Lanney, to stay in his place behind Helgurdda.

Ahead of Helgurdda, her warband poured down the slope to the road, turning the Evrozings' own tactics against them, ambushing the ambushers. They smashed into the supposed brigands and howled that they'd made contact with the enemy.

Thanks to the fog, Helgurdda's warband's timing was off—Wyl didn't hear Eirgei's warband's howls answering theirs as they crashed into the fighting along the road.

Wyl added his own howl to the others', but once down beside the road himself, he couldn't see the Evrozings. He could only see Helgurdda and beyond her, the backs of her guardsmen blurring into the curtain of fog.

Bronze sabres crashed against bronze-bound, wooden shields with deafening force. Moments later, the howls of Eirgei's warband came from somewhere in the fog ahead, beyond the closest fighting.

The fog made it difficult for Wyl to judge the enemy's numbers, but by the way Helgurdda's charge had come to a sudden, violent halt, they faced more than a single warband of twenty Evrozings. Against just one warband, her charge should've broken through to Calderek's minions in the middle, even without the simultaneous impact of Eirgei's warband. Eirgei would surely quiz Wyl later on the reason why their attack stalled—which was because the odds were not one Evroza warband against Calderek's, but at least two of them against Eirgei's three.

He silently cursed Calderek and his pride. Though these three rebel warbands were each capable of meeting the Evroza on even terms, Eirgei always avoided such battles, calling them *foolish opportunities for mutual annihilation.*

Calderek should've howled more than a warning. He should've howled for help once he'd realized his ambushers outnumbered him by two to one, even if they'd been brigands and not Evrozings.

Wyl cursed the absent scouts under his breath, because this ambush, this battle, shouldn't be happening. *Quiz me about the scouts, Eirgei!*

Helgurdda's warband's front line pressed forward. Wyl shifted his shield higher and adjusted his grip on his sabre, but he remained in position because Helgurdda stayed put, allowing more of a gap to open between herself and the closest line of her veteran guardsmen.

Now that she knew she fought Evrozings, if one of them wanted the bounty on her head, he'd have to earn it. She wouldn't risk herself without cause, but her presence always inspired the minions of her warband to fight at their considerable best. Most of her guard were former nobility—some of them were Calderek's renegades, some were Traditionalist Evrozings; all were disowned and outlawed by their birth clans and adopted by Helgurdda.

Wyl had watched countless battles and skirmishes unfold from the relative safety of a treetop. To his experienced eye—based on what he could see of the fighting—both Calderek's minions and the Evrozings seemed evenly matched in skill.

Helgurdda snarled curses as she withdrew back up the slope, both to claim the advantage of the high ground against any Evroza minions who won through her guard and to try for a better view of the battle. Firebrand fretted and danced in place as he obeyed orders, and waited and watched from behind Helgurdda. How ridiculous was it to position a bodyguard behind her? But those were his orders. He and Lanney guarded Helgurdda's back, not her front.

His head jerked at the unexpected sound of faint howling from the direction of the rest of the menney that they'd left behind. He turned his head to listen.

According to those howls, the rebels who had been left waiting were now also being engaged by the Evroza. *They* gave the howl for an attack by an overwhelming force.

Both Helgurdda and Lanney heard it, too, and turned to look at Wyl.

"That's impossible," he protested, in his own defense. "I was in Myymor for the Moon of Hay and most of the Moon of Harvest, and I counted the Evroza forces myself. That was not even two weeks ago!"

The long blood-feud had sapped Evroza clan of young men old enough to bring into their menney, and the lesser clans of Milkdales had been successfully resisting any additional levies into the auxiliary menney. Blood-feud was, after all, a private clan matter. If Evroza gold could have bought enough Tokari mercenaries to outnumber Helgurdda's minions, the news of it would've outrun those hirelings across the width of Trascolm, all the way to Helgurdda's ears—Wyl was not her only spy.

That the rebel menney was being overwhelmed, he didn't doubt, but it had to be by the Evroza's superior skill and not by superior numbers.

If his suspicion was right—that this was the whole of the Evroza menney, pitting themselves against the whole of Helgurdda's menney—then the overall odds were more like one to one, in numbers.

In fighting prowess, the odds were much worse. Despite Eirgei's brutal training, the fighting skills of most of Helgurdda's minions were still worse than those of the Evrozings and better-suited to brigandage than war. Given a choice, Eirgei never committed any of his warbands to battle unless the numbers were overwhelmingly in his favor. In the past, both Eirgei and Royenne Sharei had picked their clashes with care, seeking clear victories and avoiding being drawn into losing battles.

But this time, they were in a full-scale battle, menney against menney. This was no accidental meeting, not with an ambush and the presence of the Evroza's mages, who continued to baffle Wyl by not striking.

Thanks to Eirgei's disgraceful scouts—who were probably leagues away, taking their ease, terrorizing the Folk of some hamlet—Helgurdda's menney had become engaged in an even, but unequal, fight on ground of the enemy's choosing.

Helgurdda's warband howled like a pack of wolves, and the sound of the fighting became ferocious—that would be the surprised Evrozings turning from battling Calderek's minions to face the twin attacks on their flanks.

Something suddenly exploded overhead with a lightning-bright flash, dazzling Wyl's eyes and making the ground shake underfoot.

Evroza magery—the faint, spoiled stink of it was as unmistakable to him as the explosions were to everyone else.

Their horses snorted and skittered. Wyl pressed his hand gripping the reins hard against Firebrand's neck to keep her in place, and she reared.

The terrible noise of the explosions resounded through the woods, along with the cracks and booms of falling trees. The fog turned into smoky, lightless shadows.

"See! I was right!" Wyl exclaimed angrily.

"Maybe you guessed right about the mages," Lanney snapped at him, as she fought with her panicking horse. "Fog must've confused them—should've struck first in their ambush—*ockh,* their magery's just as dangerous to them as to us."

He made no reply.

The reason why the Evrozings' magery had gone astray was because the mages were close enough to be affected by the *luck* charm he'd scored under Calderek's saddle flap without the warlord's knowledge. He'd made that charm years ago, when he'd been first learning spit-craft, and it remained one of his best efforts.

More magery exploded overhead, and the noise built into a furious barrage. The blasts snapped and toppled trees on either side of the road like a garden fence flattened by stampeding aurox.

Behind Helgurdda, Wyl sheathed his sabre so he could use both hands to hold Firebrand in position. He counted the blasts, one per mage, until the tally matched what he knew of their numbers. Then, the chaos and violence of the magery attack abruptly stopped.

"*Heh,* those mages did more harm to the trees than they did to us," Lanney laughed, with amazed relief. "They wasted a day's worth of magic-gathering. They couldn't hit any of us without hitting their own people, so they must've been just trying to scare us into running. Eir-gei'll be pleased."

Not so. Eirgei would be scornful—he considered the Evroza's in-sistence on using magery a poor substitute for real tactics. Evroza magery had done nothing to aid them in the fighting here, so Eirgei would feel vindicated by that failure.

Eirgei didn't know about the spitcrafted *luck* charms also under the flaps of his, Helgurdda's, and Lanney's saddles. Even if he had known, he'd never give credit to any kind of magic—and especially not to low-ly spitcraft. Eirgei believed Helgurdda's victories were proof that mages were no match for well-trained minions, and that seers were no substitute for good scouts.

Wyl believed in *luck*—and he took care to be discreet, but diligent, in his devotions to MiPaatet and to TolDaanyo, the Horned Hunter, Her Brother. This situation clearly called for TolDaanyo. He drew a throwing knife and nicked his arm above his bracer through one of the ragged holes in his sleeve. *He* wasn't too proud to beg for aid.

"TolDaanyo, help me," he whispered under his breath. He clung to the hope that the blood offering would make a difference, though being self-inflicted rather than drawn in battle, he risked drawing the ancient Folk God's ire rather than His aid.

A horse screamed, and an Evroza minion with a bloody sabre came out of a curl of heavy fog and spurred towards Helgurdda.

Wyl caught Lanney's eyes with his and when she nodded, he sent Firebrand charging forward to head off the Evrozing, who swerved aside to intercept him.

The Evrozing hesitated for a fatal moment when he got a good look at Wyl.

As the Evrozing stared, Lanney burst out from behind Helgurdda in a charge of her own. She rammed her Gerisari horse into the Evrozing's Gerisari horse's flank, and at the same time, Wyl lifted his sabre from his shoulder to make a cut at the Evrozing. He did it slowly enough for the Evrozing to counter, but rather than letting him parry it away, Wyl twisted his blade under the Evrozing's. He tried to disarm him, but settled for putting the other's sabre in a bind with his own.

The Evrozing's horse staggered when Lanney's horse hit it, and on impact, Lanney brought her sabre across the side of the Evrozing's neck in a vicious swoop. Her jegurit-bronze blade bit into the jegurit-bronze aventail protecting his neck.

With its magical, artisanry edge, Lanney's sabre was stronger than ordinary jegurit mail, but this mail was well-wrought. It would take more than one blow.

Wyl pushed off against the Evrozing's sabre, taking advantage of the shock of injury. Sitting tall and shifting his weight in the saddle, he spun Firebrand around, still on the Evrozing's left side, and clashed shield to shield with him. He didn't unseat the Evrozing or even push him very far, of course, but the distraction allowed Lanney's second swing to bite into the damage done by her first one.

Mail rings didn't erupt, as sometimes happened when badly-made mail gave way, nor was there a great wash of blood when Lanney wrenched her blade free, but the Evrozing collapsed in his saddle, then fell to the ground. Dead or alive, he was out of the fight.

Wyl and Lanney returned to their positions behind Helgurdda.

Lanney gave him a smug grin, as if they were in a contest and not a battle. Being half-Folk, half-Dremn, and all mercenary, maybe Lanney wasn't eager to die for the rebel cause, but she loved a good fight— which was any fight that allowed her to claim the rich spoils off a noble Evrozing corpse.

Wyl was too tense to grin back. He could only hope that no more Evrozings would make it past the guardsmen. He knew it was foolish, but he wanted to get through this battle without getting Evroza blood on his sabre. In spite of the blood-feud, he still shied away from killing members of the royal clan.

Royenne Sharei had wrongfully condemned Helgurdda to appease her Gerisari allies, and most Tras considered Evroza clan's honor tainted by her decision, but how could he fault Evrozings for choosing to remain loyal to their baronne?

As part of Wyl's training, Eirgei often quizzed him about how nobles thought. *What are the noble virtues? Which is the greatest of them?*

Naturally, of valor, loyalty, and cunning, Eirgei's answer would be *valor*.

Wyl disagreed, though he was smart enough to keep his mouth shut about it. He hated the Evroza, but he had to respect what they'd sacrificed to be loyal to their clan and the royenne, Evroza clan's baronne.

The stifling fog had finally started to thin, yet the putrid smell remained, and by the crawling sensation on Wyl's skin, that odd magery was still at work.

The Evroza gave Helgurdda's minions a spirited fight, and that gave Wyl an uneasy feeling. Whenever they'd fought the Evroza in the past, Eirgei had seen to it that the rebels had had the advantage of numbers. Wyl feared they'd grown used to easy victories.

A strong, chill wind abruptly began to blow out of the southwest, freezing him through his layers of surcoat, *byrnney*, and sweat-dampened undertunic. He coughed.

The remaining wisps of fog swirled and rose from the road, revealing that the front line of Helgurdda's guardsmen was under renewed pressure, enough to make it bulge backwards toward her.

He straightened, adjusted his grip on his sabre, and shook off the bite of the wind, but the second line of Helgurdda's guard had already reinforced the weakened front line before the Evroza could break through. Her guardsmen hacked their way forward again, leaving him, Helgurdda, and Lanney behind—all of them unscathed, for which Wyl gave credit to their *luck* charms.

Two over-bold Evrozings, who had thought to break through Helgurdda's warband, lay motionless on the ground.

No one took prisoners.

Now, Wyl could get his first clear look at the fighting around him. It was also his first look at it from a battlefield rather than from the safety of a treetop, and he tried to lay aside his lingering apprehension. Helgurdda's warband looked likely to overcome their share of the Evroza ambushers, just as Eirgei had intended when he'd still thought them only brigands. Her guard and the vanguard still had the advantage of numbers here, even against two warbands of the Evroza's caliber.

When Eirgei finished with these ambushers, his minions would be free to savage the Evrozings attacking the rest of his menney. Eirgei would find the pivotal portion of the Evrozings' attack, and with surprise and the same maneuver that worked so well here, it should be enough to tip the battle in Helgurdda's favor.

But, Wyl still had a bad feeling. That nightmare stink remained as strong as ever.

Overhead, the rising fog thickened with unnatural speed, transforming the gray sky into great, dark-towered clouds. The filtered sunlight darkened, and abruptly, tiny bits of hail rained down, falling at an angle with the wind.

Wyl closed his eyes. His skin still prickled from the presence of magic, and the wave of pressure coming from the southwest felt even heavier than before. Yet the clear focus of it made him suspect it came from only a single mage. The fog had gone, but his gut feeling remained convinced that the hail was no more natural than the fog had been.

He opened his eyes.

Why hail? Small as it was, it seemed a peculiar weapon.

He tucked his head down against the wind-driven bits of ice.

The hail fell in sheets, and the hailstones collecting in the folds of his rolled cloak were becoming larger with each successive gust of wind.

If the hailstones grew big enough, they might shift the momentum of the battle.

Wyl wasn't the only rebel unsettled by the hail. Some of the rebels were forced to take notice of the hailstones when their mounts, without the protection of leather barding like what the Evrozings' horses wore, began to snort and churn amid the fighting.

Wyl raised his head, wincing at the sharp impacts against the exposed skin of his face and glad for his helm and *byrnney*—they were certainly better than nothing.

Firebrand objected to the barrage, and shifting his position behind Helgurdda so the mare's tail pointed into the wind didn't appease her. She objected so strongly that he again had to hastily sheathe his sabre so he could use both hands to keep her under control. Despite Firebrand's war training, fighting on a battlefield was as new to her as it was to him, but he couldn't let her carry him off, leaving Helgurdda with only half her protection.

Firebrand fought him, rearing and shaking her head as his hands, seat, and legs insisted she stay where she was.

He saw a couple of horses fleeing riderless through the mêlée—both of them rebel mounts.

Firebrand squealed, and Wyl kept her moving in tight, angry circles behind Helgurdda.

As his mare turned under him, what he saw dismayed him. He'd seen enough battles unfold to recognize when the momentum of the fighting had shifted in Eirgei's favor. This time, from his vantage on the slope above the road, he sensed it shifting *against* them.

It was the birth of a rebel disaster.

Eirgei recognized it, too.

Wyl could hear ferocious howls from somewhere below him to the north as Eirgei attempted to rally his warband. Helgurdda took up her uncle's howl and did the same.

The stinging hail had already grown to the size of Wyl's fingernail.

The magic he sensed pressed as hard as ever, but how could a mage be responsible for the hailstorm? Wyl had spent four campaign seasons spying inside the Evroza clanhold in the frontier town of Myymor. He'd learned a lot of Evroza secrets, but he'd never heard of any mage who could do more than scry or loose magery blasts.

But what else could account for the fog and then the hail, all carried on a wave of that strange, hair-raising pressure he always felt before a magery attack—it couldn't be a coincidence. Nor did he feel it coming from someplace close by. Distance didn't seem to handicap this mage like it did those who used blasts of magery.

Wyl looked all about him. Helgurdda's minions and the Evroza alike were being bombarded by hail.

So, if *he* were the mage casting this violent storm, where would he be?

He'd be on the other side of the wind and not here on the road, too close to the fighting and being battered by the hail like everyone else.

In his mind, he searched through terrain he'd come to know well over four winters, both the rocky dales that ran down to the river and the fire-scarred forest that linked them. The Evroza could field only one warband of mages, and they had just one warband of archers to protect them. If they sent another mage as far away from the battle-field as the weather-mage seemed to be, the Evroza wouldn't divide their warband of archers—they could guard the weather-mage with minions, no fewer than a hand, but probably not a full warband. The mage's guards would seek out a road or an open space where any ap-proaching enemy would be exposed, and where they could take ad-vantage of their individual prowess.

Wyl knew of such a place. But to put a stop to the hail, he'd have to leave Helgurdda and Lanney. Yet, if he stayed, and the hail continued to grow until it reached the size of sling stones, the rebels would be unable to control their horses and fight. There'd be no stopping the Evrozings, whose own horses were protected by leather barding, from slaughtering them.

Did he have time to hunt down the mage before the Evroza could crush them?

A defeat now, with the entire rebel menney committed, would mean the end of everything. All of them would die, the lucky rebels in battle, the rest hanging from the walls of Crossroads Keep.

He looked over either shoulder as Firebrand circled under him, gauging the course of the battle now that he could see even more of the mêlée. He wished his first impression had been wrong. Tempting as it was to use his bow, his bow was worse than useless in the chaos of close-quarters fighting.

The Evroza's warband of Folk archers had to be somewhere close by, but they wouldn't risk shooting into the mêlée, either. They'd be reduced to standing guard with their hatchets—as if Eirgei would waste time and minions attacking used-up mages.

Wyl skimmed his eyes over the fighting, making a quick reckoning of numbers. He'd been right in his guess about the Evroza's strategy here. They'd committed no more than two warbands, likely the pick of their menney, to ambush Calderek's vanguard. That they'd set a trap for Eirgei with so few minions confirmed his suspicions—the ambush had been a deliberate diversion to draw Eirgei away, leaving the rest of his menney virtually leaderless and ripe for attack. That wouldn't have happened if Eirgei had been warned he faced Evroza and not brigands.

Wyl now understood why the Evroza had so much confidence in their young warleader, Lord Goffray, but it galled him that the Evroza reckoned two of their warbands could hold their ground against Eir-gei's three best warbands, while the rest of the Evroza destroyed the rest of Helgurdda's menney—but it seemed to be true, thanks to that hail.

Helgurdda's guardsmen and Calderek's vanguard fought to control their hail-struck horses while exchanging blows with the Evrozings. That handicap undermined their advantage in numbers.

A plan began to take shape in his mind, and Wyl quickly tallied Hel-gurdda's initial odds—three warbands of twenty minions, along with her, Eirgei, Calderek, Lanney, and himself, against two Evroza warbands of twenty, their two warlords, one warband of unseen, ex-hausted Evroza mages, and a like number of Folk archers left idle first by the fog and now by the mêlée. He knew of three Evrozings down, but nothing of Eirgei's own losses.

He glanced aside, still wrestling Firebrand with both hands on the reins. Lanney and Helgurdda struggled one-handed with their more seasoned mounts, while a wave of Evrozings hacked their way towards them through the confusion.

Wyl tensed, taking his left hand from the reins to grip the hilt of his sheathed sabre, but once more, Helgurdda's warband beat back the Evrozings. It was only a matter of time, though, before the hail put all of them at the mercy of their horses and the merciless Evroza.

Stopping the hail would prevent that—but only if he acted now. No one else knew the hail was unnatural, and no one else was in a position to do something about it. He just had to hope Helgurdda would be safe, and that Lanney wouldn't need his help before he could return.

Firebrand screamed, humping her back and plunging under him, struggling against his hold, and as she again whirled away from the fighting and half-reared, he released the reins and let her bolt.

Racing-bred Firebrand shot down the road like an arrow from his bow.

Without the hail, Eirgei's cunning leadership and his decades more experience as a warleader ought to turn the battle back against young Lord Goffray. From everything Wyl had heard in Myymor, Lord Goffray was well-regarded by his clan's minions, but what could be more rash than to commit all the Evroza menney to this battle? Lord Goffray gambled with his royal clan's survival. He'd come out of this battle with victory or with nothing left.

As would Helgurdda.

Stop the hail, and Wyl had confidence Eirgei would put a swift end to Lord Goffray's folly. Then, what remained of their three rebel warbands could join up to hammer the Evrozings attacking the rest of Helgurdda's menney—and strike the Evroza menney a blow from which it would never recover.

Destroy the Evroza menney today, and complete victory and the crown of Trascolm would be just a siege away. Once Crossroads Keep fell, and the royenne's daughter surrendered, the blood-feud—and the rebellion—would both end, and Helgurdda would be royenne.

Then his rebel family, his outlaw clan, would finally be safe.

All he had to do was kill a weather-mage.

CHAPTER 3

THE HUNTER

Once past the bend in the road and away from the fighting, Wyl checked Firebrand's headlong gallop and got her back in hand in time to swerve off the road and onto a narrow trail he knew well, a shortcut through wooded terrain too rugged for carts and wagons. A half-league's hand-gallop to the southwest along this twisty path brought him out of the woods at an overgrown sunken lane.

He halted Firebrand and peered down past her shoulder to confirm the fresh hoof prints, large enough for Gerisari horses.

Maybe his *luck* charm worked after all.

He knew where that lane led—to an open field and the remains of the manor house of a member of Evroza clan's Traditionalist faction. The burned-out, siege-engine-ruined manor would be Wyl's pick if he were a mage who didn't want to risk being caught up in a battle. The open, surrounding fields could be easily defended by horsemen. The remaining walls of the ruins were like a maze, offering cover for the mage if he had to elude capture on foot.

As Eirgei often said, in that dry, sarcastic way of his, *always assume the Evroza are at least as clever as you are.*

Wyl figured his years of successful spying on them gave him the edge in wits and daring, but only an idiot would tell Eirgei that.

He crossed the sunken lane and rode Firebrand up the opposite bank, travelling deeper into the woods. Then he reined-in, dismounted, and tied Firebrand to a bare-branched tree sturdy enough not to sway in the strong wind. He hung his shield behind his saddle. On the other

30

side of his saddle was his quiver. He took off his gauntlets, tucked them into his belt, then pulled his unstrung bow from its sleeve and struggled to string the small, fiercely-recurved horse bow while now-acorn-sized chunks of hail struck him. He took out half the arrows from his big oilcloth quiver to make room for his bow, tugged the drawstring top closed, and slung it over his head and shoulder. Then, he ran bent over through the hail and up the rise overlooking the little lane with its view of the open field beyond it. Just before he reached the crest, he flopped down on his belly, then crawled as close to the edge of the woods as he dared.

The ruined manor's wide swath of overgrazed demesne proved the local goat herders hadn't forgotten it.

Neither had the Evroza.

A smoke-stained barn was nearly intact, and by the light streaming from several holes in the thatched roof, he glimpsed horsemen moving inside. One in Evroza colors trotted out of the barn and headed for the lane that ran on through the woods to the northeast. Once in the open, the Evrozing urged his horse into a gallop, obviously a courier bound for whoever directed the ambush.

Given that most Evroza accounted Lord Goffray as bold and brave, Wyl reckoned the young warleader would be directing the ambush in person, so that message would be for him.

But who would be sending messages to the warleader in the midst of battle?

Wyl felt tempted to go after the courier and intercept the message. He knew these woods, and Firebrand could easily overtake the Gerisari horse.

Then the wind gusted, and a warband of horsemen shifted restively into view from behind the barn.

When Wyl saw their spears, his heart stopped.

For one terrible moment, it looked like the Evroza's Gerisari allies had decided to join in the blood-feud, though only a couple weeks ago, in Myymor, his spying had uncovered no hint of it.

Then the spearmen shifted farther into the open, and he could see they and their gaily-caparisoned mounts were in Evroza scarlet and green, not the blue and gold of Doromont, the royal house of Gerisar—and, if the truth be told, the Evroza's masters. But these were Evrozings, despite bearing the same kind of arms as the Gerisari—stout bear-spears with streamers snapping in the wind from the short cross-pieces.

This Gerisari-style troop of Evroza spearmen was something new, and its location was puzzling. If the Evroza were holding it in reserve, it was badly placed for it, too far from the fighting. Lord Goffray was young, but Eirgei hadn't called him an idiot. There could be only one reason why a warband of exotic spearmen would be here and not creating havoc out on the road. No mage was worth this much protection!

Four years ago, Eirgei had burned this forest to drive the Evroza out of the dales, and the years of drought since then had stunted the returning undergrowth. Now, on the brink of winter, the only cover Wyl could use was the riot of brambles. He spider-crawled his way along the edge of the woods, then lay flat, and strained for a better view inside the barn.

There were horsemen there, but no sign of any archers. The Evroza, even more than other noble clans, disapproved of archery for their minions—the royal clan, tainted by the scandal of the blood-feud, hoped to restore its reputation by overcompensating in how Evroza upheld its honor in other matters. They fielded only as many outcast Folk archers as they needed to defend their mages, so the lack of archers here was no surprise.

Near the barn entrance was the profile of a mounted man in a conical helm, a long, white Tras moustache, and gray hair pulled back and wound into a heavy war-knot. He was built along the same lines as Eirgei—tall and strong—and like Eirgei, he appeared as comfortable in his mail as if he'd been born in it. He had an air of command Wyl could sense even at a distance, but that Evrozing was much too old to be Lord Goffray.

Though Wyl couldn't see the Evrozing's face, he knew every royal Evrozing, as well as those Eirgei considered the most notable of the merely noble ones, like Lord Goffray. Wyl knew them, if not on sight, then by description, expertise, and habits. He'd never actually seen this old man before, but he could only be Prince-Viceroye Osbart, Royenne Sharei's new viceroye and her longtime spymaster—not Eirgei's equal in war or valor, but his master at intrigue. *Not brilliant*, Eirgei had said of him, *but infinitely patient and with a long memory.*

Wyl caught his breath and wondered if he weren't seeing a chance to do something better than killing a mage.

Viceroye Osbart should have been far across Milkdales, in Crossroads Keep like he usually was, a deadly spider at the center of the web of Evroza plots and intrigues that spanned all of Trascolm. How had he managed to be here, in the middle of nowhere, with the entire

Evroza menney and without alerting the locals?

Could it be because of an Evroza seer?

Foresight was a rare talent, and Wyl had thought they'd just one seer left, Prince-Magus Odomazer, who was too old and frail for war. Apparently, they'd found another and had ensured his existence remained a very well-kept secret.

A great deal of planning had gone into this impossible meeting of menneys in the middle of rebel-held territory—further support for his suspicions. The Evroza truly *were* gambling everything, even their survival, on the outcome of this battle—they'd thrown everything and everyone they had fit for war into it.

For years, Eirgei had drilled Wyl relentlessly on the particulars of the royal clan. Discounting ancient Prince-Magus Odomazer at his school in Hundyyga, after Prince-Viceroye Osbart, Wyl knew just one Evroza prince remained to serve Royenne Sharei—Prince Warheim, the only child of Royenne Sharei's younger sister and still in the Young Court. There was just one other royal cousin, Osbart's peculiar nephew, Lord Sterren, a man whose blood was scarcely more royal than that of the merely noble Evroza. So, if the Evroza were forced to seek a replacement for Prince-Viceroye Osbart, they might tear themselves apart even more than the blood-feud that had already divided them into pro-Gerisari Loyalists and Helgurdda's Traditionalist supporters.

The Evroza couldn't afford to lose Prince Osbart.

Wyl gauged the distance to the barn and looked in vain for some cover that might let him get within bowshot of the viceroye. The field was too open.

When he looked back into the barn, he could see something glinting next to Prince Osbart. He had sharp eyes, so when he narrowed them, he could see the real reason why all these guardsmen and spearmen were here, rather than on the battlefield.

Sitting her horse next to the viceroye was a woman in mail with hair worn royally-long and loose like Helgurdda's, only her hair wasn't a brilliant gold. Her golden glint came from the spiked, gold battle-crown at the base of her helm. He couldn't see her face, but during the Moon of Hay, the whisper on the streets in Myymor had been that Royenne Sharei had fallen grievously ill.

Maybe that was a false rumor spread by Prince Osbart to mislead Eirgei or maybe it was the truth. By the Moon of Harvest, Wyl had been too sick himself to find out the truth of it.

But if the rumor were true, if Royenne Sharei was indeed too ill to accompany her menney in the field, then this woman had to be the royenne's daughter, thirty-one-year-old Princess-Heir Ragna—the focus of Helgurdda's banked rage for thirteen years.

If Ragna had finally quit Crossroads Keep and taken the field, this would be the first time she and Helgurdda might come face to face in battle since the two had first sworn blood-feud against each other all those years ago.

Making a woman his target made Wyl uneasy.

To the Folk Goddess, MiPaatet, nothing could be more sacred than women and children—though She protected only *gentle* women, not those involved in violence or war. Surely, as a principal in the blood-feud, Ragna was no more under MiPaatet's protection than Helgurdda was.

That didn't relieve his uneasiness.

Most of the trees around him were winter-naked, but nearer to the barn, in the middle of the field, was a clump of tall, narrow cedars. They were close enough to the barn for him to get a better look at the woman, though he still wouldn't be within bowshot of her.

Wyl made one more stealthy trip through the woods. This time, he came out with the stand of cedars between him and the barn. He covered the expanse of open field to the cedars at a dead run, though he'd seen no sign of sentries.

The Evroza were very sure of themselves.

Even here, the hailstones grew larger as the wind got stronger.

He looked up at the swaying top of the sturdiest cedar and hooked the hilt of his sabre to its sheath by its wrist strap. He adjusted the quiver on his back, tossed his aurox helm to the ground, and began to climb.

Under the outer greenery of the tree, close to the trunk, were spokes of naked twigs and branchlets. It wasn't a big space, but he could manage it, breaking a ladder for himself as he climbed, ripping through the clutter whenever his quiver or sabre hilt caught on a twig—in the rising wind, he could risk speed over stealth and silence.

When the cedar's bobbing top started to dip wildly under his slight weight, he retreated downward a few branches, then pushed his head and shoulders out of the quivering green fronds, putting the bulk of the cedar between himself and the Evrozings. Maybe he wasn't well-hidden, but who'd be looking up into the wind and hail?

He straddled the narrow trunk, put his right arm around it, and leaned his shoulder against it to hold himself steady on the springy branch under his feet. He shifted his quiver to hang at his left hip and pulled his bow and a war arrow from it.

Then, he hesitated.

Despite the jektrar warheads on his arrows, he had only ever used his war arrows to hunt large game. This wasn't the same thing. He had no target, either, though he'd a choice of potential ones just out of range. Unfortunately, none of them included a scarlet-robed mage.

"*Horned Hunter hook them*," he swore under his breath. More than anything, he needed to kill the weather-mage—he had to stop the hail before the battle turned against Helgurdda.

Yet, with the crowned woman and Prince-Viceroye Osbart here, maybe he had a chance to do more than help win a battle. Maybe he could win the war, put an end to the blood-feud!

Excitement stiffened his resolve to shoot.

The two Evrozings made irresistible targets: the woman, either the royenne or her heir, and the man, the irreplaceable viceroye and spy-master.

If either came a little closer, he could get off one shot before they'd know he was out here. At this distance, he didn't think he'd get a second shot. So, without a mage to shoot, which of those two was his next-best choice?

He peered at the crowned woman, trying to make out her features, the details of her crown. In the dim interior of the barn, her hair could as easily be dark and heavily gray-streaked as it could be light brown.

He wished he could see her face. He'd seen Royenne Sharei several times in years past when she'd come to Myymor for the fall tribute.

This woman sat erect on her horse, rather than hunched-over like the care-ridden royenne he remembered. But he couldn't be sure, and that meant he couldn't risk shooting her.

Helgurdda had one standing order: Ragna must die by *her* hand.

If he killed Ragna, Helgurdda would be furious. She'd orphan him as punishment for spoiling her vengeance, no matter how today's battle played out.

When it came to her vengeance, Wyl knew better than to rely on Helgurdda's sanity.

He wouldn't risk her anger any more than he would MiPaatet's, so he didn't dare shoot the woman. Besides, even if the woman were Royenne Sharei, killing her wouldn't give Helgurdda a final victory. Wyl might put the Evroza into temporary disarray, but he'd also be making Ragna the new Royenne of Trascolm, giving her the power to pursue the blood-feud more aggressively than Royenne Sharei ever had.

He clung to the tree, wrestling temptation and dread.

No, ending the blood-feud was a matter best left for his elders. Once Eirgei destroyed the Evroza menney, Helgurdda could deal with this woman, mother or daughter, at her convenience.

He nearly sagged with relief that he had a good reason not to shoot an unsuspecting woman, bloody-handed or not.

Yet nothing barred him from shooting Prince Osbart and becoming an assassin himself. But what else could he do? Prince-Viceroye Osbart would be worthy prey. Taking down the royenne's Right Hand and spymaster would be a crushing blow and throw the Evroza menney into chaos.

He shifted his weight, trying to make himself more comfortable for a long wait in the treetop. If he did have to settle for shooting the vice-roye, he'd still have to wait until he ventured into bowshot.

Until then, what could he do?

He tugged his wax charm with *luck* still inscribed on it from under his *byrnney's* collar and cupped it in one hand.

This time, his concentration was all it should be. He felt the tingling of magic spread from the charm in his hand to throughout his body. He tucked the charm back under his collar, next to his skin, and felt its warmth.

He waited, clinging to the cedar treetop like a squirrel, nervously adjusting the wide archer's rings on his thumbs.

The sky rumbled, and multiple lightning bolts flashed from cloud to cloud, reminding him of the Evroza mages' earlier, thwarted magery.

It still made him grin, that his humble spitcraft charms had thwarted all the magery the Evroza could muster.

But his amusement didn't last—not while he remained at the top of a tall tree in a lightning storm. Hailstones, now grown heavy enough to pass through the greenery, stung him. He shielded his head as best he could among the fronds.

Maybe his *luck* charm wouldn't be enough after all.

How long did he dare wait for a good shot while Lanney and Helgurdda could be fighting for their lives without him?

✦

Lady Breieroz sat on her horse, holding the reins of her aunt's mount inside the ruined barn and waiting on her mentor, Prince-Viceroye Osbart. She watched her aunt work, and tried hard to over-hear what Princess-Heir Ragna said to Prince Osbart.

Though crushing the rebellion meant political survival for her clan, it would not do to forget that, for Princess Ragna, this was personal.

Aunt Constanz looked up from the sigils she obliterated from the dirt floor of the barn and looked outside. She was still a young woman, but the strain of the past hours made her face look worn. She frowned at the hail still falling.

Then, she gasped, loudly enough to break into Princess Ragna's ranting to Prince Osbart about Helgurdda. The two turned and looked at her.

"Lady-Magus Constanz?" Prince Osbart said, with the old-fashioned formality that was the hallmark of the royal Evroza. "What is amiss?"

Aunt Constanz silently stared at the sky and grew paler by the moment.

Prince Osbart followed her gaze. Breieroz did, too.

The hail that had forced them to seek shelter continued unabated, but the rising fog now divided and darkened into distinctive thunderheads.

A bolt of lightning streaked from one cloud to another, its thunder far more earth-shaking than that of any blast Breieroz had ever seen a mage cast. She felt her confidence in the outcome of this battle waver. She had seen what lightning could do to a man in bronze mail. Not even a year ago, a sentry back at Crossroads Keep had suffered a slow, agonizing death from his burns.

Aunt Constanz scrambled to her feet, then ran out of the barn, looking around wildly before kneeling in the open on the other side of the barn from the spearmen. She snatched her athame from its sheath and started carving sigils into the turf.

"Stop the lightning!" shouted Prince Osbart. He had to be remembering the sentry, too.

Fear showed on Aunt Constanz's face when she looked back at him as she crouched, one arm shielding her head from the hail. "I am trying to stop it!" she cried. "But it is like the hail—it is out of control!"

Prince Osbart winced as another chain of lightning flashed from one towering cloud to another with a vast *boom*.

"Do not dismiss your storm!" Princess Ragna shouted, her blue eyes hot with battle-fever.

Though the blood-feud that fueled Helgurdda's rebellion had gone on for all Breieroz's life, this marked the first time the royenne had permitted her heir to risk the battlefield. Breieroz had always assumed the royenne meant to protect Princess-Heir Ragna, but now she suspected the reason was much worse—Princess Ragna was as mad as Helgurdda when it came to this blood-feud.

Thanks to Osbart's cunning, Helgurdda did not know Princess Ragna was here in the north, nor that the princess-heir knew *exactly* where *she* was.

Breieroz sympathized with the princess-heir, who wanted Helgurdda's blood in the worst way. Her cherished Gerisari prince-consort had been murdered by Helgurdda in defiance of Royenne Sharei, despite him being judged innocent of murdering the runaway slave who had been Helgurdda's consort.

All that had happened before Breieroz had been born, when her brother Reichert had been little more than a baby. The blood-feud had dragged Evroza clan and the royal barony of Milkdales into a perpetual state of civil war ever since.

"Send the lightning to where the fighting is fiercest!" Princess Ragna cried.

"But, Princess," Aunt Constanz shouted back, "even if I could direct the storm, that is also where our minions are fighting hardest."

And where Uncle Goffray, Aunt Constanz's younger brother, and his warband would be.

Breieroz looked anxiously to Prince Osbart. Surely he would not sacrifice the best of the royal menney to this preternatural storm? They might win here, defeat Helgurdda and Eirgei, and end the blood-feud, but war loomed in southern Trascolm, another civil war and one Royenne Sharei feared Evroza clan would lose if they took heavy losses today. Lord Goffray's audacious battle plan, backed by Princess Ragna, had barely prevailed with the royenne.

"And that is where Helgurdda will be!" Princess Ragna turned to Prince Osbart. "I would pay any price to have her head today!"

"Killing Helgurdda will not be enough to end the rebellion," Prince Osbart said bluntly.

And Princess Ragna would not be the one to pay that price. Just the thought made Breieroz squirm in her saddle.

"How can I make you see?" Prince Osbart asked. "To end the rebellion, Eirgei has to be our first target, not Helgurdda!"

"Why, are you afraid the goddess will punish you for killing a woman?" Princess Ragna mocked. "I assure you, Helgurdda is armed and fighting out there, so she certainly is not entitled to divine protection!"

"You do not understand! Even if Helgurdda falls, it may be a terrible blow to the rebels, but it will not make their Traditionalist sympathizers—especially those within our clan—into pro-Gerisari Loyalists. The Traditionalists will simply look for some noble Evroza woman willing to sanction Eirgei's efforts on her behalf." Prince Osbart made a frustrated gesture. "That is all Eirgei will need to legitimize his fight against your mother, and surely somewhere, he will find a woman willing to risk herself in exchange for the crown of Trascolm. I hope your plan succeeds and that Helgurdda dies or is taken. But unless Eirgei is, too, all you will do is force him to find a new leader quickly."

"He will not find one," Princess Ragna snarled, "not so long as Helgurdda's head rots on a pike above the gate of Crossroads Keep."

"If, as you say, the rebels' search for a new leader takes long enough, Helgurdda's rebel menney could disintegrate," Prince Osbart said, in a wary, conciliatory tone. The Evroza were known for quick tempers, and none more so than the royal Evrozing women. "But even without a menney, he is still Helgurdda's uncle, still her champion, and he will avenge her—and like you, he will reckon no price too high."

If that happened, Breieroz foresaw no winner in this blood-feud, save the Baronne of Jegurett clan in Redmont barony, who would surely seize that moment to cross Milkdale's barely-guarded southern border to lay siege to Crossroads Keep and claim the crown for herself.

"Such dire predictions," Princess Ragna said scornfully.

The princess-heir showed no sign of concern for her ailing mother, nor for her own thirteen-year-old daughter, Breieroz's good friend, Princess Sheinhild—nothing else mattered to her with Helgurdda nearly in her grasp.

"Without Eirgei, Helgurdda would have only Calderek left to be her warleader, and he is no match for Goffray," Prince Osbart said. "So long as Goffray does not have to face Eirgei, I am confident he can easily deal with Helgurdda's rabble and put an end to thirteen years of blood-feud and madness—immediately and forever."

Princess Ragna just stared out into the worsening storm.

Breieroz watched with concern as Aunt Constanz spent long moments with her hands under her robe's hood, pressing them against her temples. Then, she leaned over on her knees to carve more sigils around herself. She kept flinching from the impacts of the hailstones, clearly having trouble concentrating.

Prince Osbart dismounted, snatched up his shield from behind his saddle, and went out to stand behind Aunt Constanz, close enough to hold the shield over her head without getting in her way.

✦

Movement caught Wyl's eye, and he straightened on his perch. Someone in a hooded, scarlet robe darted from the barn and knelt.

The mage *was* here!

So, he hadn't been wrong about where to find the weather-mage. But why was the mage out in the hailstorm?

He strained to see what the mage did. The Evrozing appeared to be holding a knife and carving something into the ground. Despite the masking effect of his *luck* charm, Wyl could still feel a powerful magic spreading outward from the mage.

Next to that magic, his spitcraft was so weak, it might as well not exist.

The crawling feeling on his skin became more intense. He could smell the awful magic and that now-familiar stink had grown stronger—this mage was indeed the source of the weather-magic.

He steadied his stance on the cedar's limbs, his bow in his right hand. He carefully shifted more to the left to brace both his right hip and shoulder against the tree. Drawing his bow would be awkward, and he'd be facing his target from an almost full-on stance that might take away too much of his range. He hoped his *luck* charm could make up for it.

Then, Prince Osbart left the barn to go to the mage and held his shield over the mage's head.

Wyl nocked an arrow and drew down on the mage, sighting past the wicked barbs of the warhead, focusing on the mage's chest. He angled his own chest as best he could to lengthen his draw, shifted his feet, and raised the tip of the arrow above the mage's head, allowing for the wind.

He closed his eyes and tried to set aside a sudden qualm. Up in the cedar, waiting for a target to step into range, he'd had too much time to think stupid thoughts, like how this would mark the end of his resolve not to kill an Evrozing—easy enough to keep when spying, but truly an idiotic resolve on a battlefield full of Evroza enemies.

From the day Lanney had first been allowed to teach him archery, he'd known in his heart this day would come. What could it matter, when he already had blood on his hands? But this felt different, killing a person—especially a noble Evrozing—at a distance and in cold blood. He hated assassins even more than he hated brigands, yet he was about to become one.

But how was this any different from when he killed an assassin with a blade—simply reacting the way Eirgei had trained him?

It was different because his target, his victim, was an Evrozing with no means of defending himself from his arrow.

There would be a certain justice in loosing his arrow—let the Evroza learn what it was like to live under constant threat from assassins.

He took a deep breath, cleared his thoughts as if readying himself to face Eirgei in a training bout. He exhaled, opened his eyes, took a short breath, and again took aim.

A wind gust caught the mage's hood and blew it back, revealing nobly-long, disheveled blonde hair.

And that the mage was a woman.

He let his bow go slack.

MiPaatet might turn a blind eye to him killing one of the principals in the blood-feud or a woman minion trying to kill him with a sabre, but an unarmed female half a league from the battlefield? In the eyes of MiPaatet, the only thing worse than killing a gentle woman was killing a child. Killing this mage merely for meddling with the weather would anger the Goddess. His spitcraft was already unreliable, but She could make it totally useless. If he killed the mage, he could be fatally out of *luck* the next time he needed it—which could be as soon as he loosed his arrow.

MiPaatet was a gentle goddess, but She had TolDaanyo as Her Right Hand, and men lived or died at the pleasure of the Horned Hunter. Wyl didn't dare provoke Her anger. Especially not while up to his neck in a blood-feud. His good idea about killing the weather-mage now seemed a very bad one.

Even impious Eirgei said that leaving noncombatants unharmed proved the righteousness of Helgurdda's cause, that they were not, as the Evroza accused them, nothing more than brigands.

If she'd been an ordinary mage, her magery really would have been useless on the battlefield at this distance, and she'd truly be a noncombatant, no threat to anyone.

But this was no ordinary mage, and if she didn't die, if he didn't stop the hailstorm....

His stomach clenched and churned.

Outcasts, renegades, and half-reformed brigands though they were, Helgurdda's menney was all he really had for a clan, for his kin. Kin protected kin. Helgurdda, Eirgei, Lanney, and even Calderek—the lives of everyone he considered close family—depended on him doing what had to be done. Surely, TolDaanyo would understand he had no choice. If he didn't act, his rebel clan—his true family—would pay for his failure in blood and death.

He tried to make his stomach settle. Time was precious. The battle might be lost while he wrestled with his fear of TolDaanyo and the misgivings of his conscience. He had to calm down and shoot. This would be a difficult shot, requiring the utmost concentration, with only one chance to make it. He had to make it count. Stop the hail— nothing else mattered.

But he couldn't help thinking about afterwards, wondering how he would live with what he was about to do.

Assuming TolDaanyo let him.

CHAPTER 4

THE HUNTED

Breieroz watched while Prince Osbart held his shield over Aunt Constanz's head and she stretched to inscribe another sigil.

An arrow passed between Aunt Constanz's nose and her wrist.

Breieroz cried out as her aunt fell backwards into Prince Osbart's legs, staggering him and scuffing the markings behind her as she tried to scramble to her feet.

The arrow skidded weakly along the ground on the other side of her sigils.

Breieroz looked out across the barren manor demesne, tracing the arrow's path even as her mentor steadied Aunt Constanz and disentangled himself from her.

It had been a long shot—the arrow had been nearly spent. Without so much as tall grass in the field to hide in, the arrow had to have come from the woods. Without leaves, the trees gave a vantage, but were too far away and provided little cover. So, where was the assassin?

Then a movement caught Breieroz's eye. It came from up near the crown of the tallest tree in a clump of spindly cedars in the middle of the field in front of the barn—not proper trees, really, and surely not large enough to hide an archer. A *good* archer, to have come so close to killing Aunt Constanz in this wind and at that angle, without so much as a ranging shot.

"Prince Osbart!" she cried and pointed.

The archer bounded down from the top of the cedar, invisible under the greenery, but making the branches jerk more wildly than the wind did.

"There!" Prince Osbart roared to Lord Jerrek, who had been watch-ing Aunt Constanz from the other side of the barn.

Lord Jerrek was the warlord of the troop of Gerisari-trained spear-men outside the barn—and the most skillful of them. He also was a close cousin to Aunt Constanz, as well as to Breieroz herself.

"Go!" Prince Osbart pointed.

Lord Jerrek sped across the field with his spear upright, the pol-ished mail of both horse and rider gleaming gold in the ominously gray light, his fluttering streamers like a spill of blood from the long, leaf-shaped blade.

Breieroz caught a glimpse of the would-be assassin at the base of the tree, snatching up an archaic Folk helm before fleeing. Small and quick, the archer had the shaggy black hair of the Folk visible above a russet Folk shoulder-hood. She glimpsed the archer's face and saw no sign of the moustache worn by male Tras and Folk alike.

A Folk woman? The archer was small enough. But outcast wom-en—Folk or Tras—were extremely rare, unlike outcast men. Yet that archer had to be such a one because she was wearing a rebel surcoat and a *byrnney*.

The archer ran across the open field, blending against the back-ground of dead grass, little more than a blur heading for the woods.

✦

Wyl ran hard, but pounding hoofs gained on him. He shied off to the right and flinched as the polished, leaf-shaped, jektrar-bronze spearhead narrowly missed him, its shaft passing over his left shoulder.

Now the spearman had put himself between Wyl and the woods. He turned and charged.

Wyl kept running, and at the last moment, he dodged to the right again.

The spearman tried to swerve with him, but he couldn't bring his spear to the other side of his horse fast enough.

Wyl dove to the ground.

The spear passed over his head. The spearman charged past him, failing to ride him down.

Nothing now lay between Wyl and the woods. He jumped to his feet, dared turn his back on the spearman, and ran.

He could hear the spearman again drawing close behind him. If he kept running, the spearman would simply sink that spear between his shoulder blades. The woods were just too far away.

His mind raced through all that lay in his power, all that might save his life, but there was damned little he could do.

Then, an idea came to him.

As he ran, he felt for the lump under his *byrnney's* collar—his *luck* charm—and snatched it out. Though *luck* was still cut into the wax, he couldn't rely on spitcraft, not given his obvious disfavor with MiPaatet.

Time to try something else, something stronger than *luck*, a little *something* he'd learned in Myymor, though he'd never been desperate enough to try it.

Bloodcraft.

Sorcery.

He bit his lip hard as he ran, put his spitcrafted charm wax-side down onto the bubble of blood, and held it in his teeth. He panted around it, tasting blood as he frantically groped inside himself for an elusive, spine-tingling feeling, one that should be so much stronger than the feeling he got with his spitcraft—and not at all like what he'd felt coming from the weather-mage.

He wasn't sure what to expect.

On the streets of Myymor, they said once someone started down the blood path, there was no turning back from becoming a murdering, black-hearted sorcerer.

But turning back would only be a problem if he lived through this.

Something welled up with startling ease from within him.

His hair stood on end.

He could feel the heat rising in the bit of wax and wood against his lips, and when it did, it meant his humble, harmless spitcraft *luck* charm had become a bloodcrafted *hex*, stronger than *luck*—and nearly as criminal as outright sorcery.

A wave of sudden weakness rippled through him. He staggered, nearly falling.

He hadn't expected that. His spitcraft had never affected him physically, except maybe to give him a headache from concentrating too hard. This was something else entirely.

He shuddered. Just what had he done?

He couldn't let it distract him. According to Lanney's Folk tales, a sorcerer's blood-magic required concentration for as long as he needed it to work.

But there had been no time to calm down, no time to focus his will the way he would've in spitcrafting a charm. He'd made the thing, this *hex*, with nothing more to guide him than an impulse and a desperate will to live through this, with or without MiPaatet's blessing, and that couldn't be good for the *hex's* effectiveness.

Yet, he could sense the magic in the charm, though he had no idea what, if anything, his *hex* could do.

Rather than letting himself be skewered from behind, he turned his back to the woods and its beckoning safety, and faced the oncoming Evrozing horseman.

Two more spearmen had moved out from behind the barn and were galloping towards him.

He was running out of time to make his escape.

The spearman bore down on him, his long, strong spear lowered as if he were hunting wild game—or the Evrozing meant to make a game of chasing him.

Wyl shuddered and hardened his resolve not to give in to his fear and bolt.

He took the bloody *hex* from his mouth, then stared at it in disbelief—the blood that had pooled in the writing had somehow sunk into the wax itself. But, no time for puzzling over what had happened. He stuffed it back under the collar of his *byrnney* where it could lay against his skin, then clenched his sweat-drenched hands, waiting to feel something happen, for some change to come over him.

Nothing did.

He tried again for some inspiration to get him through this. Foolish to rely on an unpracticed *hex* any more than he would his well-practiced *luck* charm.

Now he could see the murderous expression on the spearman's face and the whipping ends of his long, drooping, Tras moustache.

If this was a game to the Evrozing, it was the kind brigands played, with someone else's life at stake.

Time seemed to slow, just like it did sometimes when he defended himself against Eirgei in a punitive training bout.

The horse approached with strange, languorous, bounding strides.

Wyl's mind raced for some way to counter the spearman's attack.

Lacking better inspiration, he snatched off his helm, howled Eirgei's eerie signal for attack, and hurled it by one horn cheekpiece at the Evrozing's horse.

"*Horned One hook you!*" Wyl yelled.

The big gelding reared, spooked, and spooked again when the helm caught on its reins and slammed into the underside of its neck. The horn cheekpiece on the other side of the helm snagged on a link of the horse's mail.

The horse swerved, and the spear blade jerked upward. Not much, but enough that when Wyl flung himself flat on the ground, he was neither stabbed nor trampled.

The horse ran past him.

He leaped back up and ran after the spearman, who was now once more between him and the distant woods.

The spearman pivoted to face him, blocking Wyl's view of the bramble thicket he hoped would save him. An angry snarl lifted the spearman's dark moustache as he charged. Again, the horse galloped towards Wyl at an unnaturally-crawling pace.

But this time when Wyl suddenly dodged right, the spearman was ready for him. The Evrozing smoothly crossed his spear over his horse's withers and legged his mount sideways, still on target and closing on him with that uncanny slowness.

Wyl quickly reached over his shoulder and slipped his hand through the loop of his sabre's leather keeper, unhooking and drawing the blade from its sheath in one move. He clasped the hilt in both hands in a low guard and set his feet.

He knew he presented a perfect target for the spear as he waited for the surreal charge to reach him.

The spearman grinned viciously and took aim.

Wyl saw the spear tip poised to plunge down into him. He focused on nothing but that leaf-shaped blade.

He waited for it, palms sweating. His left eye began to twitch.

Now!

He swung his sabre in an upward parry with everything he had in him. His sabre blurred as the flat of its blade slammed into the spear's stout shaft, flush against the crossbar. The spear tip swung up just enough to pass over his left shoulder, even as the force of his parry whirled Wyl around and knocked him down.

He scrambled back up. His fingers stung from the hit that had jarred the sabre out of his hands, leaving it hanging from his wrist by its keeper. He flipped his wrist and swung the hilt back into his grasp.

The spearman brought his horse to a skidding stop.

The still-moving spear shaft smacked into the side of the horse's head hard enough to make the horse jerk back and veer off.

The *hex* worked! It gave *bad luck* to his enemy!

Wyl didn't stay to watch. He flew for the woods with a burst of desperate speed and a death-grip on his sabre's hilt.

His sense of time jolted back to normal—there were now three spearmen closing the gap with him at full speed.

He didn't slow when he reached the trees just several horse-strides ahead of the first spearman.

The spearman hurled his heavy spear, but it overshot Wyl and thunked into his path.

He dodged past the angled shaft of the spear and kept running. He pulled his leather hood up over his head and smashed his way, head-down and sabre raised hilt-first before him, into a vast thicket of brambles and half-strangled saplings.

He used his sabre in front of his face to lift and push aside the arching, thorny canes, heedless of the lacerations on his knuckles. The canes flexed and slid off his blade and his leathers with their horn scales, but the thorns on them tore at the cloth of his surcoat and undertunic sleeves. Thanks to his *hex*, though, the thorns didn't hold him.

He wove his way through to the other side of the huge thicket as deftly as a rabbit and made his escape. He kept running, heading for Firebrand.

The stink of failure, of weather-magery unaffected by his *hex*, wafted after him.

✦

The other two spearmen arrived too late, and Breieroz knew the rebel archer had made good her escape. Lord Jerrek's spearmen couldn't maneuver through brambles and brush with their Gerisari spears, though they tried thrusting their shafts into the thicket, only to have to wrestle the spears' crossbars free.

She heard Prince Osbart groan in frustration. He and Uncle Goffray had prepared against a possible raiding force of rebels mounted on swift, agile Tras horses coming for Princess Ragna, not a lone Folk archer in a tree targeting Aunt Constanz, a harmless—and female—seer.

It just didn't resemble something the honor-obsessed Eirgei of Prince Osbart's tirades and curses would do.

"It is getting stronger! We have to get away—I cannot control it!" Aunt Constanz cried, pointing upward as she ran to where Breieroz held her horse.

Breieroz looked up at the sky.

The color seemed wrong. Then, jagged bolts of lightning started spearing into the ground, worse than hailstones, arrows, or even magery. But, off to the west, the way the clouds rotated and bulged downward disturbed her most of all.

Nothing Aunt Constanz had done with her magery today could be called natural. Just as the fog had been followed by hail and then by the lightning storm, Breieroz had no doubt that the lightning storm was about to be followed by something worse—with deadly consequences for anyone, Evroza or rebel, caught in its path.

Prince Osbart stared up at the clouds with concern on his face.

Uncle Goffray and his minions were engaged with the enemy, and Lord Sterren, with his archers and mages, was still on the fringe of the distant battle. None of them would be watching the sky.

Prince Osbart beckoned to Evroza clan's bannerman. Today, it was her brother, Reichert. As one of the young Thorns, it was his turn to bear the Evroza banner and carry the signaling horn. He had ridden to Prince Osbart's side at the first sign of trouble.

"Blow retreat!" Prince Osbart commanded. "Now!"

Reichert's horn blared insistently.

The hailstorm abruptly stopped. Then, sheets of rain came down on their heads.

Breieroz squinted up into the rain, afraid of what she might see. She heard a monstrous roar and felt the rumble of it even up through the legs of her horse. Was this the wrath of the Goddess? But who would it fall on, the rebels or the Evroza?

"That way!" Prince Osbart waved to catch Princess Ragna's eye from where she sat her horse in the doorway of the barn. He gestured south through the torrent of rain to where the lane would allow a fast escape. "Go!"

The heir's guard, with Princess Ragna in their midst, quickly obeyed. At her mentor's impatient gesture, Prince Osbart's own guard followed, taking Aunt Constanz with them, but neither Breieroz nor Reichert budged from his side.

Prince Osbart swore under his breath, but let them remain. He had to be worried about Uncle Goffray and the rest of the menney, as well as his nephew, Lord Sterren, with his mages and archers—all of them trapped in the fighting on the road, with the rebel menney between them and the fastest route to safety—the way the rebel menney had come.

Lord Jerrek arrived at Osbart's side with his regrouped spearmen. Prince Osbart cast a grim eye towards Breieroz and Reichert, then turned to Lord Jerrek.

"That whirlwind is heading straight for the battlefield! Stay out of its path, but do not lose Eirgei!" he shouted above roar of the rising wind. "If he perishes in the whirlwind, I want his head. But, if he is not dead after it passes, he will try to rally his rebels in some hamlet. Find him! Get him back onto the river road and keep him on it or north of it. Drive him westward. I will be coming up the road from Almyyga to intercept him. Delay the rebels until Lord Goffray and I can cut them off. Whatever you do, do not let Eirgei slip away south into the hill-country!"

Now Breieroz could see the whirlwind, a great funnel cloud in the distance, drilling mercilessly into the ground with bolts of lightning surrounding it, as if Aunt Constanz had tapped the very mother of the explosive magery ordinary mages used. Chunks of debris shot into the sky above the trees as it headed in the direction of the battlefield.

✦

Wyl was in a lot of trouble. He hadn't the slightest hope that his absence from the battlefield had been overlooked.

He had finally reached the hamlet Eirgei had picked as a rallying point back when they'd first taken the dales from the Evroza four years ago. The Folk hamlet was little more than a collection of thatched huts surrounding a large common green, now brown and dusty from the drought.

He came out of the woods and into the lane, worrying over how to explain about the mage.

Firebrand checked and gave a fluttering, uneasy snort.

Until now, the cloud of dust in the road swirling around Firebrand's knees hadn't alarmed him. He expected the other rebels had already arrived ahead of him.

But he didn't expect to see spearmen on the common, stabbing fallen rebel minions.

A handful of terrified rebels whipped a burst of speed out of their horses as they fled the hamlet towards Wyl. They charged down the lane with defeat showing in every line of their bodies.

Wyl hurried to clear their way.

They didn't notice him on Firebrand, standing stock-still amid some yaupon bushes on the roadside. Likely they wanted nothing more than to escape into the hills and take up brigandage again.

He should've shot that mage.

That thought wouldn't leave him. He couldn't stop thinking about his misjudgment with every fresh disaster.

Within minutes of escaping the spearmen at the manor, he'd known he hadn't done enough. His arrow had startled the mage, but she hadn't been frightened so badly that she couldn't maintain her magic. It hadn't kept her from sending a whirlwind cutting across the battle-field just as he had returned to it.

He warily made his way alongside the lane and then, even more cautiously, he left the road entirely and entered the hamlet from between a pair of huts.

Fighting continued, raising dust over the common. Across the common, he could see Helgurdda's hair. He could see Lanney, too, right where she belonged at Helgurdda's side. She and Helgurdda were both engaged by several sabre-wielding Evrozings.

Helgurdda's personal guard should've blocked her from his view, but they lay in heaps on the ground, some with spears still lodged in them.

Eirgei fought at Helgurdda's other side, where Wyl should've been, chopping through spears and spearmen with his famous black merkusar sabre.

Wyl reined back behind the nearest hut and used the other huts for cover as he circled the outskirts of the hamlet to get behind the fighting, anxious to reach Helgurdda's back.

He wasn't the only one with that idea.

A pair of Evroza spearmen were ahead of him, doing the same thing.

Another spearman rode out from between a couple huts, taking him by surprise.

"Get out of here, girl!" the spearman cried as he charged up to Wyl, spear still upright.

Wyl flushed—he hated being mistaken for a girl as much as for a child, but he wasn't stupid enough to correct the Evrozing.

"Go find the rest of your people and stay away!" the Evrozing snapped and barely glanced down at him as he passed.

The Evrozing was so fixed on killing Helgurdda, he didn't seem to see Wyl's shield, his *byrnney*, or even his rebel surcoat. Maybe the *hex* distracted him, or maybe Lanney had been right, that the Evroza would only see him as Folk.

A Folk *girl*.

Wyl charged after him and drew his sabre. Firebrand easily caught up with the spearman on his mail-shrouded steed. Wyl shouldered her into the other horse. Before he could swing his sabre at the man's back, horse and spearman went down, knocked over by the force of Firebrand's impact.

He sent Firebrand racing after the other two spearmen as they emerged from the cluster of huts and started across the common behind Helgurdda. He picked the right-side spearman as his target.

The spearman had no way of defending against an attack from the rear.

Even as the Evrozing realized Wyl was not the third spearman and started to wheel around, Wyl chopped hard at the Evrozing's forearm. Then, Firebrand crashed into his horse.

The larger horse kept its feet, but Firebrand stumbled over the rebounding spear when Wyl's blow disarmed the spearman.

Out of reflex, Wyl whipped a long back-knife from its sheath at the small of his back even as the spearman drew his sabre and brought it down towards his naked head.

Wyl countered the blow by crossing his sabre and knife. He trapped the blade and tried to wrench the Evrozing's sabre from his hand even as Firebrand recovered from her stumble and slammed into the spearman's horse again. The spearman sailed out of his saddle and partially into Wyl, surprising both of them.

Wyl recovered first, legging Firebrand aside, and used the pommels of his crossed blades to punch into the spearman's face. He felt the spearman's sabre glance off the back of his *byrnney*, and then the spearman tumbled to the ground.

Eirgei howled retreat.

Before Wyl could draw the breath for a warning howl of his own, Eirgei proved he had eyes in the back of his head.

Eirgei spun his Gerisari horse around as the remaining spearman closed on Helgurdda. He chopped the spear to a stub with a mighty blow of his merkusar sabre and snapped his left-hand back-dagger into the spearman's eye. The spearman fell to the ground.

For a moment, Eirgei's eyes met Wyl's own. Eirgei's amber eyes widened, then narrowed under his conical, jegurit-bronze helm.

Wyl took a breath, but before he could say a word, Eirgei and Lanney were in full flight at Helgurdda's back.

Wyl didn't follow them.

Instead, he halted Firebrand, sheathed his sabre, and pulled out his still-strung bow and an arrow from the quiver still strapped on his back beside his sabre.

In the distance across the common, he saw spearmen skewering some of the surviving rebel minions.

He nocked an arrow and waited for his chance.

Calderek's warband, now reduced by half, fled past him. Calderek gave him—or rather, his bow—a shocked look, an honor-bound Traditionalist to the end.

The Evroza spearmen didn't follow. Most were busy ensuring all Helgurdda's fallen minions were dead. But one spearman, then another, and another, broke off and started across the common in pursuit of the survivors.

Wyl raised his bow.

Someone blindsided him, grabbed his bow arm, and wrenched at him, swinging Firebrand around. The arrow fell from the string as Wyl reached back and whipped out his left back-knife.

He was face to face with Eirgei.

The rebel warleader ignored the knife at his throat. "Ride!"

"No! I've got enough arrows, I can account for them all!" Wyl rolled his eyes at the approaching spearmen, quickly sheathed his knife, and fingered another arrow from his quiver.

Instead of releasing Wyl's arm, Eirgei yanked Firebrand's reins and started hauling her after him.

Wyl swore, losing that arrow, too. "*TolDaanyo gore—*"

"*Get up there and stay with Helgurdda!*" Eirgei snarled, in a voice of pure evil.

Wyl shut up and obeyed.

CHAPTER 5

ROUT

Several hours later, Wyl drooped wearily, his hands braced on the cloak still rolled and tied to his saddlebow, careful not to touch the ridge of drying gore where he'd wiped his sabre after the last time they'd clashed with the Evroza spearmen.

His resolve not to draw Evroza blood was long-broken.

He and Lanney rode behind Helgurdda and Eirgei at a jog, letting their horses catch their breath while watching for fresh trouble or a glimpse of those damned, demon-spawned spearmen.

Whenever the rugged hillsides offered a chance to escape to the south, Eirgei left the road to lead them into the hill-country. But every time, *TolDaanyo gore their guts*, those spearmen appeared out of nowhere to cut them off.

Ever since the whirlwind and the disaster at the hamlet, they'd been on the run, struggling steadily westward on the river road, never daring to stop even for a moment, leaving the wounded to look after themselves as best they could. In time, those who couldn't fell from their horses, and the rebels' numbers dwindled.

Behind them, in the east, the whirlwind was still on the ground. It moved west, following the river road—and the rebels. Due to the continuing influence of his *hex*, Wyl couldn't sense any mages or magery ahead, but obviously, they were being herded into yet another trap.

Helgurdda's menney now consisted of no more than Calderek, the remainder of his renegade warband, and several broken warbands of former brigands, who trailed behind them like a ragged rear guard. If any other rebels still lived, they'd been scattered beyond any hope of regrouping.

Their situation was desperate.

When Wyl had lagged behind to shoot Evrozings at the hamlet, it hadn't been bravery on his part, it had been guilt. It was his fault that the battle that should've given Helgurdda a complete victory had turned into a disaster, a complete rout.

He wished now he'd shot that weather-mage while he'd had the chance. That he'd deliberately missed her had won him no favor with MiPaatet. If he'd killed the mage, he'd have been no worse off than he was now. He'd still have lost MiPaatet's favor, but there would've been no whirlwind.

The rebels would've won the day—and perhaps even the war. He'd have had dreams of what he'd done, but what would it have mattered? One way or the other, there'd be dreams.

But he hadn't killed the mage, and because of it, Eirgei had suffered his first real defeat after thirteen years of rebellion. It might be his last defeat as a rebel, as well—the Evroza had broken the back of the rebellion, and this battle couldn't be salvaged. They'd be lucky to salvage their lives.

Thanks to Eirgei's foxy maneuvers through the rugged, broken terrain whenever they left the road and to the valor of Calderek's minions, whenever the spearmen forced them back onto it, the rebels who survived had managed to thin the spearmen's ranks each time and increase their small lead. Eirgei had room to maneuver, but not enough to escape the Evroza hounds entirely—or the rest of the Evroza menney that they all knew lay somewhere ahead of them, unscathed by the weather-mage's castings.

Not even Eirgei, backed by all of Helgurdda's elite guard—had they survived—could prevail against the Evroza's now-overwhelming numbers.

Wyl swallowed, his mouth dry with fear. He wasn't going to have dreams about any of this. When they met the Evroza menney on the road, the final battle was already a foregone conclusion.

They were all going to die.

✦

Breieroz and the Evroza menney reached the river road in time to trap the surviving rebels between them and Lord Jerrek's spearmen, just as Prince Osbart had planned. Now, her mentor anticipated Eirgei's absolute defeat.

Breieroz hoped it was not premature.

"I will accept nothing less than the total destruction of the rebel menney. It has to be finished off and the old Wolf with it," Prince Osbart told Uncle Goffray, with a couple glances aside to eye her and Reichert.

As he spoke, Breieroz squinted into the uncannily bright, cold sunlight from a cloudless afternoon sky. It was in stark contrast with the black sky to the east, where Aunt Constanz's unnatural whirlwind still raged, moving slowly, but implacably, westward.

The plumes of road dust ahead of the whirlwind marked where Helgurdda's rebels and Lord Jerrek's pursuing spearmen were.

"My prince," Breieroz said to Prince-Viceroye Osbart. "Will not the dust raised here by Uncle Goffray's main force betray the closing trap to Eirgei?"

Prince Osbart turned towards her. Breieroz saw an odd shimmer in his blue eyes.

Grief? Not over the rebels, surely!

But maybe for the end of a legend?

"There is no help for it," Osbart said, his voice thick. "No minion in all of Milkdales knows the northern dales the way Eirgei does. He knows Goffray intends to intercept him at the next junction, where the river road meets the road to Almyyga, but he has nowhere to go that will not deliver him and Helgurdda into our hands."

"But this time, Uncle Goffray will not have the advantage of surprise," she pointed out, with some concern. At the start of the day, her elders had emphasized the importance of having that factor in their favor.

"And this time, he will not need it to defeat Eirgei. I have great confidence in what will happen when Lord Goffray's forces meet what remains of Helgurdda's. Your uncle has a tremendous advantage in numbers now, but he will not grow careless, thinking victory is assured."

She desperately hoped Prince Osbart was right. It would be a tragedy if more Evrozings died needlessly while disposing of the broken remains of Helgurdda's rebels. It had already been a bloody day, and it would get worse when they tried to take Eirgei and Helgurdda. The rebellion was finished—all but for the final fighting, killing, and dying.

She did not look forward to that part, the culmination of two moons of secrecy and misdirection. She feared that witnessing the final, utter destruction of the rebels would be part of her training as the future spymaster.

Eirgei and Helgurdda would not let themselves be taken alive, and she was glad of it, though, with no hope of escape, Eirgei and his niece would fight like cornered rats. It was better for Evroza clan if the two died in battle here, rather than risk more Evroza lives trying to take them alive and bring them back to Crossroads Keep for execution.

Not only would that make a pitiful ending for legendary Eirgei, but—after what she had overheard Princess Ragna say in the barn—she feared the princess-heir would lose all restraint once Helgurdda was in her hands for the journey back to Crossroads Keep. The scandal of the blood-feud would scarcely be alleviated if Helgurdda had obviously been tortured before she was publicly executed—and after so many years, the executions would have to be public to fight rumors, a final indignity to Evroza clan's battered pride.

A deep rumble from behind the brush and scraggly trees to Breieroz's left told her the road had wound closer to the Tor. Prince Osbart rose in his stirrups to survey the road ahead, looking past Uncle Goffray and the menney, all of them waiting for the rebels.

Then, she saw the rebels come around a distant bend in the road. They checked when they spotted Uncle Goffray's minions waiting for them and swerved north, off the road.

That meant they would either put their backs to the river and die to the last man—and woman—or they meant to prolong their agony by doubling back, trying to outflank Lord Jerrek's pursuing spearmen, even though fleeing east meant running back towards the unnatural whirlwind closing on them, lightning flashing among its clouds.

Where would Eirgei choose to fight his last battle? The choice would be his to make—ground of his own choosing, even to the end.

The rebel force broke into several clusters of minions as it left the road.

"Breieroz," said Prince Osbart, squinting, "can you tell me which of those are Calderek's renegades and which are Helgurdda's rogues?"

It was easier than she expected. The foremost group of rebels was still organized and heading north. They were in sharp contrast to the larger, lagging group, which shed a few rebels desperate enough to try to hide in drought-dry gullies.

"Those heading for the river are Calderek's minions, and those trying to get away to the south are Helgurdda's brigands, but I think Eirgei and Helgurdda are with Calderek."

It was a futile effort for the rebels. Now that they were in full flight northward, there was no need for further herding from Lord Jerrek's minions, so his spearmen turned and gave chase to the brigands trying to escape southward through the gullies.

She looked away as they rode down those strays.

Uncle Goffray called a command to one of the hand-leaders in his warband, dispatching a hand to go after the spearmen and collect heads to turn in to the outlaws' former clans for the bounties. The spearmen were free to execute them on the spot, a more merciful death than an Evrozing might expect from the rebels, had the situation been reversed.

✦

The rebels made their own way northward, recklessly using their horses to smash through brambles, scraggly yaupon bushes, and stunted river oak saplings until they came to a rocky bluff overlooking the wide, wild Tor River. Below, water roared through the deadly cataracts, a broad, massive jumble of jagged rock.

Ahead of Wyl, Eirgei scarcely looked before sliding his staggering horse over the edge of the bluff and down onto the shingle beside the river.

Helgurdda followed. As soon as her horse got clear, Wyl unhesitatingly slid Firebrand down to the riverside, in turn.

The long drought had made the Tor unusually low. The treacherous river looked more deadly than ever: larger expanses of its rocky teeth were exposed, rising high above the rainbows formed in the mist from the whitewater churning through them.

Wyl walked Firebrand back and forth along the river's edge, letting her blow as he waited for the others to slide down.

With another enemy force coming out of the west, he did his best to hide his panic at the thought of being up against the river with nowhere left to turn—except Eirgei never put himself in a position where he didn't have an escape route.

Wyl knew how Eirgei thought. He stared out at the churning water and shuddered at what Eirgei intended with this unexpected tactic.

Firebrand, her coppery neck white with lathered sweat, shied back from the water's edge.

Wyl coughed and shifted uneasily in the saddle, trying to swallow past a choking tightness in his throat. His skin had stopped crawling from Evroza magic, but he hadn't stopped shaking, despite the distance they'd put between themselves and the whirlwind. He had survived too many traps and close calls with the spearmen herding them to their doom to worry about maintaining a brave appearance. He was alive, and he wanted to stay that way.

His surcoat had new slashes from the glancing blows of Evroza spears and sabres. Some of the horn scales were missing from his *byrnney*, yet underneath, thanks to a miracle—or maybe his *hex*—the tough aurox hide remained intact and so did his skin under it.

He could see Lanney and Calderek, still atop the bluff, also realize what Eirgei intended. Lanney's jaw dropped, but she growled at her horse to get it moving and sent it sliding down to the water's edge.

Calderek balked and didn't descend, though the four of them waited beside the river for him and the rest of the survivors to join them. Instead, he reined back, preventing his horse from following Lanney's. Behind Calderek, what remained of his vanguard of deserters did the same.

"This is suicide!" Calderek shouted hoarsely over the thunderous noise of the river. "We cannot cross—the Dremn will kill us if the river does not first!"

"Better that than Ragna!" Eirgei bellowed. "We are too badly outnumbered now to fight! Come with us and live to fight another day. Sometimes surviving is as good as winning!"

"I will take my chances surviving on this side, Eirgei! If nothing else, I will draw them away, and you will only have to contend with the river. I am going to head back east to the Black Mountains. If we have to, we will make a feint into the Forest of Alshemir and let the ghosts help us deal with the Evroza."

"No, Uncle! I will not leave Milkdales!" Helgurdda shouted, tugging at Eirgei's arm. "I will not give up!"

Eirgei shook his head at Helgurdda's objection and stood firm, shocking Wyl.

He'd never seen Eirgei refuse even Helgurdda's most insane orders outright, and this was the worst possible time for an argument.

"Fare-well! Let the Evroza think they have won!" Eirgei shouted up at his Right Hand warlord and old friend, ignoring Helgurdda's furious tugging. "When we meet again, I will have a Dremn menney!"

"You are either brilliant or crazy!" Calderek shouted down to Eirgei. "The Dremn will never ally with you—they will kill you on sight!

You have killed too many of them!"

"I will take my chances—Osbart and that pup Goffray will not be able to say that they finally defeated me!"

"Fare-well, indeed!" Calderek called, turning his horse. "I will keep my listening post in Myymor operating. Send me word if the Dremn take leave of their senses, too!"

Calderek and the remains of his warband turned and stormed out of sight.

Eirgei's makeshift rear guard arrived at the top of the bluff. The former brigands brought their horses to a wobbling halt at the brink, gaped down at the river and turned away, whipping their horses to catch up with Calderek and his minions.

✦

Turning her head away from the slaughter in the gullies, Breieroz watched Calderek's renegades flee north, only to abruptly halt at the bluff overlooking the river. They stood there, while the pursuing spearmen drew closer. Then, in answer to some signal she could not hear above the roar of the river and the pounding of hoofs around her, they suddenly wheeled in formation and spurred east.

The lagging brigands also halted at the bluff, then turned and followed after Calderek and what was left of his warband, though every man rode for himself, all of them scattering like quail.

She could see Calderek attempt to outflank Lord Jerrek's spearmen, heading back towards the advancing whirlwind. She strained to pick out individual riders among them. Calderek was easy to spot at the head of the fleeing rebels: no mistaking the one-time warlord of the Evroza's auxiliary menney, his massive, square form dwarfing a stout Tras horse.

No Gerisari horses ran with Calderek's warband, nor did she see Helgurdda's bright hair, or Eirgei, or even the woman bodyguard who Prince Osbart said always shadowed Helgurdda. All she saw was a dark-moustached rebel warlord riding at Calderek's side on another Tras horse.

"My prince!" she called to Prince Osbart, trying to draw his attention from the road. "I think Helgurdda is trying to escape!"

Prince Osbart looked at her. "How does she hope to do that? The road is too open to hide three rebels on Gerisari horses and that narrow strip of woodland between the road and the river is already being cut off by part of your uncle's menney. Escape is impossible!"

She saw Uncle Goffray, at the head of the main body of minions, raise a hand.

A horn sounded, and Uncle's bannerman, Prince Warheim, an older Thorn, dipped his flag eastward, pointing in pursuit of Calderek and his renegades. The main body of the menney turned away from the river to join the chase.

Prince Osbart frowned and gave Breieroz a considering look, then gestured for her and Reichert to follow and dug a last burst of speed out of his tired horse to catch up with Uncle Goffray.

"Prince-Viceroye?" Uncle Goffray sounded surprised.

"I am taking my guard to the river," Prince Osbart shouted over the noise of the river smashing against rock. "Eirgei is not up there with Calderek. Your niece has a hunch he is trying to sneak Helgurdda past us."

"I am sure you know best," Uncle Goffray said dubiously, then brightened. "Take the princess-heir and her guardsmen with you. When we catch up with the rebels, they are going to be desperate. I do not want Princess Ragna anywhere near them."

✦

"Fools!" Eirgei said, spitting past his horse's shoulder. He looked disgusted, not at all surprised like Wyl was when the last of Helgurdda's minions fled the riverside. "If Calderek does manage to draw off the Evroza, they will only be slaughtered."

"I will not go into exile!" Helgurdda reached over, grasping one of Eirgei's reins to hold his horse. She shook his arm like *she* might shake sense into *him*. "You will be killed the moment the Dremn lay eyes on you!"

"*Ockh*, it'll be a clean death, compared to what Royenne Sharei intends for us," Lanney cried, above the roar of the river.

Lanney was outlawed in Dremnar, but Wyl knew what would happen to her if she stayed behind. The Evroza would kill her—once, for riding with the rebels, then again for good measure, just for being Dremn.

"I know what our choices are. It's worth the risk," Lanney urged Helgurdda.

Wyl still trembled. He desperately wanted neither choice of deaths offered—not a rebel's death at the hands of the Evroza, nor something equally horrific at the hands of the barbarian Dremn, who hated the Tras as much as the Tras hated them.

He had to trust that Eirgei wouldn't give up so easily, that he had a scheme that would work—provided they got across the Tor alive. He agreed with Eirgei. Playing for time made room for a miracle—and for the last thirteen years, Eirgei had been a master at creating them. Wyl had absolute trust in Eirgei's canniness.

He furtively tugged his *hex's* thong out from under the neck of his *byrnney* and examined it. Though the smear of blood still stained the wax, the word itself was barely legible. The heat rising off him had softened the wax until the *luck* gouged into it had slumped into a formless smudge. The *hex* had kept him alive so far, but he doubted its effect would last much longer. He had no time to remake either part of it, though his desperate focus on survival was still strong. He had to hope that the faint, spitcrafted *luck* inscription that formed the basis for it would still be enough to draw the flickers of luck and coincidence that had so far kept him alive against all odds, even with the loss of MiPaatet's favor.

Fortunately, the old *luck* charms scored into the undersides of the others' saddles still seemed to be working—wearing his *hex*, he couldn't sense lesser magic. He wished now he'd scratched a *luck* charm into *his* saddle—keeping his ability to detect magic or to experiment with spitcraft without a charm's interference seemed a poor trade-off now.

He swallowed hard and stuffed his *hex* back under his collar, where it lay cupped in the hollow of his throat. If it still possessed any heat of its own, his skin was too overheated to tell.

"If Calderek doesn't draw them off," he called from the riverside to the base of the bluff where the others waited, straining to make himself heard, "we'll be overrun here. If we're not giving up, then we've got to cross now!"

He followed up his words by savagely spurring sensibly-reluctant Firebrand into the water. Eirgei wouldn't have brought them here unless he believed this was possible.

"Wylheim, no!" Helgurdda cried. "I will not be an exile in Dremnar!"

He didn't stop driving Firebrand forward towards the cataracts, not hesitating to use his spurs. "*Ockh*, I'm not falling into the hands of the Evroza," he turned to cry back. "And neither are you! Think of the uproar in Crossroads Keep when the Evroza learn you've gone over to the Dremn! This will be our most famous escape yet, but only if we do it now!"

He forced Firebrand to the edge of the whitewater, then turned his head, coughing, to see if anyone followed him. He wasn't crossing just so he could face hostile Dremn by himself. If he was going to die, he wanted it to be with his family.

But Helgurdda entered the shallows. "Hereres, please, come back!"

He closed his eyes and grimaced.

Helgurdda wouldn't follow *him* into the river, but she'd do it for Hereres, a man thirteen years dead. Calling Wyl by that name meant Helgurdda was on the brink of her old madness—a chilling thought if he was right about Ragna leading the Evroza.

He hadn't told Helgurdda that Ragna might be present for fear of a suicidal confrontation. He didn't doubt that Helgurdda would choose death if she could be sure of taking Ragna with her, but she'd also take him and Lanney—likely even Eirgei—with her, too.

He had seen death, even caused it, but today had been a bloodbath. He didn't want to die. He didn't want any of them to die.

He urged Firebrand back into motion, trying to find a path through the massive jumble of rock and rushing water and spray.

When he glanced back again, he could see Eirgei in the water behind Helgurdda, guarding her back—or preventing her from changing her mind.

Eirgei shouted something to him, gesturing at the towering rocks upriver and the lesser ones cast against the riverbank on the Tras side of the Tor, but the noise of the churning water drowned out his words.

To his surprise, Lanney's horse had yet to get its feet wet.

Wyl silently urged Lanney to come with them. No law would protect her in Dremnar, but she had to know nothing would save her in Trascolm, either, not if they got away and she were all the Evroza had to show for the day's death toll.

He began to breathe again when Lanney finally sent her horse into the water after Eirgei.

He again drove Firebrand forward into the jetting water. His determination didn't protect him against the shock of how miserably cold the Tor had become from passing through the glacial ice bridge to the east at Iceroad Pass.

The river channels that roiled and braided through the rocks got deeper the farther Firebrand slipped and staggered among the angularly-fractured boulders.

The water was now over Firebrand's knees. When she got to what appeared to be the calmer, rock-free channel in the middle, it would be more than deep enough to float her off her feet, if the force of the water through the cataracts didn't knock her off them first.

The current was treacherously fast. The rocky, unseen riverbed under the froth threatened to trap a hoof with every step, while the icy water numbed whatever it touched. He worried his hot horse would succumb to muscle cramps, with fatal consequences for them both.

His throat tightened, and his breath caught as death, rather than escape, became the more likely possibility.

Firebrand snorted and advanced in fits and starts, scrambling for footing. Once she stepped into a hole and was smashed sideways against a huge rock—and only that kept them from being swept away and battered to death on the rocks downriver.

All his attention was on her next lurching step, guiding the mare, sensing more than seeing where the water was shallowest, the current less swift, the footing least treacherous. He whispered a plea to MiPaatet, to TolDaanyo, but his last bit of hope clung to the remnant of his *hex*.

A horn called from the riverbank on Milkdales's side.

When he encountered what was almost a calm eddy—compared to the rest of the whitewater—he let Firebrand brace herself and pause for breath. As her sides pumped like bellows, he looked back.

The Evroza had caught up. Calderek's attempt to draw them away hadn't been entirely successful. What looked like two full warbands of fresh Evrozings remained, assembling along the top of the bluff, then dividing and sliding down to the riverside.

No turning back now, not with forty minions to the four of them. Given a choice of the Evroza capturing him or the river killing him, Wyl picked the river. Neither fate offered mercy, but at least the river held no malice born of a festering blood-feud.

The Evrozings spread out along the riverside. Surely their sense of self-preservation ought to make them balk at entering the water? They didn't have the same incentive to cross that he and the others had.

And would they be so eager to take their chances in the river, once they realized Eirgei would be waiting for them on the other side?

At the top of the bluff, Wyl could make out the crowned woman, who he could now see had to be Ragna. The scarlet-robed weather-mage sat her mount beside that of the princess-heir.

Seeing the mage brought back his shame and guilt.

He wished he'd killed her. Who'd have guessed a mage could be capable of summoning fog and hail, or be able to pull a whirlwind out of a wicked lightning storm—and all on the same day? The only thing she hadn't done was cast an explosion like an ordinary mage.

If not for her, it would've been the Evroza menney that had broken today. It would've been Ragna being pursued to her death, not Helgurdda.

The Evrozings' polished mail glinted in the sunlight as they searched among the massive, flat-sided columns of rock braced against the riverbank. They threaded between the blocky riverside boulders and slabs rather than looking out into the wide, deadly river.

Wyl could see no Folk archers among them, and that was a relief. He'd been afraid of getting picked off by an arrow while they were easy targets in the water. Now, if they were spotted, the Evroza would just have to watch helplessly as the four of them made their escape.

CHAPTER 6

VICTORY

On the road in the distance, Breieroz could see how Lord Jerrek's spearmen lagged behind as Uncle Goffray and the rest of the Evroza menney tried to cut off Calderek's escaping minions. Under the scarlet silk caparisons, the spearmen's Gerisari chargers were armored in mail like their riders, and they were now too utterly spent to prevent Calderek's minions from punching through their line.

Calderek's renegades swerved south, off the road, up the loose rock of the first of the foothills and into the woods that marked the edge of the brigands' haven that was Milkdales's hill-country.

They were getting away!

Lord Jerrek raised his hand, and a horn sounded the spearmen's withdrawal while the rest of Uncle Goffray's menney, their horses fresher and themselves unhampered by spears, continued their pursuit of Calderek, scrambling up the hillside after the rebels, then passing into the woods and out of sight.

Lord Jerrek's spearmen turned back to rejoin Prince Osbart and his guardsmen at the bluff.

Prince Osbart motioned for the riders in his guard to check the rocky outcrops overlooking the river. "Look for caves, deep crevices, any place they could hide!" He turned to Breieroz. "It has to be done, but I expect the search to be futile. Hiding is not Eirgei's style, yet if he's not down there somewhere on the riverbank, where else could he be?"

He rode to the edge of the bluff.

"Eirgei! Helgurdda!" he bellowed over the noise of the river, so loudly that his searchers turned towards him. "It is over! There is nothing left of your rebels. Surrender without a fight, and I personally guarantee a private, easy death for both of you!"

Honor demanded he offer some sort of mercy for capitulation, but Breieroz did not expect anything to come of it. She knew all the stories. Only an utter fool would imagine Eirgei—the Wolf of Milkdales—surrendering, not so long as he was alive and on his feet. When Eirgei died, he would make them pay dearly for his head and take as many of his enemies with him as he could.

Helgurdda, of course, was insane, too mad to surrender if Eirgei would not.

Breieroz scanned the river's edge, looking for inspiration.

"It is not like Eirgei to let himself be trapped against the river," Prince Osbart said.

She looked at the seething expanse of rainbow mist, white spray, and gray rocks. "But where could they have gone?"

"Where Eirgei is concerned, something unthinkable would be his first choice in strategies."

Then, amid that monochrome backdrop, she spotted a bit of color *in the river.* "Look!"

Prince Osbart did. "Damn! Sterren and his archers are still leagues away at the other end of the Almyyga road."

That her mentor would even consider using archers against Helgurdda and Eirgei told Breieroz how badly he wanted this to end.

The picket line of saddle horses for Lord Sterren's archers and mages had broken loose during the chaos of the hailstorm, even before the whirlwind had approached the battlefield. Many of Uncle Goffray's minions had escaped the whirlwind with their horses bearing double. Once all who had survived the battle were safely away from the storm, Uncle Goffray had been forced to leave the mages and archers behind on foot. Everything had depended on making it to the northern end of the Almyyga road before the rebels did.

A flash of faded red caught her eye, then disappeared behind hulking rocks and whitewater spray. But, now that she knew where to look, she saw another bit of red downriver. She scanned the broken rock pylons that formed the cataracts and saw another rebel, cloaked in glinting gold, move momentarily into view.

Helgurdda!

Even farther downriver, in the lead and at mid-river—and completely unexpected—was a fourth rider.

The two women on Gerisari horses had to be Helgurdda and the bodyguard. The rider of the other Gerisari horse between them had to be Eirgei.

"Who could that first rider be, the one leading them across?" she asked her mentor. The rider was bare-headed and bare-faced on a native Tras horse—by size and coloring, a Folk woman. "Do you think she is a guide from Dremnar?"

"No, surely not! Fleeing into Dremnar would be suicide for Eirgei and an ugly one," Prince Osbart said.

"But why else would Eirgei risk crossing unless he was sure of his welcome?"

"Hmm," Prince Osbart mused. "If he is, that would make Eirgei a traitor to his people as well as a rebel against Sharei." He shook his head. "He would never do such a thing. No, this must be an elaborate feint, hiding in the river."

But as they watched, the Folk rider entered the open channel at the midpoint of the Tor, clearly intending to go all the way across.

But into Dremnar?

"This makes no sense," Prince Osbart muttered. "Before Eirgei became a rebel, he spent the better part of his life along the northern border here, fighting Dremn raiders. What refuge does he expect to find amongst them?"

Breieroz saw the fast current of the deep channel snatch and carry the Folk guide over a drop. Both horse and rider went under.

"They will never make it across," Prince Warheim said, as he came up beside her. He was by far the youngest of the three remaining Evroza princes, just three years older than Breieroz. "I would have thought Eirgei would prefer to die fighting rather than drowning."

Much farther downriver, she saw something bob to the surface. When she looked more intently, she could see a horse's head and neck outstretched, and something trailing behind it.

"We have trouble," Aunt Constanz said, riding up to them. She pointed to something upriver.

Breieroz looked and saw nothing.

"The storm still has not died out. I can feel the *yyther* flowing towards us," Aunt Constanz said, as if that were an explanation.

She turned away and quickly rode to a rock outcrop atop the bluff. She dismounted, careless of her reins, and climbed to the top of the flat expanse of bare rock as her horse wandered off. She crouched and began drawing with chalk the same sigils Breieroz had first seen her make that morning after her scrying in the barn had become something more than scrying.

Aunt Constanz had surprised them with what she had done that morning. She had taken the same *yyther* that she had used for scrying and rechanneled it into what she had described as a modest, ambush-concealing fog using the water of her scrying basin. Aunt Constanz had told Prince Osbart afterwards that she had not expected anything to happen.

But, if that were true, then why would she have thought to try it? What exactly was Great-Granduncle Odomazer up to at the mages' school in Hundyyga?

Prince Osbart leaned forward to see around Aunt Constanz and make eye contact with Breieroz. "Watch for Helgurdda."

Breieroz looked back upriver, at the spot where she had last seen the outlawed rebel leader.

"Wherever she is, Eirgei will not be far from her." Prince Osbart motioned to Reichert.

Her brother's horn called the searchers back. As they turned, they, too, saw the escaping rebels and began looking for where the rebels had found a way across the river.

Prince Osbart turned in his saddle as Princess Ragna rode up to him, shrieking, "Helgurdda! What are you waiting for?" Her horse half-reared as her hands clenched hard on the reins. "We still have my guardsmen—after her! Those fools down there do not see where she crossed."

Before he could reply, she gestured at her own bannerman, who blew the release for her guardsmen on his horn. They spurred past her, descending to the riverside with wild whoops, and charged to where tracks in the gravel showed where the rebels had entered the river to start their crossing.

The lead rider of the heir's guard splashed into the river and rode with unchecked speed into the whitewater.

Almost immediately, horse and rider were swept off their feet. They smashed first into the nearest of the stone pylons and then into the next one. The whitewater carried them into the fast current of the cataract. Horse and rider went under. Clad as they were in bright, jegurit-bronze mail, neither surfaced.

The next riders, proceeding with belated caution, failed to find a way across. A few more were swept away to die smashed against the rocks, their bodies sinking into the depths of the Tor; the rest wisely withdrew to try to better retrace the path the rebels had taken.

"It is no good, Princess!" Prince Osbart said. "You will only lose your guardsmen, either to the river or picked off one at a time on the other side, if they survive. None of them is a match for Eirgei one-on-one. All he has to do is wait for the river to deliver them to him."

"I will not let her escape!"

"Whatever they may think they are doing, they are not escaping," he said. "Let the river have them! If they make it across, the Dremn will kill them for us."

Breieroz fervently hoped so.

"Our menney is pushed to its limit," Prince Osbart told the princess-heir. "We cannot risk losing more of them, nor put all our trust in the auxiliary menney, not with the southern baronies plotting an uprising."

"Helgurdda has to die!"

"Yes, and Eirgei, too, but it would be better if the Dremn did the killing—let them suffer the losses Eirgei will inflict on them to do it. We need enough of our menney to survive to reinforce the barony's borderguards before Jegurett clan realizes the guard we left behind is a sham."

Breieroz looked out across the river. Had Eirgei decided to die fighting—but fighting the way he had begun, against the Dremn? Maybe, despite what everyone said, the Wolf of Milkdales had a secret, sentimental streak, if he would rather kill Dremn than other Tras— even Evrozings, despite the blood-feud.

"Fool! We have to be sure of them on this side of the Tor. I must have her head!" Princess Ragna said. "Only her head on a pike will send a clear message to our enemies!"

"Better to let the river or the Dremn kill them," Prince Osbart repeated, trying to calm her. "The blood-feud will still end, and without Helgurdda and Eirgei, the rebels have no cause to fight for and no warleader, either. The Traditionalists will not go away, but without Eirgei, they will back down from open defiance. No Traditionalists will back brigands and that is what Calderek's minions will be in a year's time—if they last that long. Calderek is no Eirgei."

Breieroz felt her spirits lift as he spoke. The truth of the matter hit home. It was over!

"We have beaten them, Princess!" Prince Osbart said. "We have won!"

Dremnar

Yet another rock battered Wyl. An unshod hoof struck him on the shoulder, but he doggedly hung onto Firebrand's tail as she swam and pulled him along with her. Her thrashing legs touched the riverbed, and she surged up into a shallower stretch of the Tor.

He scrambled behind her, trying to pull himself upright as she dragged him over rocks framed by harsh whitewater, still gripping her tail.

When the mare paused in the lee of a tall, slanting boulder, straddle-legged against the swirling force of the river, he finally got his feet under him and caught hold of a stirrup, flinging an arm over his saddle. He hung on, gasping for breath, his heart hammering. He shuddered with cold and breathed hard enough to rock Firebrand.

He looked back.

All he could see of Helgurdda were bright, sunlit flashes of her hair between the massive rocks as she picked her way across. He knew she'd seen what had happened to him because she'd veered and entered the deep channel upriver from where he'd been swept away.

The current in the deep channel took her, too, but it didn't drag her under, and she crossed back into the whitewater before she could be carried over the drop that had nearly killed him.

Close behind her, following her course, came Eirgei. Lanney was only a third of the way across, but coming on steadily, despite what she'd face in Dremnar.

Several Evrozings on the Tras riverbank looked like they were gathering their courage to follow.

Something invisibly began to press against Wyl's skin.

That putrid stink had come back.

A tremor radiated from his core—he felt just like he had when the mage had cast the whirlwind on the battlefield.

He took another look over his shoulder, up at the top of the bluff.

The mage had dismounted. She crouched on a large, flat slab of rock overlooking the river and she did something up there, though what, he couldn't see.

His breath caught in his chest.

What would she inflict on them now?

Despite all the river water that had gone down it, his throat was choking-dry, and he couldn't swallow. It took him three tries to heave himself into the saddle as the force of the water repeatedly knocked his shaking leg out from under him and tried to wash him away.

Firebrand didn't need to be urged forward—she was as anxious as he to reach the other side.

He now had cause to be grateful for the rocks. Better to be smashed against them than be swept away again, but he worried about Firebrand's legs, battered against the water-washed, splintered columns of rock leaning in all directions. His own were battered, too, but they were too numb from the icy water to feel anything more than the thud of each impact through the protection of sodden riding boots that reached halfway up his thigh.

He felt a tremor from under the saddle. If Firebrand encountered another hole or had to swim again, it would be too much for them both.

But finally, no more icy spray from the river splashed onto him. In front of him were only dry, jumbled boulders to scramble through, then a mud flat, and then Firebrand was out of the river and on the narrow stretch of shingle on Dremnar's side of the Tor.

He painfully unclenched his fist from Firebrand's mane as he hunched and coughed.

Across the river, he could see the mage now standing and gesturing upriver.

Helgurdda and Eirgei were almost across, but Lanney had just gotten to the deep channel. Lanney's unpolished jegurit-bronze mail was lighter and stronger than mail made from the more common jektrar alloy, but still not so light as his humble horn-and-leather *byrnney*.

If he'd been wearing mail when he'd gone tumbling over that drop, he'd never have had a chance to grab hold of Firebrand's tail and would never have come back up. This once, he was grateful for his *byrnney*.

The roar of the river against the rocks suddenly diminished. A series of louder, cracking noises echoed off the sheer walls of the gorge the Tor had carved across the base of the steep, southern slopes of the Icepeak Mountains.

He looked farther upriver and froze at what he saw.

A wall of water surged around the bend from the east, where the mage's whirlwind still blackened the skies. The monstrous flash flood looked solid and muddy.

And it stood three times as tall as Lanney and her horse—who were directly in its path.

✦

Milkdales

Some distance downriver, Breieroz saw that the first rider, the Folk guide, had somehow survived being submerged and swept away. She was back on her horse and had reached the other side.

Well upriver of her, Helgurdda, on her Gerisari horse, clambered up the steep bank into Dremnar, and Eirgei, still mounted, followed right behind her. The last rebel, the Dremn bodyguard, was halfway across the river, as well.

They were all going to make it—and that was just not possible!

None of Princess Ragna's minions had even made it through the whitewater as far as the channel: the bravest, most determined of them had drowned in the attempt, and those with more prudence than valor had turned back.

Part of Breieroz's training under Prince-Viceroye Osbart had been to help find ways to insert spies into Dremnar, but the fate of Princess Ragna's guardsmen confirmed the truth of what Folk mountaineers had told her. No one had ever survived an attempt to cross the Tor between the Barony of Moorlands to the west and Iceroad Pass to the east—not by swimming, not in a boat.

Certainly no one had ever even attempted to cross on horseback—least of all, on the exhausted horses of rebels who had been fighting and running all afternoon.

But there, before her eyes, Eirgei and Helgurdda reached the top of the far bank and started downriver towards the first rider, the only one of all those who had been swept away by the current to surface and reach the other side alive.

This was just not possible!

She saw how Princess Ragna did not take her eyes off the river, avidly studying the route the Dremn bodyguard took.

Prince Osbart saw it, too. "Princess, do not do it!"

"Not until Eirgei is out of sight," Princess Ragna said, still watching.

"Even if you cross successfully, manage to defeat both Eirgei and Helgurdda—and take their heads—how do you expect to return to Milkdales without falling victim to the Dremn yourself? Risk another crossing like this one? Risk the Dremn hunting you like we hunted Helgurdda? They would force you east to the Black Mountains where the brigand scum there would also be on your trail!"

Breieroz imagined her mentor trying to explain to Royenne Sharei that her heir had drowned trying to swim across the Tor into Dremnar on horseback. Princess Ragna was as mad as Helgurdda to even think of trying it.

Then, Princess Ragna gasped. "*Aaii!* The river!"

Her horse grunted as she dug in her spurs and it launched itself away from the bluff.

The minions still down at the riverside, checking their courage for the crossing, all stared upriver. Then they, too, sent their horses scrambling up the bluff.

Breieroz looked upriver.

Aunt Constanz's magic had not stopped working or changing. The torrential rain that had come with the whirlwind had fallen suddenly on the dry, parched soil to the east.

The consequences had just caught up with them.

Dremnar

Wyl stared upriver, paralyzed.

Driven by the distant whirlwind, an enormous bulge of water thundered down the ancient gorge of the Tor. It had to be magical in origin. The unnatural flash flood rose in a wave impossibly higher than either riverbank, scouring the riverside down to bare rock as it travelled downriver, churning whatever it took into the torrent behind it. Whole trees spun and splintered on the giant rocks in the foaming whitewater.

He saw the Evroza menney hastily retreat up the bluff, heading for higher ground.

Lanney turned her head to see what came at her, and urged her horse to greater speed, but they were swimming in the deep channel. Before her horse found footing again, the mass of water and debris smashed into them.

She and her horse went under, and Wyl stared in horror, only waking to his own danger when Firebrand snorted and scrambled higher up the rocky bank to get away before the water raked by.

The steeply-angled bank on the Dremn side of the Tor was higher than that on the Milkdales side, and though the flash flood washed over its top, it didn't reach far. As soon as the daunting wave passed,

Wyl turned Firebrand and followed it downriver along the narrow top of the bank, splashing through puddled water, craning his neck to look for Lanney.

Though he eyed the river with desperate hope, he could see neither Lanney nor her horse among the branches and tree trunks left snagged on the massive rocks in the flash flood's wake. Then the riverbank he rode along disappeared into a sheer drop, and he could go no farther.

He cursed and turned, and made his way back upriver.

A shout came from his left. He looked among the trees high above the bank until Helgurdda's hair drew his eyes to her and Eirgei.

"*Ockh*, we have to help Lanney!" he called up to them.

Eirgei shook his head and called back, "There is no helping her now. If she survived, she has been carried into the swamps of Moorlands."

She'd be safe there—if she was alive. The border between the baronies of Moorlands and Milkdales was either cataracts or swampland. No pursuit could enter Moorlands from Milkdales. He hoped the *luck* charm under Lanney's saddle still worked and that she'd not been swept from her horse when that wall of water and debris had hit, that she hadn't drowned in her mail.

In grief—and in anger, as much at himself as at the mage—he urged Firebrand farther upriver along the riverbank until he was opposite the bluff where they had started their crossing, as close to the Evroza as the flooded Tor would allow.

He could see the Evroza menney had pulled back from the bluff, but not far enough to escape the trapped floodwaters that covered the scrub brush north of the road.

✦

Milkdales

Across the Tor, Breieroz saw that the Folk guide who had almost drowned in the crossing had returned upriver and rode along the edge of the riverbank, staring out at them, close enough that she could make out her youthful, delicate features.

She scowled, certain that this was not the Dremn woman bodyguard she'd heard about. This girl was much too young for such duties. Yet there was something about her that seemed familiar. Breieroz returned the stare across the water, working over the puzzle. What clan would risk a girl on so perilous a mission as guiding the rebels across an impassable river? No Folk clan would do such a thing.

She became less and less certain that the other was a Folk guide...or even female.

She had forgotten, in the urgency of the pursuit, that the mercenary bodyguard who had died in the flash flood had a Folk fosterling, an outcast who occasionally rode with the rebels. She'd have thought the foster-son older, from the nature of the occasional reports that mentioned his ruthless behavior in the rebel camps.

That *he* was the mysterious fourth rider in the river was more believable than that Eirgei had met up with a guide to take him into Dremnar.

The pretty Folk boy was obviously too young for either a Tras moustache or a Dremn beard to confirm Breieroz's guesswork about his origins. But when the boy reached over his shoulder, producing a strung Folk horse bow, she then knew him with certainty: this was the archer who had tried to kill Aunt Constanz at the manor ruins!

She watched the rebel boy brace his bow against his stirrup and change his wet bowstring with calm deliberation. He seriously intended to shoot, despite the impossible width of the river.

She looked back at Prince Osbart's scattered troop. Princess Ragna was still on her horse, splashing through the flooded scrub towards the road, gesturing at Lord Jerrek and all but invisible to someone across the river. Aunt Constanz, however, crouched atop her rocky outcrop on the bluff, surrounded by water. Long strands of blonde hair from her single braid whipped about her face in the wind. In her scarlet robes, she would be an irresistible, but difficult, target.

The rebel archer had tried to kill her once before, and Breieroz was sure he was about to try again. It would be a long shot with a powerful crosswind from the east, but she could not ignore the threat. That archer was too determined to kill Aunt Constanz.

Prince Osbart had reached the same conclusion.

"Cuz," he called to Aunt Constanz, riding through the water to her. "Let me take you off that rock before—"

"—No," Aunt Constanz called back, shaking her head and pointing at the sigils she had laid down in chalk. "I have to try to draw the *yyther* out of that storm."

"All the same, you need to move back," Breieroz's mentor said. "That is the archer who tried to put an arrow in you out by the ruins. He is trying for you again."

Aunt Constanz looked up from her work and glanced at where the viceroye pointed. She bit her lip, looked over her shoulder at the flood surrounding her, then shook her head. "There is no time! I have got to find a way to dissipate the storm before it floods all of northern Milkdales and drowns our Folk in their homes."

Across the river, Breieroz could see the archer nock an arrow and draw his bow. He held it at full draw, making a serious attempt at aiming despite the strong, gusting wind. As she watched, the archer shifted his aim farther upwind and released.

"Aunt Constanz! Get back!"

The arrow shot out across the river. The wind seized it and curved its path back toward her aunt, its flight impossibly long.

Then, the arrow slammed into the base of the rock slab on which Aunt Constanz crouched, sending chips of rock flying. Her aunt flinched back, brushing at a graze on her cheek.

The feat astonished Breieroz. She watched the archer angrily ride back and forth along the top of the bank, snatching another arrow from his quiver.

Prince Osbart spurred his horse towards Aunt Constanz in splashing bounds. "Cuz! Jump!"

This time, she gave him no argument. She dove from the rock, trusting him to catch her.

The next arrow shattered against the sigils where she had just been crouched.

Prince Osbart caught Aunt Constanz under her arms, awkwardly settled her sideways over his saddlebow and hurried to carry her well out of range before the archer could shoot again.

Across the river, Breieroz saw the archer stand in his stirrups, shaking his bow, looking angry and frustrated. Then, the boy turned his horse upslope, climbing up the flank of what was the southernmost of the Icepeak Mountains, going deeper into Dremnar and disappearing into the trees, trailing after Helgurdda and Eirgei.

Breieroz rode splashing to Aunt Constanz's rock and retrieved the first arrow from where it floated in the floodwater with its fletching upright like a fishing bobber.

The second arrow had hit with such force that its brittle jektrar warhead had shattered against the rock—far from spent, despite the distance. If Aunt Constanz had not jumped, that second arrow would have killed her.

Breieroz frowned down at the wicked barbs of the first arrow's warhead, the jektrar-bronze tip blunted by impact against the rock—no hunting arrow, that. She looked up and saw her mentor coming to her.

"I no longer know what to expect from Eirgei," he told her in a low voice. "The Wolf of Milkdales is outside the protection of the law and thus not bound by honor, code, or custom. Anything is possible with him, now—an archer-assassin, even taking refuge in Dremnar. I am afraid to wonder what is next—using poisoned weapons?"

Breieroz had a disturbing thought. "If Eirgei can survive the Tor, could he survive the Dremn, too?"

"No, that is impossible—if there is a single man in all of Trascolm whom the Dremn hate with a passion, it is Eirgei. Unless he manages to incite them into attacking him against hopeless odds so he can go down fighting, the barbarians will capture him. Then, with great creativity and at their leisure, they will kill him—and Helgurdda, too, if she lets herself be taken alive." He stared across the water. "Perhaps that would be a fitting end for them both."

"Yes," Breieroz agreed.

Hampered by the political situation created by thirteen years of blood-feud, no Evrozing—not even Princess Ragna at her bloodthirsty worst—could make those two suffer enough for what they had done to Evroza clan, to Milkdales, and to Trascolm.

But the Dremn could.

CHAPTER 7

EXILE

Dremnar

W yl warily looked about as he trailed Eirgei and Helgurdda. Dremnar's side of the Tor was very different from the Milkdales side. For most of the length of the river, the southern border of Dremnar was all sheared cliffs, the source of the great, jagged rocks that made the Tor impassable. Eirgei's knowledge of Milkdales's terrain amazed Wyl. He'd led them from the chaos left by the whirlwind to what had to be the only place between Iceroad Pass and Moorlands where the north side of the Tor wasn't bordered by vertical cliffs.

But now they were in Dremnar. With the exception of some famous, long-ago winter campaigns through Iceroad Pass to the east, Dremnar was unfamiliar terrain, even for Eirgei.

Instead of Milkdales's familiar pastureland and rocky garden plots surrounded by woodlands of oak and maple, yaupon and brambles, the land here rose steadily, with barren rock making clearings in expanses of hemlock trees and mountain laurel that weren't so dense as the woods in Milkdales.

He felt exposed as Eirgei led the way north, going uphill in the open, trackless forest. The climb taxed their exhausted horses.

Wyl coughed and shivered in his sodden clothes, but at least his skin had stopped crawling from the presence of magery, and that stink had vanished with it.

He felt relieved when Eirgei called a halt at the first bit of level ground far enough from the Tor that they couldn't hear the water, but he was still uneasy. As outlaws in Milkdales, he knew all too well that they could be hunted and dispatched with no need for a trial. There wouldn't be a trial in Dremnar, either, where a Tras could be a long time dying. The Dremn had been preying on Trascolm—and the barony of Milkdales, in particular—for untold generations.

He knew all about the Dremn from Eirgei, who had fought them long before he'd fought the Evroza. To Dremnar's tribal warlords, hostilities with Milkdales were what passed for thrilling midwinter entertainment, once the glacier in Iceroad Pass froze over and earned its name. This early in the season, Milkdales was safe from Dremn raids— the glacier remained rotten with great chasms and slush. Even a Folk mountaineer on foot would be in peril of his life attempting a crossing. Eirgei hadn't so much as looked aside at where the river road had crossed the overgrown track that ran over and through Iceroad Pass.

Eirgei had chosen to take his chances with an equally suicidal course—attempting to cross the Tor River itself—and in succeeding, he had surely added another tale to his legend.

"We're camping here," Helgurdda decided. "The horses are finished, daylight is fading, and now that we are in Dremnar, we need to go over what comes next." Her voice sounded bitter.

Wyl dismounted and unlashed his saddlebags from behind the cantle of his saddle, turning them over to let water drain out. For the first time, he realized he'd lost his shield in the Tor. He stripped the wet tack from Firebrand and dropped it in a heap.

Then, with her body between him and the others, he threw his arm over her neck and rested his head against her. He just breathed and shook for a time. Firebrand didn't betray him by moving, but stood stock-still, her own head hanging low.

When Wyl had escaped the spearmen at the ruined manor, he'd been *so sure* that his shot had left the mage too rattled to concentrate on more weather-magery. He'd been wrong. Instead of protecting his rebel kin, he'd gotten them killed.

What had he expected to happen when he'd pulled that shot at the ruins—that an Evroza mage would hold back in return?

Lanney's absence felt like a sickening accusation. If Helgurdda and Eirgei had still been in the river with Lanney, they all would've died.

And for what?

His misplaced mercy hadn't saved lives—he'd sacrificed Lanney and the closest thing he had to a clan just so he didn't have to kill one woman, a female mage. But he couldn't bring himself to confess his guilt—the risk of breaking down like a youngling was too great. Bad enough that he knew it was his fault—what could Eirgei possibly do to him to make him feel worse? If Eirgei killed him outright, it would be a mercy he didn't deserve.

Helgurdda had cleared a bit of ground for a fire, kicking the forest litter into a pile for tinder. Then, she squatted and struck her flint against her firemetal-set ring until the sparks caught. Despite the huge storm the mage had caused earlier—far to the southeast of where they were now—the long drought remained unbroken; there was no shortage of dry fuel.

On the other side of Firebrand, Eirgei knelt, examining a gash on Helgurdda's horse's foreleg.

As soon as Wyl stepped clear of Firebrand, Eirgei looked up and glared at him.

Eirgei must have seen him shoot across the Tor at the female mage and miss.

Wyl squatted to finger the assortment of scrapes and swelling bruises on Firebrand's legs, then left her loose to graze the dry, dead grass; she was far too tired to stray.

He spread her wet saddlecloth over a laurel bush to dry and surreptitiously peeked at Eirgei to be sure he wasn't still being glared at before he pulled his wax charm from under the neck of his *byrnney*.

As he had suspected, his bloodcrafted *hex* was gone, and where *luck* had been written, there was no longer even a ripple in the wax. No surprise, not after he'd missed the weather-mage twice with his arrows. He hid the exhausted charm in the oilcloth robber's pouch under his surcoat.

He still shivered, but it had to be because he was cold and wet, not because he was that badly nerve-shaken. *Never admit to fear or weakness—* that had been his first lesson when Eirgei had finally agreed to let him become his pupil seven years ago.

He needed to get dry, though his only change of clothes—the ragged Folk outcast disguise he wore in Myymor and kept packed in a saddlebag—was as wet as the rest of him. He undid the knots tying his waterlogged wool cloak to his saddlebow and wrung river water out of it. He struggled to spread it over another clump of laurel—it felt as heavy as mail. He had little hope that it would be dry before the sun went down, and the temperature dropped in earnest.

He pulled his quiver's strap up over his head. Just looking at it filled him with heartache. He took his bow from his quiver, unstrung it to let its limbs coil back into shape, and hoped dousing it in river water and then shooting it hadn't ruined the horn lamination.

He unbuckled and removed his sabre's shoulder harness, pulled his surcoat off over his head and with it, the rag that kept his hair out of his eyes. He untied his robber's pouch from around his waist, then tried to unlace his *byrnney*, only his near-drowning in the Tor had made one of its leather ties swell into a knot at the base of the high, bronze-reinforced collar. He tugged at it in frustration—he felt embarrassingly panicked by its tightness.

He walked to the small, crackling fire Helgurdda had started, worrying and tearing at the knot with his fingernails. He hunkered down beside the fire on his heels, fitting neatly between his wicked war spurs, and hung his head so he could hide behind his still-dripping hair—the short half of it.

He had started cutting his front hair to humble Folk-length for the sake of disguise when he'd begun spying in Myymor four years ago, though Helgurdda had never given him permission to sacrifice it—she'd been furious when she'd seen what he'd done.

He peeked out through the lank locks of hair.

Helgurdda and Eirgei weren't crying over Lanney, so he couldn't, either. Of course, it wasn't *their* fault Lanney was dead—it was his.

How many times had he begged Eirgei to let him ride with the rebel menney on a raid, begged to do more than spy or lie in wait for vengeful brigands or hireling assassins?

The worse thing was, he couldn't swear that he hadn't instinctively pulled that first shot across the river, too, though by that time, it'd been far too late for him to win back MiPaatet's favor. It hadn't been prudence that made him miss, not that time. It had been pure squeamishness.

He knew that to Eirgei, the weather-mage was no different from an ordinary mage—harmless because of the river's great width. By Eirgei's lights, that meant he'd had no justification for trying to assassinate her as a threat.

Hit or miss, he would still be in trouble with Eirgei, who hated his bow, but hated incompetence just as much.

Wyl hated the tears welling up under the ragged fringe of his hair. Tears were pointless, childish, a sign of weakness, and he was *not* going to give in and cry just because he'd known Lanney half his life. Tears weren't going to bring her back. He needed to stay alert—he couldn't indulge in guilty grief while they were in enemy territory.

He shifted closer to the fire so it would dry his eyes as well as his hair. He coughed.

By the rigid expression on Helgurdda's face, he could tell that she was also upset about Lanney's loss: Lanney had been the only other woman among the rebels.

For the past six years, he and Lanney had guarded Helgurdda against assassins in winter camp. Lanney had always been at her back during the spring and summer raiding seasons, when Wyl's spying missions took him away from sharing that responsibility. Lanney had been the only other person besides Eirgei who knew Helgurdda's most closely-guarded secret. She'd had Helgurdda's rare trust, just as she'd had his own.

He watched as, across the fire, Helgurdda unslung her sheathed sabre from her shoulder.

"What is your plan, Uncle?" Helgurdda asked, in a tightly-controlled voice. She drew her blade, which made Wyl's skin throb, and absently sighted down its edge—old habit rather than necessity. Gerisari artisanry gave her sabre an edge that would not easily dull or be notched. "Is it that we throw ourselves on Royenne Errengard's mercy?"

"You would prefer to hang upside-down off a wall at Crossroads Keep?" Eirgei said sharply.

Helgurdda made no reply.

Wyl's skin throbbed even more when Eirgei drew his merkusar sabre and also caught the firelight on the black blade with its unmarred, red edge.

Merkusar was a closely-guarded secret of the Gerisari, a metal so resilient that it had to be made using artisanry—which was probably the magic Wyl sensed in it. A merkusar sabre was superior to those of jegurit-bronze, even artisanry-sharp ones, and it would never break or bend or grow dull, would never be marred by any means. It had been created with the help of artisanry, and Eirgei said there was no known way to destroy a merkusar weapon.

Eirgei wiped down the hard-used sabre, then laid it aside to clean an artisanry-touched back-dagger.

Wyl thought it ironic that Eirgei respected the subtle Gerisari artisanry that bound a craftsman's intentions into what he crafted, and that it was only powerful, explosive—but difficult to direct—Evroza magery that had Eirgei's scorn.

He didn't want to imagine Eirgei's reaction if he ever found out about his spitcraft. To Eirgei, anything unreliable was useless, whether man or magic.

Helgurdda threw more kindling onto the fire, causing it to flare, and Wyl saw the firelight reflect off wet tracks on her cheeks.

He paused in his work on the knotted tie, took a deep breath, and coughed.

He'd never seen Helgurdda cry.

Well, except over Hereres, but that didn't count. Helgurdda wasn't herself when it came to her dead consort; Hereres was the reason they were all rebels.

"Niece," Eirgei said, in an odd, subdued voice. Wyl suspected Eirgei also had seen those tears before she'd turned her back to the fire.

"I never meant for us to cross the river, just to conceal ourselves behind the rocks of the cataracts where we could make a stand if we were discovered."

Wyl stared across the fire at Eirgei in disbelief.

"Luckily for us, the boy has more guts than wits, or we would have all died like Lanney in that—that—*freakish*—flash flood."

Wyl looked down.

"Why did you think to do that, Wyl?" Helgurdda asked, her back still turned to hide her face, but without any emotion in her voice. Once, she had been Eirgei's pupil, too. "No one has ever crossed the Tor and lived. Did you not know it?"

He shrugged warily, staring down at the ground. He didn't dare admit he'd been so afraid that he'd entrusted their lives to spitcraft, even when he'd known it might not work.

"I guess I felt lucky."

Eirgei grunted and eyed him critically.

Helgurdda suddenly whirled back to face Eirgei and snarled, "So, we try to parlay with the Dremn? Do you expect me to trade your life for mine and Wyl's?"

Wyl knew the viciousness in her voice was a measure of her fear for Eirgei; he shared her fear. He lifted his head to watch the exchange, but said nothing.

Eirgei's face was set in stubbornness as he shoved a bit of crumbling log into the fire. "I expect you to negotiate to get the best price for it. Even the rumor of an alliance between us and the Dremn will make Sharei apoplectic, especially since there is not a thing she can do to stop us."

Wyl envied Eirgei for seeming so fearless, not at all disturbed by anticipation of his own cruelly-prolonged death at the hands of the

Dremn.

"But this is exile! I cannot just abandon—"

"—First," Eirgei interrupted, "assume Osbart already has agents in Nornholm—but they will only be observers. He will not want to compromise them. It will be some weeks before Ragna's assassins can make it here and start to plague us, but whether you are in Milkdales or not, she will not rest until you are dead."

Nothing new in that assessment: dealing with the threat of assassins was second nature to Wyl, a fact of life for all of them.

"While Sharei would prefer to forget the whole thing," Helgurdda said, and her voice broke.

Wyl looked at her as she resumed cleaning the dried gore from the hilt of her sabre.

She kept her head down. "Well, I may be in exile, but I will find a way to make sure she does not forget me. I am not a problem that is ever going to go away!"

"I am not proposing you do," Eirgei said. "I am proposing, as I told Calderek, that you persuade Royenne Errengard to back you with a Dremn menney. It is the kind of gamble that might appeal to the old vixen. Granted, I had intended to negotiate it through messengers from the Forest of Alshemir, but being in Dremnar will speed the process."

Wyl gaped at Eirgei. He'd thought Eirgei had just been putting on a brave front for Calderek—he'd believed none of it. He coughed.

Only Eirgei would consider actually taking refuge in the haunted Forest of Alshemir. The Forest was in the foothills of the Black Mountains, not far from Myymor, and Wyl had heard plenty of bad, uncanny stories about it. Anyone with sense stayed clear of that place. He was glad now he'd misread Eirgei's intentions about crossing the Tor. He had enough things haunting his sleep. He didn't need to deal with vengeful ghosts while he was awake, too.

"How do you propose I do that?" Helgurdda asked. "It will be hard enough to keep them from killing you!"

"Niece, you know there is a way. This is no time for foolish pride. Do whatever you must to raise a Dremn menney—an Icebear clan menney—and I promise you, we will defeat whatever Osbart can throw at us. We came so close with barely-trained rabble, even with, even with—"

Wyl watched Eirgei struggle for words. The most brilliant warleader in Trascolm loathed the very idea of magery proving superior to valor in battle, but surely Eirgei had to admit, after being defeated by that strange weather-magery, that they couldn't fight magic with virtue. No matter that they had a righteous cause, loyal supporters, and Eirgei's valor and cunning, what use was it without some kind of magic of their own?

Though after today, he didn't know if anything could counter weather-magery—not Evroza magery, maybe not even the foulest, black-hearted sorcery—and certainly not his own humble spitcraft.

"It was clever of Osbart to take advantage of that freak storm," Eirgei said. "But after Goffray committed all of Evroza's menney to battle, if those cowardly brigands in *our* menney hadn't run, we would have destroyed them."

Wyl looked down, hiding behind his hair again.

He owed his own survival to two things: the waning influence of his bloodcrafted *hex*—despite his loss of MiPaatet's favor—and Firebrand's amazing speed. He, too, had fled the whirlwind. He'd run so far, in fact, that he'd been the last to rejoin the survivors of Helgurdda's menney at the hamlet, arriving just in time to see the spearmen slaughter them.

Helgurdda sighed and grimaced. "I suppose I can bring up Prince Valdurren's name to Royenne Errengard, but he may not be much help. It has been a long time, and there is no telling what other trouble he brought down on himself after his return to Dremnar."

Wyl didn't doubt that, somehow, they'd be back in Milkdales, riding at the head of a Dremn menney to fight the Evroza. Eirgei didn't boast or threaten—or give up. The Wolf of Milkdales made promises and kept them.

And when they returned, *Wyl* swore he'd make sure that weather-mage paid for what she had done today! He swore he would never again spare an enemy, even if that enemy was a woman. Kin protected kin—and avenged them. His restraint hadn't kept MiPaatet's favor, anyway, and his conscience wasn't worth the lives that had paid for it today.

While Helgurdda and Eirgei quietly discussed what arguments and incentives they might use to persuade Royenne Errengard to back them with a menney, Wyl propped his leather shoulder-hood near the fire. He finally shrugged out of his *byrnney* and laid it out next to Firebrand's tack and his ragged, outcast clothes.

He took off his long riding boots with their roweled war spurs and fresh bramble scratches. He removed the hidden knives sheathed inside the cuffs, then found sand when he felt deep inside the boots for the hiltless hide-out blades under the felt insoles. He unsheathed the long, thin, spine blade hidden under his *byrnney*, along with the back-knives from his belt and the throwing knives hidden under his bracers. All needed the sand cleaned away.

But he laid his sabre and one back-knife away from the fire to keep bits of gore from baking on them. Those two would require more attention.

He stripped off his leggings and scowled down at the red blotches on his thin legs that would ripen into deep bruises by morning. He had no tunic to remove, so he started to strip off his ragged, worn-thin undertunic, then hesitated and thought better of it. He didn't want Helgurdda or Eirgei to see the marks of his injuries—old or new—and revive the old arguments about his age and fitness for the work he did. He withdrew out of sight of his elders before he removed his undertunic.

He wrung out his clothes as much as he could, then pulled the wet clothing back on and resigned himself to shivering as he returned to the fire.

He checked the condition of his bow. He was relieved. The lamination seemed sound, so he took the quiver of arrows closer to the fire. He crouched there, trembling with cold, and went through his remaining arrows, snapping off the valuable jektrar heads of the ones with shafts broken from being smashed against river rocks. He wrapped the sharp points in the rag that had held back his hair and dropped the warheads into his oilcloth robber's pouch, next to his oilcloth-wrapped packet of spare bowstrings.

The bread that he'd wrapped in a rag and stashed in a saddle bag that morning was a foul mush now. He dumped it in disgust. There would be nothing to eat between the three of them that hadn't been drenched and spoiled crossing the Tor.

He took a codex from his other saddlebag, along with a slate, a lump of chalk, a small roll of parchment, a couple stripped goose quills, and a carefully-wrapped little jar of ink. He fanned through the codex with its vellum pages bound between thin wooden boards decorated with inked sketches of Firebrand.

The codex was a book on horse training that Eirgei favored, both for its content, and for coding and decoding messages. Wyl had learned to read using it, so he was relieved to find no real damage to it. He carefully opened it and laid it out flat to dry, not too close to the fire.

But his charcoal sketches on the rolled parchment mapping the streets and alleys of Myymor—and rendering a few unrecognized Evrozing faces—hadn't survived the swim across the Tor.

"Let us speak of something else," Helgurdda said to Eirgei.

Wyl looked up as the two of them shifted to look across the fire at him.

"When you did not arrive at the hamlet with her, Lanney told me you had ridden off on your own *before* the whirlwind hit, not afterwards," Eirgei said, in that deceptively mild voice that meant Wyl was in serious trouble. "I have not spent seven years training you so you could run off in the middle of a battle, even if it was your first real battle! *Especially* because it was your first battle—you were supposed to stay with Lanney!"

"I wasn't running away!" Wyl protested. He hadn't thought about how it would look. He'd just worried about stopping the hail. "There was a mage—"

"That unarmed woman you shot at from the riverbank?" Eirgei growled, his eyes narrowing. "Maybe if she still had any magery left, she could have destroyed us all in the river! But she didn't, so she was no threat to us. Where was your honor? I thought I had taught you better conduct than that! And then you missed her, anyway. I have told you time and again, if you are going to stoop to fighting with a bow, you had better be as good as Lord Sterren with it. Sterren would not have missed that shot."

"No one could have made that shot in that wind, at that distance!" Wyl protested indignantly. "But at least I stopped her from unleashing more of her weather-magery on us."

"There is no such thing, boy," Eirgei said, in an ominously flat voice.

Wyl rose warily to his bare feet, conscious of the treacherous clutter about him and the distance to his sabre, his knives—and the pitiful defense they'd offer against Eirgei if he fell into a rage. "She caused the storm—the whirlwind—the flash-flood that killed Lanney!"

"Coincidence," Eirgei said and spit. But to Wyl's relief, Eirgei stayed seated on the other side of the fire. His anger didn't quite override the weariness in his voice. "This is the Moon of Storms, when things like that are commonplace. That is no justification for acting like a murdering brigand and trying to kill an unarmed, powerless woman—even if she was an Evrozing and a mage. There are limits, even in a blood-feud! We do not destroy the helpless, no matter what the Evroza stoop to doing. And do not start crediting Evroza mages with supernatural control over the weather. You have seen their magery before. Today, it was next to useless to them. That freak storm was just bad luck."

Actually, it was amazingly *good* luck that the three of them had survived it—that only Lanney's *luck* charm had failed.

Useless to protest further about magic. He had lost that fight long ago, when he'd first started his training with Eirgei. He took a knee where he was and humbly bowed his head towards Helgurdda, in the hope that an appeal to her would avert one of Eirgei's armed thrashings.

"Oh, get up!" Helgurdda said irritably. "It is over. Next time, obey your orders."

He ducked behind his hair, incredulous that there'd be no disciplinary training—that was what Eirgei called his sabre-thrashings. Eirgei didn't forgive his pupils' failings and Wyl's least of all.

But he felt hopeful that if Helgurdda could imagine a *next time*, then maybe the rebellion wasn't over, and their exile wouldn't be forever.

He rose from his knee and stole wary glances at the two of them, not entirely certain the matter was really settled. But when he looked closely at them in the firelight, he could see his elders were both truly exhausted.

Eirgei looked seedy and ancient. He actually hobbled as he went to tend to the rest of his and Helgurdda's gear, too tired to hide that his knees were hurting. Helgurdda perched on a rock, listlessly combing the knotted mess of her hair so she could wind it back into a tidy, practical war-knot. She looked grim and withdrawn.

"Take the first watch and try not to go running off," Eirgei told Wyl, when he returned from the horses. "You have responsibilities, Wylheim, so start taking them more seriously. Or do I have to treat you like an overgrown youngling who needs constant supervision?"

"I'm not a youngling!" Wyl snarled defensively, then regretted it. Like Lanney, Eirgei knew how to get his back up in an instant.

"Then do not act like one! You say you want to be my successor as Helgurdda's viceroye and her warleader? You will have to do better than you did today!"

Wyl bit back a resentful retort—Eirgei was right, after all. Knowing what he knew now, there was no good excuse for his failure to kill the mage when he'd had the chance to do it without Eirgei knowing about it.

As Wyl gathered more firewood to build up the fire, Eirgei and Helgurdda wrapped themselves in their damp cloaks and lay directly on the ground. They dropped off to sleep almost immediately.

He sat beside the fire, cleaning his blades and sheaths. Mostly, it was just a matter of wiping away the sand that had gotten into everything when Firebrand had pulled him off the bottom of the river and into the shallows. He didn't want the sand to grind off the dark patina that allowed him to draw his blades unseen in the night.

The bloodstains on his sabre and a back-knife were another matter.

After escaping the hamlet, he'd wiped them clean on his cloak as soon as he'd dared sheathe them. The icy river water had washed most of the blood from his cloak, but those two blades needed more thorough cleaning than a swipe and a dunk. Blood had dried around both weapons' hilts.

His sabre and back-knives were good quality, but just ordinary jegurit-bronze without any artisanry in them. Though their edges were bright from honing, he'd used them hard today. They'd been nicked and blunted, and they needed attention.

He sat by the fire with a rag and a whetstone, gritting his teeth against his stiffening bruises and trying to hold back the recollection of how his blades had gotten this way. He didn't want to remember the narrow escapes he'd had—that they'd all had—after being driven from the hamlet where Eirgei had tried to regroup and bring order back to his shaken and frightened minions.

In the end, Wyl had been so desperate to get away, nothing else had mattered except giving Firebrand room to run.

He didn't know if he'd killed anyone to get it.

Once they'd been driven away from the hamlet, the Evroza had kept trying to capture him alive whenever they'd appeared. They'd tried to separate Wyl from the others, while other spearmen had been cutting the rebels off from the safety of the hill-country and sending them fleeing back onto the road. Thanks to Firebrand and the skills Eirgei had drilled into him until they were practically an instinct, though the Evroza singled him out often enough, they hadn't taken him.

He'd rather be killed on the battlefield than be paraded as a prisoner through Crossroads Keep to meet a rebel's slow death on its walls. He'd fought himself clear of the spearmen on the strength of that fear, but he had no real memory of the fighting after escaping the hamlet, just a blur of fear and reflexes, blades and mail, and lean, hard-eyed

Evrozing faces.

He didn't *want* to remember more than that.

When he'd finished cleaning and restoring an edge to his blades, he rooted through the piled contents of his saddlebags again. He found a jektrar needle, and with thread from the unraveling hem of his surcoat, he neatly stitched the newest slashes on his surcoat's torso. With his last stitch, he was out of excuses to avoid examining his *byrnney*.

He reluctantly took it up.

Those Gerisari-style spearmen were a new thing with the Evroza—yet another example of Lord Goffray's influence? What the storm and the whirlwind had started, their surprise attacks in the hamlet and then on the road, had finished.

By the evidence of the gore and countless bright scratches in the patina of his weapons, he knew he'd done some damage to those he'd fought. Likewise evident from the damage to his *byrnney*, he'd almost died doing it.

He credited his bloodcrafted *hex* with his survival.

Looking at his *byrnney*, his memory of the rest of the day's clashes before they'd reached the river started to come back to him.

In their next encounter with the lancers after fleeing the hamlet, the Evroza had surprised them. Wyl had been overwhelmed by two Evrozings, one a spearman, the other a sabreer. Those two had worked well together and had not held back because of his youth. While Wyl had been desperately avoiding being skewered by the spearman, the sabreer had almost taken off his head—Wyl had failed to avoid the beheading slash, but the sabre cut had been too low, missing its mark by a blade's width, leaving a line of bright gold scored into the jegurit-bronze strips on the front of his *byrnney's* high collar.

Wyl involuntarily flinched when he fingered the matching bruise on his throat.

Fierce as the fighting had been, somehow bruises were all the harm he'd taken.

His *byrnney* had been better protection than he'd expected, but it had paid a heavy price. In one section, over his belly, the firelight showed where the scales were sheared away—more likely from a glancing sabre slash than from a deflected poke with a spear. Whichever weapon had caused it, it had left the backing of aurox hide deeply gouged.

He fingered the gouge and shuddered—he'd seen men gutted. It was a particularly awful memory and he shied away from stirring it back to life.

He hated brigands, but they'd taught him a lot, too. Thanks to growing up surrounded by them, nothing he saw on the battlefield, on Myymor's streets—or even in camp—could stagger him, shock him, or stop him from doing whatever needed to be done to keep Helgurdda safe. Today, that numbness had helped save his life.

It was only now that he'd a chance to think about what had happened and what he'd done, that the numbness left and those memories rose to trouble him.

Lanney was gone.

Death was nothing new, but Lanney was the first of those he cared about to die. He knew, as long as the blood-feud endured and the rebellion went on, she wouldn't be the last, but that was no comfort.

The tears he'd fought earlier now refused to come, though there was no one to see them, so he checked on his drying gear rather than think about Lanney any longer.

After he'd tended to his gear and rearmed, he caught and picketed the horses, then posted himself in the brush by them, where the firelight wouldn't keep his eyes from adapting to the growing dark. The horses would give him first warning of something approaching—he wasn't at his best for standing watch. He was tired and his body felt like one big bruise. Unlike Eirgei and Helgurdda, though, he hadn't fought a battle before being chased by the Evroza all afternoon and then plunging into the Tor. They needed the rest more than he did.

But he couldn't stop returning to what had happened at the river.

He well-remembered life before Lanney had become a constant presence beside him, and he dreaded returning to it.

For the past six years, the other rebels had thought of him as Lanney's odd, half-Folk foster-son, and Lanney had never corrected them. It had pleased him, her acting like he was close family.

Lanney, not Eirgei, had been the one who'd taught him how to handle himself in the roughest company. She'd gone everywhere with him, except on his spying missions to Myymor, where her strong Dremn accent would have betrayed her. In the brigand camps, Lanney and he had watched each other's back as well as Helgurdda's, while Helgurdda and Eirgei recruited for her cause—aside from outcast rebel Evrozings, few of the other outlaws in Milkdales's badlands had been unjustly cast out of their clans the way Helgurdda and Eirgei had been.

Under Eirgei's command, those recruited outlaws made passable, but unreliable, minions who were at their most dangerous off the battlefield. Only Eirgei's brutal discipline kept the former brigands under control, and even then, there'd always been someone ambitiously plotting to seize the rebel treasury or Helgurdda herself, forcing Eirgei to kill the upstart.

Over those six years, Wyl had known other warlords and advisors close to Helgurdda and Eirgei, all of them lost to the blood-feud, treachery, or disease—but never his Lanney.

Not until now.

No use trying to fool himself. Lanney surviving what had happened at the Tor was as likely as him putting an arrow into the weather-mage from across the river.

He couldn't—wouldn't—think about Lanney. He needed to keep his mind focused on watching for local foresters, whose alarm at finding them camping in their hunting grounds might provoke an attack before he could yell *parlay*. With the cliffs and the Tor guarding Dremnar's southern border, there was little danger of encountering a warband patrol here—that danger would only arise when they proceeded north and eventually approached Dremnar's royal stronghold, Nornholm.

After the moon had set and the night sky remained cloudless, he figured foresters would have no reason to be blundering through the woods in the dark, and a little of his tension eased. He watched through a gap in the hemlock branches overhead as the uncaring stars rotated with the passing hours.

To take his mind first off Lanney and then off the spearmen who had chased him, he dwelled instead on how responsibility for the whole of the rebel disaster could be traced back to him. If he'd killed the mage when he could've, none of this disaster would have happened.

He brooded over his mistakes until the night grew cold enough for a damp wool cloak to be appealing. He returned to the fire and fed it, and tried to dry the cloak while wearing it. He wished he could make a spitcraft charm that would help. He didn't know one, so he occupied his numb mind with trying to make up a *drying* charm until the cloak had dried on its own.

When the stars and his body told him the night had entered the dead hours, he cautiously woke Eirgei to take his turn on watch, approaching not quite an arm's length away.

He coughed.

Eirgei lunged up for him. One of his hands snapped up towards

Wyl's throat, while the other hand, with a short blade in it, flashed around behind Wyl, aiming for where his kidney would be, if he were taller.

But, after such a day, Wyl had expected Eirgei to wake up fighting, so he ducked and dodged aside, out of reach and unscathed.

He doubted his own dreams would be any more peaceful.

The jerk from missing the grab and blow jolted Eirgei fully awake. The rebel warleader blinked owlishly up at him, glanced up at the sky, and grunted as he climbed to his feet.

"Get some sleep, boy."

Wyl nodded, too tired to argue over Eirgei's choice of words. Wrapped up in his cloak, he lay in the warm spot where Eirgei had slept, coughed, and pretended to obey.

It was a night made for nightmares.

CHAPTER 8

PARLAY

2ⁿᵈ Day of the Moon of Storms, 113 G.E.

The next morning, Eirgei led the way farther into the Icepeak Mountains, climbing northward in what he said was the general direction of Nornholm. They travelled slowly for the sake of their bruised, worn-out horses, though Firebrand had enough energy to resent being made to follow behind the more worn-out horses and muscled her way into the lead at the first opportunity. There was no trail, just a direction, keeping the morning sun on their right.

Wyl thought on their current misfortunes and dreaded what was to come—first, there had been Eirgei's fatal misjudgment of the scouts' competence, offset by his own lucky confusion about Eirgei's intentions at the riverside. This was a new and disturbing reality: Eirgei made mistakes, too, just like he did—and Eirgei's could be just as dire.

Which meant the negotiations Eirgei envisioned with the Dremn royenne—his lifelong enemy—might not end favorably for them.

They descended into a ravine.

Suddenly, unarmored, dark-bearded Folk hunters dressed in tunics and shoulder-hoods, their black hair jaw-length, came out of the woods and surrounded them with their bows drawn. Their dark eyes were narrowed and tense.

If she'd been alone, Helgurdda's golden hair might have let her pass for a Dremn, but not with Eirgei and his long, graying-brown Tras moustache riding beside her.

Wyl held his breath, but Eirgei surprised him by leaving his black

95

sabre in its sheath—only its anonymous, rough leather-wrapped hilt and scarred sheath showing. He called to the hunters before they could do something hasty that they'd all regret.

"We have come to parlay with Royenne Errengard! Helgurdda of Milkdales has come to parlay with Royenne Errengard!"

Eirgei didn't name himself, and the emphasis he gave to Royenne Errengard's name was heavy-handed. Nor did he seem embarrassed for not pairing Helgurdda's name with that of a clan, bold acknowledgement of her outlawry.

Wyl wished Eirgei wouldn't tempt them. If they chose, these Folk could feather them with arrows, kill them out of hand, and never be called to justice for it.

The Folk he'd known in Milkdales had all been disowned—dead to their clans, rogues of one sort or another, and too proud to ever admit to who they'd once been. Those of them who had taken up brigandage before moving on to rebellion had been very good at killing.

But Eirgei had read their situation with these Dremn accurately. These Folk were hunters, not outlaws. The three of them didn't get shot. Perhaps these *were* decent, law-abiding Folk, but Wyl didn't trust they were safe with them.

He knew better than to trust anyone except Eirgei and Helgurdda— and Lanney. For an outlaw, trust was a character flaw—which was why it astonished him that Eirgei trusted these Folk not to let fly at them. But then, Eirgei had more courage than anyone he had ever met.

"Take the Tras to Royenne Errengard. Let her decide what to do with them," a hunter advised the one who seemed to be in charge.

"Release the boy, and surrender your weapons," the leader of the hunters said.

Wyl ducked his head to hide his reaction. With his hair, shoulder-hood, and *byrnney*—and riding the only native horse of the three—he had been mistaken for one of them, one of the Folk.

He quickly got his face under control and scooted Firebrand to the hunter's side. He assumed his Myymor identity, that of a young Folk outcast disowned by his clan for cause.

"MiPaatet's favor on you, sir," he said, in a humble manner, thankful that here in Dremnar, he could speak—sometimes, just opening his mouth in Myymor could be dangerous after six years around Lanney's accent.

"Did they hurt you?" the hunter asked. "Harm you in any way?"

Wyl shook his head, keeping his eyes downcast, wishing he'd kept back some of his *upala* infusion to make his eyes look more Folk. But he hadn't thought he'd need *upala* while settled into their winter camp—no more than he'd expected to end up in Dremnar, still trying to pass as Folk.

"Come with us, boy. You'll have to tell Prince-Viceroye Frekkei what you know, then Royenne Errengard will see about returning you to your people. She may even give you a reward for finding these criminals first."

"Thank you, sir, but I—I'm disowned. My clan doesn't want me back." He hung his head in practiced shame, letting his hair screen his face and his so-not-Folk eyes.

The dark-bearded Folk hunter looked at him thoughtfully.

Wyl watched him through his hair, saw how he took note of his angled cloak and the *byrnney* under it. The hunter's dark eyes narrowed, no doubt spotting the sabre hilt sticking up between the folds of his pushed-back hood and his quiver.

"Hmm...carrying a blade like that, I can see why. Were you playing with swords before they disowned you or after?"

The Folk were hunters and herders, not minions, though Wyl's *byrnney* was called Folk armor. All the Folk clans had turned their backs on war long ago, and some Folk clans were so morally strait-laced, they'd even disown a youngling boy just for playing at war. The Folk shunned their outcasts, and Wyl counted on that now—only one of the Folk might see through his pose, and he'd ensured they'd shy off from contact with him.

"Before, sir," Wyl muttered, lifting his head when he had enough hair overhanging his eyes not to rouse suspicions that anything was wrong about them.

It was a wise precaution. The hunters' leader looked him over, his eyes narrow and critical. "These rogues didn't take you prisoner, did they? You're their guide—you hired yourself to them, even knowing they're Tras."

"He's probably not much better than them, either," one of the other hunters said, with distaste. "He either stole the sword and horse, or earned them on his belly. Pretty boy like that, I'll bet he didn't have to steal anything."

Wyl bit his tongue hard against retorting with a slur of his own and ducked his head again, as if in shame. He should be relieved—the hunters had accepted him as Folk, albeit the worst of their kind. Out the corner of his eye, Helgurdda and Eirgei looked shocked, which he found darkly amusing. What else could these Folk think of him?

A boy didn't stay honorable or virtuous when far from clan or kin. This wouldn't be the first time he'd been accused of underage bedsport or even outright whoring. Everyone knew disowned boys were notoriously willing to do anything to survive. When posing as an outcast while spying in Myymor, he'd received such insults before from Folk trying to drive him out of town. The only real difference between being an outcast and an outlaw was that he didn't have a price on his head. Without a claim on a clan's protection, there was little in the law of the land to protect an outcast. An outcast lived by his wits, or died for lack of them. Against so many—if these hunters hadn't been honest, upright Folk—he would have been fair game for any sport. His was a good disguise, but a dangerous one.

"And either way," another of the Folk hunters said, "he's right, no clan will take him back."

"So we'll let the viceroye figure out what to do with him," the leader decided. "He's just a stripling. How old are you, boy?"

"Fourteen," Wyl contradicted hunter with a lie. He liked fourteen. Fourteen was a good age for a boy to be—a youth, not a stripling, and old enough to be treated with more respect, while still accounted, under the law of the land and by most people, as too young to hang. If they got a close enough look at him to know he'd lied, then they'd also know he wasn't Folk.

If only he hadn't used up all his *upala* before he'd left Myymor!

"The viceroye will probably see him fostered until he's of age," one of the hunters said to their leader. "He's young, maybe he'll learn enough honest behavior to avoid being bonded once he's sixteen."

The leader looked at Wyl and didn't trouble to hide his disgust. "Best keep your mouth shut about what you've done since you were disowned and maybe you'll get a second chance as a reward. Keep your bow, but give me that sword so there won't be questions asked when we get to Norn Holm. Just say these Tras forced you to be their guide, and you might even get a few silver denarreis for leading them to us."

Wyl disliked tamely giving up his sabre, but the hunters thought they were doing him an undeserved kindness and no other reaction would be in character for even the most corrupted Folk outcast temporarily restored to the toleration of his own people.

They were lucky these hunters were Folk and not Dremn. These Folk hunters had obviously never served alongside a noble Dremn clan's menney—they didn't think to check Wyl for other weapons, like the pair of back-knives under his cloak that he hadn't tried to conceal, but now didn't dare reveal. The back-knives were for a Tras style of fighting no rustic, disowned Folk boy in Dremnar could know. The hunters wouldn't know it either, but since Wyl also didn't want to be any more disarmed than he had to be, he said nothing of them.

The hunters disarmed Eirgei and Helgurdda without examining the weapons they confiscated or searching for hidden ones, either. But because the hunters were on foot, they took Helgurdda and Eirgei's horses.

They weren't thieves—they let Wyl keep Firebrand, but only after she bit the hunter who tried to catch her by the bridle and then kicked him when he moved to strike her for it.

A couple of the hunters thought they'd ride the Gerisari horses alongside him, but those horses weren't as docile as Gerisari horses were expected to be—Eirgei had given them war training, too. Though their ground manners were still Gerisari-schooled and they would follow whoever led them—making them so easy to handle, even a five-year-old could steal one—these wouldn't let a stranger ignorant of warhorse ways mount.

The Gerisari horses served to reduce the hunters' effective fighting strength by two—the hunters who were leading them—but the horses were too valuable for the hunters to let loose, and the Folk were likely reassured that they still outnumbered the three of them by two to one.

"Don't try anything stupid, boy," the leader said, still rubbing his kicked thigh and obviously concerned that Wyl was the only one still mounted. "I'd make you walk, but you'd slow us down too much. Just remember, if you don't come to Norn Holm with us, you won't get any reward."

Helgurdda and Eirgei were tied up with more leather thongs than Wyl thought necessary, a compliment to Helgurdda's aggressive glower at the hunters. It relieved him that she had successfully distracted the hunters from giving much attention to Eirgei—the only reason Eirgei still lived. Once recognized, he'd soon be a dead man.

The hunters tied the two of them together at the neck like common criminals, with one hunter leading Helgurdda and another positioned to hold Eirgei back, keeping the tether taut between them.

When Wyl rode past Eirgei to get to the front of the group, Eirgei gave him a cold stare, as if he were nothing more than a chance-met stranger, but he could read Eirgei well enough to see the approval in it. If throwing themselves on the royenne's unlikely mercy didn't work out, Wyl had ensured he had the freedom to help them escape.

The Folk hunters led them through a series of ever-higher mountain passes overlooking forested valleys. These were the Icepeaks, and it seemed that they'd be climbing all the way up to the ice. They didn't make good time—Eirgei limped, and Wyl didn't think it a ruse.

His sleepless night had left him still exhausted. It took everything he had left in him to stay in the saddle as Firebrand climbed up and scrambled down into an endless succession of mountain valleys. The frigid air tightened his lungs and made him cough more, which he muffled in his cloak. He didn't want Eirgei to have any doubts about his ability to keep up or do his share of the fighting if they had to make a dash for freedom.

But nothing raised an alarm in Eirgei; he and Helgurdda had troubles enough to distract them. There was no need to launch an escape attempt—the hunters would know the fastest route to Nornholm and Royenne Errengard.

They spent their second night in Dremnar with Eirgei and Helgurdda as prisoners in a high mountain meadow where the hungry horses were loosed to graze. The hunters shared their bread and cheese with Wyl, but their grudging generosity to an outcast boy didn't extend to sharing their venison jerky. As far as Helgurdda and Eirgei were concerned, their generosity was limited to water.

Wyl lay huddled in his cloak and focused on Eirgei's low voice murmuring somewhere in the darkness to his right. With his keen, spy's ears, he could make out all their words as they devised a contingency plan if the meeting with the Dremn royenne went all wrong. He closed his eyes, tracking their hushed discussion and the part he was to play in that plan.

Why had he thought Eirgei intended to surprise the Evroza by crossing the Tor? Why hadn't it occurred to him that a successful crossing would eventually make Eirgei a prisoner of his oldest enemies? That these unsuspecting Folk hunters had found them so quickly meant those *luck* charms under their horses' saddles were still working. Wyl might've lost MiPaatet's favor, but Helgurdda and Eirgei clearly hadn't. If the three of them had gotten deeper into Dremnar, they'd have eventually encountered a menney warband on patrol and with it, the possibility of meeting an old minion, some veteran raider who might have recognized Eirgei from before the rebellion, even after thirteen years.

These hunters hadn't even asked Wyl for his name or Eirgei's—

they were too dazzled over capturing Helgurdda, the most notorious outlaw in three lands. All the talk around the hunters' fire that night centered on the reward Royenne Errengard would give them for capturing outlaws and on ideas about how they might also collect on the bounty being offered by the Evroza royenne of Trascolm for Helgurdda's head.

With Helgurdda bound and helpless, Wyl tried to stay alert to watch over her and listen to the talk among the hunters by the campfire. If they decided to sport with her, only Wyl—and not the law of the land—could protect her. But his miserably sleepless night and the horrors of yesterday all caught up with him, and weariness made his head spin.

His half-waking dreams were all bad ones—nothing new except that Lanney's drowned body now had a guilty place in them. He felt like he was again underwater in the Tor, with a death-grip on Firebrand's tail and no clear sense of which direction was up.

✦

3rd Day of the Moon of Storms, 113 G.E.

At dawn, Wyl watched through slit eyes as the hunters sent one of their number ahead to Nornholm with their news. What kind of welcome would be waiting when they arrived?

A couple hunters tended to Helgurdda and Eirgei, but though Helgurdda pointed out that they would voluntarily accompany the hunters to Nornholm, the two of them remained bound and afoot.

The hunters eventually led them into a broad valley.

Wyl could see a distant fortress towering over the tops of the hemlock forest surrounding it. It sprawled across a terrace partway up a massive, jagged pinnacle of rock near the center of the valley.

They arrived at the town of Nornholm—which had been hidden by the forest—by midday, when no shadows from the quarried peak hid any part of the fortress. The mountain, the hunters said, was Mount Norn, and it formed the royal stronghold's north and east walls.

Wyl stared up at it and felt the bottom drop out of his stomach.

Nornholm—the fortress and the town outside it—was bigger than Myymor on Milkdales's eastern frontier. The Evroza's fortified clanhold within that town had been imposing, but even at a distance, Wyl could see Nornholm's citadel was far more massive. The town of Myymor had been his only experience of any place larger than a village,

and Nornholm made Myymor look like a Folk hamlet. On the outskirts of the town was a Folk village composed of clusters of *cruk*-
houses, large huts built around a massive central tree. In the town itself, the shops and cottages were made of stone, despite the plentiful
timber from the hemlock forest surrounding it.

Wyl hadn't reckoned that the barbarians of Dremnar were rich—or
so civilized.

The fortress's outer curtain wall began halfway up the slope of the
mountain. The wall loomed over the hunters' party. Behind it, higher
on the mountain, the stone walls of the inner bailey overshadowed
those of the outer bailey, and behind those walls were the tops of towers he could barely see.

He counted the sentry posts along the lower bailey battlements—all
of them manned by black-bearded Folk archers.

Once inside, it would be hard to get out again.

The hunters took the wide lane that ran through the town and up
the open and sloping demesne that lay between the town and the
stronghold. At the end of the lane, a pair of halberd-wielding guardsmen allowed them to pass through Nornholm's open outer gates. Inside, they picked up a small escort, a hand of Icebear minions.

They climbed the wide, shallow, stone terraces of the lower bailey
to where another pair of guards stood aside to let them pass through
the open inner gates.

At an Icebear minion's command, Wyl dismounted in a stone
courtyard carved out of the rock of Mount Norn. When grooms arrived to take the horses, Firebrand pinned her ears and snapped at one.

"War-trained," Wyl warned apologetically, hanging his head. He
held her steady as the grooms took the Gerisari horses away. When a
groom returned with a brass muzzle, Wyl stripped off her bridle and
attached the muzzle to the halter underneath. He watched the groom
lead Firebrand away to the same nearby stable where the Gerisari horses had been taken, a stone building that seemed to have grown out of
the rock. The weary Gerisari horses had plodded behind the grooms,
but Firebrand still carried her head and tail high, ears pricked and nostrils flared in snorting suspicion under the war-muzzle as she took in
her first taste of civilization.

He swallowed hard.

Another warband of minions surrounded the three of them and the
Folk hunters, too, and escorted them inside the sprawling palace. Wyl
spared a moment from his gawking to size them up. They wore white

and black-speckled, half-sleeved fur surcoats with the fur on the inside muffling the rustle of the full-sleeved mail underneath. They had an assortment of straight swords and axes strapped over the outside of their surcoats.

Wyl took in his surroundings with the eyes of a spy. The corridors were faced with well-fitted ashlar stone. The ceilings looked high enough for a full-grown man to use a longsword. The narrowly-spaced rafters high overhead supported a slate roof rather than the thatch it would have been in Myymor. In a few places, he saw pallets rolled up along the walls. Oil lamps hanging from old, blue, jektrar-bronze cressets lit their way rather than windows.

He couldn't ignore the foreboding he felt, that they might not be able to escape this place if this meeting went badly.

He felt a draft. Ahead, he could see a curved wall—the wall of a tower. Just before they reached the tower, they passed a jagged set of stairs going downward, the source of the cold draft. At the base of the tower's curved wall facing the corridor, a door was open, and he could see into its guardroom.

Their escort took them around the tower and continued down the corridor. Every time the corridor came to a tower, there was another guardroom, and his concern deepened. If this went wrong, their chances of escaping looked ever bleaker.

He could hear Eirgei hobbling behind him. Eirgei would be unable to escape unless he could do it at his own speed—and stealthily, because not even Eirgei could fight his way out of the heart of Nornholm against the kind of odds Wyl saw.

He desperately hoped Helgurdda's parlay with Royenne Errengard would be successful. Otherwise, they'd have done better to have drowned in the Tor than be captives of the age-old enemies of their people.

Outside the entrance to Nornholm's great Crown Court hall, he saw a handful of Dremn noblewomen already waiting with sweet words of welcome for the hunters to put them at ease. Inside, the great hall was empty. The viceroye had gone hawking, and they were to await his return. The servants separated Wyl and the hunters from the prisoners. Helgurdda and Eirgei sat on the floor against the back wall farthest from the doors, still bound.

More servants appeared, both Folk and close-cropped blond bondsmen, and offered everyone except Helgurdda and Eirgei delicacies to eat and drink.

Wyl stared uneasily down at the scuffed toes of his boots from under his hair and wished for Lanney's familiar presence beside him.

A bondsman offered him a piece of sweet bread baked with dried fruit. He wolfed down, wishing there were more of it. The bondsman then brought him a bright silver drinking horn. It didn't contain wine or water, or even beer, but rather something a paler gold.

"Watered mead," the bondsman told him, raising a brow at his wariness, then looking him up and down the way the hunters and then the Folk servants had, trying to figure out what he was.

Wyl was careful to keep his head tilted down.

The bondsman was Dremn, but shorn of his beard and with his blond hair left a finger-thickness of stubble, as befitted a bondservant. He had an uncommonly lofty manner, but he gave Wyl a kindly smile and pretended he hadn't noticed Wyl was an outcast; for their part, the Folk servants avoided him.

Wyl was in the wrong disguise. His Folk identity was better suited to Myymor's streets than to noble company. A Folk boy disowned for cause had no place here in a royal palace or even in the company of respectable Folk, but it was too late for him to try to look *not*-Folk.

He coughed, keeping his eyes downcast, trying to mask his suspiciousness as a young outcast's ignorance. He took a careful sip of the mead and tried to look ill-at-ease rather than worried that the responsibility for somehow devising an escape rested with him.

The servants departed, and the minions standing guard stepped outside and closed the doors behind them. He could do nothing more than lean against a stone pillar and stare up at the clerestory windows letting in the cold and light, ponder the high ceiling's rafters above them, and wait.

After long minutes, he heard an odd scratching sound behind him. He looked to the far side of the hall where Helgurdda and Eirgei sat.

Helgurdda beckoned him with a twitch of her head.

Wyl looked toward the hunters. They'd grown bored with waiting on the viceroye's pleasure and huddled together on the floor between the pillars playing some gambling game. No one took notice when he padded from pillar to pillar, carefully silent despite his boots and spurs. Once he reached Helgurdda's side, he crouched to avoid drawing anyone's attention.

"My hair," Helgurdda said, in a low voice. "I am not meeting the Royenne of Dremnar looking like a common outlaw. I need to look like a royal outlaw, fit for a crown."

He nodded and glanced aside at Eirgei.

Helgurdda's uncle rested with his chin on his chest. Though he seemed asleep, he was slumped in a position that kept most of his face obscured.

Wyl unwound Helgurdda's hair and finger-combed it out of its twists so that her burden of honor rippled loose down her back like a golden waterfall and pooled on the floor around her. Then he returned to his place.

No one had taken any notice of him.

He tried to do as Eirgei did and feigned sleep with his chin on his chest.

Some time later, he looked up at the sound of voices and a clatter of boots outside the doors.

Prince-Viceroye Frekkei had arrived, accompanied by Dremn nobles, women and men, all in hunting attire. Prince Frekkei, in white and black, was dressed for hawking in a garnak trimmed with speckled ice bear fur at the hood and wrists. The royenne's son was perhaps ten years younger than Eirgei's fifty-three years. He was tall and muscular, typically Dremn in his blond hair and blue eyes. Under a viceroye's circlet, he wore his long hair in a war-knot held with a silver and onyx hairpin in the shape of a bear's claw. He had a neat, light-brown beard—and he grinned as the hunters explained who they'd bagged.

The viceroye courteously heard out the Folk hunters. His eye skimmed over Wyl and then over Eirgei, who still leaned against the wall with his head down. All the viceroye's attention riveted on Helgurdda, who was pale, exhausted, dirty—but still beautiful.

Helgurdda gathered herself and rose, despite her bound hands, as he approached. Wyl admired the casual, clever way she shifted aside so the viceroye's eyes would not rest on Eirgei.

"So, you are Helgurdda, the notorious outlaw and rebel leader," the viceroye said. "Why have you come to Dremnar?"

"It is a matter for your royenne. I have a proposal that will interest her, an alliance that will be to her advantage as well as mine."

"But the risks will not," he said dismissively.

"The risks will be well-worth it. The prize is the crown of Trascolm for me and a treaty dealing with the Gerisari for Royenne Errengard. There is no harm in her hearing me out."

"The royenne does not converse with common felons."

Helgurdda lit up with genuine amusement.

Wyl relaxed a little—Prince Frekkei wouldn't be the first enemy to succumb to her charisma.

"You must admit, I am a most *uncommon* felon. If she does not agree to my proposal after hearing me out, then sell me back to the Evroza."

Wyl was first stunned, then horrified at her defiance, that she'd throw away a life so dearly preserved with blood and sacrifice—and then tried to restore a neutral expression to his face. Luckily, Helgurdda's words had ensured everyone's eyes were still on her and Prince-Viceroye Frekkei.

"But sell me to the Evroza unheard, or execute me, and Icebear honor will never recover. I claim the right to deal with Royenne Errengard—"

He heard a thin, grating laugh that didn't come from within Prince Frekkei's company.

"An outlaw talking of honor and claiming rights?"

Wyl looked toward the other end of the great hall. An elderly woman with the long, sweeping hair of a crowned royenne had entered the Crown Court hall from behind the large tapestry to the rear of the dais.

He hadn't been trained to recognize royalty outside Evroza clan, but because the Dremn courtiers immediately went to their knees, this could only be Royenne Errengard—she wore her gold crown over a gauzy white, dark-spangled veil covering her hair. Her trailing, white silk robe was liberally sprinkled with clusters of gleaming black jet beads—the royal Icebear clan took the bear's colors for their own.

She took her time crossing the hall to the dais, long enough for servants to spring out of the shadows, set up a curule chair sheathed in gold on the low dais and drape the seat with a thick ice bear pelt. Prince Frekkei directed a handful of his minions to take charge of Helgurdda and Eirgei, and went to meet his mother.

The viceroye greeted her formally, dropping to one knee one stride from Royenne Errengard's feet. Then he rose at her nod and gave her his arm for support as she stepped up onto the dais and made herself comfortable in the chair. At her nod, the viceroye's noble companions also rose from their knees and arrayed themselves among the pillars for a better view of the proceedings.

Royenne Errengard thoughtfully tapped her fingers on one golden arm of the chair and gave Helgurdda a shrewd and leisurely survey.

CHAPTER 9

ROYENNE ERRENGARD

Wyl thought Helgurdda looked a desperate outlaw, dressed in her battle-worn, faded-red surcoat and high, bramble-scarred riding boots. Her boots disappeared under the tattered edge of her red quilted aketon, itself barely visible beneath the bright-scratched, brown jegurit mail covering her from neck to wrists to knees.

Her clothing contrasted with her gleaming hair, well-kept and reflecting her care for presenting a royal appearance despite the privations of an outlaw's life. The golden curtain of it hung loose almost to the floor, giving her a regal air.

The Dremn royenne leaned toward Prince Frekkei at her right side—there was no consort on her left—and her son bent to listen.

Wyl strained his ears to hear from where he stood among the hunters gathered with a hand of Icebear minions behind the noble courtiers. He watched their lips to better make out their low words.

"Have the prisoners given any trouble?" Royenne Errengard asked her son in a hushed voice. "Have they committed any crimes in Dremnar?"

The answer to both was *no.*

The royenne pursed her wrinkled lips thoughtfully. "If I am to converse with an outlaw, I would prefer not to be reminded of that fact. Release their bonds, and if there is any trouble, do as you please."

Prince Frekkei's lips tightened and his eyes narrowed as he looked over at Helgurdda and then at Eirgei, then back at Helgurdda.

Wyl ducked his head, hiding his interest behind his hair.

What Prince Frekkei pleased clearly didn't involve loosing a pair of desperate outlaws in the same room as his mother.

Nevertheless.

"Unbind them," Prince Frekkei told the guardsmen.

The guardsmen, too, looked unhappy, but they obeyed. They first removed Helgurdda's bonds, then Eirgei's.

Eirgei cautiously rubbed his wrists, not making any sudden moves. By the way he flexed his fingers, Wyl worried Eirgei's hands were numb, too numb to hold a weapon if this went badly.

The guardsmen brought Helgurdda a couple steps closer for their royenne to better see and hear her. Behind her, they prodded Eirgei to his feet and brought him forward, his head still cast down, hiding his face.

One of the nearby guardsmen poked Wyl and directed him toward the dais. "You, too. The royenne will decide what is to be done with the likes of you."

So he quietly walked forward until he was just behind Helgurdda's back on the right, the defensive bodyguard's position that had been his for six years and mirrored where Eirgei had positioned himself on her left—where Lanney should have been.

He glanced away.

"Let her approach," Royenne Errengard said.

Helgurdda shrugged a guardsman's hands off her arm and quickly strode forward towards the dais. Eirgei and Wyl moved fast behind her, staying between her and the guardsmen. When Helgurdda didn't stop at half the distance to the dais, the surprised guardsmen converged on her.

She did stop, then—a mere three strides away—and went to both booted knees, bowing her head.

Instantly, Eirgei dropped to both his knees, putting him two strides behind Helgurdda. His forehead touched the fragrant, matted floor, and he kept it there in the profound obeisance of a bondsman—or a doomed man.

Wyl took Eirgei's actions as a prompt, only when he went to his knees, he remained upright at Helgurdda's heels—their second night in Dremnar, Eirgei and Helgurdda had spoken of this moment, and though they'd not spoken directly to Wyl because of the hunters, they'd expected him to have understood his part in it.

The guardsmen surrounded them, nervous hands on longswords, and Prince Frekkei stood between them and his mother, his own sword drawn.

The old royenne scowled. "If you intend to beg for your life, you are a fool to offend me with unwarranted familiarity, outlaw." She gestured for Prince Frekkei to stand aside.

He did, but he didn't sheathe his sword, merely rested its point on the floor.

This wasn't a promising start—Wyl did what little he could to improve matters by also bowing his head to the ground like Eirgei, only with his arms crossed under him, fingers poised to draw his hidden throwing knives.

"I permitted you entry into Norn Holm," the royenne said to Helgurdda, "for the sole purpose of hearing you beg, outlaw."

Wyl stole a look at what was happening.

Helgurdda raised her head, her entire posture one of serene confidence. "I am outlawed unjustly. I came to Dremnar—and to Nornholm—to take refuge with my royal kith in my time of need."

Wyl quickly ducked his head back down. He couldn't see anything except the scarred knees of his riding boots, but in the sudden, shocked silence, he could practically hear everyone in earshot running through Icebear clan genealogies in their heads, looking for Helgurdda.

"Prince Valdurren is long dead," Royenne Errengard said, the first to figure out the connection Helgurdda meant.

The Dremn nobles who had accompanied the viceroye shifted where they stood, showing intense interest and started murmuring.

"Though your cousin, my sire, was in disgrace," Helgurdda said, regally ignoring the reaction of the courtiers, "he still had standing in Icebear clan, and he had been formally betrothed as consort to my mother and acknowledged by her as my sire. I claim protection and a welcome from Icebear clan on his behalf."

There was a long silence.

Royenne Errengard was renowned even in Trascolm for her cunning political maneuvers. Wyl knew a welcome here would make Royenne Sharei furious, but he knew nothing of the Dremn royenne's mind, whether she'd reckon tweaking the Royenne of Trascolm's nose worth the trouble sure to follow. Would she realize that trouble would include a relentless stream of hireling assassins and bounty hunters eager for the price on Helgurdda's head?

Wyl swallowed hard and called on everything Eirgei had taught him to keep his fear in hand. He concentrated on the feel of the releases for the knives at his wrists, recalling his last glimpse of the Icebears around him to pick his targets despite his bowed head.

"Your claim on my protection," Royenne Errengard said at last, speaking as Icebear clan's baronne and not as Dremnar's royenne, "as mere kith is rather shaky, but Ice Bear clan looks out for its own, kin or kith, no matter how insignificant or notorious that person may be elsewhere. I grant you asylum here in Norn Holm, so long as you keep the peace in accordance with the laws of Dremnar."

"So long as that law," Helgurdda said, and her giving conditions caused more murmuring among the Dremn courtiers, "still recognizes the right of one wronged to have justice or the right to vengeance when justice is denied."

"Of course! Dremnar still keeps the old laws, customs, and traditions." Royenne Errengard didn't sound offended by Helgurdda's words—likely because of the insult to Trascolm and the Evroza. "See that *you* keep them, too."

Wyl began to breathe easier when the royenne called for her attendants to bring a stool for Helgurdda, also gold-sheathed and with a cushion that imitated ice bear markings. It was public acknowledgement of a relationship—and a claim—Royenne Errengard could've easily denied, had she not seen an opportunity for something.

"Who are these others with you?"

Helgurdda reached around and put her hand on the back of Wyl's still-bowed head.

He closed his eyes to enjoy the moment, his scalp tingling under her fingers.

"This is my son, Wylheim—"

His eyes flew open, and he went rigid with shock.

Until the blood-feud was over and Helgurdda was safely crowned as Trascolm's royenne, his relationship to her remained a secret worth his life. He'd never been acknowledged as Helgurdda's son, not to her inner circle—not even to Calderek. There was no price on his head, but he'd be a valuable prize in the blood-feud, a prime target once the Evroza knew he existed. His value lay in the assumption that killing him would be a devastating blow to Helgurdda, one that might tilt the war in the Evroza's favor.

"—by my beloved consort, Hereres." Helgurdda concluded.

Just once, he wished Helgurdda wouldn't force him to share her attention with a man thirteen years dead.

Then, he felt Helgurdda tug his braid out from under his shoulderhood and *byrnney*. He flushed with embarrassment and kept his head down.

It had to look bizarre. The front half of his hair had been short-cropped like a humble Folk's, though it had now grown out to the bridge of his nose and just past his jaw, still too short to stay tucked behind his ears. The rest of it was gathered in a long braid, a burden of honor worthy of a prince—Helgurdda's idea, not his. She made him grow it long, despite all the moons he spent in Myymor spying on the Evroza in the guise of a Folk outcast. He cut the front hair every spring before he arrived in Myymor—a long-standing irritant between him and Helgurdda.

The audacity of that braid, if it had ever been discovered in Myymor, would have seen him shorn and beaten—or worse—which was why he always tucked the damned thing under his clothes and wore a Folk shoulder-hood to cover it at the back of his neck.

"I recognize a remote connection to Ice Bear clan through you to your son," Royenne Errengard said. "Rise, Wylheim, son of Helgurdda. Take your place at her feet."

The royenne gestured with a gnarled finger.

His place was at Helgurdda's back in a situation like this, but as he straightened, there was no mistaking the demand for obedience in Helgurdda's face. He stayed low and took a knee at her feet as she had silently commanded.

Then Royenne Errengard's voice grew harsh. "But I know who this old man must be, and I recognize no relationship, kith or kin, to the outlaw Eirgei, whose hands are red with Dremn blood!"

With that, Wyl knew Royenne Errengard would have Eirgei dragged off and summarily executed. He tried to keep his face unconcerned, to act as Eirgei expected of his best pupil and not show fear to the Dremn. He coughed and pretended boredom, while Helgurdda appealed for the life of her mother's brother, who indeed had no claim on any clan in Dremnar.

Eirgei remained silent and prostrate on his knees, out of the ensuing negotiations between Helgurdda and the royenne of Dremnar.

Ignored at Helgurdda's feet, Wyl subtly scanned the great hall to locate the Icebear minions among the courtiers. He mapped out a course to the double doors that avoided them, playing out in his head how each minion would likely react if the three of them attempted an escape, trying to predict the flow of battle. The courtiers carried only their noble side-daggers, but the Icebear minions were well-armed.

He listened to Helgurdda and Royenne Errengard with an ear only for a critical change in tone while he worked out in his mind the fastest route through the crowd of courtiers.

Helgurdda spoke for some time, using the same eloquence that had swayed so many brigands into swearing loyalty to her in sudden willingness to give up the rewarding business of robbery and murder for the hardships of rebellion. The brigands and outlaws did it for a chance at redemption by fighting for her honorable cause, with adoption into Helgurdda's upstart clan—what would be the new royal clan—as their reward.

But the old royenne was made of sterner stuff than any outcast. She countered Helgurdda's arguments in a cracklingly dry voice, making no secret of how badly she wanted Eirgei dead, despite Helgurdda's earnestness and unfeigned sincerity.

Wyl could feel the hostility in the hall as if it were Evroza magery, heavy and suffocating. His palms began to sweat as he tightened his focus, first settling on the minion he'd take by surprise when he drew his spine blade from under his *byrmney's* collar. Then, he shifted his gaze to consider the next minion. If he were quick, it wouldn't be unreasonable to hope to take that one by surprise, too—and after his initial attack, he wouldn't be acting alone. Eirgei and Helgurdda also carried spine blades, long, thin, three-sided blades narrow enough to pierce mail links.

Fighting without shields, Eirgei would draw his spine blade and move up on Wyl's right so each of them could act as a shield to the other. Then, escaping the hall would be inevitable, with Helgurdda following in their wake with her own spine blade drawn. Getting out of the Crown Court hall might be simple enough, but escaping from Nornholm and then Dremnar would be another matter.

That would require valuable hostages to hold as surety.

Wyl studied the courtiers in the hall, but he didn't know anything about the Dremn court. Which nobles in that crowd were sufficiently in the royenne's favor to secure safe passage for them if held hostage?

A brief shift of his attention to check on the progress of the negotiations told him Royenne Errengard was making an excellent case for Eirgei's execution over Helgurdda's dogged assurances and promises—all of which could only be fulfilled when she became Royenne of Trascolm—in exchange for sparing Eirgei's life now.

Wyl's attention returned to the problem of escape with renewed urgency.

Then, the sudden addition of a male voice into the tense negotiations grabbed his attention.

"No one can transform rabble into a menney like the Wolf of Milk Dales," Prince Frekkei said. The Dremn prince gave Wyl's homeland's name the Dremn pronunciation, as two words. "His ability to create great minions was second to none before he was outlawed. I cannot fault him for rebellion—no one in Dremnar could have stomached what Royenne Sharei did in pandering to the Gerisari, not and still have hoped to keep their honor."

It surprised Wyl to hear open admiration for Eirgei in the viceroye's voice; those words gave him hope. He watched the royenne give her son a narrow-eyed, unyielding look.

Prince Frekkei fingered his beard thoughtfully. "Since Eirgei is so careful of his honor, perhaps—in exchange for his life—he can offer us restitution for the many deaths he has caused during the years he spent helping the Evroza war against us."

Wyl masked his hopefulness, as well as his anxiety for Eirgei, and awaited the royenne's response.

"There is no restitution that can meet the price paid in so many lives," snapped Royenne Errengard. "And if I am not mistaken, the rebel treasury did not cross the Tor with them."

"What I propose, Mother, is to allow Eirgei to make restitution in kind. Let him swear to serve under me as a warlord, leading my minions wherever I direct him, and giving them training in his skills. Then, those sacrifices made by two generations of our people will not be wasted. Dead, he is just so much jackal-meat; living, he will give us an insurmountable advantage over the Tras. He knows the Evroza, and he knows Milk Dales. Let him keep his head, if he will serve me in restitution."

"There must be a limit on his service," Helgurdda said, her voice as bland as Wyl had ever heard it. "I did not come to Dremnar to concede victory to Sharei. When I am royenne of Trascolm, I will require my uncle to serve as my viceroye. But until that time, I believe we have mutual goals regarding the Evroza and Trascolm, and he will help us both achieve them."

"You are bold to dare set conditions, girl," Royenne Errengard said.

"If I do not avenge Hereres and become Royenne of Trascolm, then I would as soon be dead," Helgurdda said. "But if I do become Royenne of Trascolm, it will be with the aid and backing of an honorable ally—Icebear honor is surety everywhere."

"As Evroza's honor is not," sniffed Royenne Errengard, but Wyl could tell the flattery had an effect.

"When I am Royenne of Trascolm, I will keep my word—and the old ways—and bring great credit and distinction to my Icebear kith, who would be made welcome in Crossroads Keep and anywhere else in Trascolm they might wish to visit."

"Even Trascolm's Crown Fair, to bargain with the Gerisari traders?"

The coyness in the old woman's tone made Wyl blink. Now he understood why they were all still alive.

The Dremn hungered after Gerisari arms and armor, but the Gerisari regarded the Dremn as barbarians and refused to trade with them, or even to acknowledge Dremnar as a country. Everything Gerisari in Dremnar had been taken as spoils from winter raids into Milkdales, the Tras barony closest to Gerisar—dominated by the Evroza and ruled by the Royenne of Trascolm as its baronne.

Royenne Errengard sat still, rheumy blue eyes focused inward.

Wyl worried that Prince Frekkei's intervention hadn't been enough to save Eirgei and gathered himself to spring at his first target.

"Cuz, kith to Ice Bear clan," Royenne Errengard finally said to Helgurdda, "I cannot find it in me to refuse your requests. You will take your place in my court as my honored kith-kin, and your uncle will earn his life under my son's command.

"I give you welcome to Norn Holm and to Dremnar."

That caused the greatest murmuring of all from the watching Dremn.

Wyl stiffened, ready for trouble, but these were noble courtiers, not lawless rogues. No one barged forward to protest Royenne Errengard's decision even though, by those words, Royenne Errengard allowed Trascolm's most famous—and infamous—warlord to turn traitor as well as rebel by aiding Dremnar, Trascolm's ancient enemy.

He knew enough about Royenne Sharei to know she and all the Evroza would take this as a mortal insult warranting a response just short of a declaration of war on Dremnar—not out of any restraint, but solely because blood-feud was a clan matter, not a crown one.

Royenne Errengard looked very pleased with herself.

Nornholm's palace had just become Wyl's new home, but that didn't mean he didn't have to be on his guard. He was still Tras, and no matter that Helgurdda's Icebear kith were giving her a formal welcome, that Eirgei looked cool and relaxed despite his brush with death, and that the old royenne smiled to herself, they were still trapped in

Nornholm.

This was part of the price for his crazy impulse to spare the weather-mage, leading first to so many deaths, exile, and now this. This treacherous bargain Helgurdda had struck in allying with the hated Dremn was his fault. He wished he'd taken that first shot at the mage and killed her—none of this would've happened.

Then, he heard his name.

"Of course, Wylheim—I suppose I should call him *Prince* Wylheim," the royenne said ironically, "will join my granddaughter's Young Court. I am sure he would think the doings in my Crown Court boring. He will find the Young Court much more to his liking. He should enjoy making friends with my favorite grandchild, Crown Prince Norren and his young menney, the Bear Cubs."

Wyl blinked, hoping he'd heard wrong while caught up in his thoughts. He was an important part of Helgurdda's personal defenses because strangers overlooked him. Now he'd be the source of more trouble—Royenne Errengard wouldn't take Helgurdda's refusal to part with him very well.

His traitorous left eye twitched, and his stomach clenched with pre-battle nausea as he again considered their route out of the hall.

"Of course. My son will welcome the chance to be with others his own age," Helgurdda said smoothly, astonishing him.

He reeled as he turned on his knee to gape at her—feeling betrayed and by his own mother! What kind of bargaining ploy required him to be thrown to the enemy Dremn?

He tried to make sense of what had just happened, why Helgurdda would consent to being separated from the last of her bodyguards—Eirgei given into the hands of the Icebear minions and now him to the Young Court. She had to have seen a way to wring an advantage out of this, but how?

The answer came to him in a heartbeat—hostages.

Eirgei had often told him not even Evrozings would deliberately let their children come to harm, but Wyl himself placed no confidence in the Evrozings' family feelings. The Dremn, however, should cooperate to the utmost if he threatened the royenne's granddaughter and her Young Court. With her in his hands, the Bearcubs should be easy to control. The whole maneuver should be simple enough to do on his own.

What this meant was that, if the royenne's favor suddenly soured, it would be up to him to provide the valuable hostages they'd need to barter for their lives. Now, Helgurdda's consent to sending him to the Young Court only made sense.

But when Prince Frekkei came down from the dais, Helgurdda gestured for the prince-viceroye to wait.

"Leave your blades," she said, turning to Wyl.

He'd risen with his fingertips hovering over his boot cuffs, cautiously poised over two of those blades. He didn't like strangers and disliked even more the idea of walking off alone with this one, no matter that this stranger was Royenne Errengard's son and viceroye, and his own kith-kin. The thought of doing it *disarmed* made his throat tighten.

He looked over at Eirgei, who nodded.

They really meant for him to give up *all* his blades?

He frowned and tossed the hair out of his eyes to mutely plead with Helgurdda. There would be at least one Evroza agent in Nornholm already. Of the three of them, he was the one most likely to discover the spy. He'd need his blades when he did. He coughed.

Keeping those remaining blades would also be a great relief to him. He already felt naked, first, without his sabre and now, exposed as Helgurdda's son. He still carried his bow and quiver of arrows, but those wouldn't be much help in winning free of the palace—and a bow was useless at close range for threatening a hostage.

Helgurdda gave him back a harshly unmistakable look that demanded obedience. Either she felt the Dremn were too nervous to risk provoking an overreaction, or she didn't trust him not to use his weapons afore time. The Dremn did seem nervous, but that had to be on account of Eirgei, not Wyl.

He unbuckled his back-knives' belt and drew them out from under his cloak to give to Eirgei.

Hands moved as startled Icebear minions reacted, their hands flying for the hilts of their swords.

Wyl let the belt fall, freeing his own hands to reach for his wrists and the nearest of his own weapons—the throwing knives under his bracers.

The belt with his back-knives clattered to the floor.

All around him, he heard the scrape of swords clearing sheaths.

He clawed at his throwing knives, but someone slammed him to the ground from behind.

He twisted, trying to reach any of his five remaining blades, but that someone held him pinned down with his arms out-flung. The feeling of a heavy body on top of him sent Wyl into a kicking, clawing, biting frenzy.

A hand gripped his hair, and he tried to wrench free before his head could be smashed against the stone floor.

Then Prince Frekkei shouted, "Stand down!"

The Icebear minions checked. Someone swore.

The man on top of Wyl let go of his hair and when he did, Wyl bit the hand holding the man up, sinking in his teeth and clamping down for all his life was worth. The minion yelled and smacked Wyl's ear, but Wyl didn't let go.

Eirgei barked, "Wyl—enough! *Hold!*"

He let go of the man's hand, freezing at Eirgei's command, his heart beating hard. The belt of back-knives had hampered him just enough to create a fatal delay. He'd been much too slow in getting to his throwing knives.

If these had been brigands rather than royal minions, he would now be wishing he were dead.

He still might be.

The Icebear minions, their swords still drawn, stood uneasy and restless, their faces reddening with either fury or chagrin. Then they lowered their swords and sheathed them.

The man crushing Wyl hastily rolled off and stood, shaking his hand, marked with blood from Wyl's teeth. He reached down, offering Wyl his other hand.

"*To/Daanyo gore your guts!*" Wyl swatted it away, furious and still shaking, and scrambled upright on his own.

Prince Frekkei snapped a sharp reprimand at the hand-leader of the guardsmen—the one who had been crushing Wyl—for allowing someone to be brought thus armed into the royenne's presence.

Wyl didn't dare move to pick up his back-knives' belt. He'd intended, out of habit, to hand them to Eirgei. Now he could only bend over, like he was trying to catch his breath—instead of fighting the urge to puke—with his hands braced above his knees, and not-coincidentally, close to the hilts of the long knives hidden in his boot tops.

He looked to Eirgei for some hint in his amber eyes, some clue of what was expected of him in this situation.

Eirgei's face held an odd expression, trying to tell him something, but what? Something to do with the Young Court?

Eirgei gently stepped back, giving the Icebears uncontested access to the back-knives.

The hand-leader, the Icebear who'd tackled Wyl, came forward and snatched up the belt of knives with a murderous look for Wyl.

"You will not need those blades to take your proper place among your peers," Eirgei told Wyl, ignoring the Icebears surrounding them.

What did he mean by that?

But Eirgei didn't demand he also surrender his hidden blades, so Wyl breathed easier. The disarming had just been a show of trust, not the real thing. Helgurdda and Eirgei were so good at deceptions, they'd even fooled him.

As Eirgei had said, Wyl wouldn't need his primary weapons. His wits were to be tested, not his bladework.

It relieved him that Eirgei wouldn't leave him defenseless, but it also left him puzzled by his family's intentions in revealing the weapons that had thus far escaped notice.

The only thing he could figure was that, once they were back in Milkdales, they'd be short of rebel warlords. Eirgei meant to use the Bearcubs to test Wyl's readiness for command. To be a fit warlord for their scouts, Wyl would need cunning as much as skill with weapons. He had to prove he could control the Bearcubs without weapons, otherwise, how could he hope to command brigand-scouts? He wouldn't be much use to Eirgei if he had to kill half of the scouts to gain their respect. If Eirgei's plan to obtain a Dremn menney prospered, Helgurdda would need warlords like Wyl, who already knew all Eirgei's signals and maneuvers.

And if the Dremn betrayed them rather than aided them, then he could still take the Young Court hostage and barter the royenne's granddaughter for their lives because he'd have already cowed the Bearcubs, leaving them too fearful to move against him.

He liked Helgurdda's plan, now.

No one demanded that he surrender his quiver and unstrung bow, but he wasn't surprised. The nobility of both Trascolm and Dremnar considered a bow a Folk hunting tool, not a weapon fit for a minion. A minion would no more use a bow than a hoe in place of a sabre—any minion not close enough to look his enemy in the eye when he killed him could be accused of murder. A minion who carried a bow might be labeled a coward and would have to prove himself.

Wyl was too young to be a proper minion, so he wasn't the least bit self-conscious about carrying a bow—he knew better than to let an enemy bigger than him get into grappling range. He wasn't proud of his attack on the weather-mage, but he didn't regret anything except missing her. Results were all that mattered.

"Remember your manners and play nicely," Helgurdda said to him.

He stared at her.

She spoke as if whatever manners he knew would be suitable for a Young Court.

He knew how to deal with what Helgurdda recruited from among the outcasts and brigands of Milkdales's lawless hill-country.

He didn't know how to play, nicely or otherwise.

Part Two

CHAPTER 10

THE YOUNG COURT

Prince Frekkei led Wyl up the winding stairs to the Young Court hall on the third floor of the Heir's Tower, in a different wing of the sprawling palace. The first thing Wyl saw through the open portal was a large, open space with curved walls hung with a dozen fine tapestries showing strange animals like none he'd ever seen in Trascolm. Reed mats, still green and fresh, covered the wooden floor. A pair of youths sat at each of about twenty small tables scattered about the room.

As soon as he saw the young courtiers, he felt awkward and out of place—half the youths were girls. He swallowed nervously, but couldn't help staring.

His rebel surcoat and *byrnney* were what he considered his good clothes, compared to his ragged outcast's tunic. But in Nornholm, in royal company, his good clothes made him look like some sisterless mercenary, disowned and reduced to beggary, little better than a brigand.

He followed the viceroye through the arch of the doorway and resisted the urge to scurry across that open space. He tried to cover his uneasiness at standing out so starkly by putting on his war face and studying the enemy.

About two score young courtiers attended the crown princess, Royenne Errengard's underage heir. They all looked older than he, more or less, though all the boys were significantly older and most of the girls were less so.

On second glance, he realized some of the girls, despite their height, could be no more than striplings, between ten and thirteen years old.

He was uncertain about the girls' ages because he'd never actually seen an underaged girl this close. Save for merchants in village marketplaces and the occasional, close-cropped bondswoman in Myymor, he had only rarely laid eyes on *any* females. Except for Lanney and Helgurdda, there'd been no women among the rebels—and certainly no girls.

In any of his identities, whether rebel or outcast, respectable clans would keep someone like him away from their cherished, all-important females.

Though he looked carefully, none of the youthful nobles seemed armed with anything more than the small, jeweled side-daggers that the Tras nobility also favored to guard their honor. No one drew one of those daggers as Prince Frekkei led him across the hall on a random path between the little tables.

It relieved him to see that the Young Court was relatively informal, compared to what he'd seen of the Evroza baronial court in Myymor. Oh, he saw a brigand's drunken fantasy's worth of jewelry as he wound through the room, but there wasn't a crown in sight. He picked out the three princesses and three princes—one pair was among the younglings at the back of the hall—by the archaic gold torcs around their necks.

The princesses and assorted young noblewomen all wore long, straight, heavily-embroidered, fur-lined tunics with sides slit to the waist to show thin layers of delicate undertunics. Those, too, were slit, but only to the hip, enough to display the decorative quill-work running down the outsides of their leggings and into the tops of their soft, low boots.

The underage noblewomen of the Young Court were scattered around the frigid yet sunny court hall, sitting at the tables, playing some game with the underage noblemen, who had to be the girls' brothers or cousins. All the boys were attired in similarly-styled but shorter tunics.

The six royal scions wore what he now knew were the Icebear colors of white and black. The score of male youths—undoubtedly the Bearcubs—along with the two older princes, wore half-sleeved Dremn surcoats of ice bear pelts with the fur on the inside and rolled outside as trim, the speckles showing even on the bearskins. Underneath, the young minions' tunics were in a variety of unfamiliar clan colors.

Despite the presence of a surcoat, by the way the young minions moved, easily and without a telltale tinkle, Wyl knew none of them wore mail under it—or even a *byrnney*, for that matter.

This wasn't a young menney, it was a *baby*-menney.

He tried to take heart from that, tried not to dwell on how badly he was outnumbered. None of them were openly armed, but—as with him—that meant nothing.

About a dozen grubby, blonde younglings played obliviously at the back of the courtly gathering, where they were farthest from the stairs. They looked to be between five and nine years old. The Icebear prince of the royal pair playing there stood a head taller and looked a little older than the others. He might be a stripling, but he laughed and played like one of the younglings.

Prince Frekkei led Wyl towards a youthful royal couple sitting at a small table. The room quieted with each step they took as the Young Court noticed them and stared.

The crown princess looked older than Wyl, but younger than the crown prince beside her, obviously her brother or a close cousin. She wore her hair long and loose like Helgurdda, and had a stiff-backed, regal air, despite being a barbarian princess in a barbarian court—though this Young Court, like the Crown Court, was rapidly impressing him as being anything but barbarian.

He had been wrong—this Dremn Young Court easily matched the formality of the Evroza's baronial court in Myymor, just minus all the exotic Gerisari fripperies the Evroza had adopted.

The crown princess looked at him coldly.

He expected that. He could have played a harmless, waif-like outcast, the way he had for the hunters who'd brought them to Nornholm. But, as a Tras faced with Dremn royalty and high nobility, if he was to be scorned, he preferred the scorn be defensive rather than sneering.

He saw a thoughtful expression on the crown prince's face. Like the crown princess—and most of the noble Dremn in the room—he had blond hair just like Helgurdda's. His even had Helgurdda's famous metallic glint and he wore it in the same war-knot she wore when not flaunting her defiance of Trascolm's royenne—or claiming kith to the royal clan of Dremnar.

"He looks just like a smaller version of the full-grown brigands our minions capture and hang upside down beside the gate," Wyl heard the crown princess remark in a soft aside as he approached.

She couldn't know he heard her.

The crown prince beside her stared out at Wyl and answered. "You are right, Sister. He has the same defiant look those brigands have—just before they get pushed from the parapet."

"Well, he is certainly no cleaner than a brigand. I can already smell horse, and he is not even close enough to kneel. I am just grateful that he will have to keep a distance from us, one appropriate to a Folk boy, if not a brigand."

Wyl hid his growing anger, continuing the pretense that he couldn't hear them. As a spy, he'd learned knowledge was power, and he would need every bit of power he could get to succeed in his mission here.

"He's not under guard," the crown prince pointed out, "so I suppose he cannot actually be a brigand."

Prince Frekkei brought Wyl to within three strides of the crown princess before he rather pointedly made him kneel.

"Both knees," the viceroye said acidly under his breath, so only Wyl could hear him.

Wyl knelt as ordered and nodded his head at the crown princess the way Eirgei had taught him was polite, then sat back on his heels, between his war spurs, and sized up the older boys in the room.

"He is not only odd, but rude, too!" the crown princess said, this time loudly enough to be heard by the rest of her court.

And by Wyl. His lips twitched, nearly losing his war face to a snarl. He wasn't being rude, he was just being sensible. He was surrounded by enemies, after all, and being on his knees made him vulnerable enough—only a fool would bow down and hide his eyes, as well. This girl was *not* Royenne Errengard!

She frowned at the viceroye.

"Crown Princess Kotakei, Crown Prince Norren, I make known to you Prince Wylheim, the son of Helgurdda, the famous Tras outlaw and rebel leader from Milk Dales. Your grandmother has just granted Helgurdda asylum in recognition of a kith claim on Ice Bear clan—and on the crown of Trascolm."

Crown Princess Kotakei was dark for a Dremn, her hair the color of clover honey, her brows and lashes much darker. Prince Frekkei's words made her gasp and her pale blue eyes flashed with outrage. "Are you serious? What is Grandmother thinking!"

"She is thinking of supporting Helgurdda's bid to win the crown of Trascolm. On the strength of that connection," Prince Frekkei continued, "she has permitted me to take Helgurdda's uncle, Eirgei, the Wolf of Milk Dales, into my menney and has given you Helgurdda's son for schooling befitting to a prince."

Prince Frekkei dropped all that on her, then took his leave before she could say another word. Wyl almost felt sorry for her.

Crown Princess Kotakei turned to her brother. "What kind of schooling befits a rogue Tras?"

Crown Prince Norren shrugged, looking as puzzled as she.

Wyl glanced at the crown prince, then at the taller, powerfully-built youth next to him—both obviously foes to be reckoned with—then looked over the rest of the Young Court, picking out the older of the two remaining princes as yet another potential threat. There were several other boys worthy of his attention, but the girls...? He doubted they could be any threat to him.

He turned back to the crown prince and the tall boy at his back, and wondered which would be the more accomplished fighter. It didn't matter, really. He could take either of them, singly. They were just big children.

The crown princess looked annoyed by the situation, but since she was no threat to him, he ignored her.

She spoke softly to her brother. "I expect you to waste no time putting this, this *Tras* in his place. Make sure he understands that he is as welcome among us as summer fever, and," she frowned, "he looks as dangerous."

Wyl tossed the hair out of his eyes and sized her up with reluctant approval. She seemed to see him for what he was, which was unusual. He normally had to give some sort of bloody demonstration before strangers could see past his appearance and give him the warrior's respect he was due.

She stared back into his eyes with hostile fascination until he became uncomfortable—and therefore determined not to be the first to look away.

Then she surprised him by turning to her brother and whispering, "Those eyes! If the sire looked anything like the son, I can understand why his mother betrothed a foreign slave—and started a blood-feud to avenge him."

Not her, too! Could he never escape the shadow of his sire?

He gave her a defiant stare, narrowing his left eye, the one that would have been twitching if she'd been a brigand. He'd worked on that rogue's glower, and Lanney had assured him that it made his eyes looked darker, harder, and full of sinister calculation.

The effect on the crown princess was not as complete as he'd wanted.

She flushed, but didn't look cowed. "There are grown minions in Uncle Raldorrei's menney who are not as menacing-looking as this boy. You and Lord Martei need to take care in how you deal with him," she whispered still more softly to Norren, not taking her eyes off Wyl, not knowing he could still hear her. "I think Grandmother will soon regret taking in these rebels and championing their cause."

From across the hall, he felt the older of the other two princes staring. He turned and shared a glare with him, but rather than being intimidated, that prince merely looked regally bemused. The lordling beside him at the game board had his head down and his shoulders were shaking in evident amusement. Wyl's glare had no effect on him.

When Wyl turned back to the royal siblings in front of him, he caught the crown princess staring at his hair. She looked offended.

He hadn't tucked his braid back under his collar after Helgurdda had shown it off to Royenne Errengard.

She whispered to her brother. "Whatever he is, half-breed Folk or something else, there is something wrong about him, like he is somehow too old and—"

"Too beautiful," her brother grinned mockingly down at her.

She turned her glare on him and away from Wyl. "—And much too dangerous to be in my Young Court. Or among the Bear Cubs."

The boy at the crown prince's back scowled at the crown princess's caution and openly showed his disapproval of Wyl. Oddly, the crown prince himself looked merely amused.

Wyl looked away and accidentally met the eyes of another princess, the one across the hall with the other formidable princeling. She was flaxen-haired and willowy, and—was that a wink? She followed it with a dazzling smile.

When he averted his eyes, he met another girl's eyes. He hastily returned his gaze forward in time to see the betrayed glare the crown princess directed at the princess who'd winked.

The other girls in the hall had looked intrigued, but the crown princess looked furious, though he had done nothing.

Except, maybe, breathe.

The crown princess turned to her brother and hissed, "What are Uncle and Grandmother thinking? I know enough about the rebellion in Milk Dales to know that Helgurdda is a deluded madwoman, Eirgei, an evil monster—and both of them have had a hand in making *that!*"

Wyl stiffened. She was deliberately trying to provoke him, as if she could do that and not fear the consequences.

He disliked being surrounded by so many enemies while partially disarmed, on his knees, and now insulted. He curled his feet under him and rocked back to rise straight up in one smooth motion with all the menace in him. As he did, he kept his hands poised close to his boot knives.

Better to take the offensive and offend, than to look weak and be preyed upon. That was especially important now. Eirgei would judge Wyl's readiness for his own command by how he handled himself here.

He intended to pass this test.

Crown Princess Kotakei frowned up at him. "You may rise," she snapped.

He ducked behind his hair in sudden embarrassment.

Remember your manners, Helgurdda had warned him and already he'd forgotten what few he had.

He warily scanned the crowd around him.

Take your proper place with your peers was simple enough to understand. To be one of Eirgei's warlords, he had to prove he could keep touchy, not-quite-reformed brigands under control and following orders, but without killing too many of them.

With the Bearcubs, killing one or two was out of the question, so he could best demonstrate his readiness for command by undermining, then overthrowing the youth who was their current leader and taking his place. That would give him control of the Bearcubs.

He had an important mission. Kith or not, the Dremn couldn't be trusted. He fully expected his hostages would be needed sooner rather than later. That meant doing whatever was necessary to put his hostage-escape plan in place as soon as possible.

His plan already had taken shape. It started with him becoming the new warlord of the Bearcubs and teaching them to respect him. Then, they wouldn't dare oppose him when he took his hostages. He needed to be able to take those hostages at a moment's notice and have them in hand so he'd be ready as soon as Eirgei needed them.

This time, no more soft-hearted failures.

With the exception of the crown princess, the other young noble-women seemed happy to have him in their company, but he couldn't imagine why—it had to be some baby-Court intrigue. He was sure of it when the crown princess suddenly gave him a brilliant smile that didn't quite reach into her winter-sky blue eyes.

"Welcome to Norn Holm, *Prince Tras*," she said, without the least sign of welcome in her voice. There was an edge in the way she named him.

In Dremnar, *Tras* was a foul insult. Lanney had said so.

"*Ockh*, no need for such formality," he said, matching her hauteur with an edge of his own, his pride smarting. He knew little about how ordinary families acted, but he did know he was entitled to at least the courteous *Cuz* of close friends or distant relatives. "Just call me Wyl."

"Won't!" Crown Princess Kotakei snapped back, which provoked a wave of laughter from the Young Court.

It made his hackles rise.

A fleeting expression passed over Crown Prince Norren's face.

Wyl involuntarily took a defensive step back to give himself room as the crown prince rose and shifted with deliberate protectiveness between Wyl and his sister.

Wyl could sense currents of tension, a tension that hadn't been present until the Crown Prince had moved—not that he needed proof that the crown prince would be a formidable opponent. He had known that since his first appraising glance. Wyl could take him, but not without a serious fight.

Crown Prince Norren was a tall, older youth with a man's frame, but not yet starting to acquire a man's well-muscled build. Wyl estimated the crown prince had to be close to sixteen years old and his coming of age ceremony, when he'd leave the Young Court to take his place in the Crown Court. He could only hope the crown prince would change courts—and take his tall friend with him—before Wyl needed to take control of the Bearcubs. Wyl was certain he could take him down, but the crown prince didn't look to be an easy conquest if he had to take care not to kill him.

Crown Prince Norren reached down, lifted his sister's hand, and drew her to her feet. She, too, was taller than Wyl.

She whispered to her brother, "I do not want this Tras boy in my court. Make Grandmother take him back—put him in with Uncle Raldorrei's menney or something."

Wyl blinked at her in surprise.

That was an excellent idea!

Proving himself among the Icebear minions alongside Eirgei would be more appropriate than scaring children—and he'd surely be allowed his weapons, which would greatly simplify taking the Young Court hostage once the need to flee Nornholm arose, now that he knew where to find them.

Crown Prince Norren scowled down at his younger sister and whispered back, "Do not be silly. He is too little to belong with Uncle Raldorrei."

Wyl bristled, but Crown Prince Norren's attention stayed on his sister.

"He has to remain with us," the crown prince continued, "if for no other reason than to acquire some royal polish, in case his mother does actually become Royenne of Trascolm."

"What does that have to do with us?" Crown Princess Kotakei asked.

"Obviously, Helgurdda cannot take *that* into Cross Roads Keep with her," Crown Prince Norren said matter-of-factly, "not now that everyone knows we are kith. He will disgrace Ice Bear clan! I will not have us branded uncouth barbarians because of him."

Wyl was tempted to draw a knife at that insult, but these were *children*.

This was not the first insult he'd been forced to swallow, nor the worst, but it was his first as Helgurdda's acknowledged son and not as a Folk outcast or Lanney's half-Folk foster-son, both of whom drew insults like flies to a corpse—and took appropriate retribution for them. Those insults had never bothered him—he'd always taken them as a compliment on how well he'd fooled everyone with his disguises.

But now, insults that should've been mere words if he were in disguise, cut unexpectedly deep.

What kind of just retribution could he take against children?

The crown prince gave him a faint smile and took no notice of his sister's frown. Then, he turned to address the Young Court. His voice was loud enough to carry even to the younglings at the back of the hall, who looked up as he started to speak. "You will join my Bear Cubs, of course, Prince Wylheim, and attend me—I think that will be the fastest way for you to learn how to comport yourself as a nobleman and a real prince."

Wyl clenched his fists, his fingers aching to tell the *real prince*, in thieves' finger-talk, what he thought of his idea. He liked the crown princess's *real menney* idea much better.

But, then again, the easiest way to bring down a nobleman was as an insider, maybe even as a trusted part of his inner circle. Lull Crown Prince Norren, then when the time came, as it surely would—no peace with the Dremn lasted for long—Wyl's takeover of the Bearcubs and then the rest of the Young Court would take all of Nornholm by complete surprise.

He liked surprises when he was the one springing them.

An interesting expression flickered on Crown Princess Kotakei's face as she looked at her brother, one that reinforced his vague sense that there was some trouble between the two of them. Perhaps that was the source of the tension in the rest of the Young Court?

If so, all the better for his plans. A Young Court already divided against itself would be easier to control.

Crown Prince Norren didn't take notice of his Bearcubs' universal disapproval. Instead, he smiled at Wyl with a kindly expression on his face.

Wyl didn't trust it in the least—and not just because the crown prince was Dremn.

"Tell me, Cuz," Crown Prince Norren said, "How does a Tras rebel come to be in Norn Holm?"

"I swam my horse across the Tor."

The entire Young Court gave him a disbelieving stare.

"Right," said the crown prince's tall friend, from where he stood behind Crown Prince Norren's shoulder. "He's a liar. Nothing with legs can cross the Tor. Maybe a gigantic mountain roc flew him across?"

Giant mountain rocs existed only in Folk mythology.

Wyl shrugged off the sarcasm with a sneer and a cough. "I'm here, hedge-get. Believe what you want—it's nothing to me."

The tall youth's smile vanished, and Crown Prince Norren's smile tightened.

"Martei, my friend, when it comes to the Wolf of Milk Dales," Crown Prince Norren said, "the impossible is the only reasonable explanation. Why not swim horses across the Tor? Who would imagine the infamous Wolf of Milk Dales as a part of the Ice Bear menney— that is equally impossible! If anyone could find a way to cross the Tor, it would be Eirgei."

Wyl couldn't help letting his hackles come down in response to the crown prince's respect for Eirgei.

✦

The Tras boy's eyes shifted away from hers, and Kotakei could see how he bristled under Norren's benevolent, if condescending examination. Though the Tras boy's expression was guarded, before it had emptied, she'd have sworn she'd seen something dangerous, even predatory in him. Now, despite her brother's evident awe of Eirgei, there was nothing genuine in Eirgei's grandnephew's bland expression, and though he appeared to relax his guard, Kotakei felt he still crackled with brittle tension. But no one else seemed to notice it—were they all blind?

"May I see that bow?" she asked. Something about the rapport she felt building between the Tras boy and her brother made her unaccountably anxious to break it. Why would Norren want to befriend this boy?

A year ago, Norren would never have allowed such a dangerous stranger near her, and that was before she had become the heir. Now, instead of being even more protective of her, he seemed less so, and lately had begun avoiding her outside the confines of the Young Court hall.

"Your bow?" she repeated.

The Tras boy hesitated, then unslung his quiver. From a sleeve on the outside of it, he pulled an odd bow grip with a pair of spiraling horn coils for its limbs and a loose, dangling bowstring,

She was startled when he gave it to her. She had been expecting him to pull an undersized Folk forester's bow from his quiver. "What a strange bow!"

The Tras boy folded his arms, fingers casually tapping one of his bracers, but the tension underlying the way he did it made the gesture seem anything but casual.

She turned the grip in her hand, examining the laminated wood and horn construction, fingering its odd tips and the scuffed areas around the nocks on the outside of the coiled tips. She turned it by its leather-wrapped grip and frowned, trying to deduce how it worked. Even the grip felt wrong.

"Folk horse bow," the Tras boy said nonchalantly. "The double recurve makes up for its size."

That was not as informative as he seemed to think it should be, and that annoyed her. Her people were not famous for archery—or fighting—from horseback. She handed the bow back to him. "I want to see what it looks like strung."

So the Tras boy strung it.

Apparently, stringing it was no easy feat, and she did not bother to hide her amusement as she watched him struggle to make it look easier than it was.

An ominous silence came from the rest of her Young Court, especially from the Bear Cubs, who had gathered around to watch.

Once the Tras boy had it strung and flexed into a bow shape with graceful curves from grip to nocks, she nodded her understanding. "Now it looks more like a bow."

With a sidelong look at the young minions, the Tras boy handed his bow back to her. At her gesture, and with obvious reluctance, he pulled an arrow from his quiver.

She expertly nocked the arrow, a little puzzled by the other arrow rest on the right side of the bow's grip, and frowned at the extra effort needed when she tried to take the little bow to full draw. Then, she snap-shot the arrow out an open window. The distance to her target was twice what she normally shot at, but the arrow covered the distance in a nearly flat trajectory, something she had not expected. She'd tried to compensate for the drop from the third floor to the courtyard, the same as she would have done with her forester's bow.

"A hit!" she exclaimed. She did not say it had not hit where she had aimed.

She ran down the stairs to the guardroom, and with the full Young Court at her heels, she ran out into the wide corridor, down two more flights of stairs, through the tower's kitchen, and past the servants bustling in the scullery, and then out into the adjoining courtyard.

When she looked back, she could see the Tras boy trailing behind, looking somewhat apprehensive—did he think she had shot a bond-servant? She could only imagine what someone like him, a brigand in all but name, might consider fun.

She almost laughed aloud at his expression when he reached the courtyard and saw she had hit a tree growing from a wide fissure in the stone underfoot.

She ran to the arrow and struggled to pull it out, but the branch kept moving with the arrow. The branch was small enough for her to wrap her fingers around it halfway. It surprised her how deeply the arrow had sunk into it.

Norren came up with a superior smile and displayed some impressive muscle-flexing, but did no better in his attempt at freeing it.

The Tras boy walked up, visibly annoyed.

Rather than trying to pull the arrow out, he went up on his toes and reached high to grip the arrow shaft with one hand and the branch with the other. The branch split, and he hung from the branch to flex it enough to make room for the fletching to pass through. He struggled to throw his weight against the arrow until the tip and its wicked barbs came out the other side of the limb, leaving enough shaft exposed to grasp. He pulled out the arrow.

Despite his effort to salvage it, the feathers did not pass through intact. He looked at the ruined fletching with disgust. "*Ockh*, never do that again! War arrows aren't meant for trees."

She blinked at his hostile tone. Never in her life had someone spoken to her like that!

Norren scowled and stepped in close to the Tras boy to loom over him. A year ago, he would not have done such a thing. Of course, a year ago, he had not yet reached a man's height.

The Tras boy stood his ground and ignored him, examining his arrow instead.

"Here is your first lesson in courtly manners," Norren said. "You do not talk to my sister—or any noblewoman of this court—like that!"

When the boy looked up, Norren locked eyes with him and deliberately placed his hand on his hip, drawing attention to his jeweled side-dagger.

That got a reaction.

The Tras boy sidled back out of reach, his fingertips twitching in a way that made Kotakei wonder if he had a weapon hidden inside his left boot. But, if there was one, he did not draw it. Instead, he shifted his right hand's grip on his ruined arrow, and she suspected he intended to use it like a thrusting spear if Norren drew his side-dagger.

"So, *that* is a war arrow!" she exclaimed, disingenuously. "I was so fascinated by the bow, I never noticed the arrow. I have never shot one of those before."

That much was the truth. But there was not going to be a brawl between the Tras boy and Norren if she could prevent it. A year ago, Norren would never have stooped to picking a fight with a younger, smaller boy, especially a newcomer. Now, given the criminal influence being forced upon her court by the Tras boy's presence, displaying the foundation of nobility, the Three Virtues—cunning, loyalty, and valor—were more important than ever. Let the Tras boy see how far he would have to reach if he aspired to be truly part of her court. She wondered, not for the first time, what was going on in her brother's head—and why did he not share it with her?

"Now give me a target arrow—I want to try the bow again."

She sensed the mood of the Bear Cubs ease as Norren stepped back, his thoughtful look restored, though his smile was not.

Kotakei had learned what that meant over the past year, and it meant nothing good for the Tras boy.

"Don't have any," Prince Tras said, breaking the jektrar head off the damaged arrow and tossing the shaft aside. He hesitated, then dropped the warhead into his quiver.

She turned and snapped her fingers at a hovering, unhappy Folk servant. The woman sniffed and gave the Tras boy a superior sneer as she came to Kotakei.

"Zeldey, bring me target arrows."

Kotakei turned back to the Tras, who was still watching the Folk woman. Between the unkempt locks of his hair, she could see his brows come together. Suspicion narrowed his eyes.

She turned her head to see what prompted it.

Zeldey had just received an unnecessary nod of approval from Norren before she walked off.

The Tras boy glanced at Kotakei, and she pretended to be oblivious to that strange, even disturbing, exchange between Zeldey and Norren.

Zeldey was her servant, not Norren's.

She looked down at the bow in her hands.

For the first time, she noticed the markings painted in yellow and black on the blood-red stained wood. "What are these?"

The Tras boy looked at her, then down at his bow. "*Heh*, Folk hunting charms."

"Ah, Folk superstitions," she said. "The effect is beautiful. Do you think the charms work?"

The Tras boy looked uncomfortable and shrugged. "They're harmless."

That didn't answer her question.

Zeldey returned with quivers of blunt arrows and a number of forester's bows, while a bondsman set out a straw target in the courtyard.

Norren talked with Martei and her cousin Sammei, showing no interest in the archery. He ignored Zeldey's return.

Perhaps the change inside her brother was related to the changes on the outside of him? He was nearly full-grown, and lanky with it like his friend Martei, who had outgrown him by a handspan and as quickly as Norren had topped Kotakei. The two boys—young men in all but name—explained their frequent disappearances as studying their coming of age rites in preparation for when they turned sixteen years old.

Martei would do so just after the new year and Norren two moons after him.

Did Norren feel he had outgrown her Young Court already?

Kotakei wondered about that as the other young women of her court eagerly took turns shooting the Tras boy's bow. Afterward, she gave in to temptation and decreed a contest.

Her cousin Tirrengard and the baronnes' heirs of her court were all keen to test their skill against the Tras boy, but he scowled at the target across the courtyard between the palace and the stables like something was wrong.

"Is the distance too great for your bow, Prince Tras?" she asked, with a touch of malice, still smarting from his reprimand over the arrow.

"It's not very realistic for practice," he said. "Any archer who tries to stand his ground and lets an Evrozing get this close is going to die."

"How fortunate that there are no Evrozings here, Prince Tras. You should be safe enough."

He shot her a wary, sidelong look, perhaps realizing for the first time that he had put his foot wrong with her.

She aggressively stared back into his beautiful, dark-rimmed, silver eyes. There was something uncanny about them, and she tried to decide what it was.

His gaze narrowed. He did not back down from that contest, so she was happy to make him uncomfortable with her scrutiny until he finally glanced away.

The Bear Cubs stood aside and watched him line up beside the girls with open derision on their faces. Even Norren thought the contest a bad idea. He stood with his arms folded, one hand covering his mouth, his brows drawn together as if he were rethinking something.

CHAPTER 11

ARCHERY CONTEST

TolDaanyo gore that hell-spawned girl! Wyl silently cursed the crown princess and her archery contest, and resisted the urge to throw a knife at something. Or someone.

Noblemen didn't use bows, not even for hunting. When noblemen hunted, they used javelins, spears, and sabres, practicing for war on worthy game like stags, boars, bears, wolves, and aurox. Eirgei said so. *Noblewomen* shot targets, but neither warred nor hunted with their bows.

Only commoners and Folk—and Wyl, in the guise of Lanney's half-Folk foster-son—hunted game with a bow, out of necessity, for the pot.

He wondered about the crown prince's ill-concealed disapproval. Was it aimed at the archery competition that he and the other young noblemen wouldn't participate in, or at something else?

The youths of the Bearcubs all glared at Wyl, reflecting the change in Crown Prince Norren's mood.

Why did Wyl care what the Dremn youths thought?

The crown princess stared at him again. She had lined up on his left, where he couldn't help seeing her, and now she tried to catch his eye with an untrustworthy smile. A gold signet ring glinted on her forefinger as she drew her bow.

He shook more hair between him and her, and tried to ignore the hostile, male portion of his audience.

He needed to pay attention to his shooting. Noblewomen regularly practiced archery, and he could see the girls' skill as arrows began to fly.

The youths of the Bearcubs were all standing behind him, making his skin crawl. Maybe these Dremn boys weren't his enemies, but that didn't mean he could trust them at his back.

He wished Lanney were here.

He'd learned all about youths their age in the streets and alleys of Myymor—they were bold as brigands, when it came to stranger-boys, and as vicious.

He kept a wary ear cocked to sort through the random scuffling noises, so typical of boys amongst themselves, listening for the more purposeful ones of the attack he awaited.

He pulled one of the target arrows he'd been given out of his quiver. As he set it on the string, the skin between his shoulder blades prickled almost painfully. He would never have turned his back like this in Myymor and couldn't believe he'd let himself be put into this situation.

"That is a silly way to draw a bow," Lord Martei commented, as Wyl used his jektrar thumb ring in a horseman's release, "even being wrong-handed."

He tried to ignore Lord Martei and sighted on the painted straw target.

Just as he was about to let fly, someone behind him coughed loudly—and sounded closer to him than anyone should be.

He jerked and before his shot hit the target—wide of the center mark—he'd whirled and had another arrow nocked.

Lord Martei had come a step closer and gave him a calculating stretch of his lips that wasn't at all friendly.

Wyl returned him an outlaw-quelling glare, with his left eye deliberately, menacingly narrowed to hide the twitch. That was all the warning he would give these Dremn pups. If this young nobleman tried to jump him when his back was turned, the Dremn would have to live— or die—with the consequences.

He turned back.

The girls' arrows were clustered neatly around the center of the target. His arrow stood out alone near the edge of it.

The servant plucking arrows from the target stepped clear.

Wyl sighted on the bull's-eye again, trying to relax his left eye while preparing for another ill-timed cough. Despite his determination to do so, he couldn't ignore the youth's presence behind him.

The traitorous muscles under his eye jumped as he sensed movement. He spun to sweep his right side, his blind side, with his bow still drawn.

Behind him on his right, Lord Martei had taken several more steps forward and now stood just a sword-lunge away—had he possessed a sword.

The youth's hands were empty. He scratched his head with a mocking smile that dropped away when he looked the wrong way down the shaft of an arrow at full draw. His eyes bugged out. He took a step backwards.

"*Ockh*, don't crowd me," Wyl said tightly, his heart pounding. He coughed.

"Do not point arrows at the warlord of the Bear Cubs!" Crown Princess Kotakei snapped from behind him. "Or at anyone else!"

He didn't understand why she was so angry. As a left-handed archer, the only way for him to clear his blind side and flank was to pivot right.

Ockh, but in the process, he'd swept his bow along the line of the crown princess's attendants—all girls and doubly sacred in MiPaatet's eyes for being children—before he'd had Lord Martei in his sights.

Did she think he would shoot girls?

He couldn't hold to his righteous anger, not while remembering the long, blonde hair of the weather-mage whipping around her face and her all-too female curves. He couldn't forget that he'd shot three arrows at *her*, and at least one of those arrows had been meant to kill.

But the weather-mage hadn't been a child, and she'd destroyed the entire rebel menney without ever setting foot on the battlefield.

He had no intention of threatening girls. His ears burned as he eased his draw, even as Lord Martei foolishly scooted backwards rather than closing with him.

He glanced at the pair of guardsmen who'd accompanied them outside the Heir's Tower. They were gawking at him, their swords useless in their sheaths. Crown Prince Norren, who stood beside them, snapped something in a low, angry voice.

"We have rules, Prince Tras," the crown princess said, drawing his attention back to her.

He bridled at the name—another reason to ignore her.

Rules were for other people.

"You're lucky," he snarled at Lord Martei, as if the crown princess hadn't spoken. "I don't shoot *children*. But make another move at my back like that, and I'll make an exception for you."

His cough diminished some of the effect he wanted, but though Lord Martei scowled at being called a child, his eyes were still riveted on the arrow.

"Another rule," Crown Princess Kotakei said furiously. "You do not threaten members of my court!"

He turned away from Lord Martei, deliberately pointing his arrow at the ground as he turned past the crown princess and back towards the target, but still keeping his bow partially drawn. "Not a threat, Crown Princess, just a friendly warning."

"If that was friendly, then you have a great deal to learn about friendship!" Her voice was sharp and tart.

He certainly wasn't going to learn about friendship from her!

The two guardsmen belatedly drew their longswords and held them at the ready.

Wyl turned his attention back to the target and tried to steady his hand against the nervous tide of energy inside him, but it wasn't enough. When he released, his arrow again hit wide of the mark.

He looked over his shoulder as he pulled another target arrow from his quiver, but all the youths remained a prudent distance away. The two guardsmen remained beside the crown prince.

He rolled his shoulders, trying to ease his tension and calm down. He nocked the arrow.

He'd never had to shoot with his back to armed enemies an easy run-and-cut away. He tried to find the detachment he felt when hunting, but this time, he felt like the hunted.

"Best concede the contest to the crown princess," someone said loudly, just as he loosed his arrow.

In spite of himself, his back stiffened. The arrow flew wide of the entire target and smashed against the courtyard wall behind it.

He wheeled to glare at the boy who'd spoken, this time without an arrow on his string.

"What?" Lord Martei asked. "We cannot talk, either?"

The baby minions were converging on Lord Martei, backing their young warlord, the crown prince's Right Hand, who silently dared Wyl to do something stupid.

Wyl turned back and closed his eyes, rolled his shoulders, and took a deep breath, but he just couldn't relax and concentrate with two bared swords and a mob of scowling youths behind him. Every hard-earned instinct screamed for him to run or draw the sabre he no longer had.

He rolled his shoulders again. His eyes were on the target, but his ears were still fixed on the noises behind him. He was ready for the first sound of the guardsmen's running steps or for the first flicker of light on a polished sword out the corner of his twitching eye. But it was the sound of the youths jostling each other that unnerved him most.

He would rather face a band of slavering brigands than a like number of boys with the same intentions. He'd no qualms about killing brigands, but he'd never killed a child, nor a youth, not even in Myymor, where he'd learned that nothing surpassed the creative cruelty of a mob of boys. It didn't help that these particular boys were Dremn and would happily cripple or kill a Tras boy.

But he'd sworn no more soft-hearted failures, even if it meant making an example of Lord Martei. He had to be ready to do whatever would help his family escape Nornholm—no matter that just thinking of what he might have to do sickened him.

A rebel had to be practical—even unscrupulous—to survive. And have a strong stomach.

One good thing about this situation—today, *practical* meant not killing anyone.

"You would have better luck hitting the target with a rock," Lord Martei cracked, just as Wyl released his arrow.

He was better prepared for it this time. His arrow hit close to the center.

He could do this. He rolled his shoulders and pulled another arrow, again ready for a deliberate distraction. Or so he thought, when he drew down on the straw target.

At the moment before he released, Lord Martei said, "Maybe he will do better if we paint the rear end of an Evrozing on the target."

He stifled an involuntary, nervous laugh. His arrow wobbled past the target and bounced off the worn stone of the ground behind it.

"And we do not taunt during a competition," Crown Princess Kotakei scolded Lord Martei.

Only then did he realize Lord Martei's Evroza joke had been an insult aimed at *him*, not the Evroza. A nobleman always fought at close quarters, looked his enemy in the eye, and never cut one down from behind.

Or was there a more personal insult also hidden in that taunt?

Killing *that* boy suddenly seemed appealing.

Wyl shot his last arrow, and this time, anger guided it. It sank deep into the center of the target, but too late to give him a respectable showing in the competition. All the crown princess's arrows had hit the center and no one else had wasted two arrows by missing the target completely.

It was an embarrassing performance.

"That is enough archery for today," Crown Princess Kotakei said, not sounding the least bit pleased, though she had won the competition.

"Let us play senet instead," said Crown Prince Norren. It sounded more like a decree than a suggestion.

Crown Princess Kotakei pressed her lips together as if upset by something, but she said nothing.

Wyl wondered what went on between the royal siblings—and how could he best make use of it?

✦

Crossroads Keep

Breieroz gazed down from the gallery overlooking the royenne's scent garden as the Crown Court took its ease.

Royenne Sharei looked too gray and sickly. She ought to have stayed in bed, as Prince-Viceroye Osbart had advised her, rather than holding court outside, but Royenne Sharei had ironically assured him that she wouldn't drop dead from the strain of walking in her favorite garden.

"Royenne Sharei," said the Gerisari envoy, catching Breieroz's attentive ear.

Prince Kreseyn approached the royenne from out of the informal crowd of courtiers scattered among the flowers and herbs. The elderly diplomat went gracefully to one knee in the walkway of bruised and aromatic chamomile.

"Please accept this token of amity from my empress. Though we could not come to an agreement over harvesting the timber in the Forest of Alshemir, Empress Jerhafyne still considers Evroza clan a valued ally and friend."

Breieroz came sharply alert as, at the elderly prince's gesture, a Gerisari slave came forward from under the gallery across the garden, where he had been concealed in the shadows between the pillars supporting it.

The slave bore a small, gleaming silver casket, its sides and lid inlaid with gold incised into tiny diamonds that caught the light with a golden glint. Prince Kreseyn took the casket and opened the velvet-lined box to display a goblet of similarly-incised silver, only its bright sparkle put that of its container to shame. A dazzling display of light came through the rubies, emeralds, and topazes set into the silver in the shape of an evening rose still bearing its thorns.

"It is endowed with sufficient artisanry that the jewels will sparkle in any light and the silver will never blacken—just like the friendship between Trascolm and Gerisar, despite Empress Jerhafyne's disappointment in this matter."

Royenne Sharei took the proffered goblet and held it at arm's length to peer at it.

"I thank your empress for this royal gesture, but the dispute has already been forgotten on my part and soon will be forgotten on Empress Jerhafyne's part, as well, once she sees the quality of the timber from southern Milkdales. The Gerisari trade fleet will not suffer for obtaining timber from deeper within Milkdales." She gave Prince Kreseyn a pained smile. "It is difficult for even the rest of Milkdales to understand the sacred nature of the Forest of Alshemir. The Forest is haunted by the spirits of Evroza martyrs, and those ghosts defend it with no help from the living. The mighty oaks there are under divine protection and must be left untouched by axe or saw. No one, not even an Evrozing, crosses into the Forest without the ghosts rousing against them. Those who attempt to take from the Forest suffer the wrath of TolDaanyo."

Prince Kreseyn inclined his head. "It was not Empress Jerhafyne's wish to offend the ancient deities of the Folk nor to distress those to whom that place is sacred. It is our hope that this gift will bring you peace from any misgivings this unpleasantness has caused you."

"Convey my appreciation to Empress Jerhafyne and assure her no offense was taken." Royenne Sharei grimaced. "If only peace from this blood-feud could be had so easily."

The Gerisari envoy smiled and bowed his head.

✦

Nornholm

As they returned to the Heir's Tower, Wyl couldn't help constantly looking over his shoulder to check the positions of the two guardsmen following with their naked swords. Their excessive caution flattered him, but all the same, it was a relief when the guardsmen did not follow them up past the guardroom on the second floor.

"This is my favorite game, as well as my brother's," Crown Princess Kotakei said, with a distinct lack of enthusiasm. She directed him to where he'd first seen her, at the low table under one narrow, deep window and in the full light—and scant warmth—of an open west window across the Young Court hall.

A pair of stools were at the table and the table held a board marked into squares. Crude pictures with odd scribbles under them filled some of the squares.

"We play every day—it is good discipline for the mind and," she said, quirking a false smile at him as they sat opposite each other at the small table, "I am very good at it. I will teach you the rules as we play."

Wyl had a hard time understanding the rules, but eventually, after she'd won five games, he'd gotten some idea of how the game was best played.

It wasn't the way she'd been teaching him.

"That is enough for today," Crown Princess Kotakei said, just as he was ready to test his suspicion. She beckoned to a Folk servant to bring refreshments.

"Not yet, Kotakei!" the other youthful princess, Tirrengard, said. "I have not had a chance to play!"

The handful of young noblewomen clustered around the table watching them begged for a chance to play, too.

He looked up at them, surprised to find them so close. They hadn't intruded on his awareness like the Bearcubs had during the archery contest.

The girls seemed truly upset not to get their chance to play. Was everyone in Dremnar obsessed with the damned game?

But then, when Princess Tirrengard caught him with her eyes, he suddenly realized the girls hadn't been watching *them* play—they'd been watching *him* play.

He casually leaned away, feeling uneasy. Perhaps they were, in their own way, as dangerous as the boys?

He took cover, shaking his head to shift his hair so it hung over his eyes. He hated that people stared at his eyes.

"I hope you enjoyed playing with me, Prince Tras," Crown Princess Kotakei said, with an easy familiarity, though the smile she wore seemed more calculating than sincere. She alone hadn't been trying to catch his eye—and she continued to use that hateful name.

He had no trouble understanding it meant she didn't accept him in her court, no matter that she'd been forced to accept him as kith; he'd never expected otherwise.

So, for whose benefit was she smiling?

It wasn't meant for him; it just happened to be aimed in his direction—or was it aimed behind him, across the room to where Crown Prince Norren and his young minions played and plotted? Had all this been a performance for her brother?

"Senet is more fun with a strong opponent," she said, in a voice loud enough to carry across the hall. "If we had kept playing, I am sure you would know all my tricks. I cannot believe you have never played senet before—already, you are almost good enough to play my brother. No one can beat him at it. He is much better than I am, but I keep trying. After all, the only way to become really good at something is by facing the best at it."

The handful of girls around the table giggled. For a moment, the other young noblewomen elsewhere in the hall looked over at them, then returned to their games.

Wyl wondered if Crown Princess Kotakei and he had been playing on the same board. He'd been no challenge to her at all. But he had learned one thing: given that pure luck played as much a part in winning as skill and strategy, he couldn't believe no one could beat Crown Prince Norren. Either the young courtiers let him win or the crown princess lied.

He suspected she played another game besides senet, a deeper one without boards, and that she had just now tried to make him one of her playing pieces. A piece she'd happily throw to the gape-mouthed swamp lizards on the last row of the board if it served her purposes—whatever those might be.

But the strangest thing was her pretense that he had given her any kind of contest. Why defeat him five times and then imply otherwise, stopping just short of an outright lie? Was she setting up some sort of rivalry between him and her brother?

If she wanted to make him look good to the Bearcubs and her brother, why pretend he'd won instead of just *letting* him win? Was she too proud to let someone like Wyl beat her?

There was another possibility.

The Folk said that the outcome of games of chance spoke the will of MiPaatet.

He wished that disturbing thought hadn't occurred to him. He suspected *that* was why the crown princess had defeated him so handily five times in a row. MiPaatet was still offended by his attempt to kill the weather-mage. With his humiliating showing in the archery contest and now this string of defeats playing against the crown princess, he was reminded he no longer could count on MiPaatet's favor.

"You pick the next game," Crown Princess Kotakei said. "Show us what kind of games you played in Trascolm."

"I never played any games—not like this," he hastily added, thinking of Eirgei's version of hound-and-hare, which wasn't at all suitable for children. He avoided looking at her and pretended that it cost him nothing to admit that. "Let's play senet some more. I think I'm getting a feel for it."

She declined, but he played more games of senet, this time with Princess Tirrengard, the tall, flaxen-haired princess who'd caught his eye when he'd first arrived. She was about the same age as Crown Princess Kotakei, but unabashedly good-humored. After her, he played more games against other noble girls.

Whether he wanted to or not, it became very clear to him that he didn't belong here—no more than he had among the outcast boys in Myymor. In Myymor, though, he could keep his distance and the boys who ran the streets had learned to let him. The rest of Myymor had treated him like any other disowned boy—as either invisible or a public nuisance.

A good spy could blend in anywhere, he'd always thought, but he'd never tried to do it among the nobility. These were just *children*. His life was hardly at risk among them—which was fortunate, considering the ridiculous mistakes he kept making. If they'd been brigands, he'd have dealt with them easily enough. Why did he let *children* affect him this way? He coughed.

None of the other young noblewomen played senet as well as the crown princess, perhaps because, all the while as he played, each girl ogled him mercilessly from across the board—further proof, to his mind, of MiPaatet's unhappiness with him, though his evolving senet strategy nearly counterbalanced his unrelenting bad luck throwing the sticks.

After senet, he watched the Young Court play singing games—a fascinating novelty. Then he followed them back down into the courtyard to watch a game that involved a leather ball and baffled him.

There were a lot of groans, jeers, and mockery as the Young Court played, yet no one drew a weapon.

But everyone, male and female, watched him.

Whenever someone—usually a girl—spoke to him, her words felt like coy traps. He was convinced there were subtle messages being conveyed by nuances of voice and gesture between members of the Young Court—a palace version of thieves' finger-talk, with himself as the unsuspecting mark.

As the afternoon dragged on, he felt more and more out of place rather than less.

It was like the world had turned on its head. Things that he'd never even known existed before today were suddenly important, while the skills that had always been matters of life or death to know—things he'd taken pride in mastering with sweat and blood—didn't seem to have any place at all in the Young Court.

He tensed as Crown Prince Norren and Lord Martei walked over to him. Crown Prince Norren's face was impassive, and his Right Hand—and obvious favorite—only betrayed his feelings with a faint sneer and a bored expression rather than the open loathing he'd shown earlier.

"Come," Crown Prince Norren said. "Walk with us."

CHAPTER 12

A DEEP GAME

Wyl worked at concealing his uneasiness as Crown Prince Norren led him up the spiraling stairs of the Heir's Tower to the sixth floor with Lord Martei following too closely at his back.

Crown Prince Norren turned aside at the door in the wooden inner wall.

Wyl wasn't breathless from the climb, but neither were the two Dremn youths. Whatever else they might be, they weren't soft and lazy like he'd always imagined ordinary noblemen—those who weren't Evroza—would be.

"This is where my Bear Cubs sleep," Crown Prince Norren said, gesturing at a barracks of raised pallets, clothes-presses, and trunks.

He had been right about these Dremn boys. The Bearcubs hadn't been armored in court—every raised pallet had two cross-poles standing behind it, one bearing mail, the other the quilted aketon in clan colors that was worn under it. Some of the mail had golden jegurit torsos, but most were entirely that faint, green-under-gold sheen that jektrar-bronze took on when burnished to imitate jegurit-bronze.

At the other end of the barracks, a doorway marked another, smaller room. Crown Prince Norren crossed the room and opened the door. "And this is where I sleep."

Wyl looked at it curiously.

The crown prince's chamber held a curtained bed and a couple of large, closed cupboards in addition to furnishings like those in the barracks.

He suffered instant jealousy when he saw Crown Prince Norren's armor was wholly true, jegurit-bronze mail polished to a golden sheen. Jegurit mail for an underage boy likely to outgrow it overnight?

Eirgei said a boy was man enough to wear mail when he stopped growing and started shaving.

Though the crown prince had achieved a man's height, he hadn't finished growing into a man's muscle. Nor did he have a beard to shave or—being Dremn—to not shave.

Wyl struggled to hold back a resentful scowl, reminding himself of how much even jegurit mail weighed. It was the one advantage his *byrnney* had over other armor, and his quickness was his greatest advantage over an opponent.

The rest of Crown Prince Norren's panoply leaned against the wall, all of it equally princely in quality. There was even fancy needlework on his aketon where no one would ever see it.

Wyl's mood soured even more.

A bondsman, polishing the faint brown patina off the golden boss of a shield, immediately stopped rubbing. He knelt to his master, forehead to the floor.

"Close the door," Crown Prince Norren said.

Wyl enviously tallied the items in the Dremn crown prince's panoply, but puzzled over the distinctive lack of weapons. The crown prince didn't sleep with a sword at hand?

Crown Prince Norren cocked his head at him expectantly.

Wyl tried not to look mystified.

Then he narrowed his eyes, and of its own accord, his lip started to lift into a nasty half-snarl. The crown prince had given that order to *him*, though of the three of them, it was Lord Martei who was closest to the door—and not a prince.

The two of them looked at Wyl.

He looked back at the crown prince and his favorite, and thought about the subtle and less-than-subtle games of dominance among Helgurdda's brigand recruits. Among Helgurdda's minions, every newcomer learned Wyl obeyed no one's orders except hers and Eirgei's.

Crown Prince Norren frowned at him, his blue eyes narrowing.

Wyl remembered Helgurdda's warning about his manners—and his own resolve to take over the Bearcubs from a position of trust. If he was to play the crown prince's loyal follower, he'd best start now.

He stepped around the crown prince to close the door.

Lord Martei folded his arms and leaned against it.

Crown Prince Norren pushed aside the heavy drapery to sit on his bed and motioned Wyl to a nearby footstool.

The gesture to seat himself, like Royenne Errengard's to Helgurdda, acknowledged their kithship, but Wyl couldn't help noticing it also doubled the height advantage Crown Prince Norren already enjoyed.

Was Crown Prince Norren trying to intimidate him?

"As part of my menney, you will sleep out there and eat with us during the midday meal, which is formal and held in the Young Court hall. We spend our mornings studying and after the meal we play se-net—which you will come to love—and then we train with the Ice Bear menney. After that we eat the evening meal with our families, then retire here for the night," Crown Prince Norren said. "I will have the Ice Bear minions who train us make allowances for your age and size. Now, tell me a little about yourself. How old are you?"

"Fourteen," Wyl replied without hesitation, then belatedly worried about the lie. If the details of Helgurdda's story were known and everyone knew Hereres had sired him, his true age was easy enough to expose—and it would be even more of a weakness, if it should become known that he had tried to hide it. But the crown prince made no comment.

"And you are addressed as Wylheim?"

"Wyl. People who like me, call me Wyl."

"Not any more," the crown prince said. "Except when you are among your peers, you will have to get used to being called Prince Wylheim. With Prince Jeik, and with Prince Lokei, and with our younger uncle, Prince Raldorrei, there is no kneeling—you will exchange the head-nods of princes." He demonstrated a slow, graceful nod. "As the Crown Prince, I am not your peer, so you will kneel as kith-kin and address me properly, as you will with Prince-Viceroye Frekkei."

Wyl scowled. More rules. "If you're a crown prince, then I'm a crown prince, too."

"Not unless and until your mother becomes Royenne of Trascolm," Crown Prince Norren said. "You will need to learn that, if you want to be respected as a prince, you have to give respect to *your* betters. Always be conscious of your rank and the rank of those around you. I imagine even brigands know to be respectful towards their chief. Be particularly mindful of the bondservants—they will jump at the chance to be disrespectful to a young noble, especially since you are Tras."

Wyl had been bristling from the moment Crown Prince Norren had said *betters*, but now he stared in disbelief at how the crown prince thought brigands behaved.

"Brigands aren't respectful to anyone. They're barely obedient and that only so long as their chief can thrash them," he said. He squirmed on his stool, irritated by the unnecessary lecture.

"Relax, Wyl," Crown Prince Norren said.

He noticed which name Crown Prince Norren chose to use with him. Apparently, he also had the idea of pretending to like his new kith, of pretending to want to be his friend.

"And another thing—can you read Teboan?"

"Well enough," Wyl said. "What—"

"You can?" The crown prince's incredulous expression wasn't flattering.

"*Ockh*, there are two things Eirgei can't abide—ignorance in boys and ignorance in horses," Wyl replied sourly. "What do you want me to read?"

"I do not—I want you to teach me Teboan. Can you write it as well as read it?"

In which Evroza warlord's hand do you want it written? But he knew better than to reveal that talent, not with the crown prince giving off the unmistakable scent of a secret. "Yes, I can teach you."

He waited for Crown Prince Norren to say more, not willing to betray his curiosity to a Dremn, now that he'd thoughtlessly betrayed his literacy—it would have been better if the crown prince thought him illiterate. Why did the crown prince of Dremnar want to learn Teboan?

"Oh, excellent," Crown Prince Norren said, with a slight smile.

Crown Prince Norren didn't seem to suspect Wyl had designs on the Bearcubs—but, then, even Wyl hadn't caught on to Helgurdda's plan, at first. With her intentions so subtle, this interplay could only mean that the young viceroye wanted to recruit him, win his loyalty as a grateful, exiled foreigner for reasons other than that they were suddenly kindred.

He had cut his teeth on the Evroza blood-feud, with its treacheries and betrayals—he expected the Dremn varieties would be tame in comparison.

"I imagine you have not spent much time in noble company," the crown prince said. "We are not pretentious here—not like Tras nobility. You will grow more comfortable with us the better you get to know us. I want you to attend me personally so you will learn what a prince needs to know as quickly as possible. I know you have never been in courtly company, so if you do not understand something, just ask me or one of my minions."

Crown Prince Norren paused, pursing his lips as he looked Wyl over, his light brown brows coming together in a pensive frown.

At least, the crown prince wasn't staring into his eyes, but all the same, Wyl stiffened, collecting himself in case he had to move fast. Nothing good had ever come from such a look.

"I can see your first need is clothing. I will have the tiring servants make up something suitable for you. We will attire you in Ice Bear colors, at least for now—just until Norn Holm grows accustomed to having Tras kith about. We do not want any tragic accidents."

Wyl scowled at the suggestion that he'd be an easy victim, but nodded, relaxing now that he knew the purpose of the scrutiny. "I'm good at avoiding fights, but if one's unavoidable, *ockh*, I'll try not to kill anyone."

Crown Prince Norren laughed. "Ah, a sense of humor! We could do with a good laugh in my menney. Lord Martei and I will come of age soon, and sometimes I think we have become much too serious in preparing for our rites." The crown prince smirked at him.

Wyl gave the Dremn crown prince his coldest stare, his face carefully inexpressive as the hint of mockery in Crown Prince Norren's laughter made him tense for trouble.

"I can see you will liven things up around here, Wyl. A sense of humor will help you become accepted more easily. That is particularly good, since you are handicapped by being Tras. So, our friendship is already off to a good start. Now, do you have any questions or need anything else?"

"I can't stay here at night," Wyl said bluntly. "I need to spend the night wherever Helgurdda and Eirgei sleep."

Crown Prince Norren lost his smile. "All my minions sleep here. No exceptions. Even the younglings on the fourth and fifth floors have learned to sleep apart from their mothers. You are too old not to be able to do the same. Here in Norn Holm, you have no reason to be afraid. No one will get past my uncle's menney, the crown princess's guard, and my own Bear Cubs."

"I'm not afraid!" Wyl snapped indignantly. "I'm Helgurdda's bodyguard!"

Lord Martei laughed aloud. "Oh, he is the *Little* Wolf of Milk Dales! What a sense of humor!"

Wyl's gut twisted as he turned towards Crown Prince Norren's friend and scowled. "Eirgei will be guarding Helgurdda during the day while she is in court, but even Eirgei's got to sleep sometime."

"Oh, this is just too much!" Now, Crown Prince Norren joined Lord Martei in laughing at him. "The dreaded Wolfling of Milk Dales protects her!"

"There are always assassins and bounty hunters to be on guard against," he said stiffly.

None of Helgurdda's would-be assassins—or the other rebels, for that matter—had ever suspected Wyl of being anything more than Lanney's young foster-son. No hindrance to them—until it was too late. Those assassins learned for themselves that he was no laughing matter.

"Well," said Crown Prince Norren, his amusement trailing off, "you will have nothing to guard against here. An assassin would have to get past two sets of gate guards and the Ice Bear menney. Your mother will be safe enough without you."

The crown prince laughed again, with what seemed genuine amusement, except Wyl's gut wasn't amused. His stomach twisted tighter. Any tighter and he'd puke.

Just the thought made him angry.

"And with our own tower guards below, you do not have to be afraid for yourself here, either," Crown Prince Norren said, letting his voice trail off and not a moment too soon for Wyl's stomach's sake.

"I'm not afraid!" Even to Wyl's own ears, his protest sounded too quick. What else would anyone think, with him jumping at odd shadows from the moment he'd entered Nornholm? "I'm just a little uncomfortable being in a strange place—I'll do better once I know my way around."

Once he knew which shadows he *should* be jumping at.

He'd recognize mortal danger long before this self-assured youth. What would the Dremn crown prince know of assassins? Royenne Errengard's full-grown Icebear menney couldn't have much experience dealing with the caliber of assassins the Evroza hired, or with bounty hunters eager for Evroza denarreis.

In another life, Eirgei had trained some of those hunters. That Helgurdda had survived all these years was a tribute to their care in guarding her, not a slight on the competence of the Evroza's assassins.

Wyl made his face a bland, disinterested mask and watched Crown Prince Norren struggle to regain a more serious expression. The crown prince's disdainful attitude worked in Wyl's favor—it revealed the crown prince as clearly naïve about treachery and betrayal. He would never suspect the real reason why Helgurdda had agreed to let Wyl join the Young Court.

"Then you may have the rest of this day to explore Norn Holm—but return here after the evening meal with your family. And you *will* be sleeping here with the other Bear Cubs."

Wyl doubted that. Closing his eyes would be next to impossible, surrounded by hostile Dremn, even if they were just boys.

There was nothing *he* needed to learn about treachery.

"Now," Crown Prince Norren said, rising, "if you have any more questions, do not hesitate to ask me or one of the others. I can imagine how strange our Young Court must be to you, especially once we rejoin my royal sister and her attendants in the morning."

Crown Prince Norren took a dismissive step, herding him towards Lord Martei and the door.

"We have never had a Tras prince among us," Crown Prince Norren smiled, as if saying those words with a smile could take the sting out of his sister's name for Wyl. "I am sure we will both learn a lot."

For the first time, Crown Prince Norren took notice of his bondsman, still kneeling with his forehead to the floor. "This is Garei. He will show you around Norn Holm and ensure no one tries to start trouble with you."

When the bondsman rose, Wyl was surprised to see he was the same bondsman from the Crown Court hall, the one he'd met while awaiting the viceroye.

Wyl instantly distrusted him as a spy, but he said nothing as he followed Garei down and out of the Heir's Tower.

After the Tras boy and Garei left the barracks, Norren lay back on his bed.

"Now, how might I put this rascal to good use?"

"It won't be easy, my prince," Martei said. "He is an ill-mannered, hill-country clod. He wasn't the least bit intimidated by noble company in the Young Court—you saw how he dared reprimand your sister over that arrow—and he didn't back down when you intervened."

"True. Making him fit in with the Bear Cubs is going to be a challenge."

"I don't know why you want to bother."

Norren gave his best friend a mysterious smile. "You will have to trust me when I say it will be worth the challenge."

"This is about that messenger-bird your hawk intercepted, is it not?" Martei asked. "If you intend to learn how to read that message by having this Tras boy teach you Teboan, you will need to be very careful."

"Of course," Norren said. "But if I could read the message and compose a message of my own in Teboan, it would be the next best thing to a secret code."

"Why not ask the tutor to teach you?"

"What, and have him wonder why? If anyone finds out I intend to secretly communicate with the Evroza, it could be mistaken for treason. What a stroke of luck that someone has given this brat a rudimentary education."

Martei shrugged. "Helgurdda and Eirgei *are* proposing to take up the crown of Trascolm and make a crown prince of this creature. I am sure he will make an appalling one."

"So what does that matter? Let Trascolm figure out what to do with their would-be prince, if that day ever comes. Right now, all that matters is that not only can he read Teboan, he can also write it."

"You know," Martei said, "there is another way to do this, one that does not depend on you mastering Teboan. A Tras refugee, dependent on your goodwill, wouldn't dare insinuate that the royenne's favorite grandchild is a traitor."

"Which I'm not," Norren growled at his friend.

"—And, even if he betrayed you, who would believe him?"

Norren flung himself to his feet and went to his window with its view of Mount Norn's west face.

"You know making peace with Trascolm will not be popular in Dremnar," Martei said. "This way, any communications that fall into the wrong hands could be traced to him, not you. No one would believe a word he said against you."

"No matter, this is merely the first step in the transformation I have in mind for our people. I'm tired of Dremnar being scorned as a barbarian wasteland. When I'm finished, even the Empress of the Teboan Empire across the Eastern Sea will bow to us." Norren turned and smiled. "That being the case, I cannot allow the Tras brat to escape and flee back to his mother's side. The first rule in taming a wild creature is to keep it at *my* side until it becomes habituated to me and my ways. Otherwise, it would make no more sense than trying to train a haggard if I were willing to let it fly back to its eyrie. The Tras brat is just another haggard, captured fully-fledged in the wild. I only have to be patient—as with my hawk, so with this boy. And you know how my haggard cliff-hawk has become a reliable—"

"—temperamental—" said Martei.

"—hunter," Norren said, annoyed. "With discipline and patience, there is no reason why the Tras brat should not also fly at my command."

"I saw how unwillingly the boy obeyed you. Putting him to use might be difficult. You're going to have to win his cooperation before you dare build a plan around him."

"That won't be hard. You saw how I generously gave him a chance to deal with his fear of being in a strange place. This will give me an opportunity to see how he reciprocates. That will tell me if I truly can make something useful of the boy."

"He's insolent."

"Well, of course, the Tras brat doesn't know his place. The little thug will have to be taught how to become part of the Young Court. Maybe he'll never be completely tame, but so long as he responds to the lure and comes back to my fist, he and his predatory ways will be mine to command." *And if this haggard thinks to escape with his master's prize rather than surrender to my will, he will soon learn that if I have no use for him, his life is worthless in Norn Holm.* "Perhaps among outlaws and brigands, his place has been whatever he made it, but here in Norn Holm, his place is wherever I put him. With his evident fear of the Bear Cubs and of you, Martei, the Tras boy will be needing my royal protection." Norren smiled smugly. "Rogues know it is better to run with the wolves than to run from them."

✦

Garei carried himself like a nobleman, and the other bondservants they passed kept their distance from him. Wyl wondered what crime the bondsman had committed. According to the nobly-born outlaws who'd joined the rebellion, most clan baronnes preferred to save face among their peers by simply outlawing their noble criminals outright rather than hiding them away in their own clanholds for the duration of a sentence of bondage.

Giving a nobly-born bondsman to serve in another clanhold—especially in Dremnar's capital—seemed a deliberate attempt to humiliate the former nobleman, no matter the embarrassment to his clan. It hinted at a private quarrel gone bad and a powerful enemy.

But dangerous criminals were disowned and outlawed outright with a price on their heads, and that had not happened with Garei, so if he truly had once been a nobleman, it made sense that his knowledge of the ways of the nobility would make him a suitable servant for the crown prince or some other member of Icebear royalty.

There remained an unanswered question: why had Wyl first met Crown Prince Norren's personal servant among the royenne's servants in the great Crown Court hall? If he was a spy, *whose* was he?

"First," Garei said, "I will show you where your mother and grand-uncle will stay."

Garei took him through a number of corridors and courtyards to a crumbling old tower squatting behind ancient breastworks at the top of the long, sheer drop that protected Nornholm's western flank. The tower's corridor was at the far end of the palace, in a wing that contained only empty, ruined stumps of towers—when Wyl peered into their guardrooms as they passed, he could see they were open to the sky.

"Your mother has been given an entire tower," Garei said. There was a touch of irony in his voice.

He looked at the bondsman sharply. Was Garei amused that just he and Eirgei remained of Helgurdda's rebel menney?

"Only the uppermost floors of the tower are actually in ruins," Garei hastily assured him. "The ground floor, guardroom, and the third and fourth floors are perfectly livable."

Wyl shrugged. He was sure even living on the fifth floor would be better than sleeping under a tree in the mud.

Helgurdda's tower seemed as far as possible from the great Crown Court hall that marked the beginning of the royenne's private wing of the palace. Nevertheless, it was still within the upper bailey, not in the lower bailey with the Folk servants, or even worse, quartering them in the town outside the gates where they'd have been vulnerable to an assassin or simply any Dremn with an old grudge against Eirgei.

So long as they stayed in Nornholm, they'd be easy enough for their enemies to find, but *where* they stayed in Nornholm would determine how difficult they would be to kill.

Garei led him through the guardroom and up a dirty set of spiral stairs to the hall.

Wyl had expected to find Helgurdda and Eirgei there. Instead, he found a handful of Icebear minions lounging against one of the bare stone walls. There was no sign of Helgurdda or Eirgei.

The ancient rush mats crumbled apart underfoot, and he scowled at everyone who met his eyes as he walked across the room. The cellar of the Evroza clanhold in Myymor was cleaner than their new quarters. The tower had clearly been abandoned for some time. He took it as a warning not to rely on Royenne Errengard's generosity.

But there were only a few water-stains showing on the ceiling planks, and the walls were still sturdy enough, no matter the condition of the uppermost levels of the tower.

Wyl was pleased—he hadn't slept under a roof since he'd left Myymor.

He remembered the layout of the Heir's Tower, the Bearcubs' barracks, and Crown Prince Norren's room. This hall was much smaller, so the room behind the flat wooden wall opposite the entrance had to be much bigger. He opened the door to what he thought would be Helgurdda's bedchamber and found an antechamber instead.

It was larger than Crown Prince Norren's bedchamber. Here, a table of trestles and bare boards was set up against another flat wall and through the open door next to it, he could see a bed like Norren's.

Helgurdda, Eirgei, and a huge blond stranger were gathered at the table. They were talking in low voices and pointing, apparently going over something on a map. Eirgei and Helgurdda both wore their sabres and had their heads together, blocking his view.

"... if Calderek...."

Then, Eirgei saw Wyl and abruptly gestured for the stranger to stop speaking.

"You've got news of Calderek!" Wyl exclaimed with relief. He'd been wanting to know what had happened to the warlord ever since they'd parted, but he hadn't reckoned on hearing news of him for weeks. "He got away, then?"

He hurried to the map table, trying to see past everyone, but Helgurdda and Eirgei didn't make room for him.

"Yes," Helgurdda said, after a moment's hesitation, glaring harshly at the smiling, heavy-set Dremn when he opened his mouth to answer. "He got away."

Wyl was taken aback by her behavior and looked from Helgurdda to Eirgei. "He hasn't gone over to the Evroza, has he?"

It wasn't uncommon for a noble rebel, offered the choice of swinging his allegiance or swinging from Crossroads Keep's wall, to choose to join the lowly penitent's warband in Evroza's auxiliary menney in hopes of earning a pardon. But, given Calderek's fame when he'd led the Evroza's auxiliary menney, and his position as a warlord and Eirgei's Right Hand in Helgurdda's rebellion, Wyl would've been surprised if the Evroza had made Calderek such an offer—or that he'd have accepted it if they had. Calderek had a stiff-necked pride that made him fit right in with Helgurdda and Eirgei.

"You need not worry about Calderek. We will take care of the rebellion. It is enough that you are finally safe here in Nornholm," Helgurdda said.

"But—"

"Leave us," Eirgei said, taking him by the shoulders. He roughly turned Wyl and gave him a shove toward the door. "Next time, knock when the door is closed and enter only with permission. It is time you learned some manners or once your mother is royenne, you will be an embarrassment, a prince fit only for the company of rogues."

Wyl turned and glared furiously at Eirgei—he was all-too-conscious of Garei's interested presence just outside the door, and no one knew better than he what gossips bondservants could be. The story of him being thrown out of this council of war would be all over Nornholm in hours. It would make his conquest of the Young Court and the Bearcubs more difficult if his family was already distancing themselves from him.

"The hall up the stairs on the next floor will be our practice area," Eirgei said, ignoring his glare. "See about getting it set up for us to use—your sabre and back-knives are over there in the corner, but you are not to wear them outside this tower. There should be a bondsman around somewhere who can get whatever you need to make this place fit for your mother to live in. Then get yourself cleaned up."

Wyl couldn't believe he was being dismissed when there was obviously news from Trascolm—dismissed to play servant!

"Go, boy," Eirgei said, in an impatient voice. "Do as you have been told."

And because obedience to orders had always been a matter of life or death, Wyl angrily took a knee and his leave of Helgurdda, and did as ordered—refusing to look at Garei as he passed through the doorway. He hadn't felt so humiliated since he'd been a youngling.

He didn't think this was the first time he'd ever been thrown out of a council of war. Something about Eirgei's tone of voice as he'd shoved Wyl out the door had stirred a bone-deep chill in him, all the more worrisome for his inability to recall the circumstances.

A spy had to have a good memory, so he'd never told anyone—not even Lanney—about the holes in his. Every time he found one, it frightened him. The memory holes were like his dreams—yet another sign he was losing his hold on the waking world; in his own way, he was likely as mad as Helgurdda.

He did what he always did when the specter of madness loomed over him: he ignored the past and focused on *now*.

"You go first," he said to Garei, gesturing at the filthy stairs, and he followed the bondsman to the next—and last intact—level of the tower.

He walked around the perimeter of the dirty expanse of bare, wooden floor. Opposite the stairs he saw an alcove and a heavy, bronze-bound door that opened onto an empty room. He examined the thick bolt on the inside of the door and the room's narrow, open window that was missing its shutters. He looked out the window, then boosted himself up and crawled out to the edge of it.

The ledge was deeper than he was tall, spanning the stairwell between the outer and inner tower walls. He put his head and shoulders out over the four-story drop to the courtyard and looked around at the weathered stonework. The window faced north and had a view of nothing but lifeless rubble surrounding an old quarry and a vertical cliff face.

All in all, the room was perfect.

Garei was still out in the hall, pacing off the expanse of empty floor. "If you are going to be training up here," the bondsman called, as Wyl emerged from his room. "You will need more light, even with the shutters open—candle trees, at least four."

Wyl went to the west window in the hall and opened the shutters. As Garei had said, it let in more cold than light from the afternoon sun. The sheer walls of the unquarried remains of Mount Norn's peak would block out the sunrise in the east.

There would be no morning light. All his dawn training bouts with Eirgei were going to focus on fighting in the dark.

He shuddered. Candles would be his next priority, once he got his bearings.

He spared time to look out the hall's wide, south-facing window. Helgurdda's tower gave an impressive view of the upper bailey and the palace, and even portions of the lower bailey. The tower stood on what was the highest ground inside the upper bailey. He could see a maze of

LEGEND OF THE SPIDER-PRINCE: REBEL

wide courtyard walls topped with steeply-peaked, slate-shingled roofs. The interiors of what remained of the original fortress's walls had been cleared of rubble and made into those slate-roofed corridors they'd passed through.

Outside the lower bailey walls some distance to the south, he glimpsed the town and beyond it, the Folk village and the gaps where the hemlock forest had been cleared for stone-walled pastures and fields.

He fixed the layout of Nornholm and its palace in his mind, then closed the shutters against the cold.

"Let us go see about the lighting," Garei suggested.

"You see about the lighting. I'm going to look around."

Garei looked ready to argue, so Wyl gave him his rogue's glower.

The bondsman blinked and involuntarily took a step backwards, giving Wyl more space, enough that he could stalk away, leaving the bondsman with no doubts about whether he could look out for himself.

And he could. Outside the Young Court, he'd simply deal with these Dremn the same way he had the brigands in the rebel menney. The Dremn might look cleaner and surprisingly more civilized, but underneath, he doubted there would be much to choose between outlaws and the Dremn.

He descended two sharply-angled flights of stairs from the corridor outside the guardroom on the second floor and entered the small, empty kitchen on the ground floor, where the hearth was long-cold and dirty with old ashes.

The underbelly of the palace was also hollowed out of the old fortress's walls and occupied the space below the second floor corridors between the towers. This tower's scullery opened directly onto a bare stone courtyard.

As he explored the upper bailey, he saw there was a kitchen for each tower. In between the towers were a variety of storerooms, workshops, spring-fed baths, and even several laundries. The stables were of stone and built near the gates letting into the lower, outer bailey.

There were two smithies—one for weaponry, the other for ordinary tin, copper, and bronzeware—just past the stables on opposite sides of the High Gate. The Dremn smiths in both gave him an appraising look that swiftly darkened into a scowl, and with baleful swings of their hammers, they ran him off before he could even see inside.

The lower bailey housed free-standing, slate-roofed workshops, kitchens, barracks for servants, sheds for carts, stables, and even a pen of wooly, mild-mannered argali goats the size of small horses.

The outer gates were barred to him by guardsmen bearing halberds. He kept in mind Eirgei's lessons about polearms and gave the guardsmen what, at a distance, might be taken for a smile. Young as he was, memory of that smile might give the gate guards enough of a pause that he could get inside the arc of those halberds if he had to open the way for an escape. He was not above using his age to disarm and surprise dangerous adults

As he made his way back towards the upper bailey, he saw Garei. He had a pair of surly bondsmen in tow with deep baskets strapped on their backs, pulling two-wheeled handcarts piled full of candle trees, trestles, planks, stools, and other household items. The two middle-aged bondsmen didn't look like former noblemen, but rather like careless thieves who likely had deserved to be caught.

Wyl trailed along behind them, hands free and unencumbered, mentally mapping and making note of interesting things and people on the way back to the tower.

Several times, the four of them trudged the length and width of the palace, and then back to what Wyl overheard was already being called *Tras Tower*. He heard that—and more—as they passed through corridors and courtyards.

Tras were not well-regarded in Dremnar and what he heard put him in a foul mood.

Garei led the way to various storerooms and collected more candles and candle trees, rushlight bowls to hang from cressets along the stairs, and the oil to fill them. He and the bondsmen obtained bedding, brooms, rags and buckets, and lastly, armloads of fresh rush mats.

Everyone they encountered stopped what they were doing to watch as Wyl approached, then let loose a frenzy of whispers behind his back after he'd passed. They seriously underestimated the range of his hearing.

The Folk hunters had been busy since Wyl had left the Crown Court hall. From the whispers, Wyl gathered that Royenne Errengard had given them a token reward worth far less than the bounty Royenne Sharei had offered for Helgurdda's head. The hunters had taken revenge by claiming Wyl had posed as one of the Folk to cover his criminal intentions towards those who had given his family asylum—a treachery no one would put past a Tras of any age.

Being revealed as Helgurdda's son hadn't made him less disreputable. Nor did Nornholm's Folk love him for his pretense at being one of them. He was, he understood, a blot on the honor of Icebear clan.

A large part of Eirgei's training had been to teach Wyl how the nobility thought, but even a fool would know Royenne Errengard wouldn't be amused by such talk, not after she'd declared Wyl kith to her. None of this would help Helgurdda's cause here, nor make Royenne Errengard eager for a closer alliance.

Two summonses arrived at Tras Tower on their heels after their last trip across the palace. Both were brought by stripling page girls squirming with the discomfort of minor clan nobility unsure of where they ranked against despised Tras who happened to be royal clan kith. One summons, from Prince Frekkei, called on Eirgei to appear at the Menney Tower. The other required Helgurdda's attendance on Royenne Errengard. The guardsmen split to escort each of them. The stranger with the map accompanied Eirgei as they left, leaving Wyl alone with Garei and the bondsmen.

Garei dismissed the bondsmen after they'd unloaded the carts and put away everything, their last task being to put together a set of crosspoles for armor and weapons. They erected them in the makeshift armory on the fourth floor, in the alcove next to the door of Wyl's room.

His quarters were now luxuriously furnished with a candle tree, a rushlight, and a comfortable pallet bed with his saddlebags for a pillow. Wyl brought up their remaining bits of panoply from the hall, hanging Eirgei's helm from the top of one crosspole and leaning both Eirgei's and Helgurdda's shields against the stone wall. Back down in Helgurdda's hall, he collected his sabre, as well as his back-knives from where they were leaning against a wall in the antechamber. He took them all upstairs to hang from his crosspole.

Eirgei had said nothing prohibiting him from wearing his *byrnney*, and to Wyl's mind, nothing about their welcome here warranted taking it off. He doubted any of their crosspoles would see much of their proper use.

Tall candle trees, unlit save for the single rushlight hanging from the one closest to the stairs, now surrounded the practice floor.

"I leave you now, Prince Wylheim," Garei said, with a nobleman's bowed head.

That was a noble courtesy when given by a nobleman to commoners and Folk, but something else when given by a bondsman to someone acknowledged as a prince in open court.

Wyl automatically kept his face carefully bland as Garei reminded him, in his cultured cadence, "Remember, you are expected to return to the Heir's Tower and the Bear Cubs after the evening meal."

Wyl nodded his understanding and watched Garei leave.

He'd suspected mockery earlier, when the former nobleman had addressed him as a prince, but had heard nothing of it in his voice. Now, there was no question of it—Garei thought Wyl hadn't recognize the insult he'd been given and thought himself clever for it.

The Evroza were masters of the nuances of noble insult, still touchy of their ignoble origins despite ruling Trascolm for four generations. Eirgei had taught him all the noble subtleties—undoubtedly, so Wyl could either insult the Evroza properly when they captured Crossroads Keep, or be assured of a swift, clean death if he were captured by them instead.

Wyl supposed he should've insisted on a proper grovel from Garei, but with no role to play for the first time in his life, he'd felt strangely off-balance around the former nobleman. Easier for him to fall back on playing Lanney's Folk foster-son than to act like a newly-acknowledged rebel-prince. In truth, despite Helgurdda publicly naming him her son, he didn't feel like her son or Eirgei's grandnephew—or even Lanney's foster-son.

He felt lost.

The tower was now empty save for him. His footsteps echoed off the bare, stone walls of the empty tower as he descended to the candle-lit third floor. He paced around each room, familiarized himself with the squeaking planks of the floor until he could cross without a sound, stalking the next assassin prowling in the dark.

He expected Eirgei to be back to guard Helgurdda's sleep when she returned from the Crown Court. But she didn't return from court, not even after true night fell.

Neither did Eirgei.

Wyl paced the stone floor of the dark second floor guardroom, figuring he'd get his first sight of them from there. But he didn't.

After a while, he gave in to his growing uneasiness and went in search of Helgurdda. Royenne Errengard had summoned her, so the Crown Court hall seemed the likeliest place to pick up her trail.

Unlike the other corridors, the one leading to the royenne's wing of the palace was well-lit with cressets that cast deep, shifting shadows outside their pools of light. He approached by way of those shadows, very conscious of the dark archways at each rushlight-lit intersecting corridor.

CHAPTER 13

ICEBEARS

Wyl encountered no one until he reached the antechamber outside the Crown Court hall. The room was big enough to hold a full warband. Opposite the entry was a double door. Two Icebear guardsmen flanked it. Coming from behind it were voices, a lot of them.

The two Icebear guardsmen were quick to block his way. Each carried a short thrusting spear and had a battleaxe at his hip, hanging from a baldric. Both were tall and imposing.

The shorter of the two sneered down at him. "What do we have here, Todreien?"

"Hmm," Todreien made a show of looking Wyl up and down. "What smells like a horse and dresses like a brigand? And is it a boy or a girl?"

"Whatever it is, it has the Folk in an uproar," said his partner. "Looks pretty ridiculous outfitted like that." He addressed Wyl. "Your granduncle know you are playing with his panoply?"

Todreien gave Wyl the kind of scornful look he'd received often enough in Myymor, playing an outcast Folk boy. But receiving that same look here from his new kith-kin shocked him.

"Is Helgurdda inside with Royenne Errengard?" he snapped, trying to cut short the insults. In Myymor, he'd endured far worse taunting than this; it stung only because he hadn't been expecting it here.

"Helgurdda? Who would that be?" Todreien asked.

"The leader of the Tras rebels, the one Royenne Errengard acknowledged as kith to Icebear clan today," he said. There was noth-

163

ing feigned in the edge to his voice. He was tired, hungry, and in no mood to be mocked or made a target for more insults.

"Do you know who this Tras trash means?" Todreien asked the other guard, with sham bafflement.

"Does she look anything like you?" the other guard asked.

Wyl had never imagined receiving this kind of treatment after the royenne had welcomed them to Nornholm, not from kith—and to his face. In that instant, he hated these guardsmen as much as he hated brigands.

"No," Wyl said shortly. "She's long-haired as a royenne—with the look of her sire, Prince Valdurren," which was merely a guess on his part, "—and bearing an artisanry sabre capable of cutting a man in half for insolence."

He scowled when the two guardsmen kept grinning down at him. There was no hint of the truth to be read in their faces, just the telltales of lies—and of amusement at his expense. "Why's she still with the royenne?"

"I'm afraid Royenne Errengard does not consult me on matters of state," Todreien said.

"If she's come to any harm—"

"Oh, now, I am really scared," Todreien laughed derisively. "What do you think you are going to do to me, little boy?"

"Now, Todreien, do not tease the youngling. You will make him cry."

This wasn't assuring him that Helgurdda was behind those doors, or safe. That he had to stand his ground against these two and try to force an answer, despite their mockery, made him furious. "Don't try to lie to me and say you haven't seen her! It says much about Icebear clan, if this is how you treat kith," he said.

Todreien grinned at his partner.

The moment the guard's eyes shifted, Wyl pulled both of his long knives from his boots and sprang at Todreien.

One knife hand darted at the hand holding the guardsman's spear. Todreien's recoil provided just enough resistance so the other knife, uncommonly sharp and already caught under the guard's baldric, cut through it like it was glove leather. The heavy axe head dropped hard on Todreien's boot.

Todreien hopped.

Wyl's kick spun the axe away, and he dodged past Todreien, pulling back on the handle of one of the heavy doors, his right-hand knife now held between his teeth.

Todreien swore and lunged, and slammed the door shut before Wyl could go through.

Wyl turned on the guardsman, snatching back the knife from between his teeth. He snarled. Fast as a hooded viper, he struck out with his left hand. The blade smashed into Todreien's mail with a shrill metallic screech, skidding under his arm, and jammed into a link of mail.

Todreien gasped. "The brat's stuck me!" There was surprise and anger in his voice, but no pain.

Wyl retreated towards the corridor entrance.

The other guardsman shifted to block his way out. "Let me show you what we do to backstabbing street scum who have no respect for their betters."

If this were a brigand camp or the streets of Myymor, Wyl would've expected something like this, but not here, outside the great Crown Court hall of Dremnar. "*Horned One hook you!* I don't want to be kith, if this is Icebear honor," he said, panting with fury.

The guardsman laughed.

Wyl weighed which of them should be his first target.

Todreien switched his spear to his other hand to probe at where Wyl had struck him. "I don't believe this—he got me! Broke a ring and scratched me through my aketon!" His expression turned angry, and he threatened Wyl with his leveled spear. "I'm going to pin you to that wall, boy!"

Todreien jabbed violently at him.

Wyl darted aside, and the spear hit the wall behind where he'd been.

The other guardsman laughed again, content to block his way out, brandishing his spear. "You aren't going to let a boy get the better of you?" he jeered at his partner.

Wyl sidled away from the second guardsman's half-hearted poke with his spear.

Todreien swore, threw down his spear, and strode back to where his axe lay.

Cut off from the way out, Wyl retreated back towards the hall doors.

"Is there a problem?" someone asked from behind him, where the closed doors should have been.

Wyl's heart seized, and he jumped like a frightened cat.

He spun aside and put his back to the corner of the antechamber, within an arm's reach of a cresset—lacking his sabre, that would be his next weapon, if he had to throw a knife.

Then, he blinked up at the powerfully-built newcomer, who ignored him and looked sternly at the two guardsmen. It was the Dremn nobleman who'd been studying the map with Helgurdda and Eirgei—only now his hair had been let down to fall to his hips over his Icebear surcoat. Not a nobleman, then, but an Icebear prince.

"We were only having some harmless fun, my prince," Todreien said.

"Harmless to the boy, or harmless to our clan?" the unknown prince asked.

Both guardsmen reddened and looked down.

The prince turned to Wyl.

Wyl glared back up at the massive Dremn, part bluff, but part deadly serious—his heart still raced from the hellish scare he'd been given. He couldn't believe someone so big had come through those doors and stepped up behind him without him knowing it.

In camp, that kind of mistake could get him killed. His knees felt weak from the shock of it. He never expected second chances to save himself.

"Put up your weapons," the prince told him, with a hard edge to his voice and a stern look on his broad face. His blue eyes flicked to the knives in Wyl's hands and became undeniably frosty. "A man having a fool's mouth does not grant you permission to draw his blood. Kin protects kin and drawing a weapon on kin, even kith-kin, is a disgrace. Draw *blood* from *anyone* in Norn Holm after this, and I will require your granduncle to discipline you. Publicly. Do you understand?"

Wyl imagined how Eirgei would react to such a demand and felt sick. "But they're the ones who started this!"

He didn't understand why *he* was in trouble—he was the one who'd been called names and taunted! Surely, a prince, even a kith prince, would be justified in drawing blood for such an offense?

The big Icebear prince glared down at him, waiting.

Apparently, Wyl was expected to accept the insult—it was no different here than on the streets of Myymor. The odds—cornered by three armed, adult minions while he had only his knives—left him with no other choice but to capitulate.

He broke eye contact and sheathed his blades. He took a knee as he would with Eirgei, except he folded his arms across his chest when he bowed his head so he could touch his throwing knives. He never took his eyes off the Icebear prince, watching him through his hair.

"This is no place for you, boy. Go back to Tras Tower. Your mother will be back there soon enough."

"I'm not a *boy!*" Wyl snarled before he thought.

The prince gave a bark of grim laughter and looked down at him, his expression inscrutable. "You are not a *man*, either. Return to Tras Tower, Prince Wylheim, and await your mother's return there."

This prince knew his name?

He hadn't seen him in the Crown Court hall when Helgurdda had met the royenne. He'd thought all the royal Icebears had been in attendance. Who was this Icebear prince? He could see traces of Royenne Errengard and even Prince Frekkei in his face and bearing, but Wyl could say the same of all the royal Icebears, even the half-grown ones of the Young Court.

He didn't like the idea that he'd been discussed after Eirgei had sent him away from his council of war, nor did he like the interest this one had taken in him. It made his skin crawl without even a whiff of magic in the air. A good spy wasn't *interesting*.

The prince went back through the doors and into the great Crown Court hall without another glance at him.

Wyl caught a glimpse of the hall through the doors. It was now filled with tables and fair-haired people, and the scent of foreign food. He didn't see Helgurdda's surcoat or her face in the crowd.

The two guardsmen hurried to close the massive door behind the prince and when they did, Wyl slipped out into the corridor.

He took a roundabout way back to Tras Tower, wandering through the understories between the various towers until he found one with a half-empty pot of stew still simmering over the kitchen fire. He helped himself to some with half his attention on the scullery where oblivious kitchen Folk were cleaning up. The other half of his attention was on the stairs to the tower's guardroom. He left as quickly as he could with his dinner.

He ate as he walked the maze of courtyards, then left the emptied bowl in another kitchen, one next to a laundry with clothes hanging by the fire to dry.

He found an undertunic and leggings that looked like they should fit, one the drab dun of undyed wool, the other dark brown. Both were nearly new, relative to what he wore, but so commonplace that they weren't likely to be recognized as stolen.

He returned to still-empty and echoing Tras Tower and built a fire on the kitchen hearth. He filled a couple of cauldrons with water from the cistern in the back of the scullery and swung them over the fire to warm while he huddled next to the fire himself, also waiting to warm—and still mightily worried.

Though he'd helped himself to food from a random kitchen and was confident that the odd flavor had been foreign spices and not poison, he didn't know whether the security of the Dremn royenne's kitchens or table was sufficient to thwart an Evroza assassin.

Surely, none of their enemies could've been expecting any of this, that Helgurdda and Eirgei would flee into Dremnar—or that they'd find a welcome. As he'd passed through the palace earlier in the day, he'd overheard nothing to suggest that the news of the battle and the whirlwind that had destroyed their menney had reached Nornholm before they had. Most of Nornholm's inhabitants had been abuzz with the news of their arrival, but they'd known nothing more about the three of them except that they were Tras outlaws who'd come begging asylum from Icebear clan.

He wanted to believe it was too soon for an Evroza spy to make a move against Helgurdda, that their sudden appearance in Nornholm had taken everyone in Dremnar by surprise. But as a bodyguard, he'd learned the hard way to be prepared for the worst, not the best, in any situation. *Your enemies will strike when you are weak, not when you are strong,* Eirgei always said. If Helgurdda already had news of Calderek, why should he think the Evroza's spies weren't equally as efficient as Royenne Errengard's?

He paced nervously through Tras Tower's kitchen and adjacent scullery, anticipating trouble that must be even now on its way. He hated waiting for someone else to make a deadly move.

✦

When Helgurdda finally arrived, he was, as ordered, clean and dry in his freshly-stolen clothing, save for his long, damp braid tucked away under the collar of his now-repaired *byrnney*. He'd sacrificed the scales from the half-sleeves to replace those sheared away from the belly.

Helgurdda was almost unrecognizable in an Icebear noblewoman's attire, her hair hanging unplaited and loose over it, held back from her face by the simple coronet of an untitled woman of the royal clan—an honor for mere kith-kin. Her sabre and pair of back-daggers added an odd, martial accent to her sumptuous court robe of blackwork-flecked, white Gerisari silk. By the awkward way it flowed, he was relieved to know she still wore her mail under it. She hadn't relaxed her guard, didn't feel herself safe here, either.

Which was why he gaped at the radiant smile on her face as she came through the door. He'd never seen such a smile on her.

She was escorted by Icebear guardsmen, who promptly left before Wyl could insist they take up posts in the guardroom below.

There was still no sign of Eirgei.

He followed Helgurdda.

She went into her bedchamber, undoing the ornate gold clasp fastening her long cloak of Gerisari silk velvet at a rakish sabreer's angle across her back, leaving the hilt of her sabre unencumbered. She tossed her sabre's shoulder sheath down onto the bed.

She turned to look at him, an excited, inward expression on her face. "Royenne Errengard has promised swift action. I think she wants us out of Dremnar as fast as possi—" She abruptly stopped and frowned. "You should not be here, Wyl."

She stepped up to him, then paralyzed him by combing his hair aside with her fingers and staring down into his eyes.

It was an intimate gesture, one that made his skin involuntarily twitch like a horse with a biting fly. The deep-seated subterfuge of their relationship—and his natural aversion to attention as a spy—made him uneasy at her touch. She'd hated that he'd cut his hair and had never let it grow back, so he was at a loss for what this caress meant.

"It is getting late. Go back to the Heir's Tower and get some rest. You have had a long day."

He stared at her.

She made that bizarre statement as if she herself hadn't spent the first part of the day bound and haltered, plodding up and down half the Icepeak Mountains on foot.

He was too conscious of the empty tower to agree to that. "I'll stay down in the guardroom until Eirgei arrives."

"No, you need to return to the Heir's Tower—did not Crown Prince Norren take you into the Bearcubs? You will be expected to sleep there."

"When Eirgei comes, he'll need to rest, so I need to be here to take first watch," he countered sensibly.

"No, Wyl," she said, with a snap in her voice. "Just return to the Heir's Tower and obey Crown Prince Norren's instructions."

He wasn't leaving her by herself, unguarded in a remote and lonely tower, surrounded by Tras-hating Dremn. "Let me stay here with you.

I—I won't be able to sleep among strangers, anyway."

"Nonsense," Helgurdda said, and her blue eyes—Icebear eyes, he knew now—narrowed ominously. "They are just youths scarcely older than you. If you can sleep in camp among my rebels, you can learn to share quarters with noble children. You need to get used to being around others your own age—and that is an order."

"But—"

"I am quite capable of looking after myself. Go back to the Heir's Tower and be sure to let Crown Prince Norren know you have returned."

She ended that command with a sudden hug that startled him into a flinch, then followed it up with a kiss on his forehead that effectively silenced him and left the skin there burning.

He trudged down the stairs to the empty scullery and kitchen, then out into the courtyard. His mental map suggested outside would be a shorter route to the Heir's Tower than by taking the corridors.

Helgurdda's odd hug and kiss hadn't felt right.

It had felt guilty.

He suspected that she meant to disown him soon.

For his own good, she'd claim, as usual. She'd betrayed herself in her excitement when she'd come in, bubbling over with news of the evening's events—and yet, how careful she'd been not to share any of it with him.

This would not be the first time Helgurdda had tried to disown him—always *for your own good*—but this would be the first time she'd tried it since he was a youngling, the year before he'd become Eirgei's pupil. He'd grown up in that year, and once Eirgei had agreed to teach him, he'd no longer been treated like a youngling.

Then Lanney had arrived, and Helgurdda had stopped trying to disown him. He'd made himself useful almost as soon as he'd begun to share bodyguard duties with the mercenary. Since then, having proven he could not only look out for himself, but also for Helgurdda, he'd thought himself finally accepted as one of her rebels—hadn't he killed enough assassins to prove his worth?

So, why was his life turning back into the mess it had been before he'd become a bodyguard?

Back in Milkdales, Helgurdda's disowning attempts had always started with her taking him to some remote Folk hamlet in the Black Mountains and abandoning him there in the keeping of a stranger—*just for the winter*, she'd say, not knowing that even so young as he had been then, he could already read the adults around him and recognize a lie.

He could follow Helgurdda's reasoning in making a fresh attempt now—she figured that with Royenne Errengard in the role of the Folk woman and with Nornholm as the hamlet, this time he wouldn't run away to rejoin her and the other rebels.

Did she really believe him so impressed by royalty and kithship with Dremnar's ruling clan that he'd stay?

He belonged with his own kin, his own clan, however small—or large and criminal.

His chest heaved but he wasn't a youngling, so he breathed hard and coughed some more until the risk of breaking down had passed. He wished he knew a similar trick to relieve the remaining ache in his chest and the tightness in his throat.

He wasn't some outcast boy whose mother couldn't or wouldn't feed him—nor was he some baby wailing at Helgurdda or Eirgei for their time or attention. He was as much a rebel as they were!

His life had always depended on *not* acting like Helgurdda's son or Eirgei's grandnephew. He'd never shared Helgurdda's tent, her meals, or anything except strategy meetings—and he'd been present at those because her inner circle knew he was the best spy the rebels had.

None of that had come easily. He'd had to grovel until Eirgei would give him weapons training. When he'd finally relented, it had *not* been because a man was expected to do that for his sister's or niece's male children, but because Wyl had already proven himself as the best, most dedicated pupil Eirgei had ever had.

Helgurdda couldn't possibly ignore the danger to herself, now that only the three of them were left. His skills made him anything but a burden or a handicap—to her or to the rebellion.

Being a mother who'd had to disown a son would make her cause seem pathetic—how could she hope to rule if she couldn't control a son? That's how people would judge matters if she disowned him for disobedience—or out of the ridiculous notion that disowning him would somehow be for his own good.

But, surely this time was different?

Maybe she was not trying to disown him. Maybe she *really had* placed him in the Young Court, away from her and Eirgei, so he'd be forgotten, unseen and eventually out of the thoughts of her enemies, just waiting for his moment to strike and take hostages when the Dremn royenne betrayed them.

A similar reason had to underlie why she would allow Eirgei to spend his days with the Icebear menney, just returning to Tras Tower to sleep, which he'd only do lightly without Wyl present to share bodyguard duty—

So, who watched over Helgurdda during the day when Eirgei trained the Icebear menney?

Wyl stopped short.

How could he forget?

Though Eirgei acted as protectively towards Helgurdda as any viceroye would to his crowned royenne, Helgurdda was still Eirgei's niece. She'd been an outlaw before Wyl had been born. Eirgei surely had trained her as he had Wyl—how else could she have survived those years before Wyl and Lanney became her bodyguards?

This was yet another of Eirgei's deceptions, that Helgurdda *needed* bodyguards.

Wyl sighed, suddenly feeling physically and emotionally drained.

It had been a long, difficult day for all of them. Things would surely seem better tomorrow, after they'd all gotten some rest.

He'd been useful to Helgurdda today—he'd taken the measure of their bondservants and accomplished a small miracle in making the tower habitable, even comfortable. For now, he'd just have to content himself with that contribution to the rebellion.

But it still bothered him that Helgurdda and Eirgei had reacted with such surprise when he'd walked in on their strategy meeting, like he'd compromised some secret.

Now that everyone knew who he was, shouldn't his family give him more attention now than they had when the world had believed him merely Lanney's outcast fosterling?

If Helgurdda *didn't* intend to disown him, then shouldn't she and Eirgei have to start treating him like a son and grandnephew—very differently from how they'd treated him all his life?

✦

The Heir's Tower, like Tras Tower, was at the end of a corridor and had only one access to the upper levels.

Wyl made a circuit around the outside of it through the surrounding courtyards—all deserted in the gloom—feeling the tower's stonework, counting the tall, narrow, faintly-glowing outlines of windows to count its floors. Finally, he entered the corridor and stepped inside the guardroom.

From out in the corridor, the guardroom had looked unpleasantly crowded with Icebear minions, but once he stepped through the open door, he saw that the guardsmen were all gathered around a table and wagering on some game. It sounded like senet.

No idle eyes scanned the room, and he delicately passed behind the guardsmen's backs like they were the town guard in Myymor, his steps first freezing, then ghosting. Other wagers were mentioned, mocking ones laid against Helgurdda's chances of surviving to become a royenne, wagers that tested his temper.

Wyl crossed to the stairs like a pickpocket through a market crowd and climbed the steps curving inside the tower wall, grateful for the dim rushlights.

He entered the dark and quiet Young Court hall one floor up. The north window had a pile of wooden toys and cloth dolls under it, so he went to the east window, the one where he'd played senet with the crown princess. He stepped up onto one of the stools under the window and boosted himself into the embrasure. He crawled head-first out to the end of the ledge and examined the stonework around the window just as he had examined that around his window in Tras Tower. Then he scooted back into the room and left, returning to the stairwell.

He climbed more stairs, pausing at the landings for the next two floors to listen at each closed door—both contain younglings, with the voices of boys on the fourth floor, girls on the fifth. The sixth floor was where Crown Prince Norren had taken him earlier, only now the barracks sounded full of male youths. He continued past it. At the seventh floor, he heard the voices of older girls behind the closed door. That was where the crown princess slept, attended by her kinswoman and high clan noblewomen.

He went through a trapdoor to the eighth floor. It had a large, covered cauldron containing rancid siege oil and a parapet walk encircled it for a lookout. The rooftop had gutters to collect rainwater and snowmelt, which was likely piped down to a cistern like the one in Tras Tower's scullery. He explored the windy lookout, examining the winch, and fingering the deplorable state of the stonework. It reminded him of what he'd found out about Tras Tower, that the fine stonework became interestingly decrepit the higher the tower rose, although this tower was not as crumbling as the upper level ruins of Tras Tower.

He descended the stairs to the sixth floor, took a deep, bracing breath, and then opened the door. The door opened—surprisingly silently—giving him precious seconds to assess the danger he'd be facing and what actions he might take.

The stone-bound room, crowded with beds and furniture, now contained about twenty Dremn youths, all of them bigger than he, but not so dangerous as rebel brigands. *They are only children.*

The nearest menace was Prince Jeik. His black-speckled surcoat stood out against the black of his high-necked tunic as much as his thick gold torc did. Wyl wondered how many weapons the prince had concealed under that bulk of white fur. The white fabric of the narrow sleeves of his undertunic was bunched at the wrists, perfect for concealing blades like those under Wyl's bracers, just as the shin-high ice bear fur-trimmed boots pulled over white leggings surely must hold boot knives, though the shorter Dremn boots would require a crouch and draw shorter knives than those Wyl carried at his fingertips in his Tras riding boots.

But as he pushed aside his qualms and gathered his tired wits, a cough escaped him. In the moment it took him to stifle it, every eye was on him.

Most of the boys simply watched and assessed, but there were several of the older young minions—Prince Jeik and Lord Martei among them—who were openly hostile.

Then Lord Martei, at the wooden east wall, rapped on the closed door, and Crown Prince Norren emerged.

"Ah, our missing Tras princeling," he said.

Wyl swallowed, then tossed the hair out of his eyes so he could glare at the Bearcubs as he defiantly stalked down the central aisle separating Prince Jeik's territory from Lord Martei's. When he was three strides from Crown Prince Norren, he automatically put a knee down, bowed his head, then raised it. "I wasn't missing. I was in Tras Tower. I'm Helgurdda's bodyguard, and now that she's back, I need to go back, too."

"I saw the Tras wandering through the lower bailey earlier," someone said, sniggering. "I think he got lost."

That got a few laughs.

Wyl darted his eyes to either side, force of habit to see who'd spoken—and who'd laughed. He yearned for an opportunity to beat some proper respect into them.

"Probably so," Crown Prince Norren nodded and looked at Wyl. "I have already said that you will stay here, so no more of this nonsense about being her bodyguard. She will be just fine without you. Now, you may rise—here in Dremnar, a bow of the head when you kneel is sufficient for kith, but it stays bowed until you are acknowledged. As kith, remember that you should have both knees down—you have never had reason to know that, I imagine. Come."

Crown Prince Norren showed him the empty bed that would be his, one bed away from Lord Martei's bed—and as far from the door as he could be, short of being in Crown Prince Norren's room.

Being close to the crown prince was an honor, Wyl supposed, but he'd rather be close to the door.

He sat on his raised pallet while the other youths stripped down to their white undertunics, all of them apparently immune to the cold. Rushlights were lit next to the doorway to the stairs and next to Crown Prince Norren's room, and the candles extinguished.

"Lie down in that bed, Tras," came Lord Martei's voice from the shadows to his left. "And if you so much as put one foot out of it before morning, I will assume it is to cut our throats while we are sleeping—and I will kill you."

By way of a reply, Wyl bared his teeth in a soundless snarl, amusing himself with the thought that, in the dark, it might be mistaken for a smile.

He meant to stay awake, his blades at his fingertips. Lord Martei's words had the ring of sincerity—and he hadn't promised to stay in bed himself.

Wyl was used to sleeping in his *byrnney*—and he certainly was not taking it off tonight!

He unpinned his cloak in the near darkness, lay down on top of the bed, and covered himself with his cloak, not just for warmth but to conceal where his hands were poised. He didn't remove so much as his robber's pouch from under his surcoat—he was now ready to rest, but prepared to come up fighting.

Through most of the night, he lay very still, hearing soft whispers around the room—he hadn't been the only one expecting trouble.

He didn't move or do anything to invite an attack, and the Bearcubs surprised him by losing interest in staying on guard—he'd been expecting a beating, no matter what he did, and had been reconciled to making sure it was a costly one for the Bearcubs.

He left his bed in the deep night of the first of the dead hours, desperate for rest, even if he had to kill Lord Martei to get it. He crossed the room, stepping in rhythm with the loudest snores, and slipped out the conveniently silent door. This time, rather than risking discovery by leaving through the guardroom, he descended only as far as the Young Court hall.

He again boosted himself up into the window and crawled to the outside of the tower. He descended slowly and carefully—while he could practically fly *up* a wall, he hadn't climbed up this one, so he wasn't sure of his finger and toe holds going down. The lower levels were a challenging climb in the dark—the workmanship was much better than that of Tras Tower. The ashlar blocks were better-fitted and required more caution—and he hated blind descents, no matter what the condition of the stonework. As always, he felt like a spider, making his way down the wall, but without the benefit of a strand of spider-silk if he fell. Then he made a foot-stinging drop into the courtyard and went to the upper bailey's stables.

He entered the dark stable and found his way to Firebrand's stall, where he intended to spend the rest of the night sleeping in the straw under her manger with the mare keeping watch.

✦

Wyl escaped the monster by waking with a desperate gasp, his eyes snapping open.

He could see stars through an open half-door across the barn aisle, and by their positions, he hadn't been asleep long. As usual, most of the dream slipped through his fingers when he came bolt-upright, and he lost the rest of it when the top of his head thumped into the cob-web-festooned underside of the manger.

The nightmare had been bad enough to banish any hope of returning to sleep. It had been like a dip into madness. Sometimes, he worried that he wouldn't be able to awaken from it, that the madness would finally take him and keep him. But not yet, not tonight.

Eventually, he stopped trembling, wiped his face, and left the stable to find the Menney Tower and the courtyard outside it.

✦

4ᵗʰ Day of the Moon of Storms, 113 G.E.

Wyl crouched motionless inside the Menney Tower courtyard with his back against the courtyard wall in the frigid hour before daybreak, nibbling a now-cold biscuit.

Here, after a small detour to filch breakfast from a tower's kitchen behind the Folk baker's back, he'd waited out the rest of the night, crouched over his heels, hunching under his cloak in a watchful doze with *hide me*, the first spitcraft he'd ever mastered, scratched into the wax charm under his *byrnney*.

Before the glow of the unseen sun lightened the mountainous horizon, he was surprised to see Eirgei's outline appear against the stars in the dark sky on the west side of the upper bailey's battlements. He disappeared, then reappeared on the ramparts to ghost through the deep shadows, heading for the Menney Tower.

Wyl rose, the motion breaking his *hide me* charm, and approached. He gave a faint cough before he got within striking range, though it probably wasn't necessary. He defied anyone to prove Eirgei couldn't see clearly in the dark.

"You aren't watching over Helgurdda?" Wyl asked, in hushed horror. He'd been so certain she had been safely in Eirgei's care this night—their first night in a Dremn fortress with nothing stronger than a kith tie through a dead man to guarantee their safety.

"There is an Evroza spy here," Eirgei mouthed back to him. "Once I have flushed him from cover and dealt with him, I will return to her side."

"*Ockh*, she's bait?" He scowled and smothered a cough with his hand.

"The very best bait—one irresistible to the enemy. Why are you here?"

Wyl just looked at Eirgei, puzzling over his question. "They've put me in with the Bearcubs and they're trying to make me sleep in the Heir's Tower instead of sharing the night watch with you. And beware of the bondsmen we've been given—they'll sell us to the Evroza at the first opportunity—probably even hold the door open for any passing assassins. How much time do you think I've got before we must leave?"

"Now that you and your mother have been acknowledged as kithkin, we are done with running. We will not be leaving Dremnar until everything is in place to take Crossroads Keep. It should not be long before we are ready to leave Nornholm and set up a training camp in the mountains."

He stared at Eirgei. "You trust these Dremn not to betray us? You don't think we'll need an escape plan while we're here in Nornholm?"

"Your mother's claim on Royenne Errengard's protection—and yours through her—is too strong for Icebear clan to refute now. There may be trouble over me being Prince Raldorrei's new Right Hand, but that will just be an excuse for trouble that has been building up among the subject clans in the hinterlands for some time. I welcome any trouble there—it will give me an opportunity to put the Icebear menney through its paces. But as for an escape plan, we are not captives, so we will not need to escape, will we?"

"Then how long before we have a Dremn menney, and we can go back to Milkdales?" Wyl persisted.

"Do not worry about that. It takes time to develop allies willing to risk their lives in a blood-feud, even for the reward Helgurdda is offering in spoils once we take Crossroads Keep. It will be at least midwinter before Iceroad Pass can be crossed, but those four moons will pass swiftly. Stay with the Bearcubs and learn as much as you can as fast as you can."

"About what?" With him already among the Bearcubs, this ought to be an easy spying mission.

And where was the harm in having an escape plan, just in case? If it were possible to see a disaster coming, there wouldn't ever be any. Eirgei certainly hadn't foreseen the disasters created by the weather-mage. If Eirgei were wrong about the Icebears, too, whether or not Wyl had an escape plan in place could mean life or death for them.

"Learn whatever they are willing to teach you," Eirgei said. "Concentrate on that, not the rebellion. We will be in Crossroads Keep before spring, and once we are there, you will not have any more opportunities to learn what you need to know about being a prince. A royal court is nothing like one of the camps. In court, an enemy can strip you of allies and strike you down with words alone, and your skill with weapons will be useless to you."

Wyl looked at Eirgei dubiously. He'd yet to be in a bad situation where pulling even a knife hadn't improved it. "I've got nothing to learn from this Dremn baby-menney."

"You will learn a great deal, none of it while holding a knife," Eirgei growled impatiently. "You will need to know how to act like a prince—how to *be* a prince—once we are in Crossroads Keep."

Wyl stared at him, confused. "You've already taught me everything I need to know." He coughed.

"Learn what you can," Eirgei repeated. "And stay away from me and Helgurdda—flushing out spies is subtle, delicate work, and we do not need you complicating it. Just make sure that when the time comes for our forces to invade, you are ready, too."

"But, our morning practice—"

"There is too much that needs my attention," Eirgei said. "I will let you know when your training will resume. Now, get back to the Heir's Tower before you are missed and have to come up with answers to awkward questions."

CHAPTER 14

MISSTEPS

Lost in troubling thoughts, Wyl strayed on his way back to the Heir's Tower despite the brightening dawn, but managed to arrive in the second floor guardroom before the guardsmen had finished searching the tower and its understory for him.

The awkward questions from the guardsmen that Eirgei had anticipated were easily answered.

Wyl looked down, acting as abashed as a youngling. "I sleep-walk. I woke up in a courtyard, and I didn't know where I was until it got light, and I could find someone to tell me how to get back here."

Apparently, because he'd come back to the Heir's Tower on his own, none of the guardsmen bothered with disputing his answer—for now, it seemed the focus was on his presence and not on how he'd managed his absence from under their noses.

Instead of taking him to their warlord for some more pointed questioning, as he'd expected, a pair of guardsmen sourly escorted him up the stairs to the entrance of the Young Court hall. They acted like Wyl truly had been given the run of the palace, even unescorted and at night, but he couldn't believe nothing bad would come of his overnight absence from the Bearcubs. He knew what to expect from Eirgei if he disobeyed orders, but he didn't know what to expect from the Crown Prince.

In the Young Court hall, he saw an older man with gray and blond hair down to his shoulder blades and a neatly trimmed, gray and blond beard, talking to the three Icebear princesses. He was dressed as a nobleman, but not in the white and black fur surcoat of Icebear clan—nor in any clan's surcoat. He didn't even wear mail.

A man who wasn't a minion?

Wyl had never imagined that such a thing were possible, unless the man was a seer. He'd never seen an Evroza man without that training, not even one of their mages. He'd just assumed other clans were like the Evroza, where every man was a minion.

A Folk servant went around the room, lighting glass-shielded candles in brackets on the wall to boost the weak daylight streaming in with the cold through the open windows.

Wyl stood in the doorway and once again, he felt the differences between himself and the Young Court.

He was half-frozen, fighting the urge to huddle in his cloak—the Dremn didn't seem to believe in having fires in any rooms save kitchens and laundries. The Young Court all looked, well, royal—even those who weren't in Icebear clan colors. The girls were all noble, high clan heirs, and the boys were all the future seneschals or warlords of those heirs. The younglings and girls all looked warm in fur-lined outer tunics, and all the older boys wore their white ice bear surcoats with the black speckles showing on the flesh side of the pelt augmented with glinting jet beads.

The Young Court stared at Wyl as he stood in the doorway.

The graying nobleman turned to see why. When he saw Wyl, his mouth opened but no words came out. Then he seemed to recover from his surprise and turned to Crown Princess Kotakei. "Who is this?"

He turned back to Wyl with an easy smile.

Wyl quickly shook his hair over his eyes. Then he advanced to his doom and knelt to the crown princess as kith, the way he'd been instructed.

"This, Lord Geilorren, is Prince Tras," Lord Martei interrupted, before the crown princess could do more than open her mouth. "Prince Tras, the Wolfling of Milk Dales."

Wyl looked up and glowered as Lord Martei gave the crown princess's scornful name for him a mocking twist that had the other Bearcubs sniggering to each other.

"He is the latest addition to the Young Court," the crown princess said to the stranger. She turned to Wyl.

"Rise and be welcomed," she said, though there was nothing of welcome in anything about her.

Crown Prince Norren looked at Wyl and gave what the crown prince probably meant for him to believe was an encouraging smile, except there was a wrongness about his eyes that told Wyl it was no true smile at all.

Wyl's lips twisted, reacting to the lie and showing his teeth.

Crown Princess Kotakei glanced back at her brother, then from Lord Geilorren to Wyl—which did nothing to relieve the bad feeling growing in Wyl because now *everyone* was looking at him.

"Yes, he is kith to Ice Bear clan—the son of Helgurdda, the Tras rebel to whom my grandmother has granted asylum," Crown Princess Kotakei said. "He is here to acquire some princely polish, so include him in our lessons."

She turned to him. "Lord Geilorren will teach you the noble arts of reading, writing, reckoning and law."

"I already read and write." The words came out as a growl through his taut lips.

The sniggering had mercifully died away, but he'd no trouble recognizing another attempt to humiliate him. He needed to quickly put an end to it. "I reckon, too," well enough for anything he might ever need it for.

Lastly, because outlaws didn't worry about keeping any laws they hadn't already broken, he added, "And it's not necessary to teach me the law—as soon as Helgurdda is Royenne of Trascolm, she'll make her own laws."

Some in the room muttered over his last words, but there was still a frozen snarl on his lips when he turned on those frowning young minions, and none of them tried to meet his eyes.

"Well," Crown Princess Kotakei said, with an expression of distaste, "so long as you are a member of this court, you will need to know Dremnar's laws—unless you intend to be outlawed here as well as in Trascolm?"

There were more laughs.

It made him angry. Some of the anger he directed at himself for creating an opening for her barb. The rest of it was for Crown Princess Kotakei, who returned his glare with one of her own.

She'd meant to provoke that mockery, and he could read the threat of more in her cold eyes.

"The law part might be a little hard for our Tras guest to grasp," Prince Jeik said to Lord Geilorren, obviously wanting to join in the fun at Wyl's expense.

By his sneer and posture—and the quarrelsome tone in his voice—
the Icebear prince promised to make trouble for Wyl, now and at every
opportunity in the future.

But sarcasm just made Wyl want to punch the prince in the nose.
He was cold, resentful, and had a throbbing headache. After his nearly
sleepless night and unsatisfactory meeting with Eirgei, he was primed
for a fight. He put his head back and sneered at the taller youth, openly
sizing him up and letting Prince Jeik know he was unimpressed.

"Best start him with the younglings," the prince said, disappointing
him. A brigand would have saved his breath and responded to Wyl's
baiting attitude with a knife.

"He is not a real Tras prince," Prince Jeik added, returning Wyl's
sneer. "I bet he has not even mastered spying or back-stabbing."

The tutor appeared shocked, even distressed, but Wyl was too angry
about being the butt of the Young Court's amusement to care how the
tutor reacted. What he wanted was a chance to get some amusement of
his own, preferably by drawing Prince Jeik's blood. But, then he remembered the big Icebear prince's warning last night.

No blood.

Prince Jeik laughed and smirked to the other youths. The disdain on
his face ate at Wyl's self-control until it was too much for him.

"Prince Jeik," Lord Geilorren was saying, "I am sure he does not do
anything of the sort! A boy his age is too young for the Three—"

"*Ockh*, I've mastered them all!" Wyl interjected, because now the tutor was making his age an issue, as well.

He was furious over Prince Jeik's mocking words. With just a little
more provocation, the Bearcub would *have* to go for his knives—only
Wyl was sure knives were a very bad idea if Helgurdda intended Icebears to be her allies.

He diverted his anger into words, seizing the first thing that came to
mind to contradict the Dremn prince, to strike back in a way that was
less likely to bring down disaster on Helgurdda and Eirgei than if he
used anything sharper than words.

"I'm the rebellion's best spy," he said, packing his words with insolent scorn. "I've even gotten inside the Evroza clanhold in Myymor
without the Evroza ever finding out!"

Let's see the coddled princeling top that!

He looked defiantly around the room, challenging anyone to say
something more.

He'd certainly impressed the Young Court. Even the servants gaped at him in astonishment.

But the abrupt silence lengthened, and the breathless stares started giving him an uneasy feeling, like he'd made a serious mistake in pursuing a quarrel with the prince. Lord Martei might be Crown Prince Norren's favorite, but Wyl had a sudden suspicion that Prince Jeik was the Young Court's favorite.

Or had his mistake been in choosing words over blows? Should he have tried to gain the Bearcubs' respect by sucker-punching the prince rather than quarreling?

He'd have to puzzle over that later—right now, he needed to get back onto safe ground with the Young Court. He needed to be on friendly terms with Crown Prince Norren so he could become part of his circle of cronies. That was the first step in his hostage-taking plan—winning the crown prince's favor and a trusted place at his side.

But Crown Prince Norren gave him a withering glare.

Maybe the crown prince thought he had backed down, that he was weak because he *hadn't* drawn a knife or punched his enemy?

Prince Jeik broke the sudden tension with some sharp-edged humor, not the least bit humbled by Wyl's challenge. "We have yet to see any *courtly* skills, Lord Geilorren, but Grandmother has charged us with trying to make a real prince of him, so perhaps some exercise for his brain instead of his mouth will help."

"There's one skill you left out," Wyl retorted. He'd reached the limit of his tolerance. There was a more direct—and much less subtle—way of winning the respect of the Bearcubs. He didn't have to draw blood to humiliate the prince and win over the Bearcubs.

"I'm also the Wolf of Milkdales's best pupil. He's taught me everything he knows." He stared aggressively at Prince Jeik. "With the prince's help, I'll be happy to demonstrate."

"No need for that," Crown Princess Kotakei said, cutting off Prince Jeik's answer and gesturing at the old nobleman.

"Come with me," Lord Geilorren said hurriedly, motioning for Wyl to follow.

Angry at yet another unexpected setback in his designs for the Bearcubs, Wyl stalked up to the tutor, tossed the hair out of his eyes, and gave him a defiant sneer.

Lord Geilorren raised his brows in mild reproof.

Wyl self-consciously stiffened as the tutor looked him up and down, taking in everything from his untended hair, to the state of his stolen clothes, to his spurred and scuffed riding boots.

But when Wyl looked up at the Dremn nobleman, he didn't recognize the expression on his face.

Usually when an adult openly inspected him like Lord Geilorren just had, he was either about to be tossed out of some public taproom in Myymor, or he'd encountered a new predator in the rebel camp who thought him easy prey. Either way, adults who gave him such calculating looks intended nothing good towards him.

He hoped the tutor would draw a weapon—maybe fighting an old Dremn lord wouldn't be enough of a challenge to impress the Bearcubs, but at least the exercise would warm him—and relieve some of his tension and mounting irritation.

But for some reason, after successfully silencing Prince Jeik's insults, this confrontation wasn't proceeding as expected. He'd crossed the Young Court's favorite prince, and whatever else that might mean, he knew it meant his attempt to gain the Young Court's respect, to become one of the crown prince's trusted favorites, had failed.

Lord Geilorren set down his box of scrolls and motioned for Wyl to take a seat on one of the floor mats.

Wyl perched on his heels between his war-spurs, poised to move in an instant.

His plan had been to show off his prowess, first by fighting Prince Jeik, then by taking on Lord Martei, whose defeat would automatically make Wyl leader of the Bearcubs. Or maybe it would happen only after besting Crown Prince Norren, if the crown prince took the oversized lordling's defeat badly.

But since Wyl hadn't been able to provoke or trick anyone, not even Prince Jeik, into starting a fight with him, his plan was in ruins.

He had to find some way to force some respect, find some way to make a daunting display of his weapon skills to the Bearcubs. If he didn't, his move to take the Young Court hostage would be bloody.

That was a fight he didn't want—Eirgei hadn't taught him to toy with his enemies. It was far easier to make an example of a brigand than a boy—TolDaanyo had no interest in the fate of brigands. Eirgei had taught him to make a quick kill and move on to the next threat— only Wyl had never killed *children*, no matter what they'd done or how big they'd been, and he wasn't about to start.

The ruins of his hostage plan felt like his dilemma with the weather-mage all over again. If he'd learned anything from that, it was that whether he killed or just frightened someone under Her protection, it would be all the same to MiPaatet.

But he had to make the Bearcubs respect him, with or without a sword. If he didn't, he'd have to hold the Young Court hostage the hard and bloody way. How else could he become a powerful insider with a group of children?

He'd get no help from MiPaatet—even if She'd forgiven him for the weather-mage, once he made his move to hold *children* hostage, he'd lose her favor again, maybe forever.

It couldn't matter.

This time, if forced to choose between his spitcraft and his family, he wouldn't try to save both.

Was there another way to win the Young Court's respect, perhaps by displaying his less violent skills?

Lord Geilorren had been fingering through the contents of his box. He turned to Wyl. "First, reading."

The tutor set a scroll in front of him and unrolled it to the first section. "Read this aloud."

Wyl looked at it and took a breath, then looked again and let it out. "What's this? This isn't writing."

"You were expecting Teboan script, that foreign scribble brought from across the Eastern Sea?" The tutor dismissed his objection curtly. "This is Runic, real writing, the writing of our ancestors—I thought you said you could read."

Wyl looked at the runes, nothing more than angular doodling to his eyes, and his heart sank. He minutely shook his head. "I can read maps," he amended.

The tutor raised a brow, but motioned to someone to bring a map. Lord Martei smirked and brought one.

"Show me Norn Holm on the map," Lord Geilorren said.

The map was utterly unfamiliar.

Of course—it was a map of Dremnar. All the notations on it—and there were quite a few—were in Runic. Wyl could find the Tor and the various strongholds and clanholds of northern Milkdales, despite the alien markings, but on the other side of the Tor, he couldn't distinguish Nornholm from several other likely marks on the map.

He coughed and tried to hide his chagrin.

"Hmm," the tutor said. "There's no point in asking if you can write what you cannot read, but can you at least write your name?"

"In Teboan," Wyl bit out, then instantly regretted showing his anger when he saw Prince Jeik's eyes narrow and gleam.

The prince whispered, and again there were sniggers.

Though Lord Geilorren had taken Wyl aside to the north window, near the pile of toys, they were still the center of attention. If Prince Jeik wanted to hold Wyl up for ridicule, Wyl had played right into his hands.

Crown Prince Norren made no move to intervene—so much for his promise of friendship yesterday, when the prince had pledged to teach him how to be the Dremn idea of a prince. There'd been no further mention of him even being *near* Crown Prince Norren since his return last night, let alone having him dutifully trot at the crown prince's heels. Was *that* what was behind this change in attitude?

Maybe his difficulties now had nothing to do with his squabble with Prince Jeik and everything to do with the enigmatic Crown Prince Norren?

But how had he run afoul of *him?* Was it because he'd disobeyed the prince's order to sleep among the Bearcubs last night?

It didn't matter that Wyl had meant to betray that pretend friendship when the time came to make their escape. What mattered was that Crown Prince Norren had betrayed him first and without cause.

Perhaps Wyl had underestimated him.

The tutor sighed. "Very well, write your name in Teboan script. Your first lesson in writing properly will be to transcribe it into a Runic glyph."

Lord Geilorren gave Wyl a sheet of parchment clipped to a laptable, then looked thoughtful as he dipped the quill pen in ink and handed it to Wyl.

But, when Wyl took it, the tutor instantly stopped him.

"No, no, not that hand, the other hand, or you will smear the ink."

The quill felt odd and not just because it was in his right hand. He'd always used charcoal on parchment to write Eirgei's orders to Calderek or the other rebel warlords, a precaution to ensure messages could be wiped away if a courier fell into the hands of the Evroza.

Or so he had until this past summer, when he'd begun to forge bogus orders for the Evroza menney using their own paper and ink, and in handwriting indistinguishable from that of Prince-Viceroye Osbart or Lord Goffray.

And he hadn't smeared the ink when he'd done it.

He took secret pride in his ability to reproduce any Evroza warlord's handwriting at a glance—but that was only with his left hand; he couldn't even imitate his own with his right hand. He used extra care, but *writing* with his right hand was the one skill Eirgei hadn't drilled into him. The long quill stuttered and sprayed ink.

"Hmm," the tutor said, looking over his shoulder when he stopped writing. "Now write the rest of it."

Wyl ensured his war face was firmly in place. "That's it."

He'd boldly, if jaggedly, written *Wylheim of Milkdales*, refusing to claim his mother's fickle clan. He named himself the same way Eirgei had named Helgurdda to the Folk hunters. By the expressions all around him, it didn't have the same effect on the Young Court as hers had had on the hunters.

He guessed it was too late to add *Prince*.

"Just Wylheim? What about your clan?"

Lord Martei laughed. "He has no clan! Even the Evroza would not take him—and I thought they would adopt anyone to fill out their menney."

"*Ockh*, no, no clan," Wyl said belligerently, now fighting embarrassment. He could feel his ears burning. He was not about to go into the circumstances of his birth and upbringing, not with everyone ready to heap even more scorn on him.

Lord Geilorren handed him a scroll. "Look through the glyphs until you find one that appeals to you. That will be the mark for your name in Runic. Since you don't claim a clan, use these two, the glyphs that mean Ice Bear kith-kin. This may take a while, so you might find it more comfortable to sit."

Wyl didn't move. He still crouched on his heels, poised to rise quickly in case he was attacked, and that was comfortable enough. He settled the laptable across his knees and unrolled the scroll of foreign scribbles.

What if he picked one that made everyone laugh?

He skimmed the scroll, and one rune jumped out at him—a stylized spider.

He couldn't take his eyes off it to look at more runes.

Lanney would have called it an omen.

No one laughed at a spider, and yet, he was not afraid of them. It had been a spider that had saved him from the monster of his dreams, though there was a hole in his memory where the details should be.

Wyl copied the three glyphs, the spider and the two the tutor had shown him, then frowned down at the rendering he'd made on his parchment. Right-handed, they lacked the bold strokes of his name in Teboan and looked like a youngling's efforts—like his own had when he'd first learned his name in Teboan.

That set the tone for the rest of the tutor's humiliating assessment: numbers that didn't look like numbers, and Dremn law rather than Trascolm's law, though both shared a common base in the law of the land—like the right to justice or revenge that Helgurdda had cited to Royenne Errengard.

"I will just start you with the younglings," the tutor concluded.

There were grins from the Bearcubs, who didn't bother to hide that they'd been listening, but the tutor didn't seem to notice. "You are a smart boy, I am sure you will soon get the hang of it. I will have you caught up and studying with the youths in a matter of weeks."

CHAPTER 15

ICE BEAR HONOR

The servants finished laying the boards and benches for the midday meal, and Kotakei set aside the codex she had been studying, signaling the end of the day's lessons.

It was also the end of the day's quiet as the younglings were released from their studies and burst into excited babble on the other side of the hall while the tutor explained Prince Tras's presence among them. She listened and noticed Lord Geilorren did not say a word about the boy's damning confession to the youths of her court that he had mastered the Three Dishonors.

She had to give the tutor credit for how well he handled the touchy newcomer. He had managed not to show disgust as he had guided Prince Tras through the younglings' lessons, though she thought his expression of delight in how quickly his new pupil grasped Runic had been overacted.

Now that lessons were done, the younglings came away from the north side of the hall and joined the rest of the Young Court. They instantly ran to the newcomer.

Prince Tras's face suddenly became an expressionless mask as the younglings rushed him. He tossed the hair out of his eyes as if he were a skittish colt, though no horse had silver eyes. Those eyes quickly narrowed to glinting, dark slits. He backed away from the raucous little mob, as wary of them as if they were wild animals rather than harmlessly exuberant younglings.

He was more like a wild animal than the younglings were. The way his hands were poised, fingertips twitching, over the tops of his boots had her worried for the younglings' safety. She was certain now that he had knives or daggers secreted in his boots. Should she wait until he drew them on the children, or call the guardsmen to deal with him now, before someone got hurt?

"You know," Tirrengard said, watching beside her, "I doubt Helgurdda would have been outlawed if her clan had known she was pregnant—or, at least, not until after Prince Wylheim was born. What kind of baronne would permit a child, even a boy sired by a foreign slave, to be born and raised outside the protection and guidance of his mother's clan?"

"Well, that not only happened," Kotakei said, "but his mother also has obviously allowed him to run amok his whole life. I do not know why Grandmother thinks *I* can do anything with him. I cannot believe she sent him to my Young Court in the first place. How could she not see past his age and realize what a danger he is to us, youths and younglings alike?"

Cousin Lokei, in the midst of the younglings' rush, said something that checked the children before they reached Prince Tras. They stood bashfully at a distance and unleashed a storm of chatter, and the Tras boy's hands remained empty.

Kotakei let out her breath in relief.

"Grandmother is not one to be taken in by appearances," Tirrengard said. "But by all the accounts I heard of her audience with Helgurdda yesterday, both Eirgei and his grandnephew were models of decorum. I doubt Prince Wylheim met many children while living among outlaws. I imagine he just has never dealt with anyone his own age, let alone younglings."

"Well, no one has seen that decorum from him or his granduncle since yesterday. You know what Prince Tras did this morning and," Kotakei said, "Uncle Raldorrei told me when I first came down this morning that Eirgei had provoked a fight with three Ice Bear minions last night. He put all of them into the Menney Tower's infirmary and got himself barred from staying in the Menney Tower with the rest of the minions."

Tirrengard's shock was gratifying.

Kotakei continued, "I do not want the same thing to happen here in the Young Court, with the Wolf of Milk Dales's grandnephew putting some of my young minions—or, even worse, younglings—into the infirmary! I will do whatever I must to keep that, that, *Tras* boy from following Eirgei's example!"

"But if he must stay in the Young Court, and he is too dangerous to be around the younglings, you will have to allow him to join the youths," Tirrengard pointed out.

"And if I do," Kotakei frowned and shook her head, "there will definitely be bloodshed. Uncle Raldorrei said he'd already told Norren and the Bear Cubs about the incident with Eirgei and warned them to treat all the Tras as if they are armed to the teeth with hidden weapons that they will not hesitate to use."

"Then why not have them searched and disarmed?" Tirrengard asked, ever practical.

"How can we do that after Grandmother declared them kith? They are not prisoners, after all."

"If that is how matters stand, then how can it be safe to have Prince Wylheim in your court at all?"

"Let alone putting him with the younglings, who are always so full of silliness and boisterous foolery? My point, exactly." Kotakei groaned in frustration. "You know how younglings can get on anyone's nerves without even trying—they bother Norren so much, he does not even like them around."

"Our kith does not look particularly ferocious, now," Tirrengard said, nodding.

It was true. Their newest and most distant relative was surrounded by younglings. He towered over them as if he were fully-grown, which made him look as awkward as he was wary. He would not let any of the younglings touch him, not even when Kotakei's young cousin and heir, Elfreida, tried to take hold of his hand to lead him. Elfreida's older brother, Lokei, the Young Court's only male stripling, directed Prince Tras to the youngling end of the dining table the servants had put together from boards and trestles under a snowy-white cloth.

Lokei was not quite as old nor as tall as Prince Tras. The contrast in bearing and expressions between the two boys made her doubt her earlier certainty that Prince Tras had lied about his age. Now that the two boys stood next to each other, it was not so much their difference in size, which wasn't all that great, as it was a certain lack of innocence and excess of knowledge in those silver eyes.

It did not matter if she was right, that Prince Tras was just a stripling—too young to be in the Bear Cubs by a year or maybe two. It would be best if everyone treated him as if he were years older, a youth—or more realistically—a full-grown outlaw. Throwing him in with bigger, older boys would be the wiser course, if she could not treat him like an obvious menace.

Surely Norren would know what to do about him.

"It is a good thing Lokei does not seem jealous and resentful about that boy being in the Bear Cubs," Tirrengard said. "When Lokei first turned ten, remember how he tried to persuade Norren to let him be in the Bear Cubs because he was the only stripling, and he did not want to stay with the younglings?"

She watched as Lokei seated Prince Tras and leaned down to speak in his ear over the din the younglings made. She glanced over at Norren, who usually disliked the shrieking and running that inevitably accompanied excited younglings.

He looked angry, but not at the younglings. He, too, had to be upset about the confession to spying.

Yet—perhaps because Prince Tras was among the younglings now—no outbreak of violence seemed as imminent as it had that morning.

She studied her brother as he watched the silliness going on down at the far end of the long table.

Over the past year, Norren had changed. His attitude of elder-brother superiority had grown to the point of grating on her usually even temper. He alone did not treat her like their grandmother's heir. At first, she had found that reassuring, that her relationship with her adored brother was unaffected by her sudden elevation after their mother's death. She had quickly come to depend on Norren to help her set up her court as if he were truly her viceroye.

But lately, he had taken to twisting her wishes, even selectively ignoring them. She was proud of how he had dealt with Prince Tras thus far, but that had not otherwise signaled a return to the way he had been before their mother had died.

She watched Prince Tras with critical eyes, hoping to find an opportunity for an accord between herself and Norren.

She sighed. "I suppose it is too much to hope that Prince Tras will remain merely an interesting distraction to the rest of my court. I am afraid we are going to return to the disruption and chaos he created this morning."

Tirrengard, seated beside her and staring distractedly down the table, made no reply.

Now, as the servants set up the trestle table and benches, something else occurred to Kotakei. "Until today, Prince Tras might never have sat at *any* table, let alone a stately one."

"Then this midday meal is perfect practice," Tirrengard said. "If he is to learn how to be a prince, he needs to learn proper behavior at table in your presence before he is fit for Grandmother's."

That was true. Here, during the midday meal, even the most casual conversation was conducted like an affair of state, with whomever Kotakei or Norren addressed obliged to stand to answer.

But not today.

Today, all Kotakei wanted was a peaceful meal so she could think about how to deal with the dishonor Prince Tras had brought to Ice Bear clan by proudly claiming to have achieved the Three Dishonors.

She had been relieved when Lokei had latched onto Prince Tras and seated him at the youngling end of the long table. One of the reasons the younglings were congregated at the far end of the table was because they still lacked courtly manners. She would have to shout to exchange words with them and thus, they were free to talk among themselves and not attend to or disrupt whatever happened at the high end—the youths' end—of the table.

It was the perfect place for Prince Tras.

Lokei cleverly put him on the opposite side of the table from her, and at its very foot, where his left-handedness would not create difficulties for a youngling next to him. With Lokei's eight-year-old sister Elfreida on Prince Tras's right and Lokei himself across the table from him, Prince Tras was as isolated from the more vulnerable younglings as her young cousin could manage.

Tirrengard leaned over and whispered, "Is Prince Wylheim staring at you or at Norren?"

She lifted her head to see—it *was* her, because Prince Tras stopped staring when his eyes, half-hidden under hair, met hers. They shifted to critically studying his silver cup and charger.

"Of course, now that I think about it," Kotakei said to Tirrengard, "he likely *is* accustomed eating from dishes like ours—there is no point in brigands stealing the wooden cups and bowls of Folk. He probably disdains my tableware as inferior to the Gerisari-made dishes and utensils he stole in Milk Dales!" She glared down the table, but could not catch his eye.

"You could have had Gerisari tableware," Tirrengard pointed out. "Grandmother's tribute-share from the winter raids."

Kotakei shook her head. "But Grandmother uses only Dremn-made table settings, all embossed with ice bear motifs, and I thought it best to follow Grandmother's lead rather than use Gerisari-made spoils from Milk Dales."

"Except your bears are cubs on silver plates and your drinking horns are just silver cups," Tirrengard said. "I would like to try some of that Gerisari wine Grandmother serves rather than this well-watered mead, like we are younglings."

"In Grandmother's eyes, that's exactly what we are," Kotakei said. A fresh grievance came to her. "How can I learn to rule if she doesn't give me control of my own Young Court and foists a foreign menace on me?"

Kotakei signaled, and the servants brought bread and then platters of food, and the meal started to slip into place. The younglings helped themselves without a break in their chatter.

"We need to talk, Sister," her brother said, his lips twisting in distaste as he stared down the table, watching Prince Tras eat with his fingers. "Now."

She clenched her teeth at Norren's unnecessary, peremptory tone and rose.

The older half of the table hastily rose with her. Prince Tras's eyes were immediately on her, though the younglings around him remained oblivious to the high end of the long table.

Once they were out of sight on the spiraling stairs, Norren prodded her to climb to the next floor, now empty of younglings. He entered behind her, closed the door, and leaned against it.

"We need to figure out how to deal with our Little Wolf."

She should have guessed that would be what this was about. "You are right, we have to find a way to lessen the damage already done, and limit his ability to inflict more."

Unfortunately, summary execution was not possible, not until he was sixteen and of age—which reminded her of something.

"The best I could come up with was to put him with the younglings," she admitted slowly, though her thoughts were taking a different turn. "I do not see how I can expel him from my court—Grandmother already knew what these Tras rogues were like when she gave them asylum."

"I doubt she knew they would ruin Ice Bear clan's reputation and smear our honor! Expelling him would be one solution. Executing all the Tras would be the perfect solution."

She frowned as her thoughts coalesced and shook her head. "You told me yourself he is only fourteen. Because he is not of age, he cannot be held accountable for his actions—it would fall on his baronne to correct him."

"Good! Then I will get Grandmother to do it." Norren sounded confident he could—their grandmother doted on him.

She was surprised he did not see the problem. "She cannot, not for this. He is only kith-kin—his baronne is Helgurdda, not Grandmother. And if he really had been a rebel spy, he had spied for her, so there is nothing to be done—it is perfectly acceptable for Helgurdda to employ spies, you know. It would be different if he were sixteen, and even then, Helgurdda would probably choose to overlook his actions—unless he had been spying for someone else or had been caught."

"We have to do something," Norren said. "We cannot just let this go."

She thought about that and about Ice Bear honor—and what lay within her power.

Why did Norren not offer any solutions? He was clever about the law of the land, and up until now, she could rely on him to always have a suggestion on how she should make use of her power as their grandmother's heir—though lately, his suggestions all seemed to be ways in which *he* could make use of it.

"The problem is," she said, "though the law of the land provides the loophole for our admitted spy to get away with proclaiming himself one, my courtiers will not recognize—or want to recognize—that there is a legal allowance made for his age. They'd rather see Ice Bear clan embarrassed."

Norren agreed. "We both know which baronnes' heirs attending this court will pass this on to their families to make the most of the situation, maybe even seize it as an opportunity to undermine Ice Bear clan's hold on power."

"The reaction will not break our hold on the crown itself."

"But, if there are enough slurs against us, it will become a matter of clan honor, and Uncle Raldorrei will have to accept challenges to defend our hold on the crown."

"I agree," Kotakei said. "It will not be enough to simply educate my court on a fine point of law. We will have to demonstrate Ice Bear clan's confidence in my reading of the law, demonstrate that we are *not* embarrassed by his claims."

"Or this morning's debacle might encourage a crown challenge to Grandmother—"

"—Which means there is no time to waste for Ice Bear clan to show itself *completely untouched* by that boy's disgraceful admissions," she said forcefully.

"Just how do you propose to demonstrate that?"

Kotakei rubbed her forehead between her eyes. "I can think of only one way to do that—show kin-favor to him, demonstrate that nothing he says can dishonor Ice Bear clan."

"What? Show this creature kin-favor for two years, until he's sixteen and I can kill him for it?" Norren was incredulous.

"Well, he is not likely to still be here when he is sixteen, and by revealing he was a spy back in Milk Dales, he obviously does not intend to act as one here. That works in our favor—we simply need to conduct ourselves as if nothing serious has happened," she said. "Take him to minion practice with you and make him your shadow."

"Martei will not like that," Norren replied, scowling. "And what are you going to do to show Ice Bear honor remains unharmed?"

She took a deep breath. "I am going to act like his best friend. I will teach him senet, maybe have another archery contest, this time without your minions causing trouble. I will do whatever I can to show kin-favor. It will be hard for Grandmother's enemies to make this a challenge matter if we openly show him favor and ignore his admission of being a spy like it never happened."

Norren grimaced. "What a terrible price we pay for our clan's honor—making up to a Tras spy and swallowing our pride. I swear, once he is sixteen, I will see him outlawed by Ice Bear clan and banished from Dremnar—or dead, if I can manage it!"

His vehemence surprised her. "He is not of age, so there is no real harm done, remember? And once Helgurdda returns to Milk Dales, he will, too, and that will be the end of this."

"He will be in my way," Norren muttered.

"In the way of what?" Would he finally tell her what was going on, what he was scheming? He still treated her as if she were a youngling and not a youth herself. Fourteen was practically sixteen! "Is it something to do with why you needed to borrow from my privy purse last week?"

But Norren had already opened the door and started down the stairs. He did not answer her question.

She sighed and followed him, and tried to prepare herself for the ordeal to come.

✦

After the meal, the senet tables were pulled out. As she had promised Norren, Kotakei took Prince Tras under her tutelage.

She kept her head tilted down so nothing in her face would give away her loathing. She pretended she was as taken with him as the other girls were by casually plying him with questions while she laid out her game pieces.

"What did you do, back in Milk Dales?"

He looked up from setting his pieces on the spaces between hers and tossed the hair out of his eyes to look at her directly. Then he looked back down at the board.

Though she tried not to stare, there was something eerie about those eyes, a nagging sense of wrongness. She didn't know why she felt that. His eyes would still have been beautiful if they had been Folk-dark rather than that impossible silver. Even with half his hair chopped short like Folk and wearing a *byrnney* in place of proper clothing, there was surely no one like him in the world. He had a striking effect on everyone who saw him—including herself, though she tried not to let it show. She refused to stare in the hope he would look at her with those eyes.

How could he have ever gone unnoticed as a spy?

But he never noticed her staring—he kept his eyes downcast and fixed on the senet board.

He shrugged in answer to her so-casual question. "We moved a lot. We fought when we could, ran when we couldn't."

"What did you do when you were not fighting or running?" she asked.

Having a light, even flirtatious, conversation where all the Young Court could see and hear would go a long way towards rehabilitating him as Ice Bear kith-kin in good standing, but he wasn't helping her.

He merely shrugged again, still not looking at her. "Plan and prepare for the next strike."

Mindful of her audience, she chose her next words carefully. "And your part in that was to spy on the Evroza?"

She could see the ripple of reaction go through her eavesdropping courtiers as she said the awful word. "How did you manage to do that?"

Another shrug. "No one notices outcast Folk boys underfoot."

That would explain his cropped hair—but why did he not boast now? He did not shy off from answering her questions, but he answered like his thoughts were on something else.

Her back stiffened. When favoring him with a conversation, she was entitled to his full attention. "That must have been something to see, how you swam your horses across the Tor."

Again a shrug. "I see it every night, and I don't want to talk about it."

She suppressed a groan of frustration and tried a different approach to getting him to open up. "I know there are quite a few rebel sympathizers in Milk Dales—they are called Traditionalists, are they not? Were you friends with any girls among them?" She couldn't believe she was reduced to practically batting her eyelashes at him.

At her question, he looked up at her incredulously.

It was the most reaction she had gotten out of him, and as if he were a wild beast, this time she did her best not to stare into his eyes, aggressively or—or, otherwise.

"Of course not! We're rebels, outlaws—and I did my spying—"

She involuntarily cringed as *he* said the word.

"—as an outcast. What kind of clan would let me into their clanhold to even see their girls?"

Of course not?

If he knew that much of honor, why did he claim mastery of the Three Dishonors? Did Tras reckon honor more loosely than Dremn? Or perhaps he was just incapable of recognizing the lack in himself?

He would not be the first person blind to his own flaws.

"What about other friends?" she asked. "Outlaw—*um*—fellow rebels?"

As soon as the words were out of her mouth, she knew she shouldn't have asked. None of his outlaw friends could claim kith-kinship with Ice Bear clan and openly attend the royal court. They would all be in the wilderness, living as brigands among their own kind, much to the embarrassment and ongoing shame of their former clans.

He looked at her warily. "There was a mercenary, Helgurdda's other bodyguard, Lanney." He abruptly looked down at the board. "She died crossing the Tor."

Kotakei had not known one of the rebels had not made it across the river.

"I am sorry about your friend," she said, feeling awkward.

He sat stiffly and said nothing. He just stared at the board.

"You said, 'other bodyguard,'" she said, doggedly persistent after an uncomfortable silence. "So that must mean there were two—what became of the other one?"

He set his jaw and pointedly tossed the sticks to determine who would move first, rather than answer.

"Did he drown, too?" She gathered up the sticks for her throw.

"Lanney didn't drown," he snarled, finally giving her another direct look—but this time, a truly evil one.

She involuntarily recoiled in her seat.

"An Evroza mage killed her, the same mage who destroyed our menney! If it weren't for that mage, Helgurdda would be ruling in Crossroads Keep right now, and the surviving Evrozings running for their lives!"

"Magic?" she asked, trying to shift the subject. "I had not heard that was what had defeated Eirgei. I know Evroza clan is famous for having dangerous mages who can do more than scry, but it must have taken every mage in Evroza clan to bring about Eirgei's defeat."

He flinched and glared at her. "He wasn't defeated! It was a tactical withdrawal because we didn't have any mages of our own. And it was just one mage—or maybe a sorceress. She could command the weather. She cast her weather-magery five times in the course of a single day, each casting more powerful than the first."

That took Kotakei's attention away from his eyes. Five times, each more powerful than the first? As she understood magery, no mage could manage more than one scrying in a day, and Evroza's unique, explosive magery was even more difficult to use. When the Evroza used that magery against Dremn raiders, their mages risked destroying themselves along with their enemies.

"According to Lord Geilorren," she said, "it takes hours for a mage to gather enough magic just for one blast. I have never heard of a mage who could manipulate the weather—or is that just an excuse for Eirgei's defeat?" She could have bit her tongue for having let that last thought slip into words.

"She's going to pay for what she did," Prince Tras said, under his breath, paying Kotakei no heed. He abruptly stopped talking and fiddled with the sweet-scented cones that were his game pieces. His eyes lost focus, as if he were blind.

"What became of the other bodyguard? You did not say—"

"—I didn't drown, either, and I don't want to talk about it—or anything else. Just play."

"You were one of Helgurdda's bodyguards?" Kotakei laughed, remembering his panicked look when the younglings had descended on him before the meal. "You cannot even protect yourself from young-lings!"

His lips tightened into a grim line. "No more talk, just play!"

She stared haughtily, but said nothing, bearing in mind her pledge to Norren to show kin-favor. She smothered an order of her own.

As they played, she tried asking more *harmless* questions like, "What is your favorite food?" or, "What do you think of Norn Holm?"

She never got an immediate answer, but rather had to persist and pry just to get short, unhelpful answers out of him.

"I don't have a favorite food," he said, and later, "Nornholm is much colder than Milkdales."

He was so guarded in his replies that no question seemed harmless once it left her lips. He never asked a question of her except about se-net, mostly protesting in favor of his own interpretation of some rule.

As Jeik had noticed that morning, Prince Tras did have trouble with rules.

But she felt unaccountably snubbed that the perplexing Tras boy acted like there was nothing special or privileged about sitting down to play senet and chat with the crown princess of Dremnar!

She had to remind herself that this performance of kin-favor was not for his benefit, it was for the benefit of the rest of her court as she tried to reduce the general scorn directed at Prince Tras—and through him, at Ice Bear clan. Though, if he were in the habit of boasting of his dishonorable behavior, he was used to being beneath contempt, a thorough rogue.

Now he stared blankly at the senet board, and she wondered if he were plotting something. It would not do to forget that he was Tras, treacherous and untrustworthy.

Those silver eyes were again half-hidden behind a tangled fall of hair, but there was tension in his mouth, his shoulders—his whole body—and he was very much aware of everyone else in the room. No one changed places at a senet table for a new match without him twitching to see, even while his thoughts were clearly elsewhere—and never on his game with her.

He was intentionally ignoring her, she concluded, frowning—and she frowned even more when her first frown went unacknowledged by him.

He played senet without any trace of a coherent strategy, though she had seen him do that just yesterday when he had played against the other girls, despite being so new to the game. Were it not for incredibly bad luck in his throws, he might have won against all of them.

Yet today, his play was horrendous.

He tossed the sticks with an economical flick of his wrist, and she tore her eyes away before he could catch her staring. She had to be careful of where she let her eyes rest when lost in her own thoughts—what would she do if he read her unwitting fascination as something more?

If she had had to push this hard towards someone like Martei, her determined friendliness would be taken as an illicit invitation—and Martei already had ambitious ideas about one day becoming her consort, simply because of his close friendship with Norren.

She no more wanted to encourage that kind of thinking in Prince Tras than she did Martei. What she wanted was Prince Tras out of her court.

An idea occurred to her.

Grandmother had strict views on the underaged participating in bedsport but Prince Tras likely knew nothing of civilized conduct or the law of the land when it came to such matters.

No! She was not going to embarrass Ice Bear clan with aggressive flirting in order to provoke a bold advance—or worse—that would allow her to send him from her court in simple disgrace! Nor would she encourage any of her young courtiers to make that—well, *sacrifice* did not seem the right word—but who would she use to bait such a trap? Tirrengard wouldn't object, but she'd made no secret of her infatuation, and Kotakei didn't want her favorite cousin hurt.

She would just have to wait for Prince Tras to make a wrong move and be ready to act when he did. It was bound to happen eventually; she just hoped he didn't distress anyone too badly before it did.

Taking the time to reflect on matters did much to calm her, but it did nothing for the quality of her senet play. Yet Prince Tras hadn't taken advantage of her mental absence to win against her. He played worse than she did, moving his cones carelessly and forgetting simple rules like throwing the sticks again when his previous throw allowed it.

As they played, she stole looks at him, wondering that he could see the senet board at all with so much hair in his eyes. Underneath it, he seemed to be brooding.

Something about him had changed. He no longer struck her as being so untamed and dangerous as when Uncle had first brought him to her court—was it only yesterday? It was too much to hope that he regretted his awful confession, but what else could be on his mind?

She studied him as he distractedly moved his cones and missed an opportunity to send two of her reeds back to MiPaatet's House of Rebirth. He looked less and less like a thug fighting the urge to hurt someone, and more and more like a lost youngling fighting tears.

Did he mean to play a game of his own with her, try to engage her sympathy by appearing younger and more vulnerable?

He was clearly ignorant of the basic rules of civilized behavior, but if he was the rebellion's best spy, he could not be stupid. Quite the opposite—to live up to his claim, he had to be convincing in whatever role he played.

So what role did he play for her and her court?

Prince Tras abruptly stood.

It said much about the impression he had made on her that she unconsciously recoiled, scooting off the side of her stool, drawing her side-dagger, and stepping back, putting herself out of range of a lunge with a sword—if there'd been a sword.

Uncle Raldorrei had trained all the young women of the Young Court to use their daggers in self-defense when they first became striplings. He would have been proud of Kotakei if he had been there to see her reaction.

It also put her out of the way of the senet table, which Prince Tras viciously kicked across the court hall, sending board and pieces flying.

The table itself skidded out the open passageway door, bounced off the wall, and clattered down the first several steps, leaving shouts of surprise in its wake.

Everyone in the room jumped and stared after it, though the table had not come close to hitting anyone, not even Kotakei.

The younglings added their startled, excited shrieks to the commotion.

When Kotakei turned her shocked astonishment back on Prince Tras, he was not there.

The court hall was abuzz as those closer to the door and the stairs tried to discover where the table had come from.

One of them was Norren, and she caught his eye.

He frowned when he took in her drawn dagger, then his gaze shifted, and she saw him realize that both her senet table and her opponent were missing.

He ran towards her, circling along the wall and whacking the tapestries as he did.

He raised only dust.

Then her brother was at her side, looking out the east window.

As always, the window stood open. Prince Tras had been seated under it, and his stool was still up against the wall.

Norren boosted himself up into the window, not deigning to use the stool. He was too tall for the height of the window, so he crouched and made his way to the outside edge to look down, then squirmed backwards and out of the embrasure. He shook his head to her, at a loss to explain how Prince Tras had utterly disappeared.

CHAPTER 16

POISONED

Crossroads Keep

Breieroz stayed grimly in the back of the royal bedchamber while Prince-Viceroye Osbart stood vigil with Princess-Heir Ragna for the two hours it took Royenne Sharei to die in agony, blue-white pale, and dry-heaving.

There was no question of it being a natural death, just of how the rebels had gotten past Prince Osbart's security precautions.

Princess-Heir Ragna knelt beside her mother's bed, holding her now-lifeless hand, crying and incoherently choking out what could only be vows of vengeance. She looked angrily up at Breieroz's mentor. "You said Eirgei would not stoop to poison, but you forgot about Helgurdda! Do you think any atrocity is beyond her after what she has done now?"

"I no longer know," her spymaster said, "what to expect from Eirgei, either. First, he is a rebel, then a traitor, and now he is a sneaking employer of poisoners—none of that is in keeping with the Eirgei I knew, who would never have stooped to assassination. His honor was sacred to him."

Breieroz winced at her mentor's implied criticism of Princess-Heir Ragna's methods. Helgurdda had been condemned and merited execution by any means, for the good of the clan.

"But it is perfectly in keeping with Helgurdda's ways," Princess-Heir Ragna said hoarsely in her grief, deaf to any criticism. "Osbart, she has made a fatal mistake if she thinks this will end the blood-feud.

All she has done is hasten her own doom. Mother never unleashed the full force of Evroza on her, but I will not hold back. Every resource will be brought to bear on her, and I will put an end to this the only way that matters—with their heads on pikes over the front gate! If anyone thinks to follow her example, that will show where it will lead!" Her voice cracked. "Leave me! All of you!"

Breieroz and Prince Osbart were in the viceroye's office when Uncle Goffray came, carefully carrying the meal the royenne had not lived to finish, her silver charger still piled with cold food. He also brought the royenne's silver goblet, the friendship-token given by Prince Kreseyn in Empress Jerhafyne's name. Sharei had scarcely taken several sips from it before she had been stricken.

"There is still a good amount of wine that was not spilled when the poison struck her down," Uncle Goffray said, grimly offering both to Prince Osbart. "But if the poison is in either of these...."

Prince Osbart nodded.

Breieroz swallowed nervously. Only close family served the royenne, bringing her food and drink. It was a precaution precisely to prevent a poisoner—unwilling or unable to poison the entire keep—from poisoning just the royenne's meal.

"Prince-Viceroye Osbart," said Uncle Goffray, "I regret to say I was one of the many minions who had long thought your responsibilities as spymaster made you overly suspicious of everyone—that you surrounded Royenne Sharei and Princess-Heir Ragna with excessive, even paranoid, protection. Now, I can see you were wiser than we credited you—I apologize for thinking otherwise and for ever having doubted you."

Breieroz wondered if this was how it would be for her when she was spymaster, that the better she was at protecting her royenne and her clan, the more those she protected would discount her.

She went with her mentor as he set about confirming his suspicions about what had killed Royenne Sharei.

He took the beautiful Gerisari goblet to the kennels where a piglet had been brought for his purpose. The goblet's bright glint of silver and gems was incongruous there. As Uncle Goffray had said, it still held a copious amount of fine Gerisari wine from a cask that had tested free of poison—Prince Osbart was as sure as he could be that Princess-Heir Ragna was safe from another poisoning. If that was how Royenne Sharei had been poisoned, it had been put only in her cup.

Breieroz watched as he poured the wine out. She leaned against the gate of the kennel, watching the piglet slurp the wine from a pannikin. It was nothing short of a miracle that Royenne Sharei's goblet had not been tipped over in the commotion or there would have been nothing to test.

The rumor Prince Osbart's spies were circulating in Crossroads Town, outside the Keep, was that the strain of the blood-feud had eaten away at the royenne's stomach and into her viscera until it killed her.

Thus far, it remained the likeliest explanation for how the royenne had died—so long as the rest of Trascolm remained ignorant of *all* the symptoms that had marked her dying. She had been ill for moons with pains in her stomach, and she had only drunk a few sips of the wine before she had taken ill, vomiting blood. But, the spymaster had pointed out to Breieroz, a stomach ulcer did not kill so quickly nor leave the sufferer nearly bloodless in a few short hours.

As part of her training, Breieroz had learned much about poisons. Ingesting *parenchy* dust from the Evroza's own Forest of Alshemir might produce similar symptoms, but the substance was rare and difficult to obtain. Only an Evrozing might dare enter the Forest, and no Evrozing would do that voluntarily.

Prince Osbart had told her that the search for the poison served two purposes: first, preserving Princess—now Royenne—Ragna's life and second, because finding the source would lead them to the poisoner. He had enlisted the help of Aunt Constanz, even Great-Great-Granduncle Odo, in an attempt to scry for the culprit, but the two seers had found no one suspicious fleeing Crossroads Keep. It was possible the poisoner might still be within.

Nor had even a trace of poison been found in the kitchen, not in the mead butts in the buttery, not in the casks in the wine cellar. No one else had taken ill, yet everyone in the keep had eaten and drunk what the royenne had.

Now, she dreaded that the piglet would confirm their worst fears, literally the last possibility they wanted to face.

The piglet finished the wine in the pannikin, oinking enthusiastically, but when it tried to walk away, it staggered, and collapsed in its tracks.

Another Evrozing—her closest kin!—had poisoned the royenne? Breieroz was horrified. How could they have missed the signs of so dangerous a disaffection?

The Folk pigherd chuckled, startling her. "You should have told me why you wanted a piglet, Prince-Viceroye. I would have picked a bigger one—this one is too small, if that much Gerisari wine got it falling-down drunk."

She held her breath and watched a little longer, but the pigherd was right. Gerisari wine was potent, and Royenne Sharei had taken to drinking hers unwatered.

The piglet got back to its feet and did nothing more sinister than squeal and totter.

Prince Osbart shook his head and looked mystified. "We still do not know how and by whom Royenne Sharei has been poisoned, but however he has managed it, Eirgei has avenged his defeat on Tor River Road."

Breieroz and her mentor left the happy piglet—the only creature inside the keep's walls that was.

At the spymaster's direction, the scraps from Royenne Sharei's plate had gone to an unsuspecting, condemned brigand chief awaiting execution, the wine being too good for him. The royenne's last meal had been bland food that catered to her painful stomach, and the brigand's suspicions hadn't been roused by the royenne's leavings. He'd finished what he'd been given—Royenne Sharei had left more than she'd eaten when she'd sickened—and he was still healthy. That was the last inarguable proof that no poison had been put into the royenne's food or drink.

Yet, with those symptoms, what else could it be besides *parenchy* poisoning?

There was one other possibility.

As Breieroz had helped with the monumental task of questioning all the servants and members of the crown household, Folk had whispered to her that it was not poison at all, that it was the work of black-hearted sorcery or an angry shaman.

Breieroz repeated those suspicions to her mentor.

"No," Prince Osbart said. "I have never seen Folk magic that actually worked. Nor has there been a sorcerer, black-hearted or otherwise, in Milkdales since our clan came to power, and there are no shamans in Milkdales—not here, nor anywhere else in Trascolm, for that matter." He stopped speaking abruptly, eyes widening. "The only place where shamans can still be found is in Dremnar!"

Breieroz frowned—that line of investigation led straight to Nornholm—and Eirgei.

They had worried about poisoned weapons on the battlefield, but not a magically-poisoned royenne at home.

✦

Nornholm

Wyl made himself comfortable leaning against the closed shutters at the back of the east-facing window ledge on the seventh floor of the Heir's Tower. No one could see him in this cave-like hiding place where he drowsed away the rest of the day after he'd finished planning his return to Milkdales and his vengeance for Lanney.

At one point, he heard the crown princess's guardsmen come out onto the parapet overhanging his window to scan the upper bailey. No one else seemed to be looking for him, which made him wary of some trick. Unfortunately, being in the east-facing window meant he couldn't see much more than Mount Norn, so he could only go by what he heard, and what little he could see of the lower bailey.

The small commotion of the search died down at dusk, when the daylight gave out. He waited longer, until faint candlelight showed between the window's shutters behind him—coming from the crown princess's private chamber, if the seventh floor was laid out like the sixth.

He carved *luck* into his wax charm, hung it around his neck under his *byrnney's* collar, and hoped it would work. Then he climbed down the outside of the tower wall.

Climbing down in the dark took much longer than climbing up it in the sunlight, but the descent was still easy enough, thanks to having climbed down the trickiest portion of that same wall last night to escape to the stables. With the courses of ashlar blocks at a convenient height for his size, and the workmanship of the stonecutters more and more indifferent the higher they'd piled the stones, there were plenty of finger and toe holds between the courses at the heights where it mattered most. The better workmanship went only as high as the third floor, where he had started—another good reason to have climbed upward instead of down, once he'd slipped out the open window and made good his escape from the Young Court hall.

Now he hunted through the sprawling palace's underbelly for the things he'd need. He travelled by the dim glow of rushlights hanging under cressets, passing overhead by way of the rafters bracing the slate roof wherever sleeping bondservants' unrolled pallets crowded the corridors.

His *luck* charm seemed to be working.

Acquiring the things he needed wasn't hard—he effortlessly took a folded tunic from beside a sleeping bondsman in a corridor to cover his *byrnney*, rolled up the sleeves, and pulled up his soft leather shoulder-hood to shadow his face. It let him play a Folk servant without drawing a raised brow in suspicion when he entered one tower's still-busy kitchen and boldly raided its pantry under the noses of its sleepy kitchen staff. He even climbed up the outside of Tras Tower to his room and then back down—the ancient tower was an easy climb up, but climbing down was more difficult when burdened with his weapons and saddlebags.

It was just after midnight when he shifted his saddlebags to carefully lift the latch on the stable door and slip inside, as silent and unseen as a shadow on a moonless night. The other horses in the stable, familiar with his presence from last night, scarcely stirred, save for the one nearest Firebrand, who expected a handful of grain.

He went to the feed room to fill one of his saddlebags with grain, and fulfilled the friendly palfrey's hopeful nicker by giving him a handful of it when he returned.

Then he went to Firebrand with another handful, heartened by her own softly-nickered greeting. He spent a few minutes with a rushlight in the tack room collecting her furniture. After that, it was just a matter of resting curled in the straw with his head on his saddlebags and waiting. He wouldn't make his move until the dead hours, that span of time between the waning hours of the night and when the Folk archers returned to duty with the first light.

In Myymor—and in camp—that had always been his favorite time to carry out secret missions.

Tonight, he'd make his move after the fresh guardsmen at the lower bailey's gate had lost their edge—during the dead hours, even the most diligent sentries struggled to stay alert. The longer he waited tonight, the easier the escape, but he couldn't wait the whole night. By dawn, he wanted leagues between himself and Nornholm, and possible Dremn pursuit. The moon had already set, and that meant he'd only make speed by staying on the road from the town until daylight allowed him to make his own way off the road in a beeline for the Black Mountains.

He lay slouched on his elbow under Firebrand's manger and absently finger-combed the chestnut mare's ruddy-gold forelock as she rooted through the straw beside him, looking futilely for some overlooked kernel of grain.

This wasn't the first time Firebrand had heard him whispering his plans in her ear—she knew all his secrets and kept them well. They were the same age, and he considered the mare not just his best friend—with Lanney gone, she was now his only friend, the only living creature who'd never betrayed his trust.

Up in the Young Court, as he'd played senet, he'd brooded over what he'd done and not done the day of the whirlwind—and the price Lanney had paid for it. He'd wanted to wallow in pain, as if his suffering would redeem him, but all the while he'd been sitting under the crown princess's critical eyes and had to guard his expression. It had been eating at him, the realization of all he had lost with Lanney and the hole she'd left in his life. That was when it had come to him, that he didn't have to wait to avenge her.

Eirgei had made it undeniably clear that morning outside the Menney Tower: Wyl had no part to play in either guarding Helgurdda or helping her recruit an Icebear menney. There'd be no swaying the old man to change his mind—Eirgei and Helgurdda were a lot alike in that.

But Eirgei had left him with no good reason to stay in Nornholm and excellent reasons to leave the Young Court—and the ruins of his hostage-taking plan—behind and go back to Milkdales immediately.

He felt guilty about abandoning his hostage-escape plan, but he'd lost his best chance to pull that off, and anyway, if Eirgei and Helgurdda didn't want his help in planning their return, then they probably thought they wouldn't need his help when the time came for them to leave Nornholm without Royenne Errengard's permission.

Neither of them seemed to understand that something had to be done about the whole reason they were exiled here in Dremnar—that motherless, hedge-gotten, weather-mage.

In Milkdales, no one had *ever* treated him like a child. But now, even Helgurdda and Eirgei suddenly seemed to think he was some flighty youngling who couldn't be trusted to wear his back-knives and not use them unless necessary!

If Helgurdda and Eirgei didn't want his help, fine, that just left him free to avenge Lanney. Four summers of spying in Myymor—and a lifetime in the camps—had taught him to think for himself as well as take care of himself. He didn't need anyone to tell him what needed doing. He wouldn't waste his time doing nothing, playing with babies in Nornholm, while Lanney lay drowned and unavenged.

That weather-mage needed killing. Why couldn't Eirgei see it? How could Eirgei discount her and the danger she posed to the rebellion and their successful return?

Well, Wyl saw it clearly enough. It would be a daring move on his part, sneaking into Milkdales and hunting the weather-mage. He hoped Eirgei would appreciate the difficulty of what he intended to accomplish. While he was about it, perhaps he could find some other ways to damage the Evroza, things that would make Eirgei proud of him, enough to make him and Helgurdda sorry they had tried to cut him out of their lives. They needed him; they just needed to be reminded of it.

But to save Helgurdda and the rebellion in the spring, he had to make his move against the weather-mage now, before the passes through the Icepeak Mountains were snow-bound and stranded him in Nornholm until mid-winter.

In mid-winter, during the Moon of Raids, Iceroad Pass would be frozen solid and offer a much shorter, direct route into Milkdales—but a crowded one, first with Dremn raiders heading south, and then with Tras minions heading north, bent on retribution.

But by leaving now, given good weather, he could make it back into Milkdales in less than three weeks. He knew—had known—some brigands Eirgei had recruited who'd prowled the Black Mountains and had raided practically to Nornholm's doorstep. According to their stories, it would take Wyl a week to cross southern Dremnar from Nornholm to the Black Mountains, then another week riding south through the wild and desolate Black Mountains to Dawngate Pass on Milkdales's eastern frontier. The leg through the Milkdales portion of the Black Mountains covered little more than half the distance of the Dremn portion, but it was the more rugged leg of the journey, with a risk of early snow.

Then he'd be in Trascolm, in Milkdales barony.

A hard-riding Evroza courier could cover the distance from Myymor to Crossroads Keep in a single day, using relays of royal post horses on the Royal Road. On just one good horse, Wyl reckoned it would still be only five days from Dawngate Pass to Crossroads Keep—even with a side trip to Myymor. He'd have to take care to avoid the well-patrolled Royal Road and keep to the hill-country of central Milkdales all the way to Crossroads Keep. The journey might take twice as long if he got caught by an early snow while he was still in the Black Mountains, or if he had to dodge brigands when he reached Milkdales' hill-country.

But once he arrived at the Evroza's royal palace on the east bank of the Bayl River, neither the Evroza in Crossroads Keep nor their weather-mage would know to guard against him, a half-blind, outcast

Folk boy.

In four weeks or less, Lanney would be avenged, and—unlike Hel-gurdda's vengeance for Hereres—he didn't need a menney to do it. He just needed Firebrand, his bow, and some under-the-counter *parenchy* dust from a certain apothecary he knew in Myymor.

Well, that and some more war arrows—clearly, if it came to shoot-ing at the weather-mage again, he might still be too squeamish to count on hitting her with his first arrow. Besides, once the mage was dead, perhaps other targets might offer themselves in Crossroads Keep be-fore he had to flee the uproar.

He'd packed what he'd taken from the pantry in the other saddle-bag, so between the pair, he'd have enough to feed himself and Fire-brand for at least half the distance to Dawngate Pass before he'd have to waste time hunting or foraging. He figured he could make up what-ever else he lacked—like war arrows—by filching hunting arrows from a Folk village once he was safely out of Dremnar. It would be a simple matter for him to replace their hunting heads with the warheads he'd scavenged from the arrows broken in the Tor.

When Wyl judged the hour favored him, he quickly tacked up Fire-brand. Her feet were bare, so there was no need to muffle them to cross the stone-surfaced upper bailey. The horse he intended to use as his decoy for the guards at the High Gate was also barefoot.

Stealing his own horse—and the one he'd made friends with—away from the unsuspecting Dremn stablemen sleeping out of sight in the loft would scarcely be a challenge: he'd stolen his first horse at age five. Nor was he particularly worried about getting through either set of Nornholm's gates—fortresses were made to keep enemies out, not a determined spy in. Easier done without a horse—or with two—but under the cover of darkness and against unsuspecting guards, not the greatest challenge he'd ever faced.

The lower gate would be easy enough to pass, posing as a Folk roy-al courier who had already passed unhindered through the High Gate—thanks to the High Gate guards' distraction with the loose horse. The sleepy guards at the lower gate wouldn't dare delay him.

He tied his bulging saddlebags behind his saddle's cantle and reached down for his quiver with its two good war arrows and un-strung bow.

His best friend failed to warn him as he straightened.

A long, lean arm reached in from the aisle, its hand grabbed a hand-ful of surcoat over his chest, and he was jerked up and off his feet.

In the dim starlight through the open half-doors farther down the stable's walls, he looked up into Eirgei's shadowy face and darkly-gleaming eyes.

They were hot and irrational—berserker's eyes dangerously close to Wyl's.

"I knew you would come back for the horse," Eirgei said, holding him face to face, letting Wyl's legs dangle in the air.

Wyl's quiver dropped from his nerveless fingers when he saw the little flecks of white foam at one corner of Eirgei's mouth under the long, graying Tras moustache.

His granduncle was furious, possibly unreasonable, and struggling was the worst thing Wyl could do. He made himself hang limp and unresisting. He dared not provoke Eirgei any more than he somehow already had.

He'd never expected this.

"The Heir's Tower guardsmen took Nornholm apart looking for you," Eirgei said, in his most dangerously gentle tone. "You threw a table at the crown princess in a fit of temper after she beat you playing some game? I am not surprised you would choose to run away rather than face me or your mother!"

"That isn't true! The table was just a diversion, not an attack. I didn't kick it at her or anyone!"

Eirgei fixed his glare on Wyl, and Wyl wished he'd kept his mouth shut. He drooped in Eirgei's preternaturally strong grip and hid behind his hair. But the absence of resistance wasn't having the desired effect.

He'd never before had to deal with Eirgei's anger, not after Eirgei had lost a menney and been forced to take refuge with his lifelong enemies, and Wyl wished he still never had. Eirgei was in a rare, towering rage, and for the first time in Wyl's life, the full weight of that rage was directed at him.

"My best pupil, running away!"

The tic under Wyl's left eye spasmed, a measure of his fright. "*Ockh*, not running away! Avenging Lanney!"

Eirgei gave him a furious look and he knew he shouldn't have answered.

✦

5ᵗʰ Day of the Moon of Storms, 113 G.E.
Crossroads Keep

By dawn, Breieroz was tired to her bones. She sat on the battlements of Crossroads Keep and struggled to stay focused on the conversation between Prince Osbart and Royenne Ragna as they stood on the parapet overlooking the menney training courtyard. Prince Osbart's first privy meeting with Royenne Ragna in his role as her spymaster had lasted all night.

Breieroz did her best to appear dozing without actually falling asleep as she sat yawning in a crenel a discreet distance away— conveying an impression of privacy even as she listened. She was emotionally wrung-out from the tragedy of Royenne Sharei's death.

Breieroz was not the only one. The need for revenge had taken precedence over all else in Royenne Ragna's mind, just as retribution for the blood-feud had with Royenne Sharei.

After simmering poisonously for over a dozen years, the blood-feud now burned hotter than ever among loyal Evrozings outraged by Royenne Sharei's assassination. Even some of the Traditionalists would rally to them rather than continue to back Helgurdda.

"It was shamanry, then?" Royenne Ragna asked Prince Osbart. He had just given her his preliminary report.

"It was some sort of magic," he replied. "I've sent a messenger bird to Hundyyga with as much detail as the bird could carry. If shamanry was what killed your mother, Granduncle Odo will know it, and tell us how to guard you against it." He bowed his head. "Sharei was well-guarded against everything else by myself and our seers, or the blood-feud would have been over years ago. Our Evroza magery is not subtle. Gerisar's artisanry is useful, but harmless in itself, and Folk magic is called spitcraft for a reason. Shamanry, though, is capable of striking magically at a some distance, depending on the shaman's personal powers, which is why my predecessors ensured that there have been no shamans here in Trascolm for at least two generations. There probably are not many shamans left even in Dremnar—but we both know who else is conveniently in Dremnar and has sworn vengeance on both Sharei and you."

"My mother's assassination demands retribution," said Royenne Ragna, "and I will have it—at any cost. This time, however, the cost will not be paid in Loyalist lives."

Prince Osbart nodded grimly.

"Offering such a treasure has to work," Royenne Ragna said, gazing down at the menney as they began the day's training exercises.

Prince Osbart shrugged. "Your offer is a fair one, yet not so generous that we will regret it after we fall out with her."

"You are so certain that we will?"

"Errengard is a cunning vixen and will run with us only as long as it benefits her. She has her own internal troubles and can ill-afford hostilities with us at this time. But even if she refuses your offer, Prince-Envoy Kreseyn will still come away with information we can use."

"Damn the timing," Royenne Ragna said. "We would have this matter finished quickly if we could use Iceroad Pass."

"Once Iceroad Pass is open, Royenne Errengard will be less interested in an accord, not with her warlords howling like hungry wolves in her ears. Going through the Black Mountains is slower, but if Prince Kreseyn reaches Nornholm with our offer before Iceroad Pass freezes over, our chances of success are greater. He should be safe enough in Dremnar after he replaces our escort for a Gerisari one from the garrison in Dawngate Pass. That should be enough to persuade the Dremn to parlay rather than kill them outright. There's no history of war between Dremnar and Gerisar like there is with us."

Breieroz nodded sleepily.

While the Evroza menney had come out of its final battle against Helgurdda much better than Helgurdda's rebels had, they could ill-afford the casualties they had taken. Evroza's good fortune lay in the unexpectedness of that final battle—the end of the rebellion had come as a surprise to Jegurett and Erythgold clans; their baronnes had intended to be ready to seize the moment, but had never expected the moment to come so soon—and then, the moment had passed.

Bringing a Gerisari legion into Milkdales was a drastic measure, something no Evroza royenne had permitted after Evroza clan had united Trascolm and forged its crown, but all the same, Royenne Ragna had little choice. Beset as Evroza clan was, she had to ask for the loan of troops.

The Gerisari would hardly refuse her request for the service of one of Empress Jerhafyne's legions. Gerisar depended on timber from Evroza's ancestral clan lands to support its massive trade fleet and navy, and traded for Milkdales's cheese and wool in exchange for luxuries and arms from Seacourt's famous workshops.

Royenne Sharei—as Baronne of Milkdales and of the Evroza—had, in turn, traded those luxuries to the rest of Trascolm, to her considerable advantage, while continuing to improve upon the impressive outfitting of her menney, making it resemble more and more an elite Gerisari legion in appearance and training.

Until the blood-feud had interrupted her plans.

"My reward for our comfortable relations with Gerisar," Prince Osbart told Breieroz, as they climbed down from the privacy of the rooftop, leaving the royenne to brood atop the keep, "is that obtaining the loan of one of their legions won't require Prince Kreseyn's diplomatic skills, merely a simple request sent through the Gerisari embassy at Dawngate Pass."

Breieroz and Prince Osbart walked the corridors to the viceroy's suite of rooms saying little, and overheard by no one. Prince Osbart entered his office and settled behind his desk.

"I also have great hopes that Prince Kreseyn can obtain appropriate additions to Royenne Ragna's bribe when he reaches the Gerisari outpost on the other side of Dawngate Pass—Gerisari treasures that will tempt the barbarians enough to buy two heads."

Breieroz did not envy the elderly Gerisari prince. It would be a grueling journey for the envoy, passing through the brigand-infested Black Mountains to enter Dremnar and then on to Nornholm, all on the cusp of winter, but an entourage of Gerisari noblemen was less likely to trigger the kind of reaction from Royenne Errengard's borderguards that a party of armed Tras would, and Prince Kreseyn *had* pledged any aid he could give in avenging Sharei's death.

For better or worse, the fortunes of the Evroza and Gerisar were intertwined. It was Prince Osbart's task—as it would one day be hers—to ensure that theirs was a partnership of equals, that the Gerisari remembered the Evroza were not barbarians to be wooed with showy gifts—gifts like those Prince Kreseyn would be taking to Nornholm.

The Evroza menney urgently needed time to recover their former reputation and the strength it was based upon. Before the blood-feud, their menney had been reckoned the equal of a Gerisari legion, but now, between the desertions of Traditionalists and years of attrition, Breieroz was afraid it would take as many years of peace to rebuild the menney as it had taken of blood-feud to undermine it.

But Evroza did not have thirteen years—according to their spies' reports, Evroza did not even have six moons' grace before they would face open revolt in the united, perennially-rebellious baronies of Redmont and Cloudcrags.

CHAPTER 17

PRICKLY SITUATIONS

Nornholm

By daybreak, the day had turned appropriately bleak and dismally sleeting.

An hour later, Wyl arrived—as ordered—at the second floor entrance to the Heir's Tower. The crown princess's guardsmen glared at him and looked like they'd enjoy pulling off his arms and legs.

That was a relief—ever since Wyl had regained consciousness, his gut had been in a knot for fear they'd laugh at his humiliating return.

The guardsmen must have been punished for losing track of him, and they didn't intend for that to happen again. Wyl was taken up the coiling stairs, flattered by his escort of a hand of guardsmen, though two of them had an excessively firm grip on his arms that made him have to climb sideways. They delivered him to the third floor, where the Young Court had gathered.

Everyone inside stopped whatever they were doing. All talk ceased. Everyone stared.

Wyl saw where the crown princess was and slowly stalked up to her with a deliberate air of defiance.

The defiance was just for show, an attempt to save face. His stiff-legged walk was merely the best he could move after Eirgei's lengthy thrashing with the flat of his sabre and the pommel of his dagger, all in the name of discipline, back in Tras Tower. Wyl was tired, sore, and angry—and looking for a fight he could win.

Prince Norren appeared and jostled his sister back so he stood be-

218

tween her and Wyl. He, too, seemed to be looking for a fight. There was no sign now that the welcoming friendship the crown prince had offered him two days ago had ever even existed.

The hostile expression on Prince Norren's face was laughable after facing Eirgei's wrath. Wyl wanted to pass on his hurt and embarrassment in the worst way, so he gave Crown Prince Norren the head-nod of equals and stared nastily into his blue eyes, waiting until the crown prince either pulled his jeweled dagger or looked away.

"You had no permission to leave court yesterday," Crown Prince Norren said, surprising him—talk being a third reaction, one Wyl hadn't even considered. "In the future, if you need to leave, you will make your request in a respectful manner, as befits the dignity of this court, so you will not have to come crawling back like a beaten dog."

Wyl blinked, angry but confused by the unexpected nature of the attack. He covered his confusion with a curled lip. Hostility rang in the crown prince's words, but the crown prince remained in control of his temper, and Wyl couldn't be seen initiating an attack on him—he had to be able to argue self-defense to Eirgei.

There'd been more to Eirgei's orders—more humiliation—but it was best to get that out of the way now. Eirgei had ways of finding out if he'd been obeyed, and the consequences of disobedience were dire.

Wyl couldn't remember having ever received a harsher beating from Eirgei—and for no reason. Eirgei's blistering words had hurt worse than the beating and had been equally senseless. He'd done nothing wrong! Certainly nothing worthy of being disowned, yet that clearly had been the threat under Eirgei's fury when he'd ordered Wyl back to the Heir's Tower.

All the same, Wyl would show disrespect to an enemy before he'd ever show weakness. *Never show weakness. Never show fear.*

He turned from Crown Prince Norren to Crown Princess Kotakei, dropped stiffly to one knee, and tilted his head towards the floor. Eirgei had specified two knees and then a profound obeisance, but Wyl had reached his limit. He doubted he could rise from both knees without a struggle—and the Bearcubs were sure to take that betrayal of weakness as a signal to attack. If the young minions jumped him, and he didn't win, he'd be an embarrassment to Eirgei, perhaps enough of one that Eirgei would finally give up on training him.

"*Heh,* I ask your pardon for my behavior yesterday," he said, deliberately ignoring Crown Prince Norren and directing his words solely at Crown Princess Kotakei.

He was pleased to see, by the way she pressed her lips together, that she wasn't taken in by him mouthing Eirgei's words.

He wasn't the least bit sorry, except that he'd been caught, and he was glad she knew it. He took some dark amusement from the situation, that she didn't know what to do about him.

"I have sworn to attend court every day and be absent only by your leave—"

Eirgei had given him more to say, but he'd already forgotten the words he was supposed to have memorized. The courtly words wouldn't be believable coming out of his mouth, anyway. "—unless my royenne's got need of me." *Even if she doesn't know she needs me.*

Crown Princess Kotakei's grim expression remained in place. It didn't suit her, but for a crown princess, she didn't seem to smile as much as he'd have expected.

"Where did you go yesterday, Prince Tras?" she asked, using that hateful name.

She didn't give him permission to rise.

"Nowhere," Wyl said bitterly, raising his head to meet her cold, blue eyes, and giving her a nasty glare that would have been sufficient to back off the wisest of Helgurdda's brigand recruits. He hoped the crown prince would intervene and challenge him over it.

Crown Prince Norren didn't move.

Damned, hedge-gotten, motherless coward.

"Then why did you leave the way you did?" Crown Princess Kotakei persisted, taking no heed of his glare, either.

Wyl shrugged uncomfortably and looked down, grimacing at the floor and counting on his fall of hair to hide his not-quite stoic expression from her. He couldn't maintain his war face. His whole body hurt—his bruises from crossing the Tor had bruises of their own now, and the underside of his jaw throbbed where the pommel of one of Eirgei's back-daggers had connected.

He'd expected the crown prince to direct the questions, not the crown princess. He'd intended to be taking out his frustration on the older boy, not to still be here, painfully stiffening at the crown princess's feet.

He was acutely aware of how he looked. He hadn't stolen another change of clothing yet, and though Eirgei never left a mark on him where it would show, training bouts with him were hard on his clothes—and disciplinary training was even worse.

Why did he even care how he looked?

It had to be the Young Court's influence that he had a new, unpleasant view of himself as seen through the eyes of these noble and royal children. Why should he care that they would make an ignorant interpretation of what accounted for the new, unstitched cuts and tears in his surcoat? His stolen undertunic's sleeves were little more than rags after desperately fending off one of Eirgei's attacks using his bronze-mounted bracers.

Until now, he'd been proud of his surcoat's countless mendings, even if the damage *was* mostly caused by Eirgei. Helgurdda's minions had known how to read the story it told. The other rebels had known him only as Lanney's fosterling, a sometime spy and efficient camp hunter, and the fact that he had survived seven years of Eirgei's brutal training—far longer than any of the other rebels—had made his reputation in that rough company. Smart rogues, once they'd begun that training themselves, walked as carefully around him as they did Eirgei. Less reflective ones learned to do that the hard way.

These Dremn *children* knew nothing of him. Their superior, scornful expressions frustrated and infuriated him. If only they weren't children!

Crown Prince Norren looked down at Wyl with narrowed eyes and an openly disdainful expression on his face.

That stung Wyl's pride. He wished he knew what had happened to change the crown prince's opinion of him. Had it been because he had disobeyed the crown prince's orders when he'd left the Bearcubs barracks that first night? Or was it his humiliation with the tutor?

Or was it just because he was Tras?

Whatever the reason, instead of the friendly smile the crown prince had worn during their private talk two days ago, Crown Prince Norren now wore a look of disgust, confirmation that Wyl had no hope of salvaging his hostage-taking plan of winning the crown prince's trust. And by Eirgei's explicit command, he was still stuck in the Young Court, in a situation that nothing in his life had prepared him to meet.

He hated Nornholm and everyone in it.

"I heard you were running away," Crown Prince Norren said mockingly. He again edged between Wyl and his sister.

A flush of anger went through Wyl, and he turned his attention to the goading crown prince.

"More like running *to*," Wyl growled under his breath, surprising himself because he hadn't intended to say anything more. Why did he care what these spoiled, noble brats thought of him?

"Running to where?" Crown Prince Norren persisted.

He defiantly tossed the hair out of his eyes. "*Ockh*, Milkdales, of course. I have unfinished business with an Evroza mage. But for now, I've agreed to remain in Nornholm a little longer, until Helgurdda's got her menney."

"What menney would that be?" Crown Prince Norren laughed. "She has already lost one."

Wyl managed a toothy, provocative imitation of a smile. "How many Dremn warlords do you really think will turn down a chance for glory and a windfall of spoils from taking Crossroads Keep? When we ride, we'll have the best warlords in Dremnar with us."

"Like you?" Crown Prince Norren sneered.

Wyl twisted his expression to show contempt, still hoping to trick the crown prince into ill-considered action. He was encouraged when the crown prince's expression went from scornful to offended before Wyl even answered. "Of course! I've seen more battles than I can count and blooded my sabre, too. I'll bet you just pretend with sticks when you train." That was as cutting an insult as he could imagine. "You're nothing but a stick-whacker." He smirked.

But though Crown Prince Norren's nostrils flared, and his hands clenched, those insults clearly weren't cutting enough. The crown prince still remained in control of his royal temper. The crown prince didn't challenge Wyl and let him beat that superior look off his princely face.

Was Crown Prince Norren a coward?

But the crown prince looked more condescending than afraid.

If anyone had fallen into a trap, it was Wyl. He still didn't know what had happened to turn the entire Young Court against him yesterday. With no hope now of pretending friendship with the crown prince and lulling him into complaisancy, he would have to take control of the Bearcubs by force of arms rather than subterfuge. If he publicly took Crown Prince Norren down now, he figured that would take the fight out of the rest of the Bearcubs later, when the time came to take the crown princess hostage. All he would really need from the Bearcubs was a moment's hesitation, and then he'd have Crown Princess Kotakei hostage. The Bearcubs wouldn't dare do anything once he had her.

Maybe the young minions didn't want to be friends with him, but he could show them they didn't want to be his enemies.

Sooner or later, the Dremn would behave like Dremn and betray Helgurdda to her enemies. Then, Eirgei would see that they needed

Wyl's hostage-escape plan. Eirgei would see that Wyl had been right about not trusting the Dremn, kith or not.

Wyl shifted his attention back to Crown Princess Kotakei rather than spend more time worrying over the mystery of his fall from favor—or fruitlessly hoping for the chance to pummel a prince.

Let the weather-mage believe herself safe for now.

Wyl would wait until Eirgei gave him his spying mission, which ought to be as soon as Eirgei and Helgurdda decided which Evroza holdings would be key to their successful return. Eirgei had to have a mission in mind for him, even if he didn't want Wyl involved in its planning. Why else make him stay in Nornholm?

One of Eirgei's instructed phrases came back to him. This time, Wyl said it to Crown Princess Kotakei like he meant it. He was desperate now to draw his act to an end, before his aching body betrayed his weakness. "I'm yours to command."

He rose while he still could. Maybe she would've given him permission, but he refused to ask for it.

And if she really believed she could command him, she was a pretty fool, and he'd have all of the Young Court jumping at *his* command even sooner than he anticipated.

✦

Kotakei was speechless, but her brother was not.

"You were not given permission to rise," Norren said. "You insult my sister with your rudeness!"

At last! Kotakei did her best to keep her face impassive and not show her relief.

"I don't answer to this court. If you've got a problem with me, take it to my baronne," Prince Tras snarled. "Or challenge me!"

Her brother blinked at the effrontery, and an angry flush started to rise in his face.

Kotakei had to do something quickly—this had to be a trap if younger, smaller Prince Tras *wanted* to fight Norren so badly. If Norren took the bait and challenged him, that would give Prince Tras the choice of weapon. She was sure he would choose something deadly.

"My brother will not waste his time fighting *stripling boys.*"

She felt satisfaction when she saw how Prince Tras flushed. Maybe she was right! Maybe he *had* lied about his age.

"Especially," she said, following up on his moment of not-quite-hidden dismay, "not rude *striplings* obviously raised in a gutter, who do not know how to behave around their *betters*."

Prince Tras glowered at her, tossing the hair out of his eyes, putting his head back to look down his nose at her, despite her being taller making him have to look up to meet her eyes. Difficult as it was to look down on someone while looking up, he somehow did it, and with an intolerable, condescending scorn, as if he had faced down giants and saw her as no challenge at all.

Never in her life had someone dared look at her that way!

She accepted his unspoken challenge. When he opened his mouth, she cut him off.

"Is that not why you have been sent to attend me, because your mother is afraid you will embarrass her if she actually becomes Roy-enne of Trascolm? You Tras and your Gerisari keepers may consider us barbarians, but my court is honorable, and you have been given to me to educate in the ways of royalty—or, at least, to civilize as much as possible. You are not dealing with clanless outcasts here. If you cannot learn simple Dremn manners, Prince Tras, you will be hopeless with all the pomp and ritual—and Gerisari dress-up—your people love so much."

He clenched his fists and shifted his weight, as if readying himself to attack her!

Just let him try—she had a dagger and knew how to use it!

"Your first lesson in civilized manners, Prince Tras, is that we do not settle discord with violence. Thugs and outcasts who do are not welcome here."

She smiled sweetly, in case her refusal to say his name, to acknowledge him in front of her court, had not already made it clear he was unwelcome. "I am doing my best to help you fit in with noble companions, but you have not made any progress. If you do not do better, I shall have to report your failure to your granduncle."

His expression of scorn drained away, taking with it all the color in his face.

So, he did fear something—Eirgei.

She smiled.

Lord Geilorren came up. "Come, Prince Wylheim, I will get you started with your studies."

Prince Tras rose and edged away from her, as if he suspected she meant to plant her side-dagger in his back.

Oh, if only she could! But that would be dishonorable, and she meant to keep virtue on her side in this.

Lord Geilorren took Prince Tras aside, apart from the rest of the Young Court, and Kotakei watched him show Prince Tras how to handle the precious parchments, papers, codices, and scrolls without damaging them.

After the angry words and threats at the start of the day, she spent the rest of the morning tense and poised to snap.

For his part, Lord Geilorren paid no apparent heed to his pupil's threatening posture. He stayed just out of arm's reach of the boy, though there was not the least waver of fear in his droning voice. There were no angry exchanges. Prince Tras's only contribution to the lessons was an occasional cough.

Hours later, the morning's lessons were finally over. Kotakei watched Lord Geilorren gather the codices brought from Grandmother's archives and replace them in the cupboard. He had impressed her by refusing to appear either angered or intimidated by his pupil's threatening attitude. Though Kotakei had kept an eye on the two, in case Lord Geilorren needed her to intervene with her guardsmen, he had dealt with his hostile pupil with aplomb throughout the morning.

Now, as they waited for the midday meal to be served, she looked down the length of the table to where the younglings ate.

Prince Tras didn't speak—and the way the younglings around him talked over each other to him, it would have been useless for him to try.

She was surprised to see a mild expression on his face. He listened to what the younglings said and looked not the least bit hostile. In fact, he looked intensely interested. In rare moments, like when the younglings paused to grab bread, she saw him speak and quirk a surprisingly gentle smile—a question, judging from the renewed babble.

Then the Folk servers arrived, breaking into her fascination, fortunately, before it became too obvious who was the object of her attention.

The main course today was porcupine. The roasted meat was cleverly covered by a cured skin, complete with quills. It was one of Kotakei's favorite dishes.

Prince Tras looked startled when one of the porcupines was placed before him by a straight-faced server. He touched the quills and tested the points like a youngling—and ended up with a fingertip full of quills.

Apparently, there were no porcupines in Milk Dales.

The younglings around him squealed and squabbled over who would remove the quills, or show him how to uncover the meat without wearing more of them.

She covertly watched and was relieved to see Prince Tras did have some sort of manners at table, even if they were Folk manners and entirely inappropriate at any noble repast. He ignored his spoon and drank soup from his bowl. He ate everything else with his fingers and knife.

Unlike the occasional Tras prisoner awaiting ransom, who generally made a show of revulsion at traditional Dremn fare, she had not seen Prince Tras take particular notice of the different dishes as he listened intently to the younglings. The roast porcupine did not put him off, as she might have expected, but neither did he show pleased surprise as he ate it, though scant minutes later, she saw him have a second helping.

"Prince Tras!" she called down the table, bracing herself to acknowledge his existence and hoping she did not make a fool of herself trying to get his attention.

Her words prompted a shocked halt to other conversations around her.

"What do you think of the roast porcupine?"

He looked taken aback by the sudden silence surrounding her question.

She could see he disliked *Prince Tras* in place of his name. A muscle clenched in his jaw, but he didn't look willing to make an issue of it.

"*Heh*, good," he said uneasily, still seated.

Her little cousin, Elfreida, at table next to him, urgently whispered to him, but it was too late. He had already drawn another's attention and ire.

Lord Martei stood. "When the crown princess speaks to you at table, you will stand so she can see you. Your brutish ways have no place in this court!"

Kotakei glanced aside at Norren. There was a little smile at the corners of his lips.

"I will not have a brawl here," she whispered to her brother. "Remember, we are supposed to be showing him kin-favor."

Norren sighed.

"Prince Wylheim," he said in a steady, neutral voice, "it is the custom of this court to conduct our meal as if we are in the Crown Court hall."

Kotakei could see the effort it took for her brother to restrict his reprimand to words.

Prince Tras tossed the hair out of his eyes, and she swore they flashed silver as he glared first at Martei, who had subsided onto his bench, and then at Norren, even as Prince Tras's tanned face paled to dirty gray. Then, he not only rose to his feet, but stood on his bench, towering over them all. "I trust, Crown Princess Kotakei, that you can see me now?"

His stiff formality, contrasted against his ratty surcoat and the ragged sleeves showing from under his ever-present *byrnney*, just accentuated how much of a misfit he was.

"Now that I have seen by your marksmanship how well *you* can see," Kotakei said, "I thank you for your courtesy, but if you will recall from the outcome of our archery contest, *my* eyes are sufficiently keen that you need not stand on the furniture for *me* to see *you*."

There was an appreciative wave of laughter from the youths at her end of the table. Her rebuke was gentle enough to pass for teasing, the humor in it more mild than cutting.

Or so she had thought.

It did not seem possible, but Prince Tras's face grew even grayer. His hands clenched into fists.

"I'm pleased to have pleased you," he said and coughed. "I didn't feel it was proper to humiliate a crown princess after just being introduced. If you like, we can try our skill again, and see how bad my archery—and my eyes—really are."

What? Her winning had been no concession from him! The condescending thug!

"My apologies," Kotakei said stiffly. "Your eyes are so colorless, and your archery so poor, I thought you were nearly blind. If you claim otherwise, then I suppose I must take you at your word."

She could feel her cheeks burning with anger.

Prince Tras glared at her, his silver eyes narrowed to black-lashed slits of fury that bored into hers. He did not look the least bit blind.

"*Ockh*, I accept your apology, Crown Princess Kotakei," he said, as if she truly had apologized, and he had gained some kind of victory over her. "I didn't know my word's been in doubt."

She could not believe he had the audacity to be affronted, after admitting to the Three Dishonors before the entire Young Court!

The youths around her laughed at him.

He stiffened. All the fire, all the arrogance—all the expression—in his face drained away. Even his eyes seemed to empty. The sudden change seemed ominous and boded ill for someone.

"I am glad we are in accord," she said, in her most frigid tone, anxious to bring this confrontation to an end while she still had the upper hand. "Please, continue to enjoy your meal. I have no more questions for you."

Prince Tras stared at her a moment longer, then hopped down off the bench.

He did not, she saw, finish his roast porcupine.

CHAPTER 18

LORD MARTEI

After the midday meal, Wyl then played a losing series of senet games against the crown princess—MiPaatet still didn't favor him when he tossed the sticks.

Then, the day having improved to merely overcast sometime during the morning, the younglings were dismissed to play in the courtyard. The stripling boy, Prince Lokei, went with them. Crown Princess Kotakei and her attendants headed for archery practice.

Finally, here was Wyl's chance to gain the respect of Crown Prince Norren and the Bearcubs, and in the process, relieve a great deal of his frustration by taking it out on them. Minion practice offered him the perfect chance to vent his rage and inner turmoil. He could make his first brutally-fast win against one of the Bearcubs look like an accident. Who'd suspect clever sword control from a fourteen-year-old?

Lord Martei stretched. It looked deliberate, calling attention to the big youth's size. He looked down at Wyl. "Come along, Tras. I am Crown Prince Norren's Right Hand, so it is my responsibility to rank everyone in the Bear Cubs. Let us see if a Tras can hold his own against our—"

"—I have changed my mind," Crown Prince Norren said, walking up to Lord Martei. "I think he is too young and too small to join my Bear Cubs. I have decided to leave him with—"

"No!" Wyl burst out, dismayed. "I'm *fourteen* and my size doesn't matter. Test me, and you'll see there's no one in the menney who can beat me!"

"Do you not mean the *young menney?*" Lord Martei barked a laugh. The young minions around him laughed.

"I challenge you, blade to blade!" Wyl spit the words at Lord Martei. "You and me!"

"The Bear Cubs only fight with staves," Crown Prince Norren said, dismissing his challenge with a wave and a mocking laugh.

Wyl was shocked speechless. How could his challenge be ignored?

"And even that would be too dangerous for you—Martei might forget you're Ice Bear kith as well as Tras," Crown Prince Norren said.

"I've fought Eirgei with real blades!"

The Dremn youths laughed even harder at him.

"I'm not afraid of an overgrown youngling armed with a stick!" Wyl snarled.

Lord Martei's eyes narrowed ominously.

"Training bouts with a doting granduncle prove nothing," Crown Prince Norren said. "Have you ever sparred with a staff?"

What was a *doting* granduncle? Had the crown prince just dared insult Eirgei? "I've always sparred with *real* weapons, if that's what you're asking. I've made my challenge—if Lord Martei thinks he can beat me, let him prove it!"

Crown Prince Norren and Lord Martei put their heads together and whispered.

What was there to talk about?

If they thought Eirgei had never truly exerted himself against Wyl, then the Bearcubs were about to be astonished.

"Very well," Crown Prince Norren said, turning back to him. Lord Martei stood at the crown prince's shoulder, giving Wyl a nasty grin while the crown prince spoke. "Lord Martei has persuaded me to give you a chance to prove yourself. But since you challenged, he has the pick of weapons—so you will face him with a staff."

Wyl sneered at Lord Martei, intending to enrage him.

Mere stick-thwacking meant he could give Lord Martei the kind of drubbing that would kill him if they were using blades—and it suddenly occurred to Wyl that killing any Dremn, no matter how justified, might be a mistake. Not just for him, but for Helgurdda and Eirgei, too.

The Menney Tower stood between the upper bailey's gates and the royenne's wing of the sprawling palace, surrounded by defensive courtyards intended to funnel an invader away from the royenne's wing and into the Menney Tower's killing ground. Today, that courtyard was quiet—Eirgei had taken the Icebear menney out for training in what he considered basic mounted maneuvers. The Bearcubs had the courtyard to themselves.

Lord Martei led the way to a rack of staves in a large—and largely empty—armory letting out onto the courtyard. All the sticks were longer than Wyl was tall.

Lord Martei selected a staff quickly—a long, heavy one—and gave Wyl a grin clearly meant to be daunting.

Wyl grinned wolfishly back in the same spirit. He was more than ready to take the next step in his hostage-taking plan—intimidating the Bearcubs. They were, after all, only children. The lingering pain from his predawn thrashing, followed by a morning of stiffness from sitting at his lessons, should be worked out by the time he was through with Lord Martei.

He intended to take advantage of Lord Martei's arrogance and sucker him in short order, though that would cost him his advantage of surprise when he moved on to challenge Prince Jeik—and he'd have to do that to prove to the Bearcubs that Lord Martei's defeat hadn't been pure luck.

He figured he'd have a good feel for his weapon after that and be ready to meet a challenge from Crown Prince Norren, who by that time, might be ready to uphold the honor of the Bearcubs and angry enough to challenge him—giving Wyl the choice of weapons.

After defeating the crown prince and gaining the fearful respect of the rest of the young minions, maybe his life would settle back to the way it used to be with Helgurdda's rebels.

He stepped up to the rack and looked over the assortment of sticks, wondering which of them would best suit him.

In a sabre fight, his advantages were quickness, agility, precision, and being a small target, so if he used the shortest of the sticks, maybe he could just pretend it was Eirgei's long merkusar sabre. Eirgei had schooled him somewhat in using an adult-sized blade, in case he didn't have the use of his own sabre, and Wyl had been compensating for an overlong, overly heavy weapon since he was ten. Though his staff was three or four hand-spans longer than he was tall—much longer than Eirgei's sabre—surely it was just a matter of compensating for its additional length and weight.

While he hefted the staff to get a feel for its weight and balance, the rest of the Bearcubs formed a large circle in the middle of the courtyard.

That circle of youths worried him much more than the staff or Lord Martei. The real danger would come with Lord Martei's defeat, which was likely to trigger a spontaneous mêlée. He would have to respect the Bearcubs' numbers, if not their skill. Fortunately, none of them held a staff, so he tried to put that danger out of his mind.

The youths parted, opening the center of the circle. Lord Martei sneeringly motioned Wyl inside the circle, as if Wyl needed encouragement.

Wyl snorted. He tossed the hair out of his eyes and stepped into the circle.

Ordinarily, distance meant safety, so when Lord Martei lagged behind him, it didn't alarm him.

On Wyl's third step, he realized he'd made a terrible mistake.

He was barely inside the circle, but he abruptly checked and whirled, swinging his staff from its balance point like an unusually long, two-handed sword.

But Lord Martei's long staff caught him hard behind his knees before he'd even made a quarter turn.

As Wyl fell, he twisted to keep his weapon up between him and Lord Martei, but his weapon was a staff, not a sword. With its balance point in the middle, its long butt unexpectedly jammed between his body and the ground, and threw him down.

Wyl lurched back up to his feet.

And immediately went back down as Lord Martei's staff again swept his legs out from under him before he could bring his staff into play.

Wyl had to take the offensive, take control of the fight!

But Lord Martei had seized the initiative, and every time Wyl regained his feet, he was knocked off them again.

As he fell, he twisted, trying to get his staff clear of his body, and this time, he caught himself and stayed on his feet. He took the staff in both hands at its balance point and swung it at Lord Martei like it was a sword, successfully parrying the older boy's next blow.

But the staff was too long and heavy—Wyl's sagging riposte was too slow.

It left Wyl open for a stunning hit to his skull.

The force of the blow made Wyl's head spin. He reeled backwards against the circle of youths.

The young minions helpfully shoved Wyl staggering back towards the center and Lord Martei.

Wyl spit out a milk tooth, tasted blood where a broken edge had cut his cheek.

He tried to bring his staff up into a defensive guard position until his head cleared, but a flurry of hard blows, impossibly fast, battered him about his shoulders and head. Lord Martei again swept him off his feet—and kept on striking him.

Wyl's *byrnney* absorbed some of the shock from the blows as he struggled to get back up.

Then another head shot stunned Wyl.

The edges of his vision blackened. He fell to his hands and knees, everything around him moving drunkenly.

Wyl tried to shake it off. He snatched up his fallen staff, and used it to lever himself upright. He brought it up to guard, still staggering and dizzy.

Again, he was attacked, tripped up by the staff's length, and bashed back off his feet.

Wyl gritted his teeth, tasted blood, and scrambled up once more, trying to parry the blows.

Lord Martei speared him with the end of his staff.

Wyl's breath exploded out of him, his *byrnney* no protection from such a hit.

He went down hard, his head in a spin, his limbs asprawl. His staff dropped from his nerveless fingers.

The Bearcubs burst out laughing.

"Martei definitely put that smug Tras in his place!" Wyl heard Prince Jeik say. "The Little Wolf of Milk Dales, hah!—more like the Puppy of Milk Dales!"

Wyl lay stunned, gasping for breath, helpless and disarmed and surrounded by enemies—it roused a sudden terror in him and he started trembling. He tried to focus on something he could use as a weapon, but his body did not respond.

Shock. It was just shock that he'd never gotten in a blow.

Wyl struggled against nausea and tried to breathe. Anything more was beyond him.

Crown Prince Norren came forward and loomed over him.

"Like I said, you are too young and too small to be in my Young Menney—not that I would have stood for having a Tras among my Bear Cubs, kith or not. Pick yourself up, and go play with the younglings. You will never catch up to the Bear Cubs, not in any of the noble arts and obviously not in the martial ones, either."

"TolDaanyo gore your guts!" Wyl scarcely had enough breath for a weak snarl at the crown prince.

Lord Martei kicked *him* in the gut instead, doubling him over where he lay. "Keep a civil mouth around your betters, Tras trash."

The young Dremn walked around him, smirking.

Wyl's head swam, and his eyes wouldn't let him follow Lord Martei's movement. It was a struggle just to breathe. He lay at these Dremns' dubious mercy, still too stunned and wretchedly nauseated to move.

"I am shocked that your granduncle lets you play with edged weapons when you do not have even the basic skills to use a staff," Crown Prince Norren said. "Here in Dremnar, we expect mastery of the staff *before* learning to use a blade."

Lord Martei completed his disdainful circle around Wyl and squatted next to his head. "You are a fool if you thought brawling with outlaw scum sufficient preparation for facing me."

Wyl made no reply. It was all he could do to continue to gasp for breath. Unfortunately, he could still hear Lord Martei's taunting over the roaring in his head.

He'd always thought he'd made a challenging opponent for his granduncle. He'd never won against Eirgei—but had Eirgei still been holding back, even during those long disciplinary bouts that only ended when he was unconscious?

✦

Crossroads Keep

Breieroz carefully picked out the tiny stitches securing the parchment and unrolled the pigeon's message. She'd been Prince Osbart's protégée long enough that decoding it took only a little longer than if she'd paged through her book of ciphers. She swore under her breath, read the message twice more, this time using her deciphering book to be sure, then ran to bring it to her mentor.

Kith-kin, it said. Helgurdda had claimed kith ties with Trascolm's ancient enemy!

Worse yet, Eirgei was not dead. Instead, he was now trusted as Prince Raldorrei's Right Hand and had somehow become a part of the Icebear menney—and how that was possible, she could not begin to imagine.

The message on the pigeon's other leg had delivered another jolt to her confidence in her mentor's spy network.

How could they have missed the existence of Helgurdda's son?

"The message says Helgurdda claimed to Errengard that he was sired by Hereres," she told her mentor. "Could our spies really have failed us so badly for so long?"

Prince Osbart gave the matter some thought. "No, it is not possible. Such critical postings go to my most skillful and trusted spies—not for them the hazards of assassination attempts."

She nodded. She had already had some experience monitoring their spies among the rebel forces and the one still in Nornholm itself. She considered what she knew of Helgurdda's close companions.

"There is that half-Folk boy who occasionally travels with Helgurdda's inner circle, but we know he is the Dremn mercenary's foster-son." Breieroz knew all there was to know about *him*, especially after she had seen the boy for herself across the Tor River.

Folk tended to be smaller than Tras or Dremn and those outcast at a young age even more so. At a distance, the Folk boy was understandably small enough to be mistaken for a younger boy—or a woman. But she knew enough about the fosterling from their spies' reports to know he was a nasty piece of work, described as Eirgei's best pupil and so vicious, there were fully-grown thugs who walked wide of him.

"But, if the mercenary's fosterling is now fighting in battles, then he is at least sixteen, much too old to be Helgurdda's secret son," Prince Osbart said, tiredly rubbing his face. "Eirgei has always had a care for his honor. He would never make a child into a thug, a killer—especially not a Folk child, not even one disowned by his clan. I am sure Eirgei would have an even greater care for the well-being of a grandnephew, if he does indeed have one. These years of outlawry have changed him a great deal, but surely not that much—there would never have been a blood-feud if not for Eirgei and his damnably inflexible honor!"

So, why had their spies never picked up even a hint that Helgurdda had a son? "A boy hovering around Helgurdda should have attracted attention—" Breieroz began.

"—Wait," Prince Osbart held up one hand, an inward look on his face. "There *was* something, years ago, from the first spy I had planted among the rebels, back when the rebel menney first began forming under Eirgei."

He took a key from a bronze chain around his neck, the sole token of his office as spymaster. There in the viceroye's hall, set into the floor behind his desk, was a Gerisari-made plate of merkusar bronze—blackened-red and priceless, and proof against the most violent thieves.

He opened the trap door and descended into his spymaster's lair. At the bottom of the stairs, he stopped and looked back at her. "Come, Lady Breieroz, and pull the trap door shut behind you."

She descended into the dark well and jumped when the lock automatically re-engaged. A Gerisari crystal overhead, as priceless as the merkusar, gave off a faint yellow light, sufficient to keep her from breaking her neck on the steep stairs.

Prince Osbart had started to peruse a rack of codices. "Lady Breieroz, if you would be so kind as to light the candles? I fear the crystal is not bright enough for my old eyes to read fading ink."

At the bottom of the stairs was another desk, surrounded by racks of codices and with a pair of candle trees flanking it on either side. Breieroz turned her two rings, one set high on her forefinger, the other on her thumb, until the bezels met. One was set with a bit of firemetal cast to look like a gem, the other was set with a well-worn flint, and when she snapped her fingers, striking the two rings against each other, a shower of sparks answered.

It was a showy enough trick that Breieroz had once heard a bond-servant mutter to another that she surely used sorcery to do it, both a compliment to her finesse and an insult, in reckoning her a sorcerer.

She caught the sparks in the tinderbox on Prince Osbart's desk and lit all the candles, then took up a smaller branch of candlesticks from the desk and joined the spymaster.

He took it from her and proceeded to jog his memory.

"There are some secrets too dangerous to commit to writing, but even more dangerous to forget," he told her. "And until now, I have been the only one who knows those secrets in their entirety. If one of them ripens, I pass it on to the royenne. Until then, they lie dormant here."

Breieroz took in the large set of racks for holding codices. She was thankful that he had to go back only thirteen years—no farther back than the incident that had triggered the blood-feud. But she could see the records of his spies' reports from those last thirteen years outnumbered the reports kept by his predecessors for nearly all the hundred years before that—all the years that the Evroza had ruled a united Trascolm. Breieroz recognized her mentor's handwriting on the spines of countless codices.

"It was perhaps ten years ago, the memory I am trying to refresh.

There was a report made by Leinvar back when he was still in the field, during the time when Eirgei went from being an outlaw to a rebel and raised a rebel menney for Helgurdda." Prince Osbart scanned the spidery spine inscriptions.

Finally, he found the one he wanted.

"Leinvar was one of my best spies and his reports were always full of important information, but the report I am looking for contained something that had struck me as no more than irrelevantly odd at the time I recorded it."

He paged through the book, looking for the incident in the spy's recounting.

"It took place just as Leinvar was forced to flee the rebel menney— only a passing observation amid pieces of Eirgei's battle strategy for the earliest of the rebel campaigns."

Breieroz went to stand beside him, peering over his arm at the report.

"Ah, here it is! It notes the presence of *a youngling boy, hardly more than a toddler*—that is the first and only time a youngling was mentioned by any of my spies or observers. *The youngling had wandered into Helgurdda's tent during a meeting of the rebel warlords.* Leinvar had been eavesdropping on them and had nearly been discovered because of that child, who had come out of the tent crying over some sharp words Eirgei had used to make him leave. I remember Leinvar said the boy made such a fuss outside the tent that he almost gave away his presence there, spying. And that is the whole of it," Osbart said, closing the codex. "Not so much as a description or a name, but the gender and age would be right. How far would a child that young stray from its mother?"

"Farther than you might think," Breieroz said, who was not too old to recall her own and her brother Reichert's early childhood adventures.

"Well, I need to learn more before I conclude that the youngling in the report is this secret son." Prince Osbart gestured for her to lead the way up the stairs and out of the secret archives. "Leinvar is no longer one of my spies. His days in the field are long over. Shortly after that incident, he had a narrow escape from the rebels that compromised his identity and his health. He now spends his days on the steward's business, using his analytical skills to delve into harvest and tribute discrepancies. He is somewhere in that warren of workrooms in the old portion of the palace. Find him and bring him to me."

Breieroz nodded. She climbed the stairs by the dim crystal's light, unlatched the trap door, and went to fetch the former spy while her mentor locked away his secrets.

Prince Osbart was back at his desk when Breieroz returned with Leinvar.

Leinvar had responded to his summons eagerly. The former spy apparently missed his days in the field: he had dropped whatever it was he did to immediately go with her.

Breieroz shut the door and settled into a curule chair while Leinvar stood at her mentor's desk and scanned the transcript of his old report.

"Early days, those," Leinvar commented. "Back then, wasn't there even an attempt by Prince-Magus Odomazer to have a rehearing on Helgurdda's charges against Princess—I mean, Royenne—Ragna?"

"That is the time period, yes. Do you remember the youngling?" asked Prince Osbart.

"The youngling?"

"The one in the report, who started babbling to you when he got run out of the tent and nearly gave you away?"

Leinvar frowned. "He was just a Folk youngling, though come to think of it, that was before Eirgei had taken to recruiting Folk outcasts and other outlaws. Why?"

Prince Osbart tapped his lips. "Was that the first time you had seen him? Who was his mother? Boy that young had to have a mother nearby."

Leinvar shook his head. "I'd probably seen him around—who pays attention to younglings like that when surrounded by full-grown traitors and cutthroats?"

Breieroz nodded. *Good point.*

"Any chance the youngling was Helgurdda's?"

Leinvar looked incredulous. "Helgurdda had a son?"

"Has one. I am told she claims he is the spitting image of his sire."

Leinvar shook his head. "Never having laid eyes on Hereres, I can't speak to that, but I can tell you this son's not the same boy as in the report."

"How can you be so certain?"

Leinvar glanced aside, started when he met Breieroz's eyes, then sighed and limped toward a window, turning his back to them both. "You always said you didn't want to know my methods or how I worked, that all you were interested in was results."

"And?"

"It can't be the same boy because I had to strangle him to shut him up," Leinvar said softly. "But there'd been no outcry afterwards, certainly nothing out of the ordinary in the behavior of Helgurdda and Eirgei, or anyone in the rebel command, nor was there a search for a missing child—I had hidden the body as best I could, and I don't know if it was ever found. I was forced to withdraw several days later, and as you know, I haven't been in the field since then."

Breieroz thought she had remained impassive, but she must have made a sound because Leinvar looked quickly over at her.

"Please, don't look at me like that," he said to her, dropping his eyes. "Those battle plans saved Evroza lives! I wouldn't have killed a child if I'd had a choice." Then Leinvar's voice grew firm, and he looked up and met her gaze steadily. "But it was him or me, and I chose to live to bring home Eirgei's battle plans—not to be a martyr for some Folk bratling who was probably going to die anyway—those outlaw camps were rife with summer fever."

Now it was her turn to look away.

Spying was not a job for the faint-hearted. Nor was there any honor in it, on account of just such ruthless acts as this—a truth she tried hard never to dwell upon. It would have to be enough that Evroza lives were saved—she couldn't have it both ways.

Leinvar turned to Prince Osbart. "So, you say Helgurdda has a son?"

Breieroz was glad to return the business at hand.

"Yes," Prince Osbart said. "And we knew nothing of him until now—my agent in Nornholm reported his presence when Helgurdda petitioned Errengard for asylum in Dremnar."

Leinvar looked at him incredulously. *"Asylum in Dremnar?!"* He shook his head. "I don't believe it!"

"Believe it," the royenne's spymaster said.

The former spy's face turned pensive. "They probably fostered the boy. That's what I'd do, if I were in Helgurdda's position—a menney's no place for a youngling, certainly not for a baby and especially not around those brutes Eirgei collected for her. Though, until Helgurdda started recruiting outlaws, there was little enough to her rebellion—no menney, nothing but rumors about her and Eirgei. Wasn't until they were able to field a menney that we even had anything to spy upon."

"True enough. My thanks."

Leinvar reluctantly departed.

Breieroz frowned. Was that the key to this whole Dremnar debacle, that Helgurdda's son had been fostered in Dremnar? "The boy had to have been fostered somewhere out of sight, but smuggling him into Dremnar in time to be presented to Royenne Errengard alongside his mother, a mere two days after they crossed the Tor?"

Her mentor nodded. "The logistics are impossible—unless this betrayal has been years in the making. Helgurdda must have given the boy over to Royenne Errengard as surety, and the royenne, in turn, had hidden the boy somewhere near enough to Nornholm for convenience, yet not so near that my spy in Nornholm would know of him."

"And that would explain why Eirgei was so sure of his welcome in Dremnar that he would risk plunging into the Tor!" Breieroz said.

✦

Nornholm

Wyl lay on a pallet in the Heir's Tower understory infirmary, his head still spinning, his guts aching and empty, and his eyes closed. He didn't care that he missed his dinner. He doubted it would stay down anyway. Crown Prince Norren had sent him here after Martei was through with him, saying he was no longer in the Bearcubs, and that, at fourteen, he wasn't welcome to stay with the younger boys on the fourth floor, either.

There was supposed to be a healer down here, but the healer was Folk, and Wyl hadn't seen her since he slumped in from the Menney Tower courtyard.

He tongued the spot with the missing molar and the matching cut inside his cheek and wondered that Lord Martei hadn't managed to break his jaw, too.

He hadn't thought he'd need *luck* to win. As it turned out, he'd been lucky to survive. Though his attempted parries had been overpowered, they still had bled off some of the killing force behind Lord Martei's blows.

The door opened, and the youngest of the Icebear princes slipped inside.

"I heard what happened," Prince Lokei said. "How badly did he hurt you?"

"I'm not hurt," Wyl said sharply. "Crown Prince Norren just couldn't think of where else to put me tonight."

Prince Lokei peered at his face and shook his head. "Your face is already starting to swell. Are you sure you are all right?"

"Of course, I am. Do you see me bleeding?"

"You are very lucky, then. The last time Martei beat someone like this, it was my cousin Reien, and he broke Reien's leg. It was not an accident, either. He meant to do it."

"Just like he meant to accidentally take my head off," Wyl said, breathing carefully to keep from throwing up, trying to hide what it cost him simply to talk.

Just then, the Folk healer put her head around the edge of the door and scowled. "Prince Lokei, you aren't supposed to be here. The Tras boy's supposed to be resting. Please leave immediately!"

Prince Lokei grimaced at Wyl and pulled something from under his surcoat.

"Elfreida made me promise to give you this," Prince Lokei said, hastily thrusting it at him.

Wyl scarcely heard the prince's words—his left hand had already yanked a knife from the cuff of his boot. Just before he drew it all the way out, he realized Prince Lokei wasn't coming at him with a knife.

It was a toy—a little stuffed horse.

He stared down at the thing, utterly baffled. *What am I supposed to do with this?*

"Prince Lokei! You must leave. Now."

Prince Lokei leaned close to Wyl's ear. "Elfreida says you like horses, so she thinks this one will help make you feel better."

Wyl picked it up. *How is it supposed to do that? Magic of some kind?* It was small enough to fit between his hands and had a horsehair mane and tail.

"Do not worry about it," Prince Lokei said. "She is only eight and thinks stuffed animals can do anything."

"Prince Lokei!"

The stripling prince glanced over his shoulder at the healer. Then he reached towards Wyl.

Wyl hadn't let down his guard, in case the toy was a ruse; when Prince Lokei moved, he flung himself off the pallet, putting it between himself and Prince Lokei, though he staggered and wobbled, and then dry-heaved for doing it.

But the prince's hand was empty of any weapon, and the stripling looked at Wyl, his hand outstretched and a puzzled expression on his face.

Then the healer came all the way into the room, took the Icebear prince by the arm, and hustled him away. She slammed the door behind her.

The sound smashed through Wyl's aching head.

✦

Later that night, Wyl lay fully-clothed on top of his infirmary bed. The door couldn't be bolted shut, so he fought the urge to sleep away his headache. He wasn't so great a fool as to take off his *byrnney*, day or night, in this place—no more than he would in a brigand camp.

Particularly after today.

He reviewed the day's humiliating events and wished Eirgei's control had slipped that morning while he'd been thrashed around the practice floor, his punishment for trying to leave Nornholm on his own. He wished he'd been struck with the edge rather than the flat of Eirgei's blade. Death, at least, would have spared him from enduring the mockery of the Young Court.

Blind? She thinks I'm blind?

Eirgei was right. Wyl needed to fight with a different sort of weapon here—he hadn't understood what Eirgei had meant, not until the crown princess had demonstrated she didn't need a sword to cut him down.

It forced him to admit the crown princess had spoken nothing but the truth. He didn't belong here any more than he did anywhere else. Even the pampered crown princess knew it.

He wished he still belonged with Helgurdda and Eirgei.

Back in the wild hill-country of Milkdales, in those frequent times of crisis, there'd be hot-tempered councils of war between Eirgei, Helgurdda, and their warlords. He'd listened to countless nights of strategizing while on guard, silent and feigning sleep on his bedroll outside Helgurdda's command tent as the warlords debated.

As part of his training as a spy, Eirgei would quiz him the next day on the strategies and tactics raised, and occasionally about the true, underlying interest in the arguments of some ally of convenience. Sometimes, as part of his training to be Eirgei's successor, Eirgei would even ask Wyl's opinion on what kind of response he'd make to a situation, and on a heartwarming number of occasions, Eirgei had even included his ideas in his final strategy. Then, after the fighting, he'd quiz Wyl again on the execution of it: what had worked, what hadn't, and why.

So, why wasn't Eirgei including him in the planning, now?

There was no longer any reason to hide Wyl's role in devising rebel tactics when all of Nornholm knew who he was.

Eirgei had often said he had good instincts, a good head for strategy. So, in the absence of Calderek and the other warlords, shouldn't his ideas be all the more welcome?

Obviously not.

And he still didn't know what Eirgei meant by *learning from the Young Court*. All he'd learn from the Young Court were skills more suited to scribes and clerks—and what was the point in studying barbarian laws useless in Trascolm? If the point was for him to learn to be a prince, then these Dremn were teaching him everything *but* that.

Even he knew that what really set the nobility apart from ordinary Tras was skill at arms and leadership in battle, things only noblemen—or rebels, clanless brigands, and mercenaries—had the leisure to acquire.

Maybe, he reluctantly conceded, the ability to read and write Runic might be useful to a spy confined to a foreign land amidst unreliable allies, but reckoning? He knew enough to convert spoils into proper shares and to estimate an enemy's numbers. He had no need to know anything more than that.

Likewise with learning the law of the land, either Dremn or Tras. One advantage to being an outlaw was that, no matter what the crown princess said, rules and laws didn't apply to him. If he relied on the law to protect him, whether facing the Evroza, Myymor's town guard, or brigand-rebels in their camp, it would only get him killed. Now that he was in exile, he couldn't afford to let his guard down, to let his instincts—the ones Eirgei had once praised—go unheeded.

Ever since he'd arrived in Nornholm, he'd felt like he was under constant, critical scrutiny by everyone he encountered, from bondservants to Folk to Dremn nobility. Though he'd felt a certain odd kinship with the outlawed Folk in Helgurdda's menney back in Milkdales, here amid Nornholm's surprisingly large Folk population, he felt like he was surrounded by enemies. Despite being under the explicit protection of Icebear clan, he didn't feel protected or safe. His nerves were constantly on edge. He never knew what to expect here from one moment to the next, and the longer he was in Nornholm, the more out of place he felt.

He missed Milkdales and his old life.

He didn't want to have time to get used to Nornholm, to feel as much at home here as he did in Myymor, or in the dales, or even in brigand territory, the hill-country containing the Forest of Alshemir and Dawngate Pass.

He'd never have thought he'd miss life as a rebel, rubbing shoulders with cutthroat, dangerously untrustworthy allies during the winter, stealing secrets from the Evroza during the summer, always in peril of his life. During his past four summers in Myymor, he'd made free with Evroza secrets, even boldly roamed the very heart of their clanhold. The worst that had happened to him in Myymor had been coming down with summer fever, and that hadn't had anything to do with the Evroza.

He didn't really care where he was, if only he could be with his family. If he could only be with them when surrounded by brigands and rebels again, then better that than being alone and surrounded by hostile, young Dremn noblemen.

More than ever, he wished he'd escaped Nornholm without Eirgei's interference. How else could he redeem himself for sparing that mage at Helgurdda's expense?

He'd never be able to rest until he did.

CHAPTER 19

KITH-KIN

6th Day of the Moon of Storms, 113 G.E.

The next morning, Kotakei glanced up from her codex of an ances-tor's decrees. She stole a look at Prince Tras, who sat at the far end of the Young Court hall with the younglings.

Prince Tras had entered the hall late, no doubt because he'd had trouble dressing himself in noble attire for the first time. He wore Ice Bear kith-colors of black and white, the Ice Bear colors reversed for kith-kin so the black predominated—a black surcoat of reversed mar-ten pelt trimmed with ice bear fur covered most of a white, high-necked tunic and a black undertunic that showed the bit of black leg-gings at the side-slits that weren't covered by his high boots. There was none of the embroidery or quillwork on tunic or leggings that enliv-ened the stark clan colors of the other, true Ice Bears—another re-minder that the Folk of Norn Holm, including the tiring servants to the Young Court, hated the sight of him.

But simple seemed to suit him. Stranger still, in noble garb, he seemed like anything *but* a child, whatever age he claimed.

In fact, with the addition of a princely gold torc, Prince Tras looked disconcertingly elegant, despite the cropped portion of his gleaming black hair—or he would have, if he were not still wearing his ragged red surcoat over his black-furred Ice Bear one. The line of his fitted black sleeves was marred by the bright-scratched, bronze-mounted bracers he wore over them, and the bulkiness of his form over his slender legs told her that he still wore his *byrnney* under his fur surcoat.

However, there was nothing elegant about his swollen and bruised face.

Word of how he had been humiliated at staves yesterday had gleefully swept through all of Norn Holm before the day was over—a sure sign that Grandmother's grudging acceptance of her Tras kith-kin was not shared by everyone.

Last night, Norren had insisted that Prince Tras spend the night in the tower's ground floor infirmary. This morning, her brother had come to warn her to be careful—Prince Tras had not taken the decision to bar him from the Bear Cubs well, despite the thorough beating Martei had given him, and he would be looking to avenge his humiliation today.

That prospect certainly did not seem to frighten the Bear Cubs.

"Here comes our newest youngling!" her cousin Jeik bellowed the moment he caught sight of Prince Tras.

Prince Tras narrowed his eyes and bristled.

"Ever figure out what to do with your stick?" Martei gave a snorting laugh, and it touched off a wave of smug amusement around the hall.

Prince Tras's jaw muscles flexed. He gave Martei a bleak and dangerous look. "You want to try it again, backstabber? Let's see how it turns out this time."

Martei flushed at the accusation. "It was a duel, fool. There are no rules. And I think one beating was enough." Martei curled his lip disdainfully.

Prince Tras's hands fisted at his sides, but he made no move to attack.

A wise decision, with the odds so much against him.

That set the tone for the rest of the morning. The Bear Cubs boldly exchanged smirks and barbed comments with Prince Tras at every opportunity, harping on his humiliation without ever giving him the satisfaction of violence, refusing to let him lure them into the fight he clearly wanted.

After lessons were over and everyone had taken their seats for the midday meal, the younglings chattered and competed for Prince Tras's attention as if he hadn't been the subject of snide jokes all morning. The younglings took no notice of the taunts, nor did they seem sense anything odd about Prince Tras the way Kotakei did.

He and Martei were two of a kind, but in Prince Tras, Kotakei thought she saw more: little signs of big trouble, hints that there was something very wrong about him. She could not have put into words what told her that, but she had a growing suspicion that he was not right in his head.

Helgurdda was mad, so why not her son, too? The conditions in which he'd lived, keeping company with brigands and surely always in fear of his life, had to have affected him. He couldn't possibly be a *normal* boy. There was something *off* about him, and the only question in her mind was, *how mad is he—and how dangerous?*

But the rapport that had developed between the younglings and Prince Tras was surprisingly strong, and it seemed unaffected by yesterday's beating or this morning's mockery from the Bear Cubs.

She frowned, watching her young cousins, Lokei and Elfreida, circling around Prince Tras, waiting for him to look up and notice them.

She could not see Prince Tras's face, only the top of his head. He was still crouched over the wax tablet in his lap—which should have been an uncomfortable position to maintain for so long. The blue-black sheen of his hair was eye-catching—as was the spectacular array of bruises on either side of his face when he suddenly looked up and caught her staring.

She quickly looked away, resenting how her eyes had been drawn across the hall to him. She did not know why Prince Tras still drew her attention—he was not so pretty now.

She watched Lokei, who now stood silently among the waiting younglings crowding close with piping cries for attention.

Lokei had always been conscious of his responsibilities as the only stripling among the younger boys and as the next highest-ranking young Ice Bear prince, after Norren. He had always been a good example to the younglings, a calming, sensible influence.

Now, however, Lokei had fallen so deeply under Prince Tras's spell that today he had been doing his best to imitate the Tras boy's arrogant bearing and predatory stalk. Despite the beating yesterday—or perhaps, because of it—an unsettling air of menace still clung to Prince Tras. Lokei had a long way to go before he could carry that off.

She couldn't help feeling a sense of looming disaster.

If only Grandmother had sent the Tras rebels back to where they had come from, kith-kin or not.

✦

Crossroads Keep

In the private splendor of the royenne's scent garden in Crossroads Keep, Breieroz casually leaned against a pillar in the open gallery overlooking the little courtyard. Below her, Prince-Envoy Kreseyn took his leave of Royenne Ragna with his usual courtly grace, serenely unaware that Breieroz had him under discreet surveillance.

"I am delighted to be of service, and when I stop at Dawngate Pass, I will order a legion be sent to help quell the spread of rebellion, should Evroza's enemies see in this tragedy an opportunity for an uprising," the Gerisari envoy said, with a courtly bow from one knee that made his long, wispy white hair brush the ground. "I will inform my empress of how your mother succumbed to her long illness and passed away."

Breieroz frowned at that.

There had been too many witnesses to Royenne Sharei's collapse to hope the truth would not spread to those who had not been present, and frankly, it would shock her mentor when she reported the envoy claimed ignorance of the true manner of her death.

They expected better intelligence-gathering from such an experienced diplomat—which was the reason why Prince Osbart had been so eager to send the Gerisari prince away on Ragna's double errand—the first, to obtain the loan of a Gerisari legion, and the second, to buy Helgurdda's and Eirgei's heads from Errengard of Dremnar. The viceroye had his own reasons for wanting those too-keen Gerisari eyes and ears out of Crossroads Keep.

"Because I will not be here to convey them after my empress learns of your mother's fate," the envoy continued, "I give you now the regrets that Empress Jerhafyne will express, along with her hopes of continuing her friendship with the Evroza, and the long and mutually profitable alliance between Gerisar and Trascolm. I assure you that I—and Gerisar—stand ready to do whatever we can to preserve your sovereignty from the rebels. I will send word to Seacourt and have treasures to tempt the barbarian ruler waiting for me at Dawngate Pass."

"And my thanks to you for that," Ragna said, offering her hand in farewell. "Your friendship, as well as that of Empress Jerhafyne, has helped us through the worst of this rebellion. Your counsel will be missed. Be safe on your journey to treat with those barbarians."

Breieroz thought it clever of Prince Osbart to send Prince Kreseyn to learn all he could about the kind of reception Royenne Errengard had given the rebels, while at the same time, depriving the Gerisari empress of the same kind of information about Royenne Ragna and what kind of reception *she* received from the great clans of Trascolm when she formally took up the reins of power in Crossroads Keep some days after Prince Kreseyn's departure.

Breieroz would not miss the envoy at all. She would be glad to see the last of the suave prince of the royal House of Doromont for a while. Prince Kreseyn made her uneasy.

She was glad her mentor employed a vast number of spies and watched over his royal charge with such obsessive—if flawed—care.

✦

Nornholm

After everyone had assembled for the midday meal, Norren surprised Kotakei by standing to make an announcement.

"Due to the icy rain outside, the courtyards are too miserable and treacherous for our regular martial training. Instead, we will play a senet tournament. Since there will be a public tournament for the prince-viceroye's birthday in the Moon of Snow, not two moons away, this will be good practice for us all."

There were enthusiastic nods of assent up and down the table. Fortunes could be won or lost betting on the outcome of a senet tourney and winning brought its own measure of acclaim.

"Also, because Prince Wylheim is no longer a part of the Bear Cubs, at his request, he will hereafter be going back to live with his mother in Tras Tower when he is not attending my sister's Young Court."

Laughter and babble broke out as Norren sat down next to Kotakei.

"You cannot do that!" she hissed. "What of your part in showing him kin-favor?"

"Where else should he go?" Norren retorted, not troubling to lower his voice to match hers. "He's not a youngling, so he can't sleep on the fourth floor, and he's no longer part of the Bear Cubs, so he can't sleep on the sixth."

She did not raise her voice, but kept it low. "And what of Ice Bear honor?"

"Well, if it is a matter of showing kin-favor, then I have already done it—he asked to sleep in Tras Tower on his first day here. Allowing him to spend his nights away from the Bear Cubs is inarguably special treatment, especially now. Of course," Norren smiled, "already you can hear unflattering comparisons being made between the Tras and the youngest younglings who sleep in the Heir's Tower and do not go home to *their* mothers. Now even the younglings have reason to despise him."

The younglings, at the far end of the table, did not act like they despised him, but Prince Tras's face was set like a stone mask. Kotakei could not tell whether he truly was pleased by Norren's announcement or not.

After the meal, as the boards were cleared, she saw the younglings were not the least bit frightened off by Prince Tras's air of sullen, bruised menace. Lokei not only stayed at his side, he put his little sister Elfreida between them where she could hold both their hands—with Prince Tras looking awkward and uncomfortable as she did.

He looked so incongruous, sitting on the floor, towering over the little ones, yet flinching back whenever they brandished toys for him to admire. Though he looked grim and out of place, he did not seem bent on harming any of the younglings.

All the same, she resolved to give Prince Tras an early release from court each day to ensure the younglings would not be left alone with him when the rest of the Young Court went for their martial training or archery practice.

She tossed the sticks and waited for her brother to gather them back up for his throw to determine which of them would move first. Across the senet table from her, Norren—with Martei, as ever, at his back—pretended not to be watching the younglings clustered around Prince Tras.

Whenever Prince Tras's gaze drifted across the hall and rested on Martei, which was often, she could swear their silver glimmer held the vengeful promise of another meeting in them.

Probably when Martei least expected it.

✦

Wyl was glad he'd been seated with the younglings for the midday meal. He'd eaten little—his head still hurt from yesterday's beating. He'd stiffened up so badly that putting the width of the Young Court hall between himself and Lord Martei seemed wise.

The younglings continued to surprise him, treating him like kin, not merely kith—and most definitely, not like an outcast. In fact, they treated him more like family than his family did. He'd even had a brief visit from Prince Lokei while in the infirmary, until the Folk healer had appeared long enough to chase him out—he hadn't seen the healer before or since. Or his mother or granduncle, either.

That didn't matter. He hadn't been bleeding, so he hadn't needed a healer. And he didn't blame Helgurdda and Eirgei for not coming to him—he'd humiliated them with his defeat. Besides, the whole point of his being sent to the Young Court was to break the connection between him and them.

But it wasn't just the younglings' friendliness that made this a fortunate seating arrangement for the midday meal.

Why was he so surprised that these younglings had so many fascinating things to say about everything he wanted to know about the Crown Court and without even having to ask? Younglings were younglings everywhere, and it hadn't been that long ago that he had been one himself. He knew first-hand that adults, whether Tras, Folk, or brigand, felt free to speak over a youngling's head. Not even Eirgei or Helgurdda had ever realized how much he'd remembered of what he'd heard them say, even if he hadn't always immediately understood it.

It hadn't taken him long to get that understanding. By the time he'd been the age of these noble younglings, intrigue had already become a matter of life or death for him. Understanding the actions and behavior of the adults around him had been all that had kept him alive, and later, it made him useful to Eirgei as a spy.

He felt like a young Eirgei with these younglings reporting to him like a troop of little spies. They told him who they were and of which clans—though only Icebear clan was familiar to him—and told him who their clan's courtiers were in Royenne Errengard's Crown Court. He'd learned more today in an hour at table than he could've learned in a moon of dedicated spying on his own as an outsider.

But no matter their ease with him, he was too old to belong with the younglings, and he didn't want to stay among them. Who would fear him if the younglings made him their favorite? If he couldn't make the Young Court fear and respect him—and soon—someone would get badly hurt when the time came to take hostages. Considering the odds, with all the Bearcubs dead-set against him and not the least respectful, that someone was likely to be him.

And the younglings were already too much at ease with him. They kept carelessly trying to handle him, tugging at his clothes to get his attention, as if they'd nothing to fear—which they didn't. He was too stiff and sore, and—as Lanney had often complained—too soft-hearted. He couldn't find it in him to make the younglings show him a respectful fear.

He felt guilty for allowing their casual friendliness towards him, and ashamed at how much a welcome relief it was from his endless vigilance, now that Lanney was no longer watching his back. But he couldn't drive them off—these younglings had just given him the means to persuade Eirgei that he was still valuable to the rebellion, regardless of whether or not they'd have to use his hostage-escape plan.

Given time to ponder and make sense of the random things these younglings had seen and overheard—and innocently repeated to him—he could now begin to put together a tidy picture of Nornholm and Royenne Errengard's court and its undercurrents of ambition and hostility. When he was finished, Eirgei would have to recognize that he needed Wyl. Even what little Wyl knew now would be crucial in any scheme his elders were setting up to wheedle a Dremn menney out of Royenne Errengard.

And if it were true, what he'd just heard, that the royenne had become suddenly, unexpectedly reluctant to meet with Helgurdda, then this was not the time for them to start ignoring his contributions to the cause.

Ever since they'd crossed the Tor, stripped of their menney and everything except what had been on their horses' backs, something had changed. Helgurdda hadn't quit the fight—she wouldn't so long as Ragna lived—so it was impossible that she and Eirgei weren't working on some fresh strategy.

That made information-gathering even more important.

Word of Eirgei's unbelievable defeat would have spread like wildfire through Milkdales. But, by fleeing into Dremnar, Wyl had already lost his best chance to overhear what the Evroza minions who'd witnessed what had happened that day on the river road had to say of it. They would've been the ones with the most facts about their mage to bandy about. Now, there'd only be wild rumors being spread by people who hadn't even been there. With this delay, by the time Eirgei did send him back into Milkdales, all he'd hear would be nothing but the most outrageous lies rather than something useful about the weather-mage.

Eirgei needed to know more about her, no matter how much he scorned mages and magery as *unreliable crutches for flawed planning.* That strange mage had caused the disaster in Milkdales. How could they expect to fight and win against something they didn't understand? Wyl's spying skills were desperately needed if they were to change their fortunes.

So, why had Eirgei and Helgurdda suddenly forgotten that?

✦

Later that night, Wyl sat snugly bundled against the cold on his sleeping pallet at the top of Tras Tower with the door to his room securely bolted. He relaxed back against the door—it was less cold than the walls—and put together in his mind what the younglings had told him, as if he'd actually get a chance to report those things to Helgurdda or Eirgei.

If Eirgei really didn't want to know about the mage, and if their prospects for a Dremn menney were so good Eirgei didn't think they'd need his hostage-escape plan, then, if he wasn't needed here, why prevent him from returning to Milkdales on his own?

He mulled that over, pretending he was Eirgei, trying to see the situation from Eirgei's eyes.

The answer was embarrassingly obvious.

Of course, Eirgei realized he *did* need to know more about the mage—which meant Eirgei needed him for a *real* mission to gather that very information about the Evroza's new weather-magery.

Getting back into Milkdales would be harder the longer Eirgei waited before sending him, but not impossible. Iceroad Pass wouldn't be firm until into the new year, but probably Eirgei intended him to use the same rugged route through the Black Mountains that he'd meant to take into Milkdales on his personal mission to avenge Lanney.

If Eirgei sent him on a real mission for Helgurdda, and did it soon, he might still reach Dawngate Pass before snow closed it. The pass itself was guarded, but the guardsmen were only up to strength during the warm trading season, when they stayed busy protecting merchant caravans from raiders—and not from stray, outcast Folk boys.

The reason for holding him back was clear now—Eirgei had to raise and assess his Dremn menney's capabilities first, before he sent Wyl anywhere. If the Dremn forces turned out to be particularly strong, Eirgei would strike out directly for Crossroads Keep and send Wyl in advance to discover what he could about the Evroza's menney and that weather-mage.

If the Dremn were—as Wyl expected—less disciplined, Eirgei

would want to join his forces with whatever minions Calderek still commanded, which would mean sending Wyl first to Myymor, at the opposite end of Milkdales from Crossroads Keep, to locate Calderek and bring him word of Eirgei's battle plans.

But if Wyl departed before the Dremn menney had been recruited, once he was back in Milkdales, Eirgei would have no means to get word to him and Calderek of his plan of attack.

No matter which direction Eirgei took his menney, Evroza's seer, Prince-Magus Odomazer, would ensure he faced that strange weather-mage again, and Eirgei had to know it, even if he didn't fear the weather-mage as he should.

Wyl intended to see to it that the next time Helgurdda's minions met the Evroza in battle, there would be no weather-magery. Eirgei would smash the Evroza as they deserved, finally ending the blood-feud, and wiping out all memory of that unnaturally disastrous day on the river road.

✦

10ᵗʰ Day of the Moon of Storms, 113 G.E.
Crossroads Keep

Royenne Sharei's state funeral kept all Prince-Viceroye Osbart's observers busy, including Breieroz. Six days after Royenne Sharei's death, the entire Evroza clan, royal, noble, and commoner, had arrived for her funeral and burning. All the great baronnes of Trascolm were present, come to renew their treaties with the new royenne. The most prominent members of every barony and major clan in Trascolm were also there—and the less prominent ones, too, just to witness the spectacle in the Royenne's Courtyard at dusk.

As Prince Osbart's secret, eventual successor, Breieroz accompanied him everywhere, maintaining the appearance of being merely a devoted page at his beck and call, just as her brother Reichert was to Lord Goffray. Whenever others were around, she was careful to present the appearance of keeping a discreet distance between herself and the viceroye's business.

Prince Osbart had said her first duties as his protégée were to become familiar with the challenges a spy faced, with the emphasis more on not being caught than on what information she uncovered. He had been at pains to assure her that there was no dishonor in it for an underage girl, especially when knowing all that passed within the walls of

Crossroads Keep would one day be her duty and the hiring of spies would be a part of that duty.

In her first lesson as a spy, she had learned that a spy needed uncommon courage and particularly keen ears.

Thus, she stood just within earshot when Prince Osbart had presented his plan for the funeral to Royenne Ragna, confirming that all the baronnes and their heirs would come to Crossroads Keep as was customary, in a show of good faith for their treaty-making with a new royenne. But it would be just a show—and the baronnes didn't know that, this time, it would be Royenne Ragna's show.

An Evroza royenne, Prince Osbart had emphasized, never took the loyalty of her baronnes for granted, even after taking their direst oaths. Hence, the surprise Royenne Ragna would unveil at the conclusion of her eulogy.

Royenne Sharei's skillfully-preserved body had been laid on its bier, the other eulogies were spoken, and then there was the dramatic application of magery by wizened, sad-faced Prince-Magus Odomazer—a small explosion over the bier, followed by a dramatic, smoky fire. When the smoke cleared, there was nothing but ash left on the stonework.

Breieroz took note of the baronne of Jegurett clan's uneasy reaction to that casual display of Evroza clan's unique power.

"…And so we say farewell to our baronne and our royenne," Royenne Ragna concluded, her voice breaking. "Thirteen years of blood-feud and defiance ground my mother down and stole away her health. I swear to you all that I will bring this blood-feud to an end in blood and fire!"

Royenne Ragna paused and gave a predatory smile to her supposedly loyal baronnes. "To that end, I have accepted the service of a Gerisari legion to reassure the rest of Trascolm that the rule of law remains in effect. Also, I am extending my hospitality to Trascolm's hope of the future—our children. All the heirs of the ruling clans and noble clans who are underage, along with the male kin and age-mate of her choosing, will remain here in Crossroads Keep as honored members of Crown Princess Sheinhild's Young Court. Those who are of age—and their companion of choice—will attend me as part of my Crown Court."

Breieroz supposed that in any other realm, that declaration would have been taken as a great honor. In Trascolm, it sparked an angry outburst from the clan baronnes, especially the baronne of Erythgold clan. Breieroz was sure the invitation to the heirs came as no surprise to the great ruling baronnes. Certainly, as Baronne of Redmont Barony as well as Jegurett clan, Baronne Radeygga had to have been prepared to part with her heir—the timing was bad for her to refuse to attend, since that meant a premature rebellion. Bringing her heir as a potential hostage would be the baronne's only assurance that she herself would be free to return to her barony. But, as Prince Osbart had warned, the lesser clan baronnes had not expected to leave their heirs behind and were dismayed to a greater degree than Breieroz had anticipated.

The hubbub quickly subsided when Royenne Ragna's newly-arrived Gerisari legion marched into the courtyard at Lord Goffray's signal.

"You are taking hostages!" the baronne of Erythgold clan cried out, clutching her young daughter to her.

"No," Royenne Ragna said, "your heirs are remaining because they are fit companions for my daughter and heir. Perhaps if they grow up together, there will be fewer misunderstandings when they take up their clan responsibilities. I assure you, they will all be treated with the same courtesy as any Evroza child, and you are welcome to come to my court to visit them as often as you please."

Over the course of the last few days, Breieroz had learned that the most troublesome clans were skeptical of the honor of an Evroza royenne, so it did not surprise her that the baronnes heard that last statement with no real relief.

Whether they believed Royenne Ragna would hold to that promise did not matter—the ploy with their heirs would ensure that all of Trascolm did not ignite into civil war. Royenne Ragna needed to buy time to settle the blood-feud with the Traditionalists—those Evrozings who had backed Eirgei and Helgurdda—and do it without risking all of Trascolm rising up behind her back.

Now she was free to pursue the remaining rebels and their supporters until no trace of the rebellion remained.

Part Three

CHAPTER 20

SPINNING A SPIDER'S WEB

15ᵗʰ Day of the Moon of Storms, 113 G.E.
Nornholm

Crown Princess Kotakei dismissed Wyl from the Young Court after the last senet game, when the younglings and Prince Lokei were sent to play, and the youths, both boys and girls, went to their martial training with staff or bow.

He left the Heir's Tower, conscious that everywhere he went, people stared at him.

He hated it.

People not only stared, they also whispered and laughed.

Even Tras Tower wasn't a refuge—the two hostile bondservants Garei had found for them were ever-so-slowly cleaning the tower and were still inclined to declare their outrage at serving unrepentant outlaws, their inferiors under the law of the land—no matter that the three of them had not violated that law in Dremnar.

He had wanted to find a private place, and since there were no sentries on the upper bailey wall except at night, he'd thought it the perfect place. But now that he was up here, he could see just how many tower windows overlooked the parapet. The best he could do was curl up in a crenel at the far eastern edge of the battlements, where only the Heir's Tower overlooked it. It was scarcely ideal, but it was still a better hiding place than on the ground on the north side of the palace, in the rubble behind Tras Tower. That lonely place struck him as the perfect spot for unwitnessed bloodshed.

He huddled in the last crenel with his feet against the face of the quarried cliff, tucked up as small as he could make himself, and hoped everyone in the Heir's Tower who was tall enough to look out a window was at martial practice in the Menney Tower courtyard.

Since the first day he had set foot in Dremnar, nothing had gone right. In fact, after his beating by Lord Martei and being thrown out of the Bearcubs ten days ago, every day had been worse than the one before.

He glanced down to his left, wondering how far it was to the ground, but instead of the ground, he saw sun-grayed, wooden hoardings only a short drop below where he sat.

He straightened with interest.

The wooden walkway looked intact, though it sagged between its supports. The hoardings were intended to hold a second rank of archers outside the parapet, raining arrows like hailstones on some enemy far below in the lower bailey.

He was sure he could stand upright on them and still not be seen from the parapet—or even from the Heir's Tower.

It was the perfect outlaw's lair.

Without a second thought, he flipped his legs over the side of the battlements and dropped onto the boards. They creaked and groaned, but held.

He was almost sorry they did.

He walked softly along the hoardings, quickly learning to beware the boards closest to the stonework where water or snow had collected over the years and left some of those boards half-rotten.

He kept walking until he was directly over the upper bailey's gate, on the other side of the battlements from the central wooden steps he'd climbed to reach the parapet.

The upper bailey's walls were more than a vertical arrow-shot tall, and there was just enough slope to the lower bailey's terraced approach to the High Gate that the edge of the hoardings hid him from below—maybe not completely, but unless someone knew he was here, no one would easily discover him on their own. He was high enough that not even the gate guards could hear anything over the clatter of boots, hoofs, and creaking carts to make them look up through the slats.

If he sat where the boards were still good, put his back to the battlements, and drew his legs up close, no one looking out from the parapet would see him, either, not without sticking a head out past a merlon to look—and letting him know his new lair had been found out.

Best of all, on the hoardings, he was finally free of the suffocating, hate-filled atmosphere of Nornholm.

The hoardings were like another world, and he was the only one in it.

Now he could explore a notion that had come to him as he'd paged through his primer on Runic, thinking about the rune that stood for his name.

He'd had a special fondness for spiders ever since he'd been a youngling, even then prone to nightmares. Rather than being the cause of nightmares, a spider had been an ally against them for as long as he could remember. And now, the spider was his name in Runic.

Lord Geilorren had said the rune represented not a spider, but rather secrets and intrigues.

That had inspired him with an idea for making a spitcraft charm to trap and reveal others' secrets, a charm based on the spider rune.

He'd always used Teboan script to inscribe his charms, but with only occasional success—tying spitcraft to the individual letters that spelled out the charm was tedious and difficult. Impossible, even, if his concentration wavered during the process.

But because Runic glyphs stood for ideas rather than sounds, he suspected it might be particularly well-suited to spitcraft, or at least, easier to use than a Teboan inscription like *luck* or *hide me*.

It made sense—ancient Folk runes ought to make a better fit with an ancient Folk magic like spitcraft than a modern, foreign script did. If switching from using Teboan script to Runic glyphs affected his spitcraft the way he hoped, he'd have a powerful charm when he finished—and what could be more appropriate for him, the rebellion's best spy, than a *trap secrets* charm?

The possibilities of using Runic to improve on the effectiveness of his spitcraft excited him. He wanted a rune-charm that would be as strong as a bloodcrafted *hex*, only without the blood. Though his *hex* had gotten him safely away from the Evroza spearmen and across the Tor, it was still just one frighteningly short step away from black-hearted sorcery, from murder for magic. Blood-magic—sorcery by any other name—put him at risk of execution if caught using it, and it would likely earn him MiPaatet's hatred rather than mere disfavor if he did it again.

He missed Milkdales, but they couldn't return without a menney, and for some reason, Royenne Errengard had lost her enthusiasm for providing one, though he didn't think she'd changed her mind about provoking Royenne Sharei.

For the last ten afternoons, he'd been banished from the Young Court—leaving him free to spy on the Crown Court from the hall's high rafters. Among the things he'd learned was that Royenne Errengard never changed her mind once it was made up.

So, if she hadn't changed it about supporting Helgurdda, then there had to be a strong reason for her to delay. And she *was* delaying—he'd heard Eirgei and Helgurdda complaining that she'd been deliberately avoiding them, and that nothing had been done to muster any warbands. One youngling girl's eager prattle to Wyl yesterday had confirmed the truth of it.

Over the past two weeks, nothing in his family's situation had changed. They had a refuge, but they had no menney, and no steps had been taken, despite Royenne Errengard's pledge of support, to raise one. Helgurdda had told him the first night they'd spent in Nornholm that she'd been promised swift action, but nothing had happened at all.

Royenne Errengard had to know there was no time to waste. Eirgei would need every day he could get with Helgurdda's new menney to train them in his commands, learn their strengths and weaknesses, devise battle plans to take both into account, and drill them using those plans.

Even if Royenne Errengard didn't recognize that, surely Prince Frekkei did—yet he seemed in accord with her delay. It added up to some secret threat to Icebear rule.

That first morning after they'd arrived, Eirgei had said there'd been opposition to him being Prince Raldorrei's Right Hand, and that there'd been trouble brewing among the other clans. Evidently, it had worsened if Royenne Errengard wouldn't send Eirgei even one Icebear warband to train for the invasion of Milkdales.

But doing nothing wouldn't change the situation in Dremnar, whatever it was. If Prince Frekkei needed Eirgei to lead his menney against rebellious clans here, then Eirgei still needed the Icebear menney able to follow his signals and carry out his maneuvers. It was less than four moons until Iceroad Pass froze over—not much time if Eirgei anticipated a campaign in Dremnar's hinterlands first. Any trouble there would have to be quashed before he took half the Icebear menney away with him into Milkdales.

If Wyl could make a *trap secrets* charm, then maybe he could uncover answers about the delay. If he could learn who the Dremn royenne's enemies were and why the old royenne was suddenly so wary of helping Helgurdda, then he'd also learn who in the Crown Court worked against Helgurdda and take steps to counter them.

So he sat above the High Gate in his new lair and took a wax tablet out of his robber's pouch. He'd kept it after his lessons, telling Lord Geilorren he would use it to practice his Runic. He grinned to himself—the old tutor had no idea what kind of Runic he would be practicing.

But spitcrafting a charm was always a wearying process, with no guarantee of success, even if the charm were a familiar one. This was, after all, spitcraft. In the past, even using his *luck* charm hadn't been enough to help him come up with a new type of charm.

He hoped that, using Runic, this time would be different.

He felt confident he could make this idea work—he'd sensed a street witch in Myymor using a similarly spitcrafted charm to compel an audience to gather around her market stall, simply by using a crudely written sign in Teboan as a charm to advertise her wares. It had been true spitcraft—though her charm had successfully drawn a crowd to her, few had actually made a purchase.

Wyl thought he could be at least that successful with his *trap secrets* charm. Perhaps, being only spitcraft, it wouldn't make anyone give up their secrets, but maybe it would make someone less careful in keeping those secrets—such a charm would still be a useful tool for a spy.

He vividly imagined a situation when he might put such a charm to good use and held it in his mind as he drew the rune in the wax. However, despite his practice drawing it, the rune didn't flow smoothly under his stylus. Though using Teboan script in a charm posed difficulties of its own, he had practiced his *luck* and *hide me* charms enough over the years that he didn't have to think about writing the words, just maintaining the prolonged concentration. But he had to think about his Runic, and after he'd drawn the spider rune, he didn't feel the tingle.

The fault had to be in the making of it—the charm had felt awkward as he'd inscribed the rune into the wax tablet with his stylus in his left hand because all his practice in the Young Court required him to use his right hand. With either hand, he'd still have to concentrate too much on making the rune instead of on his intentions in making it.

He tried to make his well-practiced *hide me* charm, substituting the rune for *hidden*, but though his oldest charm was easy to hold in his head, the rune made *hidden* seem like a completely new charm. He sighed, smudged the wax smooth, and practiced the spider rune again.

✦

19th Day of the Moon of Storms, 113 G.E.

Wyl had taken to spending his afternoons on the hoardings above the High Gate instead of spying on the Crown Court. He'd been practicing his Runic, but also growing increasingly worried about assassins. From his lair on the hoardings, he could easily see the approach to Nornholm and the lower bailey as he whiled away the hours trying to spitcraft a rune-charm. Frankly, it surprised him that there hadn't yet been an assassination attempt on Helgurdda after almost three weeks in exile. The Evroza truly had been caught unprepared by their flight to Nornholm.

He glanced down at the lower bailey gate as he smoothed out his latest rendering of the spider rune and frowned.

An old man with a younger man's stride walked up the slope to Nornholm's lower gate.

The guardsmen there came to full alert when the old man approached—something Wyl hadn't seen them do since the hunters had brought Helgurdda and Eirgei through those gates, bound and haltered. But the guardsmen didn't stop the old man.

Now that the old man was inside the lower bailey, Wyl could see that he was dressed in the most archaic Folk style—in leather, rather than cloth. His tunic and leggings were more colorful than those of Nornholm's Folk, with designs painted in red, yellow, and black on the creamy leather. He wore his gray hair long, past his shoulders—more like a nobleman rather than one of the Folk—but his white beard was wild, and he had small ornaments braided into locks of hair around his face. More of the ornaments dangled on thongs lashed to the top of his staff.

Save for the staff and a hunting knife, he appeared unarmed. Yet, he didn't seem harmless. *Wyl* wouldn't have let the old man through the gates, though he didn't know what it was he distrusted so much about him.

What really caught his attention, when the old man came closer, was his face. The entire left side—the side Wyl could best see in the afternoon light—was badly disfigured. A man with that face in their camp back in Milkdales would have had the most hardened criminals stepping lightly around him.

The old man definitely qualified as *off*, but he seemed an unlikely assassin.

Nevertheless, Wyl tucked his wax tablet into his robber's pouch, making ready to follow and see where he went.

The old man paused in the lower bailey to look about and get his bearings before approaching the entrance to the upper bailey.

Now that the old man was closer, Wyl could see more details of the terrible scar that split the length of the old man's face from the brow above his missing eye, past the corner of his mouth, and through his beard to his chin. The scarring had been made worse by puckering from haphazard stitching when the wound had been new.

The High Gate guardsmen, far from barring the old man from entering, hesitated, then took several steps back to let him pass unchallenged. One of the guards beckoned to a Folk runner-boy, spoke briefly, then sent the runner racing towards the Crown Court hall, no doubt to report the visitor to the viceroye.

Wyl picked his way across the hoardings, climbed back onto the battlements, and ran for the stairs, rattling down to the ground in the upper bailey in time to see the old man pass several staring courtiers, heading across the courtyards, straight for the northwest wing of the palace.

When the old man turned to enter a corridor, Wyl followed him inside and dropped farther back, ready to duck into a dark, intersecting corridor or down stairs, all the while keeping to the old man's blind side.

Interestingly, servants and Dremn nobility alike treated the old man's sudden appearance among them with a cautious, recoiling respect—just as the guardsmen had. Not a one of them hindered him or spoke to him, and the old man merely nodded as he passed.

With a sudden resolve, Wyl took the next stairs down to the ground level and raced across the courtyards, bound for vine-overgrown Tras Tower.

All things odd or uncanny seemed attracted to Helgurdda's rebellion, and he didn't think being in Dremnar changed that.

He took a straight flight of stairs up into the corridor leading past a ruined tower some distance still from Tras Tower. There was no sign of the old man in either direction, so he ran and entered Tras Tower through the empty guardroom.

The upper floors of their tower were vacant during the day in favor of the kitchen with its always-lit hearth. The warm kitchen would have been inhabited at night, too, but it had two entrances—impossible for one person to guard while Helgurdda slept.

Wyl had the same problem now—which entrance should he watch, the stairs in the guardroom or the courtyard entry to the scullery? He started creeping down the stairs to the kitchen, then stiffened when he heard the rustle of map parchment.

Eirgei was back early from the Menney Tower and his service to Prince-Viceroye Frekkei.

Wyl retreated back to the guardroom and climbed partway up the curving stairs inside Tras Tower, just halfway to the third floor. He sat on the cold stone steps and waited.

This strange old man had some connection to the rebellion. Perhaps he was one of Eirgei's other spies, though he seemed too conspicuous to be much good at it.

Echoing footsteps accompanied by the tap of a staff were proof his hunch was right. The old man arrived at Tras Tower by way of the corridor.

Wyl rose to his feet, preparing to retreat upwards when the old man came through the door to the guardroom, expecting him to go up to the third floor hall. Instead, he was surprised to hear the old man remain outside and descend the stairs to the kitchen.

Wyl padded out to the top of the lower stairwell in the corridor and slowly, silently, began to descend the first straight flight of stairs.

He froze when he heard Eirgei confront the strange old man at the foot of the second flight of stairs.

"Grelor!" Eirgei said, with evident shock. "It cannot be! I have thought you dead all these years!"

Wyl slithered down the stairs as far as the landing halfway down to the kitchen, hesitated, then ventured downward just a couple steps farther—just low enough to catch a glimpse of the old man from above.

He thought about his *trap secrets* charm. If ever there were an apt time to use it, this was it. He took his wax charm from his robber's pouch and pulled out a throwing knife to sketch the rune.

"Ah, shield-brother, I have missed you," the old man said. "But until now, my path serving MiPaatet has turned away from yours. You look well—"

The hairs on the back of Wyl's neck were prickling. He had goosebumps all over him.

But he hadn't drawn the spider rune-charm, not yet, so there was no mistaking it—he was reacting to some sort of magic.

It had to be the old man, but Wyl didn't know how or what he did to cause it. He obviously wasn't scrying, and Eirgei didn't make a sarcastic comment, so Wyl assumed the old man must be using some other strange, more subtle variation of magic. The only other possibility was that the old man carried something altered by artisanry, but most Folk were too poor to afford Gerisari-made goods, let alone those crafted with magic.

He supposed, with this Grelor being Folk, he could be using spitcraft, but if he was, it was a kind much more powerful than what Wyl used.

Maybe not spitcraft at all, but true Folk magic!

This time, though Wyl trembled with excitement, the spider rune for his *trap secrets* charm flowed effortlessly from the tip of his narrow blade. He felt the tingle travel through him, though it didn't block his sense of the other magic. Just to be sure it worked, he pricked his finger and liberally smeared blood across the carved rune, then watched it sink into the wax as if it were fluff.

He focused all his attention on what was being said, hoping to direct the action of the charm. He quietly retreated up the steps until he knew he was out of sight. He didn't want to risk being caught spying.

He had never managed to work two charms at once, and his wax charm had already been used for his spider rune, but he had nothing to lose by being cautious. He wet a fingertip in his mouth and wrote the Teboan script for *hide me* on the stone wall beside him. It was a strain to hold both commands in his head at the same time, and since he still felt the effects of the spider rune, he couldn't tell if the second charm worked. He sat very still and hoped it did.

"I saw you fall!" Eirgei said. "I was sure you were dead or I would never have left you!"

Wyl heard terrible, unlooked-for guilt in Eirgei's voice.

This old man had been Eirgei's shield-brother, left behind, dead or alive, on some battlefield? Then, that meant this Grelor wasn't Dremn or Folk, but Tras!

Until Eirgei's admission, Wyl hadn't doubted that the old man was Dremn Folk, despite the length of his hair—that beard and Folk clothing had completely fooled him. How mortifying to have his own kind of disguise used successfully against him—but his *trap secrets* charm seemed to be working.

Discovering that this Grelor had once been Eirgei's shield-brother was nothing short of staggering—especially the part about Eirgei leaving his shield-brother's body behind. A man of honor wouldn't leave a comrade's body—let alone a shield-brother's body—to be defiled by the enemy like a condemned outlaw's, or leave it to rot on the ground like an animal's instead of bringing it home for his clan to burn.

That didn't sound like Eirgei—his granduncle was obsessive about honorable behavior. *Eirgei* abandoned a shield-brother to run away?

"I do not fault you for it," Grelor said, more calmly than the offense merited. "MiPaatet had other plans for me. I have become a shaman and a healer, and presently live outside these walls among the Folk who serve Nornholm."

"MiPaatet?" Wyl heard the change in Eirgei's voice then, going from guilt to scorn in an instant. "A shaman?"

Despite their disastrous encounter with that Evroza weather-mage, Eirgei hadn't lost his scorn for any reliance on magic, whether innate or divinely-bestowed. He only believed in cunning, loyalty, and the power of his merkusar sabre.

"You, a shaman? What superstitious foolery is this?"

"None, Cuz," Grelor said. "MiPaatet brought me back from death and gave me gifts I could not refuse."

"You really think you've got magic now?" That wasn't just disbelief in Eirgei's voice, that was horror.

Eirgei couldn't feel the magic Wyl felt, magic centered on this Grelor. Eirgei surely thought his former shield-brother had gone mad.

Wyl didn't.

"Clearly," the old man's voice was amused rather than offended. "That was one of MiPaatet's gifts."

"Well," said Eirgei, his tone of voice changing in a way Wyl wouldn't trust, if he were Grelor. "Helgurdda could use some magic on her side—the Evroza have used mages against us time and again. Do you think this shamanry of yours can defeat their magic?"

"Eirgei, Eirgei," Grelor actually chuckled. "I know you think I have gone mad, that the blow to my head knocked out all my wits, but I assure you, I am more sane than you give me credit for being—and a good bit more sane than you, if you are trying to fight Evroza magery without any magic at all! My shamanry and the magery of the Evroza are not the same, and I do battle with forces greater than anything the Evroza have ever brought against you. That is why I have come— there is a danger coming that concerns us all, something more serious than the Evroza."

"How can you say that? The old customs, our traditions, all are being lost to Sharei's fascination with foreign ways! Surely you can appreciate the value of preserving our heritage. They would turn us all into imitation Gerisari, even down to how we wage war!"

"Oh, I do honor our traditions," Grelor said, with a rueful humor, "and certainly I keep to the old ways as best I can, but that does not make me a part of your quarrel."

"Quarrel? Do not belittle the cause that has cost so many lives!"

"Blood-feud, then. No, I do not belittle it. That is why I have come. This is no time for warring or feuds, whether yours with the Evroza, or between the baronnes of Trascolm, or between the royennes of Trascolm and Dremnar. There is a greater trouble coming. You must parlay with the Evroza, find a way to lay down your weapons and make peace."

Out of sight on the stairs, Wyl minutely shook his head, careful of his *hide me* charm. What the old man asked was impossible. The Evroza wouldn't stop fighting until Helgurdda was dead, and Helgurdda wouldn't stop until Ragna was. There was no treaty either would honor any longer than necessary to steal an advantage over the other. A blood-feud only ended when there was no one left to fight on one side or the other. Or both.

"Is that why you have come, to speak for the Evroza?"

"No, I speak only for MiPaatet. And I know you too well to believe my words will turn either you or Helgurdda from this path. I have come for the boy."

"The boy?"

"The black-haired stripling."

Wyl was embarrassed—he'd been at such pains to stay on the old man's blind side.

Then, the shaman's words sank in.

He stiffened. He was just a boy. Why would the old man know anything of him?

"His name is Wylheim," Helgurdda said, her voice startling Wyl. He heard her enter the kitchen from the courtyard entrance in the scullery. "He is the image of his sire."

"Perhaps—but having the look of his sire does not explain why the boy is here in Nornholm."

"Because Helgurdda is, and he is determined to stay with his mother," Eirgei said, in exasperation. "The boy can take care of himself—I have seen to that. He is not a danger to himself or to us."

"So long as he is with you, he is in danger. Continue your blood-feud with the Evroza, if you are determined on this path, but give the boy into my care where he will be safe."

"My cause is his cause," Helgurdda said, and Wyl faintly nodded in agreement. "Hereres was his sire. If you want to keep Wylheim safe, join me, and watch over him until the day I lead my menney down Ice-road Pass and see justice done."

"I have no quarrel with Royenne Sharei," Grelor said. "And the hill-Folk of both Dremnar and Trascolm rely on my shamanry more than you would, even if I agreed to accompany you. But nothing good can come of dragging a boy with you into war."

"I hardly drag him," Helgurdda retorted. "I have merely bowed to the inevitable. When he was younger, I tried to foster him, but he always ran away and rejoined me. Unlike my family—" the bitterness in her voice came through clearly, "—Wylheim will not abandon me."

She rarely spoke of her former clan. She had never forgiven their betrayal of her, formally and publicly backing Princess Ragna, consigning her to outlawry out of political expedience.

Yet, she still wanted Wyl to desert her, did her best to discourage him from following her, whether abandoning him in remote Folk hamlets or insisting that Eirgei's harsh training make no allowances for his age.

"When the Folk servants outside told me you had come to see me," she continued, "they said you could draw the hill-Folk to my cause as archers. According to them, even trees tell you their secrets."

"Helgurdda," Grelor said, in a gentle voice, "there is nothing I can or will do to advance your cause, unless it be to go to Crossroads Keep as an envoy to Royenne Sharei and make terms for peace between you."

Wyl winced.

Helgurdda exploded. "Easy enough for you to say! It was *my* consort who was murdered, *my* claim on Sharei's justice denied! My own clan *outlawed* me for appealing against the injustice of allowing Hereres's murderer to go free!"

"The tale I heard said you were outlawed for taking revenge against his killer," Grelor said. "After the royenne had already rendered her judgment and denied your petition."

"Denied on the basis of Gerisari law and Gerisari politics, not Trascolm's! Sharei has grown so fond of all things Gerisari that a man can be murdered in Milkdales, in front of his betrothed, for something that is only a crime in Gerisar! That is not justice! And who has better cause for pursuing this quarrel, as you call it, than the boy who was denied a sire by it?"

Wyl couldn't remember the last time Helgurdda had been so furious—but neither could he remember anyone ever trying to persuade her to make peace with the Evroza!

"So you give a stripling a sabre and do not expect him to be cut down because of it?"

"The Evroza do not make war on children. Uncle has merely seen to it that my son will not be defenseless if the heat of battle blinds them to his age."

"By disguising him in armor and putting a weapon in his hand?" Grelor's voice was merciless in his opposition and not at all intimidated by Eirgei's presence backing Helgurdda.

Wyl couldn't believe the old man was so determined to cross Eirgei. Occasionally, some rebel recruits had dared take a fight to Eirgei, either with weapons or with words, but they'd always been cut to shreds by sabre or tongue.

Eirgei had the right of it—his former shield-brother was clearly insane.

But how did this old man know so much about Wyl?

"You would do better to teach him to run from battle as fast as he can and in the opposite direction," Grelor said, undeterred. "Better yet, give him to me. I will teach him the old ways, and keep him safe until you have had enough of death and blood-feud, and this all ends, one way or the other."

"Assurances from a madman?" Helgurdda raged. "Your wits are addled if you think yourself fit to raise my boy! Look at you! You are half-starved and dressed in animal skins—a barbarian who makes hill-Folk look respectable! What do you know of children and their raising?"

"Apparently, as much as you do," Grelor retorted, losing his equanimity. "Your son will not starve or go naked, and he will not be struck down in your place by your enemies, either, which is what will happen if you keep him by your side."

"What, so I should turn him over to you, a deluded old man who thinks he has magical powers? He is only a boy, but he is all I have left of Hereres, and I say you will not have him! Uncle—show Grelor the way to Nornholm's gates and see that he leaves without my son!"

Wyl heard the two men leave the kitchen, pass through the scullery, then out into the courtyard.

He rose and eased back up the stairs. Once out in the corridor, he ran to the next tower, down its stairs into a courtyard, and then ran from there to the ramparts, leaving Folk and bondservants staring.

But by the time he reached the High Gate, Eirgei had already taken Grelor through it.

He doubled back, sprinting west to the nearby ancient breastworks along the precipice, up the stone stairs to the upper bailey battlements, then ran along the parapet to the High Gate. He hopped up into a crenel and then boosted himself atop a merlon, the better to watch Eirgei and Grelor as they descended through the lower bailey.

What shocked him was that Eirgei wasn't treating Grelor like a madman, dragging him, arm in hand, and shoving him out the gate.

Quite the opposite.

As far as he could tell, there were no more words between them. What spoke to him more than words was that Eirgei walked with Grelor on his right, his sword side, leaving the position of the stronger fighter to the old man armed only with a staff—as if Grelor were still his shield-brother, and Eirgei trusted him with his life, despite the harsh words.

Eirgei took Grelor to the outer gate and stood for a long time, watching Grelor walk back to the village sprawling below Nornholm.

Wyl watched the two of them from the battlements and wondered what the shaman meant when he said he spoke for MiPaatet.

When Lanney had first come to bodyguard Helgurdda, she had told Wyl all the old Folk tales of MiPaatet and TolDaanyo, and of the layered Otherrealms that contain their world, the Mortalrealm. According to her stories, shamans were people who had escaped death when their spirits had passed out of the Mortalrealm and into the Otherrealms, but then, eventually found their way back to the Mortalrealm and their once-dead bodies. Sometimes they'd become confused about which of the Realms they were in from one moment to the next. And always, they would come back with gray eyes, often with gray hair, and mostly barking mad.

So Lanney had said.

In some of Lanney's Folk tales, shamans were healers, but in others, they were dangerously unpredictable—undoubtedly because they were crazy. Wyl was sure that was the explanation for why the gate guards hadn't tried to stop this Grelor from entering Nornholm. A shaman could as easily hurt as heal.

So, how had Eirgei's dead Tras shield-brother become a live, crazy Dremn shaman?

Had he seen Wyl when they'd first arrived in Nornholm, when the Folk hunters took them through the town on their way to Nornholm to see Royenne Errengard?

Wyl didn't know what the mysterious old shaman wanted with him, but whatever it was, he intended to make sure he didn't get it.

CHAPTER 21

GRELOR

"*H*eh, who was that old man walking with you today, Eirgei?" Wyl asked casually, sitting on the hearthstones in the kitchen that evening, soaking up the heat from the fire, but still cold despite it. There was no cook—their meals came directly from the royenne's kitchen and always arrived just as cold as they were. Tras Tower's kitchen was where they ate and spent most of their time when not in one court or the other. His family was no more tolerant of the cold than he was.

Eirgei eyed him from the bench he and Helgurdda had pulled close to the fire, but without suspicion. Though their evening meal hadn't yet been delivered, there was a goblet of mead in Eirgei's hand and a half-full jug on the floor beside the bench.

Wyl had put the question with careful innocence—Eirgei had to know he'd been seen escorting Grelor out of Nornholm by any number of people.

"Grelor is someone I knew back when I was younger, before I became an outlaw and a rebel." Eirgei drank some mead and silently stared into the cup until Wyl wondered if he ought to repeat his question.

"He was cut down after a reprisal raid up Iceroad Pass, as we were returning from Dremnar," Eirgei said, at last. "We all thought him dead of an axe-wound to the head and were forced to leave his body behind. Apparently, he survived, but with his wits addled. He was a great man. Much of what I know, he taught me when I was not much older than you. We were shield-brothers."

"*Ockh*, you left him behind?" Wyl asked, pretending shock. "*A shield-brother?*"

He expected Eirgei to glare and try to defend himself, but he did neither. He swallowed more mead.

"He was dead, Wyl," he said eventually. "With a Dremn battleaxe half-buried in his face. We had other wounded, and our warleader had led us into an ambush."

"Warleader?" He tried to imagine Eirgei taking orders from anyone other than Helgurdda and failed.

Eirgei stared into his half-empty goblet of mead. "That became my first command," he said gruffly. "A lot of good minions died on that raid, and more died in that ambush. I lost Grelor, and we all lost our warleader. I just wanted to get us home without losing any more of us. Remember, there is a time to fight, boy, and a time to run." He paused, gazing inward, "and that was most definitely a time to run. Our warleader's foolish arrogance took us too far into Dremnar, and that was only the first of the Dremn ambushes waiting for us. I was able to bring most of us home, but we all left blood and friends behind."

Eirgei looked over at him, his eyes weary and haunted. "I became a warlord and then a warleader to try to make sure that never happened again. That is war, boy, and no one lives through one without having regrets."

Wyl thought of Lanney and felt a surge of hope. "But your shield-brother survived."

Eirgei sadly shook his head. "No, he did not. What walked through Nornholm's gates today was just an empty shell of the man he was. He is mad, and as lost to us as if he were dead. My Grelor would rather have died in Iceroad Pass than call himself a shaman, live in a cave, and fall back into the benighted superstitions of our ancestors."

Wyl tried to imagine Lanney coming back as a shaman, somehow surviving the Tor despite her mail, impacts with rocks and snags, and the brunt of the flash flood's debris. "Could Lanney—"

"No!" Helgurdda cut him off, frowning at Eirgei. "No, Wylheim, she could not become a shaman like Grelor. Shamans are people who were never properly tested for magic as younglings and had scrying talent that had gone untrained. Extreme stress can awaken the magic, but without the training to use it safely, a person's body may survive, but his mind is broken. Lanney said she had been properly tested as a youngling, but had no magic. If she had, perhaps we would have had a seer to counter the Evroza mages." She ignored Eirgei's scoff and gave Wyl a sad smile. "Son, you know she is not coming back."

Helgurdda must have seen something in Wyl's face, because she abruptly changed the subject.

"Uncle, now that you have had a chance to take the measure of these Icebears, how long do you think you will need to train them in your signals? I was thinking, because this will be a single strike to Crossroads Keep, you might use more conventional signals to save time."

"Save time doing what? In case you did not notice, Niece, you have no menney. You will never have a Dremn menney until you give them a reason to support you!" Eirgei slammed his mead goblet down so hard on the bench the mead erupted from it. "The way to get Royenne Errengard to commit her warlords and raise you a menney is to take a Dremn consort—preferably, an Icebear!"

Eirgei had already refilled his goblet several times, and Wyl knew he had to be well on his way towards being drunk—another impossible occurrence. Eirgei preached being prepared to fight at any time, and drinking to excess was something he'd been particularly scornful of in their outlaw allies.

But seeing Grelor had badly affected his granduncle. No matter their shifting fortunes, Wyl had never seen Eirgei concede defeat, never seen him give up—or wallow in grief like he was now.

"I want a menney—not another consort!" Helgurdda snapped.

Wyl sat still, quietly wet a finger in his mouth, and formed the rune for *trap secrets* on the hearthstones. He felt the tingle of success, then did it again to write *hide me* in Teboan, hoping to remain forgotten and unnoticed beside the fire, though he couldn't feel the charm taking effect.

Now, maybe he'd learn what their plans were without risking a thrashing.

He watched Helgurdda unconsciously twist the troth-ring on her forefinger. It wasn't a delicate gold ring set with a jewel like other troth-rings, or even a simple silver ring like those exchanged between a Folk betrothed and her consort. It was a massive chunk of cast bronze—jektrar-bronze, like the Folk archer's rings Wyl wore on both thumbs.

That was the only resemblance between the rings. His archer's rings were plain and workaday, turquoise-blue except where they'd been buffed greenish-gold by his bowstring. Hereres's troth-ring was unique—beautifully cast with intricate, twining knotwork and an un-marred turquoise patina.

He had never seen that exotic design anywhere else.

His sire had been a runaway Gerisari slave, and Helgurdda had giv-en him refuge. They'd fallen in love, but Hereres had had no money for silver or gold when they'd decided to pledge troth. He'd been too proud to take Helgurdda's troth-ring without a ring to give her.

Wyl had always thought Hereres's pride foolish for a runaway slave in hiding—if he'd given Helgurdda a proper troth-ring, there would've been questions about it from her kin, no matter that she'd been of age and free to take the consort of her choosing.

Two weeks after they'd secretly pledged troth, Hereres had lain dead in Helgurdda's arms, murdered by Princess Ragna's Gerisari prince-consort, who had taken part in Hereres's owner's hunt for him. That murder had been what had triggered the blood-feud—that, and Helgurdda's subsequent vengeance on Ragna's consort after her ap-peals for justice had been denied by Royenne Sharei.

Helgurdda had made Hereres's troth-ring a symbol of her rebellion, even stamping it in wax as her seal to sign orders for her warlords or messages for her allies. She never took it off.

"You need a menney," Eirgei said sternly. "Take the right consort, and you will get one. Hereres is dead these thirteen years and wearing his troth-ring does not change that. But so long as you wear his ring, neither Royenne Errengard nor any man in Nornholm will believe you are serious about taking another consort."

"I do not need another consort, I tell you," Helgurdda said.

"Yes, you do. You need a proper consort, one who brings you allies and can sire an heir. An heir will keep this rebellion alive, bring in sup-porters because they can see you looking to the future, not the past. Without an heir, your rebellion is merely the death-knell of the Evroza and not the beginning of a new dynasty. You need a daughter. Wyl needs a sister."

"I loved Hereres, so I mourn him!" That wild look in her eyes was all-too familiar. She wasn't reasonable about Hereres.

"And you have mourned him long enough. Thirteen years and all you have to show for avenging him is outlawry and now exile. If you truly want justice for him, sacrifice your show of mourning and make a show of your determination to obtain that justice. Give Hereres's troth-ring to Wyl—it rightfully belongs to him, now. Let him hold it until he becomes a consort."

"I can't be a consort," Wyl objected from the fireside, provoked into forgetting to stay quiet, breaking the effect of his *hide me* charm. "I'm supposed to be viceroye after you."

Helgurdda blinked, as if she'd forgotten his presence, then smiled sadly. "Ah, spoken like my son...like Hereres's son."

She rubbed at her eyes, took a deep breath, then let it out. "You have the right of it, Uncle. I do need a consort, if only to ensure my son's future." Her voice was the merest whisper.

"That is right," Eirgei said quickly. "Without an heir, if something happens to you, Wyl and I will have to flee to Tokar and sell our swords to some mercenary band, little better than the outlaws we are today."

Wyl stared at Eirgei, disturbed and even more put out by this vision of his future. Becoming mercenaries in the city-state of Tokar, far to the southwest of Trascolm, was yet another contingency plan he'd not been told about. Dremnar was still foreign enough to him, but Tokar? Sand and heat in place of snow and cold, and not even a common language?

But at least this plan didn't call for him to be left behind in Nornholm!

He missed Milkdales.

Helgurdda sighed again, but wrestled with the ring on her forefinger.

It was a real struggle: physically, the troth-ring was stuck. But it was the emotional toll that shocked him. Tears streamed down her face, and she cried as he'd never seen her cry before—not even when she'd first set foot in Dremnar had she actually sobbed like this.

She paused and closed her eyes, then visibly gathered her will and wrenched at the ring.

Wyl twined the fingers of his hands together, affected by her anguish.

But, at last, she had the troth-ring off, her knuckle left scraped raw and bleeding. There was a dead-white band on her finger where it had been.

She clenched it in her fist, then bent down, and held it out to Wyl, her hand shaking with the effort. "Take it!" She grasped his hand and closed his fingers around the ring.

Touching his sire's ring sent a strange thrill through him—for a moment, he felt goosebumps all over.

Then his mother released his hand and staggered back to the bench, looking wild and distraught.

He opened his hand and slid the ring experimentally onto his forefinger, middle finger, and finally, took off his right archer's ring and slid it onto his thumb, where it still hung loosely.

Eirgei frowned, rose, and went up the stairs, leaving his mead behind and using one hand to steady himself against the wall.

Wyl fingered the troth-ring's graceful arcs of knotwork and felt overwhelmed. He'd never had anything that had once belonged to his sire. The heavy ring was something that had belonged to a real person, not just a name or rallying cry. It was something from his sire more real than an ability to sketch with a bit of chalk on slate, or to stir painful memories in Hereres's still-grieving betrothed.

"Ah, Hereres," Helgurdda said, cupping Wyl's face and staring into his eyes. "You will never be forgotten!"

She sobbed on his shoulder, and Wyl tried not to squirm.

Eirgei returned with a leather thong in his hand. He coughed uncomfortably until Helgurdda looked up at him.

"Helgurdda, so long as Wyl lives, you have not lost Hereres entirely. But if you do not take a new consort, you will never have justice for him, or vengeance, either. If I go down, and you go down without an heir to rally your allies, as young as he is, Wylheim will surely die at the hands of the Evroza—and they will obliterate the last of Hereres with him."

Helgurdda bit her lip and lowered her head until she touched foreheads with Wyl. She held him to her until he started to become alarmed—she'd touched him more in one evening than he ever remembered in his whole life.

She shuddered, then released him, and watched critically as Eirgei took the heavy bronze ring from him, threaded it onto the thong, tied it around Wyl's neck, and adjusted it so the ring could be easily seen—in case no one noticed it missing from Helgurdda's finger.

"Uncle, I rely on you to advise me," she said, her voice breaking. "Find me a consort also fit to be your Right Hand."

"But I'm to be his Right Hand and your viceroye after him," Wyl objected again.

"We'll speak of what you are to be when you are grown," Helgurdda said, determination abruptly, disconcertingly, replacing her grief. "Right now, I need a Dremn menney to bolster my rebels in Trascolm and an Icebear prince to lead them."

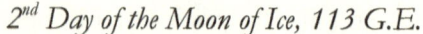

2*nd* *Day of the Moon of Ice, 113 G.E.*

It was well-over a week before Wyl spent another evening together with Helgurdda and Eirgei—tonight there was no royal banquet or some fickle warlord to woo. Word that Helgurdda had passed Here-res's troth-ring on to Wyl had stirred some interest in the Crown Court. She and Eirgei had spent the subsequent evenings talking with various warlords, and there had been some interest in her, but as a woman, not a cause, and thus far, no one was interested enough to pledge a warband to her.

Wyl still wasn't used to sharing a table with Helgurdda and Eirgei, or being included in talk about daily life when he did—ordinary talk complaining about the bondsmen, the foreign food, his table manners, wondering if he'd need new boots soon....

The peculiar small-talk was all there was left to talk about because they wouldn't discuss their invasion strategy or the persuasions they might use to overcome whatever still kept them from getting an Ice-bear menney out of Royenne Errengard.

"Son, tell me about the Young Court," Helgurdda said conversationally, breaking into Wyl's wandering thoughts as they ate the evening meal.

Her request startled him, so he licked his fingers to play for time to gather his wits.

She'd never, ever, called him *Son*, and it made him feel strange.

Did Helgurdda's question about the Young Court mean that they finally meant to include him in their planning?

Or did she have a more ominous reason for asking?

He searched Helgurdda's face for clues.

She looked relaxed. The lines of strain around her eyes and mouth had smoothed away.

Still, there was a haunted look to her, like the one she had worn the night after they'd lost Lanney crossing the Tor—or the one she got when she thought about Hereres. Was that haunted look because Royenne Errengard was acting more coldly towards them in court than Helgurdda wanted to admit?

Wyl knew the truth of their relations with Royenne Errengard—after Grelor's visit, he'd given up trying to watch for assassins during the day. Instead, he had resumed spending his lonely afternoons perched in the rafters of the Crown Court hall. Every day, he saw for himself how the royenne avoided Helgurdda.

Tonight, Helgurdda had dressed her hair in two long braids with strands of amber beads plaited through them and left them hanging over her shoulders, like those of a Dremn noblewoman, but regally longer. She still dressed as if for war in a red tunic and green leggings—Wyl had learned that she and Eirgei had refused to wear Icebear kith colors, but only when it had been too late for him to do likewise. As with Helgurdda's hair, the two of them still defied the Evroza by mimicking Evroza clan colors in their new clothes.

Wyl kept on wearing his old rebel surcoat over his warm marten fur one, which was the best he could do to echo that defiance.

He glanced anxiously at Eirgei. Where would this conversation lead? What had they kept secret from him this time?

Like Helgurdda, Eirgei, too, looked better-rested, and his gaunt face under his drooping Tras moustache had begun to fill out. He looked—and moved—like he was ten years younger.

Now Wyl felt his stomach drop.

Had something more happened between Royenne Errengard and Helgurdda when he hadn't been there to witness it? Was that the reason behind Helgurdda's question, that she needed him to have his hostage-escape plan ready to go? Much as he'd prefer to surprise Eirgei with how well he'd taken control of the Bearcubs and the Young Court, he'd do better to warn Eirgei that his part remained undone. He'd have to explain that his hostage-taking plan for the Young Court was far from ready to be put into action.

He dreaded telling Eirgei not to rely on him taking Crown Princess Kotakei hostage. But he'd learned long ago that embarrassment was better than ignorance. In Eirgei's eyes, the only unforgivable mistake was the failure to learn from an earlier one. If Wyl didn't know why everything had gone wrong with the Young Court, he risked repeating his mistake, which would earn him Eirgei's scorn and possibly endanger their return from exile.

He shrugged and looked at Helgurdda, avoiding Eirgei's eyes, fearing his judgment. He coughed and reported. "Three princesses, three matching princes—that's counting the crown princess and her brother—and nearly two-score young noblewomen attended by their nearest kin. The crown princess's guardsmen are pretty with their fancy pins and buckles, but they stay on the second floor and are better at senet than they are at guarding whenever noble adults aren't around to see."

Helgurdda looked puzzled, but Eirgei nodded thoughtfully for him to continue.

"I figure the strongest resistance will come from Crown Prince Norren and his friend, Lord Martei. There's a close cousin—Prince Jeik—but if I take Lord Martei down first and then Crown Prince Norren," he had revised his plan since Lord Martei's beating, "I'm sure Prince Jeik will back off and follow my lead. He's so popular, the rest of the baby-menney will follow him."

And Prince Jeik would be more likely to worry for the safety of the youngling hostages and not risk them by fighting him.

"Govern your words!" Helgurdda said sharply. "Call them the young menney or Bearcubs, or call them nothing at all!"

Eirgei stared at him with his goblet of mead halfway to his mouth. "Your lead?"

He looked back at Eirgei and cautiously nodded. "I had hopes of winning over the loyalty of the—Bearcubs—by fighting Lord Martei in a challenge and impressing them enough to make them switch allegiance to me, but that went wrong. Now I'll have to settle for making them afraid to go up against me, but after—" there'd been no hiding his humiliating defeat from Eirgei, not when Wyl had to spend his nights in Tras Tower after sporting those bruises, "—being thrown out of the Bearcubs, I don't think they're likely to be put off by my blades, so when it's time for me to act, someone will get hurt, and that will give my plan away and make them rally against me. So, I'm going to have to wait until the time comes—when we're ready to leave—before I make my move." He couldn't meet Eirgei's eyes for shame.

He felt a numb chill at the thought of what he'd have to do, but he'd sworn no more soft-hearted failures when his family's safety was at stake. "Then, thanks to my...poor showing with a staff...I'm sure I can take Lord Martei and Crown Prince Norren by surprise with my sabre and take them down before they know what's happening." He knew first-hand how effective that was! "After that, it's just a matter of time."

"Time for what, Wylheim?" Helgurdda asked, casting an odd look at Eirgei.

It was such a simple plan—and hadn't it been her idea?

"A menney is not like a band of outlaws, Wyl," said Eirgei, with an edge in his voice as he held Helgurdda's eye.

Something Wyl didn't understand seemed to pass between the two of them.

"Taking away their leaders will not give you control over them, not if they do not respect you—and respect among the nobility is based on more than just fighting prowess," Eirgei said.

"I suspected as much," Wyl said, relieved that Eirgei understood his problem. "I did well, at first—even Crown Prince Norren was friendly—"

Helgurdda gave Eirgei a strange look. She set down her knife and straightened on her bench.

"And then what happened?" Eirgei asked, drawing Wyl's attention back to him.

"I—I don't know. Maybe I scared them?" He felt uneasy receiving his family's rare, full attention. "I said I was your best pupil."

Eirgei snorted. "That should have impressed them, not frightened them."

"All I know is, after I said that, something changed, and everyone turned hostile towards me. I don't know why."

"Did you challenge someone? Crown Prince Norren? How many times have I warned you that in a duel with nobility, it is always better to be the defender?" Eirgei asked sternly.

Wyl remembered his disastrous challenge to Lord Martei. Having the choice of weapons as the defender would have made all the difference. But—

"No, something had happened before my...trouble...with Lord Martei. Crown Prince Norren had already changed his mind about including me in the Bearcubs."

Eirgei's assumption that he'd formally challenged *Crown Prince Norren* puzzled him. A duel was a blood-feud in miniature: no boundaries, no rules. Win or lose, a duel with an Icebear prince—any Icebear prince—would destroy Helgurdda's hope for Royenne Errengard's support.

Eirgei had to know he knew it and wouldn't risk that.

"You mean I should challenge Crown Prince Norren rather than rely on a surprise attack when we're ready to leave? You always say, *he who strikes first, controls the fight*, but I can't trust Lord Martei to stay out of a duel between me and Crown Prince Norren—and if Lord Martei joins in, the rest of the Bearcubs will, too."

Eirgei waved off his concern. "Forget the nonsense about a duel. What else did you tell them, besides being my best pupil?"

"Why are you looking at me like that? You know I wouldn't tell our secrets!"

"What else did you tell them?" Eirgei set down his mead with deliberate care.

"I told them about getting into the Evroza stronghold in Myymor—just that, no details—"

Helgurdda groaned and covered her eyes.

"What exactly did you say, Wylheim?" It was never good when Eirgei lowered his voice like that and called him *Wylheim.*

Wyl coughed, reluctantly reliving that encounter in his memory as if it were an ordinary spy's report. "I just said I was your best pupil and the rebellion's best spy."

CHAPTER 22

THE THREE DISHONORS

Eirgei slammed his hands down on the table so hard, the boards bounced on the trestles. "I knew it! Damn it, boy! Since when have you found it necessary to brag?"

Wyl shrugged nervously. He wouldn't admit he'd felt threatened by *children*, no matter how big or how many. Seven years ago, when Eirgei had finally agreed to train him, the first rule Eirgei had taught him had been, *never show fear or weakness*.

Fear, Eirgei had said, *means you are thinking defensively, not actively taking the fight to the enemy*. In his eyes, there was no greater failing in a warlord—or in someone who expected to take up his merkusar sabre one day.

"I figured it would save me a few battles, later," Wyl said, his voice wavering, still not sure where he'd stepped wrong.

"Which *later* would that be?" Eirgei growled.

Wyl swallowed, but made himself answer. "Once I have control of the baby—*Bearcubs*—I'll have control of the Young Court, as well. Viceroye Frekkei might sacrifice the Bearcubs, but he won't risk Royenne Errengard's heir, so when our welcome here goes bad, I can use her to make terms with Royenne Errengard to gain us safe passage out of Dremnar."

"If our welcome goes bad," Helgurdda said, her voice lilting on suppressed emotion, "that would be why. I do not know whether to laugh or cry, Uncle. I will leave this in your hands. Do what you think best."

She rose, her meal only half-eaten, and left the kitchen. She climbed up the stairs.

Wyl stared after her, alarmed. He still didn't know what he'd done, but whatever it was, he'd just done it again.

Eirgei had turned purple and was trying to control his breathing.

Wyl's stomach churned at the thought of Eirgei failing to master his temper. What had he done wrong?

"First," Eirgei said, at last, his voice tightly controlled, "never admit you are a spy. Think like a nobleman, boy! A nobleman may hire as many spies as he likes, but it is dishonorable to actually be one. Just accusing a noble of being a spy could be a mortal insult, an accusation of treachery. Freely admitting to it is pure folly, enough to shame a noble clan, which could then disown a nobleman for cause."

Wyl's breath caught, and he coughed.

Eirgei looked sharply at him. "But you are underage—you cannot be held accountable. That does not mean you can go around bragging about it—it is still disgraceful, but you would not be outlawed for it."

Maybe not, but Eirgei had just said he could be disowned, which was halfway to being outlawed.

Disguising himself as an outcast was hard enough to bear—he had a real horror of actually being one. For as long as he could remember, he'd been afraid Helgurdda would orphan him in the mistaken belief that it would be for his own good, but until now, he'd never imagined Helgurdda making an orphan of him for cause.

"And since there is no dishonor in employing spies, even an underage one," Eirgei continued, "Helgurdda's position in this court should still be secure. But you are her son, and she needs your name free of any taint. Never boast of such a thing again—sooner boast of thieving as spying, do you understand? And," Eirgei looked pained, "if you have done any thieving, never boast of that, either—no, I do not want to know! Just do not do it again!"

Wyl swallowed his confession and wondered how he would fend for himself the next time he was in Myymor, if he couldn't steal what he needed to survive. Nothing could be more suspicious—or dangerous—than being an outcast with money to spend. Did Eirgei mean to save him from dishonor as a thief so he could more convincingly play the part of a inept, hireling spy?

Eirgei shook his head and frowned, "I had no idea you have picked up so many criminal habits and now, one or two of the Three Dishonors, too! Where was Lanney? Even a mercenary ought to know better than to let you turn thief!"

Wyl shrugged, dry-mouthed, hoping Eirgei didn't really want to know just how many times he'd grown bored in camp and had tagged along behind certain rebel warlords, leaving Lanney to her gambling while he picked up some new skills. He'd never thought anything he did would reflect on Lanney; he'd thought all that mattered had been how well they worked together guarding Helgurdda.

"Three Dishonors?" He didn't try to hide his bafflement.

Eirgei rolled his eyes and aggravation grated in his voice. "Obviously, folly, cowardice, and treachery—spying is treacherous—and the stupidity of boasting of it is pure folly! If you were grown, you'd have brought disgrace to us all. Do not look at me like that! I taught you the Three Virtues: cunning, valor, and loyalty—the foundation of nobility!"

Eirgei narrowed his eyes, looking both frustrated and disgusted. "You told the whole Young Court you were a spy, did you not? You might as well have told all of Nornholm! *That* is why you are not a Bearcub—it had nothing to do with your age or even getting beaten at staves!"

Eirgei paused, and his glare sharpened. "Now, on to the second and more serious transgression."

Second transgression? More serious?

Wyl tried to think what else he'd done wrong. Maybe his mouth had gotten him into trouble, but he knew his behavior had been above reproach.

"Under no circumstances will you take the Young Court hostage! We do not make war on *children!* The Evroza do not make war on children! You need to be accepted by the Young Court, not in control of it!"

The last bit of warmth in Wyl froze under Eirgei's furious glare.

He was more vile than the Evroza?

"It goes without saying that if you have crossed Crown Prince Norren with this insane scheme, you need to get back in his good graces. Fit in, I said, not take over! This is a Young Court, not a band of brigands! I do not care if you have to crawl, you will repair the damage to your relationship with Crown Prince Norren."

Eirgei paused and took several careful breaths, pinching the bridge of his nose between his eyes. "Did it never occur to you that putting your foot wrong with Royenne Errengard's favorite grandchild might create problems for your mother in the Crown Court and interfere with our efforts to raise a menney?"

Wyl felt the blood drain from his face. Royenne Errengard's refusal to support them with a menney was all because of him?

"No, it didn't occur to me," he got out, barely a whisper. He coughed. "I thought it was a ruse, you taking my weapons when we got here. I thought you were testing…testing my fitness to take charge of the scouts when we got back to Milkdales."

He swallowed and couldn't continue.

Eirgei sighed, shook his head, and slowly ran his hands down his face. "You have done some damage to our cause, boy. Try not to do any more. And keep your mouth shut about *anything* you have done in Milkdales. The only people who will be impressed are brigands and outlaws—and there are none in Nornholm! Are my orders clear?"

Wyl slid from his bench at the table, put down one knee, and bowed his head until it touched his raised knee. He wanted to put down two knees, even grovel, except that would only enrage the old man—though he'd rather grovel to him than to Crown Prince Norren. But he had to obey Eirgei's orders or his family would surely be forced to disown him for cause—all their hopes depended on Royenne Errengard's favor and a Dremn menney.

Eirgei sighed again and dismissed him to his room.

Wyl fled up the stairs.

By the time he reached the fourth floor, he'd passed from shock into fury.

Who cared about *his* honor? He was what he was, whether a haughty horde of oversized Dremn younglings liked it or not. Ending the blood-feud was all that really mattered—and winning it before the Evroza could do it on their terms, with heads rolling.

The practice floor was bare and dark, except for the dim rushlights hanging from the unlit candle trees along the curving wall. Despite his presence in Tras Tower for nearly a moon, Eirgei still hadn't said a word about resuming Wyl's daily training.

Wyl shot home the bolt of his door and exploded with fury. He wanted to destroy something and kicked the wooden trunk that held his clothing across the room. It smashed into the wall, but neither wall nor trunk was damaged.

He flung himself down on his pallet, then rolled over, his arm flung over his eyes.

He swallowed, imagining facing the Young Court in the morning, now that he knew the truth about his place in it.

The coldness of the young courtiers was not merely because he was Tras, but rather the natural reaction of nobility when faced with a blatant disregard for honor. He couldn't truly blame them. The fault was with him. Not only had he boasted of his shame, but everything he'd claimed was true.

Helgurdda's situation in Nornholm wouldn't get better, not now.

Royenne Errengard's failure to provide Helgurdda with the promised menney meant her promise of asylum couldn't be trusted. That was, after all, what it meant to be outlawed—no one's word was binding, and no honor was damaged by reneging on publicly-witnessed promises.

Helgurdda and Eirgei had become too desperate, had gotten their hopes too high if they believed they were safe here. This Nornholm scheme was bound to end with betrayal—but now, Wyl had no plan for dealing with it.

Perhaps his ongoing hostilities with the Bearcubs were what had kept him from being lulled by the peacefulness here—Nornholm was really no different from a rebel camp except that, in camp, he knew how to make outlaws respect him, and he'd been able to make them deal with him like a fully-grown member of Helgurdda's inner circle—too dangerous to cross, let alone prey upon.

But according to Eirgei—and his own experience backed it up—those tactics wouldn't work in Nornholm. He was at a complete loss about what he could do once Royenne Errengard tired of their nagging presence.

He groaned aloud. Eirgei wanted him back in Crown Prince Norren's favor, but that just wasn't going to happen. It certainly hadn't happened with the crown princess when he'd come crawling back to the Young Court after Eirgei had stopped him from returning to Milkdales to avenge Lanney.

They all knew he wasn't one of them—an outlaw in fine charity clothes was still an outlaw.

The only thing his humiliating return had done was make Crown Princess Kotakei scorn him, and the rest of the Young Court had followed her lead.

Then, there was the problem of Lord Martei, who surely believed he had permission to bully Wyl—and probably did! Wyl could hardly beg for Crown Prince Norren's forgiveness, then turn around and properly defend himself against the prince's best friend if his situation in the Young Court worsened the way he expected it would.

Lord Martei went nowhere without his friends, and without Lanney watching Wyl's back, the odds would be anything from three to eight against him—and with those odds, Lord Martei could pick a fight and win.

If Lord Martei killed him, Wyl knew the Dremn would excuse it as an accident—*only to be expected when children are allowed to play with real weapons*, he could imagine Crown Prince Norren saying.

But if Wyl managed to kill Lord Martei or one of his cronies, he was sure to be judged a rogue. His family would be forced to disown him—always assuming Viceroye Frekkei didn't fly into a rage and take his head, his age be damned.

The only fate worse than his present situation would be if, in the future, he had to become consort to an enemy baronne's daughter, surety for some treaty after Helgurdda was Royenne of Trascolm—why else would Eirgei care about his name being tainted by the Three Dishonors?

So, now Wyl understood what had cost him the respect of the Young Court, but Eirgei hadn't actually told him how to get that respect back—if, indeed, he'd ever had it.

Because it just wasn't possible, not now.

Crawling to Crown Prince Norren wasn't the answer—Wyl couldn't even get the Young Court to call him by his name, and that had already been a problem before he'd disgraced himself. Following Eirgei's orders would only encourage them to torment him. Just like a brigand band, the Bearcubs would read his groveling as weakness and attack him.

Thanks to his boast of being the rebellion's best spy—even though it was true—he'd become more of an outcast in Nornholm than he'd ever been as a rebel, or even on the streets of Myymor.

Tomorrow, he'd have to face the world, finally understanding full-well where he stood in it and why.

Well, he needn't fear making more mistakes—he'd already made them all. Though he'd done his best to carry out his duty to his family, he felt hopelessly mired in failure. This exile had cost him his place in the rebellion, but there was no place for him in Nornholm, either—no more than there'd been a place for him in Myymor or anywhere else he'd ever been.

He felt helpless, lost, and very alone.

And horrifyingly close to tears.

✦

3rd Day of the Moon of Ice, 113 G.E.

The next afternoon, when Wyl left the Heir's Tower, he forced himself to nonchalantly head across the courtyard to the battlements of the upper bailey. He hadn't begged forgiveness of Crown Prince Norren for having admitted to being a spy, and tonight he might have to face Eirgei over that refusal.

He climbed up the wooden steps near the High Gate. The west side of the battlements, where the stone steps formed part of the wall's bulwark and breastworks at the cliff's brink, were too close to Tras Tower—the next to the last place he wanted to be, after the Heir's Tower.

He crossed the parapet, then climbed through a crenel far enough beyond the wooden stairs that the gate guards below wouldn't hear him easing down onto the creaky hoardings.

He walked back until he was directly over the High Gate. His lair was the one place outside his bolted room in Tras Tower where he could be sure no one could see him. He sat down with his back against the battlements.

He pulled his wax charm from his robber's pouch and hung its thong around his neck. This was not the time to experiment, so he wrote *hide me* on it in Teboan with the tip of a throwing knife while saying the word under his breath.

The immediate tingle of success failed to thrill him. He slipped the charm under the high collar of his white tunic so it touched his skin.

That was the best he could do for himself before he curled into a tight ball, his arms wrapped around his legs and his forehead on his knees, desperately clutching at his self-control.

After Lord Martei's beating, he'd had to suffer three weeks of active scorn and veiled threats from the Bearcubs—nothing he hadn't expected after his humiliating defeat. Now, though, he knew his troubles really stemmed from that stupid boast that he was the rebels' best spy, thinking to impress them. Instead, he'd damned himself to an impossible, unendurable existence. He felt like a youngling again, back in the camps, back before Lanney had come, before Eirgei had agreed to train him.

Memories from those dark, helpless days came back too easily. Only, this time it wasn't just a nightmare, it was real. He couldn't go back to living like that, with the Bearcubs tormenting him the way the brigand-rebels had.

But this time, Eirgei couldn't help him. Against the scorn of the Young Court, everything he'd learned from Eirgei was useless—he couldn't resort to his knives like he had with the vicious recruits in Helgurdda's menney, not against children.

Eirgei was right. It was his fault Helgurdda couldn't draw warbands to join her menney. Her return to Trascolm was now a distant dream, likely to be years rather than moons in the making, thanks to his mistakes.

In Milkdales, Eirgei's training had hardened Wyl to physical torments as much as twice-daily practice beatings could make him, but nothing Eirgei had ever done to him could match the pain he felt now.

The now-faded bruises from Lord Martei—and the unseen ones from both Eirgei's punitive training and his brief, belated lessons with a staff—were the kind of hurts Wyl had learned to bear without complaint—a price he had gladly paid to put childhood behind him.

But the lonely, desperate pain he felt now in his head was even worse than what he'd felt on the streets in Myymor, where he'd been casually despised and scorned as a half-blind Folk outcast—that, thanks to the *upala* leaf infusion trick that dilated his pupils and made his eyes look more properly Folk-black and unremarkable.

There was a big difference between being hated for *what* he was— Lanney's pet fosterling or a disowned street urchin in Myymor—and being hated for *who* he was. Nothing he'd ever known had prepared him for being universally hated on his own account—regardless of his shiny-new, princely identity.

Despite being Tras, he'd thought he'd found a friend in Crown Prince Norren—no matter that he'd intended to use it to his own ends—but that had quickly soured. Now he understood why—what prince would want to be friends with a spy?

Black despair crushed him.

No matter who he was—half-Folk fosterling and bodyguard, half-blind outcast and spy, or Helgurdda's half-Tras, half-Gerisari slave's get—he was a disappointment to everyone who counted.

First, for not being born a girl, the all-important heir to Helgurdda's future crown. Thanks to his history studies in the Young Court, he now knew that, as a usurping royenne's son, he'd have little control over his future and even fewer choices in it. That was really why he'd been given Hereres's troth-ring, not simply because Hereres had been his sire.

Second, as he'd grown older, he had become a painful reminder of Hereres—how many times now had Helgurdda called him by that name, then corrected herself with a mournful sigh?

Third, he was a constant disappointment to Eirgei. Back before Lanney joined them, when he'd begged Eirgei for weapons training, Eirgei had flatly refused to teach him. Oh, eventually, Eirgei had grudgingly changed his mind and agreed to train him—Wyl had been willing to learn from anyone who *would* teach him, and Eirgei had his reputation as the Wolf of Milkdales to uphold. Eirgei couldn't let him get inferior training; he'd be embarrassed if Wyl turned out to be inept with weapons—no matter that no one else among the rebels had known he was Eirgei's grandnephew.

Even after Eirgei had reluctantly agreed to train him, Eirgei had said—just as Crown Prince Norren had—that he was too young and too small for it. They'd both been at pains to prove it to him.

Learning a minion's skills had meant seven years of constant, painful struggle. Eirgei treated him no differently than he did his full-grown rebel recruits, except for insisting Wyl wear a *byrnney* instead of real mail.

When he'd been ten, Eirgei had judged him ready to learn to use a sabre, but there had been no weapon that wasn't too long and heavy for him. He had spent years learning to compensate for that sabre while fighting Eirgei, but now that he'd grown over this past summer, and his sabre was—at last!—no longer too much blade for him, Eirgei was making no attempt to move forward with his training.

Eirgei had always called training him a waste of time. Eirgei said that if he took after his sire when he was grown, he'd be pretty but useless in a fight—there was nothing Eirgei could teach him that could overcome his handicap in size and strength, now or in the future.

The truth was, for all Helgurdda revered Hereres's memory, Eirgei had despised Wyl's sire, and like Helgurdda, whenever he looked at Wyl, he saw Hereres.

When Wyl had been eight, he'd told Eirgei he wanted to become Helgurdda's champion, her viceroye and Right Hand, just like him; Eirgei's reaction had been to try even harder to make him quit training, telling him over and over that fighting against someone bigger and stronger, and of equal skill, meant he'd always lose the fight, no matter how hard he tried.

It was Calderek who Eirgei secretly favored to eventually take his place as Helgurdda's champion, not Wyl.

But there was an obvious answer to Eirgei's objections—Wyl wouldn't lose if no one was his equal. After all, he'd be no fit successor to Eirgei if there were anyone else as skilled, regardless of whether Helgurdda's enemies were bigger than he, even when he was grown. Eirgei was big, but there were younger minions who were bigger and stronger—and who were still no match for him.

Why couldn't that hold true for Wyl, too?

He angrily pressed the heels of his hands against his eyes.

None of it made any difference, anyway. The real truth was that, without Royenne Errengard's support, the three of them were nothing more than penniless exiles. And the longer they stayed in Nornholm, the likelier it would be that they'd have a falling out with the Icebear menney, especially once Eirgei's training sessions turned brutal.

Many of their rebel recruits deserted after the first few weeks of training because it was so grueling—and no few of them had come back as assassins, aiming more at Eirgei than at Helgurdda. But there was a big difference between the Icebears and Eirgei's outlaw pupils— the Icebears weren't desperate for pardons or to belong to a clan again. They had no reason to tolerate Eirgei's teaching methods. Wyl gave it no more than a moon before Eirgei had his new Icebear pupils teetering on the edge of revolt, too.

But Wyl never would.

Eirgei could keep trying to make him quit, but after surviving training bouts with him morning and night, who or what else could scare him? Now that he had been in battle, it didn't seem so daunting—even in their loss to the Evroza, the actual fighting hadn't lasted more than a few hours, and he had known he'd never be pitted against Eirgei's equal, nor would any of the fighting ever approach the long intensity of a punishment training bout.

Yet, Eirgei hadn't done any training with Wyl in the four weeks since they'd come to Nornholm, save twice—once to punish him after he'd tried to return to Milkdales to avenge Lanney, and the other, a training bout with sticks after Wyl's beating by Lord Martei. For the last moon, Wyl had been reduced to doing shadow drills to keep up his skills.

In fact, except for a few nights like last night, he'd hardly seen either Helgurdda or Eirgei. The two of them never talked about anything important around him anymore, nor asked for his ideas as they planned their return to Milkdales.

Because they planned *their* return, not his.

He stared out over the lower bailey and into the distance, seeing nothing as he sank deeper into terrible thoughts.

Sending him to the Young Court, banishing him from Helgurdda's side, it was exactly what he'd feared all along—the first step in a new attempt to disown him. Helgurdda and Eirgei had always said they stayed away from him to protect him.

But the truth was, he'd survived far rougher company in the camps than what was inside Nornholm's walls. He didn't need their protection.

The truth was clear. He just hadn't wanted to face it—that no matter what he did, they simply didn't want him.

All that he'd endured to make himself less of a burden made no difference to them. He'd fought his own battles, learned to take care of himself—yet, they still saw him as an inconvenient youngling, an untrustworthy complication who'd ruin all their plans.

Not only had *they* lied to him, *he* had lied to himself. He'd always pretended physical injuries were the only ones that mattered. If there was no blood, there was no harm done—that was what he'd always said, even to himself.

But the truth was, he'd rather bleed than feel the way he did right now.

Oh, wouldn't all his enemies enjoy seeing him disowned!

He gasped at the sharp pain that ripped through his head and knotted his stomach, and it was suddenly too much to bear. He pressed his forehead hard against his knees and arms to hide his face as he faced the hard truth.

And cried in miserable silence.

He didn't run dry until his breath rasped in his throat. Then he just sat numbly, suppressing hiccups, still hiding his face, his head pounding with the pain that had smashed through all his defenses.

Being dead couldn't possibly be worse than this—in fact, if he were dead, it would be a relief to everyone in Nornholm, including himself. No one would miss him.

It ought to be simple enough to arrange—he'd never lacked for enemies.

In fact, with the hoardings so decrepit, he could even make it look like an accident, so no blame would fall on Helgurdda or Eirgei.

No, that wouldn't work: Eirgei knew how good he was at climbing. He'd know Wyl had taken the coward's way out—a final disappointment to him.

But even that didn't matter any more.

Nothing did.

Staying here, surrounded by enemies—it was like living in one of his nightmares, only worse, because he couldn't wake up so long as Eirgei had forbidden him to leave Nornholm. Unlike in his dreams, there was no spider here to save him from the monsters. Living in Nornholm and attending the Young Court—so long as he'd thought he'd been biding his time, awaiting orders for a mission, he'd been able to endure it.

But now he knew the truth.

Once Helgurdda had her Dremn menney, she and Eirgei would return to Milkdales without him.

They meant to abandon him in Nornholm, just like they had done twice before in remote Folk villages in the Black Mountains, back when he'd been a child.

He closed his eyes, feeling hollow, drained empty of emotion.

Tired of living.

What was the point in going on like this? He had no future worth living for.

He rested his aching head on his knees.

CHAPTER 23

ANOTHER ESCAPE

The emptiness inside Wyl shattered into a sudden panic.

He woke, gasping and coughing, and staggered to his feet, drawing his boot knives and putting his back to the battlements as he frantically tried to sort out what had just happened.

It took several long moments of groggy confusion before he recognized where he was and that he'd been awakened by feet thundering up the wooden steps on the other side of the battlements.

He turned, but couldn't see through the crenel. The hoardings sagged too low at this spot. He was well-hidden if he stayed put, as safe as he ever could be.

Something thudded on the parapet. He could hear Lord Martei's angry voice snarling curses at someone in time with the unmistakable sounds of that someone getting pummeled.

Wyl sheathed his knives and searched out a couple finger holds on the wall so he could climb up and look through the crenel at what was happening.

The commotion was a fight between Lord Martei and Prince Lokei, the youngest of the Icebear princes.

Not surprisingly, the younger, smaller boy was getting the worst of it—just as Eirgei had predicted. Given that a gap of nearly four years stood between Prince Lokei and Lord Martei, and the differences in size, weight, and experience those years brought with them, Prince Lokei didn't stand a chance.

He was a fool to be in this fight at all.

Yet, Prince Lokei had never struck Wyl as a fool—he seemed to put a lot of thought into whatever he did.

So, what had Prince Lokei been thinking? Why was he fighting Lord Martei?

Then, there were more feet on the steps, and two of Lord Martei's friends appeared on the parapet to help with the ruthless beating Lord Martei was delivering.

"—and stay out of my affairs!" Lord Martei bellowed, punctuating it with another kick.

To give Prince Lokei credit, he was down, but still fighting back, grabbing and twisting Lord Martei's kicking foot. "Then stay away from my sister!"

Wyl went cold.

Princess Elfreida was only eight, a youngling.

This couldn't be happening. Not here. Nornholm wasn't a brigand camp.

Lord Martei delivered yet another kick to the downed prince. "Stay out of my way! Play time was just getting interesting—and what did you think you were going to do to me?"

Wyl felt like *he* was the one who'd just gotten kicked. Of course, why else would sensible Prince Lokei take on a fight he couldn't win? This wasn't just boys' foolish squabbling—he could guess what Lord Martei's idea of playing must be like to so enrage the girl's brother. Prince Lokei was young, but he wasn't blind—Wyl wasn't the only one who could see the brigand under Lord Martei's lordly looks.

The younger boy's stubborn determination was actually impressive. Despite his youthfulness and being overmatched—and now outnumbered—the stripling was courageously doing just as a brother ought to protect his sister.

Wyl silently slid back down the wall to the hoardings.

In the camps, he'd learned the hard way not to go looking for trouble that didn't belong to him, or if he did, not to fight full-grown and well-seasoned versions of Lord Martei on their terms.

But Lord Martei wasn't yet full-grown or well-seasoned—that had to make a difference.

There was also the matter of the beating he owed Lord Martei.

Still, he hesitated, reckoning the odds.

He felt sick, as he always did at the prospect of a fight.

He could prevail against Lord Martei so long as he fought on his own terms—Prince Lokei's beating here was proof that a *fair fight* against Lord Martei would be anything but that. The problem was that Lord Martei wasn't alone. It would be three to one or worse, with Prince Lokei down and unable to continue to fight, but still a target in need of protection.

Not his kind of odds. They'd kill him for sure.

Then the boys began to laugh.

Their mocking hoots echoed in his head. The blinding pain came back.

Wyl went very still.

In the time between one breath and the next, he had a plan. He looked at the plan from every angle, teased out every likely outcome.

There weren't many.

A weight lifted from him.

Eirgei would approve. *A warleader must seize his opportunities where he finds them.*

Wyl couldn't abandon a couple of children. Not to these monstrous bullies.

He reached up and wedged his callused fingers into the seam between the ashlar blocks, and quietly levered himself high enough to throw an arm over the bottom of the crenel, then up and onto the parapet behind Lord Martei's back.

"Beating up her brother isn't the way to win a princess's favor," Wyl said.

He enjoyed seeing all three of the tormenters spin around, startled.

The battered stripling might have startled, too, if he weren't slumped over, nearly unconscious.

"Well, if it isn't the Little Wolf, our Tras-trash prince, poking his nose where it doesn't belong."

Wyl had distracted them, but the stripling boy remained heaving on the parapet—trying to either breathe or puke.

Not good.

The young prince needed to get to his feet and run while he could, before this went from bad to worse.

But Wyl had never felt so calm, so at peace.

He laughed, really laughed, and it felt strange. He couldn't remember the last time he had. The pain in his head eased as he embraced his plan and felt relief. He didn't have to force a grin. "I can see you're brave enough, when the odds are three to one."

"You know all about being helpless, even at one to one. That pretty much describes you the last time you crossed me," Lord Martei said.

"Sounds like you've forgotten and need another beating to refresh your memory!"

"Except you're missing your big stick and about sixteen friends," Wyl retorted. "But you're welcome to try!"

He glanced behind Lord Martei to see if Prince Lokei was on his feet yet, but the boy was still dazed, feebly scrabbling at the stonework rather than scrambling to his feet and running while Wyl kept Lord Martei and his friends distracted.

Not good.

He had hoped to get in a strike against Lord Martei when Prince Lokei's departure distracted him and his friends.

"Why don't you try playing this game with someone who knows how to play?" Wyl said. "Someone a little more...challenging."

A quick look down into the courtyard showed it was empty—there was no chance of someone intervening before this went too far.

Good.

He didn't need some Dremn passerby saving Lord Martei. He wanted to finish this—the sooner, the better, before he lost his courage.

Lord Martei frowned, glancing between him and Prince Lokei, no doubt weighing which beating would be the most satisfying to deliver.

The young lord's hesitation surprised Wyl—and he felt the edge of panic. Everything would go wrong if he let Lord Martei pause and think.

So, he began backing away, creating a passable imitation of sudden fear to draw them after him and away from Prince Lokei. As he did, he waited for Prince Lokei to get to his feet.

So far, save for Prince Lokei's continued presence, all was going according to his plan. Lord Martei and his friends were more than eager to shift their malice away from Prince Lokei and towards him, but they seemed wary of a trick.

He didn't blame them. Who would take on three bigger, stronger enemies all at once? Of course, it was a trick—but he hoped it was also an irresistible temptation.

Prince Lokei finally scrambled upright, swaying.

Then, incredibly, the young prince started staggering after the bigger boys like he was still in the fight.

"Run!" Wyl bellowed in a carrying, battlefield commander's voice.

At his shout, Prince Lokei stared at him with a combination of shock and anger, until the understanding dawned on his face that Wyl was trying to help him, not joining forces with Lord Martei and his friends.

And in that moment, Lord Martei took the bait.

Wyl glimpsed the fleeting change in his face when Lord Martei decided to rush him, and Wyl made his own move at the same time. The closest way off the parapet was down the wooden stairs behind the three youths. But for once, though outnumbered by enemies older and bigger than he, Wyl wasn't anxious to escape. He already had the initiative, control of the fight.

What could Lord Martei do now, but react to whatever move he made?

All he needed now was ground of his own choosing.

So he ran to put Mount Norn at his back and turned at bay, giving a defiant rebel wolf's howl. It wasn't a cry for help—there was no hope of Eirgei hearing it, and anyway, he didn't want rescuing.

What he wanted was a chance, at last, to do something right.

The youths paused, probably not because of the eerie rebel howl, but because they knew he was cornered.

They grinned in anticipation.

Wyl feigned dismay.

"Your presence among us is an insult. You do not belong here, but if you must stay in the Young Court," Lord Martei smirked and cracked his knuckles, "I am willing to hammer in a few more lessons until you know your place, Tras."

"You're welcome to try," Wyl said. "I'm looking forward to it—I haven't murdered anyone since I got here."

His left eyelid started twitching, so he narrowed his eye into his rogue's glare to hide it.

His palms sweated—another telltale of fear, but it didn't matter anymore. He was tired of being afraid, tired of everything. Though this battle would be fought on his terms, he'd still be glad when this was over.

Lord Martei jumped forward, hands outstretched to seize him.

Wyl spun aside and vaulted through the crenel, landing on the decrepit boards. He felt the wood give under his feet when he landed, but the boards held, and he shifted along the outside of the battlements, well-out of Lord Martei's reach.

He could use the hoardings to get around the youths and get to the stairs, taking advantage of their momentary surprise. He could escape them easily enough, if he chose.

He didn't—in the moment before he'd jumped onto the hoardings, he'd seen that Prince Lokei had gone back down on one knee by the stairs, still gasping. Wyl couldn't lead Lord Martei and his friends right back to their victim.

Lord Martei hopped up to straddle the battlements and dropped heavily down onto the hoardings. A support brace gave a loud crack, and the section of boards abruptly slanted down and away from the wall.

The youth who was about to join Lord Martei on the hoardings froze in mid-straddle.

"Out of my way, fool!" Lord Martei snarled, turning to get back off the hoardings.

Wyl felt the beginnings of real panic—if Lord Martei gave up now, he'd be free to go back and deal with Prince Lokei. Everything depended on keeping Lord Martei focused on Wyl—his clever plan would be ruined, otherwise.

"What, that didn't scare you, did it?" Wyl mocked the bigger boy a little wildly, feeling the boards under his own feet beginning to sag. He gently stepped backwards to what he hoped was sounder footing directly over a support bracket. "Are you afraid of heights or are you just afraid of me?"

Lord Martei turned back towards him, his outsized fists in bony balls. "I am not afraid of heights, and I am certainly not afraid of you!"

"*Heh*, so the thought did cross your mind." Wyl was surprised he was actually enjoying this, despite the mouth-drying, throat-tightening anticipation of how this would end. "I bet you've never fought anyone tougher than your sister when you didn't have a big stick in your hands."

Lord Martei's eyes flashed fire. "Do not say a word about Kallent!"

"A word about Kallent," Wyl echoed back derisively, and groped for whatever else would fuel the fire. "And maybe a few more—I hear she doesn't think much of—"

Lord Martei lunged for him.

Two more supports cracked sharply with each bounding step.

Wyl danced backwards, the hoardings silent under his feet. "*Heh*, if this is all the better you can defend her, no wonder she doesn't think much of you!"

The planking suddenly sagged even more, jerking away from the cliff wall where it had been bolted.

Wyl backed away faster.

Lord Martei's two friends hurried along the parapet. In a moment, they'd be on the hoardings, too, and at Wyl's back, trapping him between them and Lord Martei.

The hoardings were sure to give way under their combined weight.

He felt a dark satisfaction at the prospect.

Let them come.

Lord Martei stalked forward, closing the gap with Wyl as more supports cracked underfoot.

The slope of the planking became steep enough to make Lord Martei start to slide backwards.

A support bracket and several more planks behind Lord Martei tore completely away from the wall and plummeted to the ground.

Lord Martei sprang, not at Wyl, but head-first through the next crenel, hooking his elbows over the lip. His friends ran back at his bellow to help pull him onto the parapet, while the planks from where he'd launched himself broke and fell.

Wyl was disappointed and had to force a laugh as he skittered backwards on the hoardings, tauntingly just out of reach—but now that he was alone on the hoardings, he was prepared to dive through the nearest crenel himself, if more of the decrepit boards gave way. Better to find a way to take Lord Martei with him rather than to fall alone—and better still to have one last chance to do Eirgei proud, to go down fighting rather than falling.

Lord Martei looked furiously for something to throw, but the battlements were too well-kept.

One of Lord Martei's companions threw his jeweled side-dagger at Wyl.

He swayed away. Just out of habit, he turned to mark where it fell in the lower bailey.

"*Ockh*, looks like he's stabbed your sister," Wyl jeered at Lord Martei.

He had to laugh when Lord Martei craned his head through the crenel to see past him, looking for his twin below.

She wasn't there, of course, but some servants waiting outside a workshop in the lower bailey pointed up at them.

"I warned you about my sister!" Lord Martei snarled. Then a peculiar look came over his face. "You are *jealous!* You are jealous I have a sister and you do not!"

That penetrated Wyl's bubble of blissful emptiness.

He scowled at Lord Martei. "I'm not!"

His denial was a little too quick, and Lord Martei laughed at him.

"You are worthless—you do not count for anything. You might as well be an outcast as have no sister!"

"I don't need a sister!" Wyl shot back, stung by the truth in Lord Martei's words. He groped to regain his sense of distance, of calmness. "I've got the next royenne of Trascolm—"

"Not yet, you do not! And I warned you not to say anything about my sister! I do not want to hear her name pass your lying Tras lips."

"All you do is talk," Wyl said and coughed. "You might as well be a youngling for all the good you do her. But no matter what you do, Kallent will never be anything more than heir to a petty barbarian baronne, bowing and scraping for crumbs of royal favor—just like you!"

"You take that back, Tras!" Lord Martei's eyes narrowed, looking in the distance past Wyl. He suddenly dashed ahead on the parapet before turning to climb through another crenel.

Lord Martei intended to climb back onto the hoardings and trap Wyl with the collapsed section at his back.

Wyl raced over the decaying planks to meet the older boy as he straddled the battlements with one long leg and started to swing his other leg over.

Wyl grabbed his leading leg.

Lord Martei was much bigger than he, but the youth wasn't expecting this move. His sudden weight on Lord Martei's leg was enough to tug him off-balance and down onto the planks.

Lord Martei hit awkwardly, with a thump, followed by a crack from underneath the hoardings. The crown prince's favorite rolled to get to his feet and got up as far as onto all fours—

—And Wyl viciously kicked him in the gut.

He threw everything he had into that kick, but since he lacked Lord Martei's size, it couldn't have been as hard as Prince Lokei had been kicked.

All the same, Wyl's foot smashed Lord Martei sideways against the battlements, where the lordling slumped, clutching his middle and choking.

Wyl cautiously bounced back out of reach, not trusting Lord Martei was as stunned as he seemed.

As Lord Martei's friends dithered over whether joining Lord Martei on the hoardings would help him or send them all crashing to the rocky ground below, Lord Martei struggled upright and sprang for the crenel and the safety of the parapet.

Lord Martei's friends pulled him by his arms, while Wyl jumped to clutch him by one leg, trying to pull him back down. Lord Martei kicked at him with his free foot, but Wyl jerked his head aside and held fast as the young lord dragged him up the wall. Then the lordling's friends wrenched Lord Martei out of his grasp.

Wyl had lost his opportunity.

Humiliating Lord Martei—but failing to kill him—would only make him more dangerous, his animosity towards Wyl worse.

And now there was the risk his retribution might extend to Prince Lokei and his little sister, too.

"I will get you for this!" Lord Martei snarled.

"*Heh*, not if this is the best you can do, at three against one, Lord Lame Brain," Wyl snorted. "Come on, try me, take me on! Are you afraid of a little wolf, Little Lamb?"

Though a muscle jumped in his clenched jaw, Lord Martei clearly wouldn't let himself be lured back onto the hoardings, so Wyl swarmed up through a nearby crenel and onto the parapet.

He drew his two long knives from his boots—plain, workaday jegurit bronze ones he could hold or throw. He crossed them and tapped the blades together to make them ring, like brigands did in the camps when there was a fight.

"You had your fun with sticks, so now it's my turn. Wait until you see what I can do when I really put my mind to it—how many people have *you* killed, little boy?"

"I must have hit you in the head with my staff harder than I thought," Lord Martei said. "There are three of us and one of you. Are you suicidal? What are you thinking?"

"I'm thinking I'm the Wolf of Milkdales's best pupil, and it's time I demonstrated why."

Lord Martei scowled and drew his side-dagger, but his two friends exchanged uneasy glances and muttered something about the royenne as they backed a few steps.

Wyl's attention remained on Lord Martei.

Lord Martei cast a glance over his shoulder at his friends.

"Don't tell me you're afraid of me, at three to one?" Wyl gave the lordling a snide grin. That and the name-calling ought to irritate him past bearing.

"I am not afraid of you, Tras. But you are Ice Bear kith, one of the royenne's pets. Perhaps some other time."

Lord Martei sheathed his side-dagger with arrogant dignity, as if he'd won their fight. He looked narrowly at Wyl, eying the length of his knives. "Stab me in the back, if you dare, Tras trash!"

He turned and left the parapet, and somehow he made it *not* look like he was in retreat.

Wyl stared in disbelief as they disappeared down the stairs. "Cowardly stick-whacker!"

As his adrenalin faded, his mood turned darker than before. Now, tomorrow would be even worse than today—and today had been unbearable.

He sheathed his knives and boosted himself up into a crenel with a hop. He crouched over his heels, looking through a new gap in the broken boards to the ground far below.

He'd taken falls before, of course, but never from such a height.

"Thank you for your aid."

Prince Lokei startled Wyl so badly that he all but fell over backwards when he reflexively snatched out a boot knife and spun out of the crenel to put his back to the parapet wall.

While Wyl had faced Lord Martei on the hoardings, he hadn't let his attention wander. He hadn't even thought to look for the stripling prince once he'd lured Lord Martei onto the rotting boards. He'd thought the young prince sensible enough to run away.

But he hadn't.

"I cannot believe you challenged Martei and his friends like that—and that Martei backed down!" Prince Lokei exclaimed. "My cousin Reien was the last one brave enough to call him out, and Martei broke Reien's leg."

"It's nothing," Wyl said, feeling awkward, miserably wishing the boy would go away. "I owed Lord Martei a thrashing."

"All the same, my thanks," Prince Lokei said, and he gave the head-nod of princes and waited expectantly until Wyl belatedly returned it. "I am in your debt."

"Just get back to the Heir's Tower without running into Lord Martei again," Wyl said.

But Prince Lokei seemed in no great hurry to leave. He leaned against the merlon and glanced down at the hoardings.

Or at the hole in them.

He then smiled up at Wyl with an uncomfortable intensity.

Wyl abruptly left.

He went down the wooden steps, suddenly aware that he hadn't seen where Lord Martei had gone and that several lonely courtyards remained between him and Tras Tower.

He could only hope that meant it wasn't over between them. He started walking towards Tras Tower.

As he crossed one of those isolated courtyards, he heard a scraping sound.

He whirled around, drawing both knives from his boots and settling into a crouch.

Then he saw who it was and straightened. "Why are you following me?"

Prince Lokei looked up at him with that odd intensity still in his blue eyes and just shrugged. "I do not know where Martei and his friends went, and I do not want to find out by myself."

Wyl sheathed his knives. He couldn't blame Prince Lokei for his caution.

He looked around and saw some Folk staring at him across a court-yard wall with disapproval.

"It's getting dark. I'll walk with you back to the Heir's Tower."

"You do not need to do that," Prince Lokei said, reddening.

Why else would the boy have followed him?

And he had to do it—those Folk had seen him with Prince Lokei. If anything happened to the stripling, he'd be blamed for it.

He'd deserve it, too.

If he kept going towards Tras Tower, he'd likely lead Prince Lokei into an ambush intended for him alone.

"I insist," Wyl said.

He shepherded the youngster back to the Heir's Tower, saw the boy safely inside, and hoped he hadn't seen the last of Lord Martei for the night.

"Have you seen Lord Martei recently?" he asked one of the guardsmen.

"If I have, I would not tell you," the guardsman said, looking over his head like he wasn't there.

He glared at the guard. "Fine. Then, when you don't see him, tell Lord Martei I'm waiting for him, just as soon as he's found enough guts and friends to come looking for me. I won't be hard to find."

"Pass on your own messages, Tras. I am not yours to command."

"*Motherless hedge-get!*" Wyl snarled. He spun on his heel and left, slamming the courtyard door shut on the angry shout behind him.

CHAPTER 24

RESCUE

4ᵗʰ Day of the Moon of Ice, 113 G.E.

The next morning, when Wyl arrived for Young Court, one of the guardsmen rose from a game of senet to block his way to the stairs.

"You are not wanted in the Young Court," the guardsman said.

"Why not?" Wyl was suspicious of an insult.

The other guardsmen rose from their various amusements and converged on him.

Wyl took a quick step back.

Had they somehow learned of his clash with Lord Martei yesterday on the parapet? Had Lord Martei told Crown Prince Norren...Crown Princess Kotakei?

No, Lord Martei would no more admit to being humiliated than Wyl would, but what else could have emboldened these slackers to forbid him entry?

"It is not your place to question the crown princess's orders," one of the guards' hand-leaders said, shoving away from his senet game to stand shoulder to shoulder with the guardsman blocking the foot of the stairs. "She is as sick of seeing your surly, black and blue face every morning as we are."

That got some grins and evil laughs from his fellow guardsmen. The rest of the guardsmen rose now, some moving to block Wyl's way out of the Heir's Tower.

He had no illusions about how fond the guardsmen were of him.

They'd never troubled to hide their loathing any more than Norn-holm's Folk did. Nor had the guardsmen ever forgiven him for making fools of them the day he'd tried to return to Milkdales, when they'd scoured Nornholm without finding him.

Wyl started backing towards the corridor entry.

He could pull his long knives, but if it came to a fight, it wouldn't be one he could win—there were too many of them, and for Hel-gurdda's sake, he dared not kill an Icebear minion, not even in self-defense. Except for their Icebear surcoats, these royal guards were no better than brigands—they'd kill him on any pretext to have their revenge.

"Fine, I'm leaving," he said, with every semblance of calm he could pretend.

But the guards didn't clear a path for him.

"Not so fast!" a hand-leader said, and the other guardsmen laughed.

Wyl's fingers turned icy-cold and clammy.

These were royal guardsmen. They had to be bluffing—just trying to scare him. But he didn't try hard to believe it.

He shifted to put his back to the wall.

He should've jumped yesterday while he had the chance.

Only, he couldn't have, not in front of a child.

"What? Nothing smart to say?" goaded the hand-leader.

Wyl's eye started twitching.

They probably wouldn't kill him, but after four weeks of passing through the guardroom, coming and going from the Young Court, he knew they'd stoop to anything short of it.

His throat began to close, and he couldn't breathe. The edges of his vision started to go black. He swore he could smell death.

"Prince Wylheim!"

Prince Lokei bounded down the spiral stairs into the guardroom, sporting a big grin and a set of black eyes. "Grandmother summoned Kotakei and Norren to attend her in court. The rest of us have the day to ourselves!"

As Prince Lokei descended, the guardsmen casually wandered back to their amusements.

Wyl tried not to gasp as his throat eased, and let air trickle in. He stiffened his knees so he wouldn't slide down the wall and coughed.

Prince Lokei still bubbled with excitement, oblivious to what he'd interrupted. "Come! This is a great chance to show you parts of Norn Holm you haven't seen."

And he did.

Not only did Prince Lokei get him away from the guardsmen, he took Wyl around Nornholm and openly brought him into places he had never been welcomed into on his own.

People smiled pleasantly as they passed through the byways of Nornholm.

Wyl knew the smiles were for Prince Lokei and not for him. He struggled to hide their unnerving effect on him—usually when people smiled at an outcast, an unpleasant surprise awaited.

He shared Prince Lokei's interest in the forges and stood with him, watching the smith transform ingots of bronze and brass into nails, hinges, buckles, and candlesticks. The weaponsmith fascinated him even more—he gave that smith his full attention as he worked with molten ingots of copper and tin, then mixed in several other metals and powders to forge jektrar and jegurit weapons. Wyl knew much more about the qualities needed in a good blade than those that made a sound hinge, but he'd never been privileged to watch either being made, especially not up-close as the companion of a welcome spectator.

It felt strange.

The two boys toured the stables, both the lower bailey's workaday stock and the upper one's royal and noble mounts.

Prince Lokei needed no explanations to see and appreciate Firebrand's special qualities, and he knew how to handle—or not handle—a warhorse.

That Firebrand liked him made Wyl feel easier about Prince Lokei's presence.

Prince Lokei persuaded the Folk stablehands to show off the pride of their stables. They allowed the boys to admire Viceroye Frekkei's warhorse, an aggressive, heavily-built, dappled-gray from a respectful distance. Prince Lokei even talked the grooms into letting them pet the royenne's own palfrey, and Wyl recognized the gelding as his decoy horse from that awful night when he'd tried to leave Nornholm to avenge Lanney.

After that, Prince Lokei wanted to go watch the royenne's menney while they trained. The two of them climbed up to the top of the Heir's Tower and went out to the parapet around the roof. They had a perfect, if bird's eye view, of the Menney Tower and its courtyard.

Wyl gestured at it.

"Why are they just using sticks?" he asked.

"The Bear Cubs only train with staves," Prince Lokei said. "But, after they turn sixteen and join the Ice Bear menney, they will be allowed to train with edged weapons, as well."

"It doesn't sound very realistic," Wyl said. "Who goes around with a staff besides a lame person?" He still resented his humiliation at Lord Martei's hands in front of all the Bearcubs, and his inconclusive clash with Lord Martei on the hoardings only made it rankle more.

Prince Lokei just laughed.

The prince's laugh took Wyl by surprise, and he automatically stiffened.

Prince Lokei didn't seem to notice. "You can do a lot with a staff, even more than you can with a sword, especially if you do not want to kill someone."

"What's the point of not killing someone you're fighting?"

"For practice. A friendly fight."

That must be some weird barbarian custom—a friendly fight? He'd never heard of such a thing.

"*Ockh*, when we—Helgurdda's minions—practiced, it didn't end until blood was drawn. It was always no tactics barred, just like when we fight the Evroza. Serious fights ended only when one of the fighters couldn't continue the fight or was dead—just like in a duel."

"Eirgei did not stop them?"

Wyl snorted and that triggered a coughing fit.

He gave a sinister chuckle when he caught his breath. "*Heh, heh*, Eirgei usually started it! Brigands stay brigands, even wearing rebel surcoats, and there was always someone foolish enough to call him an old man and try to take over, boasting—"

He hesitated. He didn't want to repeat what they boasted about the rebel treasury and about Helgurdda. There were good reasons why those duels with Eirgei had been to the death.

"Those challengers were sloppy," he said, instead, "and Eirgei always complained that they weren't very good for practice—*fight sloppy opponents, and you grow sloppy yourself*, he always says. That's why he likes to train with me. I help him keep his edge."

So they watched the courtyard filled with minions—and a few women—sparring with sticks and occasionally erupting into wild surges of walloping.

Wyl was surprised to see that Eirgei was there himself, leaning on a staff, though his black sabre was in its sheath at his right shoulder. He broke in on one pair, holding his staff out between the two to halt them and snap out a lecture.

Viceroye Frekkei was absent—no doubt also attending Royenne Errengard in court. A massive, middle-aged Dremn, wearing a princely bulk of war-knot held in place with a jeweled hairpin, directed who Eirgei trained next.

Wyl remembered seeing that prince on his first day in Nornholm, leaning over a map and saying something about Calderek—and then later, the Icebear prince had scared him to half to death, coming up behind him outside the royenne's Crown Court hall.

For the first time, Wyl thought how odd it was that he didn't know the prince's name—or any of the key people in the Icebear menney or Royenne Errengard's household—a strange oversight on Eirgei's part. Eirgei had taught him about all the principal minions of the Evroza menney, their strengths, weaknesses, and habits, as well as a quirky de-scription of each one sufficient for Wyl to know any of them on sight when he spied in Myymor.

The Evroza had figured prominently in the waking nightmare that had been his childhood.

Stay still, Eirgei used to say before a battle, when Wyl would watch from a treetop, *or Lord Sterren will see you and shoot you full of arrows.*

Be quiet, he'd warn, when Wyl had first started spying, not in Myy-mor, but on the Evroza menney in the field, *or Viceroye Davren will hear and cut your throat.*

Yet, here in Nornholm, Wyl didn't know so much as the name of the warlord of the Icebear menney, Viceroye Frekkei's Right Hand.

Yet another sign that didn't bode well for his future as a rebel.

"Who's that?" he pointed.

Prince Lokei grinned. "That is Uncle Raldorrei, the younger of Grandmother's sons. He is my favorite uncle." He lowered his voice. "We have even practiced using real daggers—but do not tell Norren, it will just make him jealous. Uncle Frekkei is secretly teaching him, and Norren thinks he is the only one of us Ice Bear boys learning to use a dagger while we are underage. Of course, Uncle Raldorrei has been openly teaching all the girls since they became striplings."

"Should you have told me?" People free with other people's secrets had been some of Wyl's favorite people to try to befriend as a spy, but he wasn't a spy now—and he liked Prince Lokei. The boy made him feel strange inside—a disquieting feeling, but not entirely a bad one. It made him feel that wheedling Icebear secrets from Prince Lokei, even by accident, wouldn't be right.

"Sure, you are kith-kin, are you not? Just do not tell Norren."

Secrets are weapons. There must be a reason Prince Raldorrei trained Lokei in secret.

Prince Lokei tucked up his knees and put his arms around them. "Frankly, you are lucky not to be in the Bear Cubs. Norren likes his power, and he likes to make sure everyone under him knows it."

"You aren't his friend," Wyl said, stating the obvious because the reason was not. By blood, the two Dremn princes were the closest of cousins. Shouldn't that mean they were close friends, as well?

"He thinks I am a rival," Prince Lokei said. "If anything happens to Kotakei, my little sister Elfreida will be Grandmother's heir, and I will be her viceroye, not him. That is why Martei and his friends chased me yesterday—I caught Martei alone with Elfreida, but she is only eight and Martei does not just flirt. Maybe Wolverines tolerate that sort of thing, but Ice Bears do not—we protect our cubs." Prince Lokei scowled. "I think he has given up his hopes of winning Kotakei's favor—she dislikes him as much as Norren likes him. I do not understand how Norren could have a Wolverine as his favorite, even if he is kith-kin, or encourage him to woo to his sister, especially with her being underage."

Wyl wondered the same thing. "Eirgei says you can learn a lot about a person by knowing his friends. Maybe Crown Prince Norren's just more Wolverine than Icebear inside."

Prince Lokei looked aghast. "Do not let anyone hear you say that! Grandmother despises Wolverine clan, though Norren's sire was a Wolverine, and you do not want to make her angry if she hears that you compared her favorite to them!"

"It doesn't sound like Crown Prince Norren does what he ought, not if he's been encouraging Lord Martei to pant after his own sister!" It surprised Wyl how angry that made him. Nothing like this would have surprised him in the camps, but he'd expected better behavior from members of a royal court, even if it was only the Young Court.

Prince Lokei shrugged uncomfortably. "Normally, Norren is very protective of Kotakei. Elfreida would go mad if I acted the way he does with her. He has just gotten awfully...overbearing...since she became the crown princess last year."

"She's only been crown princess a year?"

Prince Lokei nodded somberly. "Before that, my Aunt Streila—her mother—was heir, but she was killed in a hunting accident—they were hunting deer, and she came across an ice bear after she and Norren and Lord Geilorren got separated from the others while chasing a wounded stag. They had hunting swords and no one had a bear spear. Lord Geilorren went for help, but the bear killed Aunt Streila's horse and turned on her. Norren got himself mauled pulling her up onto his horse, but she was already dying. Help arrived in time to kill the bear, but too late to save Aunt Streila."

Wyl didn't want to hear about Crown Prince Norren's heroic deeds, but he did want to learn more about Royenne Errengard's heir, so he nodded encouragingly. *Nothing's more important than knowing your enemy*, Eirgei always said.

"Ever since then," Prince Lokei said, "Norren has not been the same. Kotakei is all he has left—just like I am all Elfreida has left. Our mother was killed in an avalanche two years ago, so I understand what losing a mother is like."

Wyl was surprised to learn Prince Lokei was a true orphan. "But the Icebears shouldn't abandon you so long as you have a sister," he said, to reassure him.

Lokei looked surprised. "I am an Ice Bear prince—we do not abandon our own." He abruptly flushed. "Sorry, I forgot that your mother's clan disowned you."

Wyl chewed his lip, debating how to answer.

"They didn't, actually," he confessed. "They don't know I exist. Or, they didn't until Helg—my mother—presented me to your grandmother. Once word gets back to Milkdales about me, they'll want me dead—on account of the blood-feud, you know. I'm just another way for them to punish my mother and granduncle. I want nothing to do with my mother's former clan—you might say *I've* disowned *them*. Helgurdda and Eirgei, and our rebel menney are—*were*—my clan."

Prince Lokei sat silent for a while, his eyes on the minions, but his mind clearly elsewhere.

Wyl didn't interrupt the younger boy's thoughts. He just drew a throwing knife and used it to trim his nails.

Then, Prince Lokei turned to him. "It's a miracle your mother hasn't been killed after so many years of the Evroza hunting her and with a bounty on her head the size of an heir's ransom."

Wyl shrugged awkwardly. "It's easier to guard against assassins than a bear or an avalanche. And Eirgei and I probably watch over her as closely as Crown Prince Norren does Crown Princess Kotakei—but TolDaanyo help anyone who tries to bully her the way Crown Prince Norren does his sister." He shook his head with a wry smile at the very thought. "Eirgei's very old-fashioned, and once Helgurdda makes a decision, there's no more discussion. Helgurdda doesn't decide to do things just to make him happy. She decides to do things that make sense to her—even if sometimes, what she wants doesn't make sense to anyone else. Especially if it has anything to do with my sire."

Wyl stopped speaking abruptly, appalled at himself. He'd never criticized Helgurdda aloud, voicing his own opinion about the thing she held most dear—her obsession with Hereres. Not until now.

Why was he babbling all this to Prince Lokei?

"Then your granduncle and my uncle ought to deal well with each other," Prince Lokei said, not reacting to his disloyal outburst. "It sounds like they came from the same forge."

They had nothing more to say, so the two of them watched the royenne's menney train.

Wyl silently compared how Eirgei had trained him against how he trained the Icebear menney and was relieved that Eirgei was being very selective in what he taught them. Maybe the Icebears wouldn't turn on Eirgei after all, though there was no hope that this impossible alliance of Tras and Dremn would last any longer than it would take to overthrow Royenne Sharei.

Eirgei hadn't taught Wyl all his tricks, but he was teaching far fewer of those tricks to the Icebears, just enough of them that Viceroye Frekkei or Prince Raldorrei could make no complaint of him.

Watching the minions suffer, Wyl was sure those two princes would be the only ones who didn't complain about Eirgei and his methods.

A happy pupil, Eirgei always said, *is a complaisant one*, and his granduncle despised complaisancy as much as he did ignorance. Wyl hoped Prince Raldorrei, the warlord of the Icebear menney, would still be pleased when the Icebear minions rebelled against Eirgei's teaching methods.

Since Crown Princess Kotakei's absence meant there was no formal midday meal today in the Heir's Tower, Prince Lokei showed Wyl the best tower kitchen to raid for a meal, and they scampered off to eat it from atop the battlements of the upper bailey.

It was the first meal Wyl had actually enjoyed since coming to Nornholm.

This had to be the most perfect day of his life.

"Just call me Lokei," Prince Lokei said. "No need to stand on ceremony with each other, since we're kith. That is one of the privileges of being royal kith-kin, Prince Wylheim."

"Then you do the same." Wyl still felt mocked whenever someone called him *Prince Wylheim*. The Young Court, of course, followed Crown Princess Kotakei's lead and called him *Prince Tras*. Only the younglings called him *Wyl*. "And call me Wyl. When I'm called Wylheim, it means I'm in trouble."

"Why did you do it?" Lokei asked, after they finished eating.

"Do what?" Wyl asked warily. What was he being blamed for now?

"Pick a fight with Martei yesterday."

He shrugged uncomfortably. "I try to pick a fight once a week, and this week was almost over."

"No, seriously. Those three would have killed you and called it an accident."

Wyl allowed himself a moment of irony. "As it happens, I had arranged an accident for them, too."

Lokei looked at him, frowning. "But *why* did you do it? None of us knew you were up there on the battlements with us. Those boys are three of the five most dangerous minions in the Bear Cubs—me, they would not dare kill, but no matter what Martei claims, if they thought they could kill you, they would have gotten away with it."

Wyl coughed, and idly picked up some tiny pebbles and pitched them one at a time over the battlements into the lower bailey.

How could he make his decision to poke his nose in Prince—no, *Lokei's*—affairs into something he could talk about? He couldn't tell the prince that he'd been just a means to an end. Especially when that end felt less desirable now, sitting in the sunshine with a full stomach and a friend.

So he didn't even try.

He ducked behind his hair and made himself look like he concentrated on collecting pebbles while he struggled to come up with a more heroic explanation for trying to get himself killed.

"I heard you warning Lord Martei away from Princess Elfreida. Eirgei says, *protecting kinswomen is the foundation of civilization*, and that, *only rogues and outlaws would harm an unarmed woman, whether a kinswoman or not.*"

How many times had he repeated that to himself since his failure to kill the weather-mage?

He saw the strange look Lokei gave him and hastily added, "I'm not saying you Dremn are rogues, just that Martei is."

The strange look didn't go away. "But you could have died!"

Wyl focused on selecting a pebble and didn't dare look Lokei in the eye. "And I couldn't have lived with myself if I didn't do something. Eirgei has always tried to teach me honor." He forced a nonchalant expression. "It's not his fault if I don't manage it as well as I should, but still, at least I've never harmed a woman or a child."

Even when the woman was a murderous weather-mage.

He pitched a pebble over the battlements. "And anyway, if I'd let Martei kill me, it would have been no big loss. There are hundreds, maybe thousands of boys like me, and we could all be wiped out by summer fever and never be missed."

"Not like you," Lokei still studied him, with an odd, quizzical look on his face. "You are the first person who has ever stood up to Martei and made him back down. I already told you about my cousin Reien. Sammei, Reien's best friend, tried to avenge him, and Martei immediately knocked him out. Now that Reien is no longer at court, you have seen how slavishly Sammei follows Martei everywhere." Lokei shook his head. "Yet it has been, what, three or four weeks since Martei beat the snot out of you—much worse than he had done with Sammei, but yesterday, there you were, taking him on, at three against one, and he backed down—they all did." The prince grinned at him. "Trust me—there are not a hundred boys like you."

Wyl shrugged and gave his pebbles more attention. "I'm used to dealing with Eirgei or brigands. It's hard to get excited about a fifteen-year-old—and he didn't have his big stick." He threw his entire handful of pebbles. "I don't want to talk about it anymore."

Lokei scraped up some pebbles of his own and began to toss them.

A companionable silence built between them, and after some time had passed, Lokei said, "I have got a great idea—let us become brothers!"

"Brothers?"

"Shield-brothers," Lokei said it with a grin, but the look in his bruised blue eyes was utterly sober, even grim, and at odds with his lighthearted voice.

Was this some kind of trick?

"Shield-brothers. With me?" Wyl frowned, certain he hadn't heard Lokei correctly. "We're not old enough—and your uncles won't like it."

"Why not? We are the only two stripling boys—"

Wyl flushed. Trust one stripling to recognize another.

"—in Kotakei's court, so what makes more sense than that we be friends? And if we become good friends—which we will—then it only makes sense that we become shield-brothers. What's the point of wait-ing until we are older?"

Lokei was serious!

"But shield-brothers?" Wyl breathed, excitement building in spite of himself.

"You would be right-side, of course," Lokei assured him, looking up, his eyes bright blue against their purple-black sockets. "I mean, I am sure you are much better at fighting with real weapons than anyone in the Bear Cubs, especially with Eirgei teaching you all your life—Uncle Raldorrei says Eirgei always compares our minions to you, say-ing you are the best pupil he has ever had. According to Uncle Ral-dorrei, Eirgei is serious, not just trying to goad more effort out of our minions."

Heh, Lokei and his uncle didn't know Eirgei's motivational tricks—what minion would tolerate a comparison with a mere youth—or even worse, a stripling?

When Wyl hesitated to respond, Lokei said, "You think I will be no good watching your back, because I am only eleven! But I am almost twelve, and I swear, you can trust me. With me at your back, you will not be taken by surprise. I will make sure something like what hap-pened in your match with Martei does not happen again—and with me at your side, the guardsmen will not give you any more trouble like they did today."

Wyl flushed again and cringed inside. Lokei had witnessed more than he'd hoped.

But Lokei was right. Without Lanney, his nerves were ragged from trying to watch everything at once. In a hostile Young Court, having an ally watching out for him—especially someone as popular as Lokei—would be a tremendous relief.

It was a convincing argument, but could he trust Lokei to hold to his word?

Wyl knew a little about shield-brotherhood. It was the one bond a man could enter by choice and hold to for life, as strong a bond as shared clan blood-ties, but made voluntarily, a conscious choice.

An underage stripling like Lokei might aspire to someday swearing such an oath with a kindred spirit, witnessed with great ceremony by the entire clan's menney.

Wyl had never even dreamed of it.

"But neither of us is even in the Bearcubs," he pointed out.

"That is not actually a requirement for us to be shield-brothers,"

Lokei said.

Wyl supposed having witnesses and a ceremony were frills—and what did TolDaanyo, the Horned Hunter, the trickster-brother and Right Hand of MiPaatet, care about the age of those who swore His sacred oath? The blessing for keeping it—and the curse for failing it—would be the same regardless of their age. How could he uphold his oath as a shield-brother? TolDaanyo's curse would fall on him if he failed to do as he ought—and how could he, when he knew nothing of brotherhood or even ordinary friendship?

With Lanney dead, his only other friend was a horse.

Fear of failure—and his own lingering disfavor with MiPaatet—gnawed at him.

How could Lokei trust *him*?

And what about the Evroza? Wouldn't he be dragging Lokei into the blood-feud, putting the younger boy's life at risk?

Yet despite his qualms, every bone in his body hummed. His heart thrilled and swelled like it would explode.

He jumped to his feet and turned his back on Lokei, tongue probing where a tooth had been, and bit the inside of his cheek.

Prince Lokei didn't really know anything about him. And what about the Three Dishonors? Didn't Lokei know about his idiotic boast of being a master of them?

What Lokei offered was just too great an honor for someone like him. He'd dreamed of one day becoming Eirgei's successor—the Viceroye and Warleader of Trascolm, and the Royenne's Champion—but not even in his most secret fantasies had he ever been anyone's shield-brother. And Lokei, a real prince, acted like he was afraid *Wyl* would refuse *him!*

His eyes suddenly blurred. He folded his arms around himself and gnawed at his cheek more until he tasted blood.

Then, at last, the danger of embarrassing himself had passed, and it was safe to turn around.

He still couldn't meet Lokei's eyes or trust himself to speak—silence could lie just as easily as words. He had enough of a conscience to feel ashamed that he would let Lokei become his shield-brother without telling him about the Three Dishonors. The honorable course would be to refuse to swear with Lokei—Eirgei certainly would, in his place—but Wyl suddenly wanted this with the same amount of desperation that had had him gauging the distance to the ground from the battlements just yesterday.

It would have been enough, just being Lokei's friend. What would it be like, having a brother?

But it wasn't right, carelessly involving Lokei in the blood-feud.

Why did *Lokei* want him as his brother? The boy had everything to lose and nothing to gain from it.

Lokei stared off into the distance, his brow furrowed, then looked at him. "I know you have not known me long enough to trust me," he said, obviously mistaking Wyl's silence for rebel wariness.

Wyl tilted his head down to duck behind his hair again. For Lokei's sake, he had to find the courage to refuse—and tell him why.

But he couldn't make himself say, *no.*

When he didn't answer, Lokei added, "I have always wanted a brother, a real brother."

And a prince could certainly do better than pick someone like him.

Maybe this would be safe enough for Lokei—the Evroza were ruthless, but Eirgei insisted they didn't kill children. So maybe Eirgei was right. Maybe here in Nornholm, Lokei would be safe enough from Evroza assassins reluctant to kill innocent children.

He wanted to believe that.

"Alright," Wyl said. "But no one else must know about it." That, for the sake of his conscience and his fears about the Evroza. "Come with me."

He led Lokei down from the battlements, past Tras Tower on the brink of the western precipice, and out to the barren, debris-strewn quarry on the north side of Tras Tower, where blood could easily be spilled without someone interrupting.

They sat, hidden by rubble, with their backs against the base of the cliff that towered over Nornholm as Lokei described the shield-brother oath-making, a ritual in which Wyl recognized bits of Folk magic—and even blood-magic.

Was that what made the ritual work?

He felt a nervous foreboding for them both—maybe they *were* too young for something so serious. Even grown minions didn't take the shield-brother ritual lightly.

"Alright, then," Lokei said eagerly. "Let us do it." He started rolling up his white sleeve.

Wyl looked at his black undertunic's sleeve with his leather and bronze archer's bracer buckled over it. When he removed the bracer, it would reveal his hidden throwing knife. It was a small secret compared to Lokei's secret dagger training, and strangely, he felt an urge to show his trust in his soon-to-be-brother, a secret for a secret. Revealing the location of his throwing knives was the least he could do in return for Lokei's unquestioning trust of him.

"Left arm—the rune for *brother*. You do not have to cut deeply," Lokei encouraged.

Wyl unlaced his bracer and unsheathed what the bracer's underside held.

Lokei's eyes widened.

Wyl rolled up his sleeve and without hesitation began to carefully shape the cut on the underside of his left forearm where the bracer had been. He cut deeply enough for blood to outline the rune and then trickle down to his elbow.

Lokei set his teeth and cut his own left arm. He wrote the rune for *brother* with a neat economy of strokes, and a more modest trickle started across the rune.

Wyl checked his rune against the one Lokei had neatly drawn with his onyx-pommelled side-dagger. He'd used care, but even though he wrote the way he was taught, right-handed, his Runic was still awkward, and it was even worse using his throwing knife and not a pen.

Then, at Lokei's gesture, the two of them clasped hands, bringing their forearms together, careful not to smudge the runes as they did. They transferred the marks between their arms, then separated their wrists.

"Lord Geilorren is right, you really have picked up Runic," Lokei said, examining the marks overlaying the cut runes.

Once the marks dried, they looked at each other.

Lokei grinned.

But Wyl didn't feel the familiar tingle of spitcraft or bloodcraft. He didn't feel anything.

He forced himself to grin back, surprised at his disappointment.

Despite the familiar elements, this ritual had seemed more complicated, like none he'd ever done before—but then, the only magic rituals he knew were the simple ones he'd made up himself.

So why did his spitcraft work, yet he felt nothing of magic stirring from this real ritual? Did TolDaanyo have the final say on the worthiness of a shield-brother?

Lokei clearly couldn't sense magic, or he'd also know something was wrong, that TolDaanyo had rejected them as brothers—and that Wyl was the reason.

Lokei wouldn't learn that from him! Lokei was innocent of any wrongdoing.

Which meant Wyl had yet another shameful secret.

"I feel like I have a brother," Lokei said solemnly.

Wyl forced a smile and pretended he felt a magical bond of trust that wasn't really there. The idea of being shield-brothers no longer thrilled him.

He took a breath and committed himself to the lie. "But, now that we're shield-brothers, you'll have to be the right-side one. I'm left-handed, so my strong side is on the left."

"That ought to confuse people!" Lokei crowed, delighted. "Everyone will think I am the one to watch!"

"And I'd prefer they don't watch me," Wyl agreed. Lokei would have made someone a good shield-brother.

"What now?" Lokei wondered. "That is all I know about the ritual."

"We use spitcraft," Wyl said, feeling awkwardly self-conscious, "to hide the evidence."

With a tentative grin, he spit into his hand, rubbing out the dried blood with it.

Lokei did the same.

"Hold!" Wyl said abruptly, when Lokei started to roll down the sleeve of his white undertunic to cover his still-oozing wound.

Lokei looked at him, startled.

Wyl took a deep breath and coughed. Time to start acting like a brother.

"Cover that cut with this until it scabs, or the stain will give away our bond." He picked up his left bracer. The thin throwing knife was back in its hidden sheath. He buckled it around Lokei's forearm over the cut. "And anyway, no brother of mine walks around unarmed."

Lokei's eyes widened. "Thank you, Brother, but I am not unarmed—I have my side-dagger."

Wyl snorted his opinion of that blade. "*Heh*, this is a real weapon. Don't draw it on someone unless you mean to get their blood on it."

He showed Lokei how it drew from the underside of the bracer towards his palm and the catch that held it in place. He tugged Lokei's sleeve over it. "Once that's done bleeding, wear the bracer over your sleeve—there's no point in wearing a weapon where you can't get to it. I'll find something to use for a target, and you can practice to get a feel for how it handles."

"You will have to teach me how to throw it," Lokei said. "Do not worry about me flashing it to impress anyone. I have to keep it a secret—except for our side-daggers, we are not permitted to even carry real weapons until we are of age."

Lokei suddenly grinned up at him. "When they see the bracer, everyone will think I have taken up archery, just like you!"

Wyl was surprised to feel himself effortlessly return the grin.

✦

11ᵗʰ Day of the Moon of Ice, 113 G.E.

Nornholm was still no more Wyl's home than it had been two moons ago, when Wyl had first ridden into the oppressively fortress-like palace, desperately clutching at escape schemes. Crown Princess Kotakei still pretended friendliness: she was stiffly polite and made an effort to unclench her teeth whenever she had to talk to him. He knew she hated him, so he didn't understand why she persisted in their daily senet game.

After Young Court, Wyl sat on the hoardings and waited for Lokei's release from his secret dagger lessons with his uncle so he could join Wyl in their lair. Now that they knew the hoardings were too weak to hold a youth's—or adult's—full weight, the boys had made the hoardings their special haunt.

Wyl felt peculiarly good when his shield-brother huddled next to him in the cold wind off Mount Norn. He had never sought out physical contact with another—it had never felt safe before. But with Lokei as his shield-brother, perhaps his fortunes had finally taken a turn for the better.

Of course, he'd thought the same thing when he'd first been welcomed by Crown Prince Norren, despite the scowls of the Bearcubs—only to have Crown Prince Norren turn against him.

As he waited for Lokei, he kept checking inside his dark garnak, its sleeves and hood trimmed in marten fur just like his surcoat. He fingered the wax lesson tablet under it and his surcoat, anxious for his body heat to soften it, despite the cold and wind on the hoardings.

He still worked at trusting Lokei as his shield-brother. Today, he would tell Lokei something he'd never actually told anyone, though Lanney had found out about his spitcraft on her own. She hadn't lived to pass word of it to Eirgei.

He had to know if he could truly trust Lokei. If he couldn't, this secret was juicy enough that it would be all over Nornholm in a day.

But it wasn't as if he had any respect to lose if the Young Court learned about his spitcraft. After Crown Prince Norren had thrown him out of the Bearcubs and banished him to study and play alongside the younglings, it had been clear that Wyl was meant to be further humiliated in front of Crown Princess Kotakei's court.

Maybe he would have been, if that supposed punishment hadn't made it easier for him to gain the trust of those very informative younglings—and now, to get to know Lokei.

The sensation of being the eldest, most worldly person in any group—outlaw or outcast—was something he'd never felt before, not until he'd been sent to be with the younglings. They seemed to respect him, which made no sense—but that didn't stop him from soaking it up, however little he deserved it.

He'd never felt respect before.

In the rebel camps, the warlords had looked down on him. At the time, he'd thought the warlords were jealous that Eirgei and Helgurdda trusted him as much as they did the former Lord Calderek; now he knew the truth—it had been because he was a spy, and many of the rebels had once been noblemen, with the nobility's attitude about the Three Dishonors and spies.

He didn't understand why the younglings and Lokei still looked up to him—his disgrace for claiming prowess in the Three Dishonors had to be common knowledge in Nornholm by now—but he was afraid to ask.

Yet, all it had taken to win the younglings' goodwill had been simply his willingness to listen to them. And how could he not want to listen to their stories when the younglings competed for his attention by telling him everything they knew about Nornholm and their families, all without him prompting them and betraying his own interest in Royenne Errengard's court?

He learned more every day about their mothers, uncles, and cousins—how different their families were from his!—and he'd learned how to casually ask the right questions to reveal what interests those relatives protected in the Crown Court.

Thanks to the younglings—and Lokei's more insightful comments—he was sure he now knew more about the undercurrents in Royenne Errengard's Crown Court than Eirgei or Helgurdda did.

The undercurrent in the Young Court, however, was more of a dark undertow. Overbearing Crown Prince Norren was inclined to browbeat his younger sister. For all that her brother was supposed to be serving her interests, Wyl noticed it was Crown Prince Norren's interests that dominated the Young Court's activities.

Something pricked at his awareness.

He sprang up with a snarl, throwing knife in hand.

Lokei grinned at him.

Wyl flushed, both pleased and embarrassed—he'd been teaching Lokei to sneak around without getting caught, but he'd never imagined Lokei could sneak up on him! Was the safety of Nornholm making him lose his edge?

"What are you brooding about?"

He started to deny it, then stopped.

Lokei believed they were truly shield-brothers, and shield-brothers didn't lie to each other. Now that Lokei had gotten to know him better, he might learn to tell when Wyl lied—another reason to test Lokei's trustworthiness.

"I think there's something wrong between Crown Princess Kotakei and her brother." Belatedly, he worried that Lokei would take offense at him prying into the private affairs of his two royal cousins.

"I've wondered the same thing," Lokei said, without a trace of anger.

Wyl hesitated again, then plunged in, taking out his wax lesson tablet. "I've thought of a way to find out. Using spitcraft," he added. He couldn't help casting an anxious look at Lokei's expression.

His shield-brother didn't laugh. "You know magic?"

Wyl shook his head. "Just spitcraft."

"I thought spitcraft was only a hill-Folk superstition."

Wyl shrugged uncomfortably.

"How did you learn it? I thought only shamans knew the way of Folk magic."

He shrugged again. "I dunno," he mumbled in sudden embarrassment. "I think I've always known it. There's not much to it."

He shot a quick look at Lokei and saw only eager curiosity rather than the scorn or ridicule spitcraft usually drew—and sometimes even in Folk hamlets. Folk who claimed to have the use of magic were called shamans, witches, or mad—none of those were names Wyl wanted applied to him.

"So, what will you do?"

"Make a spitcraft charm to compel people to give up their secrets," Wyl said, in a rush to put the worst behind him. "Using Runic—this rune."

He scratched a single rune into the hardening wax of his tablet. It was the rune that now formed part of his name in Runic.

"Spider?"

"For catching secrets."

"Does it work?"

Wyl looked down at his tablet, embarrassed. "Sometimes. I've got to practice the rune more, until I don't have to think about it."

A *hex* was much simpler, but he didn't trust his shield-brother's nerve to hold if he did sorcery. He doubted they'd be shield-brothers at all if Lokei had realized part of the ritual he'd led Wyl through had used a bit of blood-magic to seal the oath. Or rather, it should've sealed their oath, if TolDaanyo hadn't rejected them on Wyl's account.

So far, there was nothing in Lokei's face that hinted at anything other than curiosity—no superior amusement or haughty scorn, certainly no outright mockery. Lokei waited and watched.

Wyl began to inscribe the spider rune into the wax with his knife. Nothing happened. He smoothed the wax and drew the rune again. Still nothing. This would be the first time he'd attempted his *trap secrets* charm since Eirgei's long-lost shield-brother had come to see Helgurdda, and even then, Wyl hadn't trusted it to work on its own and had resorted to blood-magic.

Since then, he'd been practicing the spider rune as diligently as he did his shadow-fighting, but it didn't flow as naturally as Teboan script, and the very idea of this charm still felt new and alien. But both his Teboan *hide me* and *luck* charms had felt the same way when he'd first begun to make them.

He expected to get a lot of use out of this one—there was no shortage of secrets in Nornholm for it to ferret out.

He wondered if he ought to start with Lokei's.

Part Four

CHAPTER 25

THE GERISARI

18ᵗʰ Day of the Moon of Ice, 113 G.E.

Lokei and Wyl had been shield-brothers now for two weeks. Their bond remained their secret, yet somehow, other members of the Young Court seemed to sense that something lay between the two of them. Though Wyl's relations with the rest of the Bearcubs hadn't improved, neither had they worsened—it was as if Lokei's popularity had spilled over onto him. Wyl was still amazed by it.

Maybe it was because, for the first time since Lanney fell victim to the weather-mage, Wyl no longer had to fight a relentless feeling of being alone among enemies. Now he had Lokei watching his back. His shield-brother was by no means Lanney's equal in a fight, but Lokei wouldn't hesitate to take his side, even against all the Bearcubs, while Lanney's first loyalty had always been to Helgurdda.

Today, he wasn't sure when he'd see Lokei.

Young Court had been cancelled, but this time, it wasn't because the crown princess attended Crown Court.

Late last night, while Wyl watched for assassins from his perch in the ruins of the fifth floor of Tras Tower, he'd seen a courier arrive in the upper bailey. Though he'd trailed after the man, the courier had gone into the Royal Tower itself, meaning the news had been serious enough to wake Royenne Errengard in the dead hours.

Then, this morning, just after Young Court began, Crown Princess Kotakei and all the other Icebear princesses and princes had been summoned to the Royenne's Tower. There had to be some kind of crisis—all the Icebear minions, even the shirkers guarding the Heir's Tower, brimmed with hidden tension.

What it was, Wyl hadn't discovered—in his spying, he'd yet to penetrate the royal wing past the great Crown Court hall and its nearby Privy Council room. The Icebear minions whose duty it was to hold the royenne's private quarters secure were as vigilant as those who guarded the Heir's Tower were slack. Royenne Errengard's private rooms were the one place where the consequences of discovery were too dire to risk—he didn't dare do anything that might give the royenne a public, perfect reason to renege on her promised support for Helgurdda.

So, despite the snow flurries, he was up on the hoardings, trying to distract himself from wondering what was happening with the Icebears by practicing his *trap secrets* charm.

Motion caught his eye.

He stopped muttering the charm into his bare, cupped hands and stared as a cavalcade of Gerisari—flanked on either side by a warband of Royenne Errengard's borderguards—galloped out of the hemlock forest, through first the Folk village and then the town, bound for Nornholm's gate. A baggage train that would've been sufficient to provision the entire rebel menney trailed behind them.

Wyl knew they were Gerisari because they were all mounted on tall Gerisari chargers and wore gleaming, Gerisari-wrought mail—as functional as it was fancifully beautiful. The mail showed from under exotic, draped clothing—the famous *suhavi* of Gerisari nobility.

Even Wyl had heard of the *suhav*, an enormous length of Gerisari silk that took an hour to pin as it should be. He'd heard it said that no one who hadn't worn it from birth could wear it in its proper complexity. This was the first time he had seen one for himself—Gerisari merchants weren't noblemen and wore their mail with ordinary tunics when they ran the gauntlet of brigands and rebels between Dawngate Pass and Crossroads Keep.

The old man riding at the head of the cavalcade, unlike his younger companions, wore no mail. Only the *suhav* peeped from under a sleeved cloak in the blue and gold of the House of Doromont, meaning he and the nobles in identical cloaks travelling with him were kin to Gerisar's ancient empress, Jerhafyne. His cloak still gleamed despite a layer of road dust, as did those of the rest of his company.

Their clothes had to be charged with dust-repelling artisanry—Wyl could feel the throb of artisanry-magic even at this distance.

What business did Gerisar think it had with Dremnar? This had to be the reason Lokei and the other Icebears had been called away.

The Evroza controlled all access to the Gerisari traders and only permitted the rest of Trascolm to obtain Gerisari goods at the great royal trade fair held annually at Crossroads Keep, where no Dremn could go. That didn't prevent Gerisari weapons and goods from appearing in Nornholm and likely the rest of Dremnar, as well—all booty pillaged from Milkdales.

Wyl scrambled from the hoardings and down off the parapet. He ran to the old quarry behind Tras Tower so he could circle unseen to the other side of the palace and secretly get to where Royenne Errengard was sure to receive the Gerisari—the great Crown Court hall. It would be empty now—this late in the afternoon, Royenne Errengard was usually in her Privy Council chamber or meeting privately elsewhere in the royal wing. With such an event as this, he counted on her devising her strategy for dealing with these Gerisari in some private chamber large enough for a clan meeting, rather than in the Crown Court hall or even the council chamber.

Wyl circled from the quarry to the back of the royenne's wing. From there, he climbed the outside of the east wall of the great hall to the open clerestory windows under the high ceiling. He was in a hurry to get among the rafters and supporting pillars, to get into position before servants came to ready the great Crown Court hall for making a grand first impression on the visitors.

Since Wyl had begun spying on the Crown Court, he'd come to know something of Royenne Errengard, her courtiers, and her ways. Royenne Errengard was proud and self-conscious of what foreigners—even her Tras kith—thought of Dremnar's tribal clans. According to Eirgei, her court was actually more formal than that of Royenne Sharei.

During Wyl's second week in Nornholm, when he'd lurked outside the Privy Council chamber's north window for the first time—four floors up the back side of the Icebear guardsmen's tower, opposite the great Crown Court hall—he'd overheard a spy's report. According to the spy, the Gerisari in Crossroads Keep still regarded the Dremn as backwards barbarians whenever Dremnar was discussed there—and there was a great deal of discussion, now that Wyl's family had taken refuge in Nornholm.

He'd heard for himself how much that report had angered the old royenne.

Now, faced with a Gerisari delegation—Gerisar's first acknowledgement of Dremnar's existence in over a hundred years—he'd come to know Royenne Errengard well enough to predict that she'd receive them with all the pomp and splendor she could muster. She would take great pains to dazzle the Gerisari, which meant she would take enough time before greeting them to ensure her noble courtiers made the right impression, as well as to demonstrate she'd meet with them in her own good time. She'd ensure that, until then, the Gerisari had little chance to improve upon their trail-worn appearance, despite their artisanry-touched clothing.

Royenne Errengard missed no trick that might give her even the smallest political advantage. Wyl had come to have great respect for the cunning of the old royenne and her subtle political sense, as much as for her unerring hold over her quarrelsome baronnes and their warlords. Between what he'd learned from Eirgei and Calderek in Milkdales, and what he'd witnessed in Royenne Errengard's Crown Court and Privy Council, his thorough education in crafty military stratagems now included devious political maneuvers, as well.

After more than a moon of observing the noble courtiers of Nornholm, what Eirgei had taught Wyl about the ways of the nobility made more sense. He found it easier to think like one, something he hadn't learned while spying in the rustic Evroza clanhold in Myymor, where his attention had been more on military developments than on political ones.

He expected to learn even more now—the Gerisari were themselves exiles from the Teboan Empire on the other side of the Eastern Sea. Teboan treachery was a byword even in Trascolm and Dremnar— and *devious as a Teboan* was the standard by which the rebels judged their dealings with the Evroza.

Wyl hurriedly made himself comfortable in his spy's vantage atop a massive stone pillar to the side of the dais, where the angle gave him a good view of the faces of both Royenne Errengard and any who came with a petition for her.

From his tutoring in the Young Court, he'd learned the Gerisari had never so much as acknowledged the existence of Dremnar as a country, but rather had scorned it as merely a collection of tribal chieftains, as if their clans and baronnes, dominated by an Icebear royenne, were so very different from those in Trascolm under the Evroza royenne. Except for one long-ago, lost and half-frozen peddler who'd strayed into Dremnar shortly after the Teboan refugees had taken possession of all the land between the Eastern Sea and the Black Mountains, no

Gerisari had ever come to Dremnar's Crown Court.

Sooner than Wyl expected, Dremn courtiers began to arrive and fill the empty spaces between the pillars. Servants brought two curule chairs to the dais and draped them in speckled ice bear pelts.

Those chairs remained vacant a little longer, but when Royenne Errengard did appear, leaning heavily on Prince Frekkei's arm, Wyl was surprised to see her dressed in barbaric splendor. Along with her jeweled royenne's crown, chains of gold-set gems framed her face and heavy gold ornaments were entwined in the braided sidelocks of her hair. Rather than Gerisari silks, she wore a fine ice bear fur robe with her long, white hair arranged as a royal cloak over it.

Prince Frekkei was also in furred splendor. His prince's coronet held back his loose hair, the first time Wyl had ever seen the royenne's son with his hair down.

Behind them, hair also unbound, wearing heavy gold coronets and gold ornaments, and also in traditional attire, walked Crown Princess Kotakei on Crown Prince Norren's arm. Behind them walked Princess Elfreida and Lokei in their coronets, then the rest of the royal clan, including Prince Raldorrei, the warlord of the menney, every one of them with their hair down.

It was all excruciatingly formal, and Wyl pitied Lokei for having to stand through what was likely to be lengthy ceremony.

The Icebear minions, similarly attired, but still wearing their hair in war-knots, had already slipped in and dispersed into the watching crowd of noble baronnes and their supporters.

All Errengard's courtiers had their hair down, too, and were dressed in the same fashion as the royal clan. Taken altogether, the Crown Court presented a formal, yet formidably savage impression.

Nowhere in the audience hall did anyone wear so much as a Gerisari dagger.

Dremnar had grown rich off the spoils of raids into Milkdales. That Gerisari plunder would have made an intimidating display if combined with the court's surprisingly traditional appearance. The conspicuous absence of anything Gerisari in Royenne Errengard's court had to be significant. Wyl suspected Royenne Errengard was about to make this delegation pay for Gerisar's ancient slight.

Also absent was Eirgei from his usual place at Prince Raldorrei's right side; though it was never an easy feat to find Helgurdda from above when most of Dremnar's nobility were as fair-haired as she, Wyl was sure he didn't see her, either. Their absence couldn't be coincidental.

He drew a knife, etched his spider rune into the wooden rafter in front of him, then concentrated on Royenne Errengard as he nicked his wrist. He felt a satisfactory tingle as the *trap secrets* charm soaked up the dribble of blood and prickled to life. This might be his chance to learn why Royenne Errengard still hadn't given Helgurdda the menney she'd implicitly promised when she'd recognized her as kith.

The Gerisari arrived in their *suhavi*, the draped folds caught up with sparkling, jeweled brooches. Though they had long hair halfway down their backs in a variety of shades—some surely unnatural—they wore no beards like the Dremn, nor so much as a Tras moustache, either.

Wyl thought it made the Gerisari look like bondsmen, save for their long hair of nobility.

Their envoy went to one knee a precise distance from Royenne Errengard. Under a prince's coronet, the long hair fringing his bald head fell in shining white wisps that fluttered about his hips as he knelt and bowed his head. "Dread Royenne, I am Prince-Envoy Kreseyn of the royal House of Doromont in Gerisar, come as an emissary from the Royenne of Trascolm."

"So, how fares my enemy Sharei?" Royenne Errengard asked curtly.

"Poorly, very poorly indeed. I bear greetings from Royenne Ragna, her daughter and heir."

"Ragna? Sharei is dead?" Royenne Errengard asked.

The news hit Wyl hard.

He reeled, not sure how to react.

Could the blood-feud be over?

There was a ripple of reaction among the Dremn courtiers, but not a flicker of surprise from the Icebears: either they had better self-control, or they had good spies in Crossroads Keep.

"In her bed," Prince-Envoy Kreseyn answered smoothly. "During her mother's illness, Royenne Ragna often acted as regent, so she's already well-experienced in ruling and war. There is now peace in Trascolm, and it is her desire to gain experience in something new—peace between her realm and yours."

"That would be novel," Royenne Errengard said dryly. "How does she mean to accomplish this feat? I understand she is ambitious for her next consort to be a Doromont, not an Ice Bear."

Prince-Envoy Kreseyn made a graceful gesture of agreement.

From Wyl's position up in the rafters, the Gerisari envoy's balding head gave him the look of a deadly, hooded viper.

"Why sacrifice an Icebear prince to an Evroza betrothal in the name of peace when you can trade for it with the fugitives, Helgurdda and Eirgei? The law of the land exempts you from keeping any pledge you have made to condemned outlaws, and in return, Gerisar's traders will come up Iceroad Pass this winter bearing gifts from both Royenne Ragna and my own Empress Jerhafyne."

"And the price is two outlaws?"

"Who are far outside the protection of law or custom. Royenne Ragna has sent me with these gifts as a token of her appreciation that you have remained neutral in this Evroza clan matter."

At a gesture from Prince-Envoy Kreseyn, a couple of muscular, stubble-headed slaves in sleeveless tunics and goosebumps came staggering forward under the weight of a travelling chest of gleaming, golden jegurit-bronze lavishly mounted with ruddy gold and jewels. The two slaves knelt, and Prince-Envoy Kreseyn produced a key from somewhere within the folds of his flowing *suhav*.

Everyone—including Wyl, up among the rafters—strained for a look at the contents of the chest. The slaves lifted the lid.

The prickling sensation on Wyl's skin intensified when the golden chest opened, despite the masking influence of his spider rune.

Inside was a treasure in the exquisite craftsmanship of Gerisar: a beautifully-worked gold diadem sparkling with jewels and surrounded by a display of matching torcs, armlets, bracelets, and rings—all cradled on a fine-linked, blackened-red mail tunic.

Mail forged from merkusar?

That mail, with each link laboriously created using artisanry, was easily worth more than all the rest of the treasure combined.

Viceroye Frekkei gasped, but his royal mother seemed less impressed.

"I have my own crown, thank you," she said. "One that has been handed down through generations of Ice Bear ancestors. I have no need for Jerhafyne of Gerisar to gift me with a crown like she did the Evroza. And I wonder, Prince-Envoy, why should I believe protestations of peace and friendship from the Evroza, when it is a prince of the House of Doromont who gifts my warleader with indestructible armor? Is it Ragna who makes this gift, or is this more of your empress's meddling? Does Ragna even know you have come?"

Prince-Envoy Kreseyn's face suffused red, and the dark shadows of the wrinkles on his face gave him a remarkable resemblance to the scorned merkusar.

Wyl noticed the missing honorific. Royenne Errengard was making no secret of her feelings about the new Evroza royenne—or the Gerisari envoy's offerings.

The knuckles on Prince-Envoy Kreseyn's hands, resting across his raised knee, whitened under the age spots.

Was Royenne Errengard right?

Eirgei had always warned Wyl that the Gerisari were not to be trusted, but Wyl had always assumed it was because of their close alliance with the Evroza clan. Perhaps their alliance wasn't as close as he'd thought?

Lord Geilorren said that the Gerisari, with their vast, seafaring trade empire, saw Trascolm as an insignificant and backward trading partner and Dremnar as nothing more than mountainous wastes inhabited by savages.

"The royenne merely chose gifts that are the most costly and rare," Prince-Envoy Kreseyn replied, in an even voice. "And surely, Royenne Ragna's offer of direct access to our traders is only the sweeter for gifts of goods that are rare even among the Evroza."

"Royenne Ragna seems anxious for peace," Royenne Errengard said, "though we are not currently at war with Trascolm, or even with the Evroza clan. The matter of my word to Helgurdda is independent of her legal status in Trascolm. As kith-kin to Ice Bear clan through my cousin, Prince Valdurren, I have granted her asylum here, and pretty gifts cannot buy the honor of Ice Bear clan. But I do not expect a puppet of the Evroza to understand such concerns."

Wyl admired Prince Frekkei's frozen, stoic expression. There wasn't a male in the room—himself included—who didn't lust after that merkusar mail that Royenne Errengard had just refused.

"No harm is intended to the honor of Dremnar's royenne," Prince-Envoy Kreseyn said, not reacting to Royenne Errengard's insultingly cold reception. "And the gifts remain what they are, evidence of Royenne Ragna's desire for friendlier relations between her realm and yours. Whether you deliver the outlaws into our keeping—whole or in parts—or allow them to continue to impose upon you as guests of your court on account of an insignificant connection to your clan, it has no bearing on Royenne Ragna's gifts."

At a gesture from Prince Kreseyn, the slaves left the chest before the dais and crawled backwards until they were again hidden by the *suhavi* of Prince Kreseyn's noble companions.

Wyl watched the slaves intently, fingering his sire's troth-ring where it hung from his neck, and shuddered.

"These gifts are yours—do with them as you wish, bestow them on whomever you please, or cast them into Icebear Lake. Just as your honor cannot be bought, the honor of Royenne Ragna will not be bound by the fate of these gifts."

Royenne Errengard smiled wickedly. "Very prettily said, Prince-Envoy Kreseyn. You have lived up to my expectations of a Doromont prince. And perhaps I have satisfied your expectations of a barbarian royenne?"

High above them, Wyl stifled a snigger of laughter.

"You may carry a message to generous Ragna, Royenne of Trascolm and Baronne of the Evroza clan: we are content in our current dealings with Trascolm, and with Milk Dales and her clan. Peace would make my warlords as soft as the Evroza, who seek to buy what their prowess cannot win and send foreigners in their place to beg for what is not in my power to give."

Wyl could feel the tension in the hall rise as Royenne Errengard paused.

"If the Evroza wish their honor restored, it will not be by negotiating with *me*. Let Ragna's justice satisfy the claim on it Helgurdda has made. It reflects badly on Ragna's honor, trying to disguise her private dispute with Helgurdda as a matter of state. I refuse her gifts."

Prince Kreseyn quickly bowed his head, but from above, Wyl had a clear view of the red again rising up the back of the Doromont envoy's neck under the thin veil of white hair.

The audience was clearly over. Royenne Errengard coldly extended the hospitality of Nornholm overnight and promised an escort in the morning to see the Gerisari swiftly taken on the long, difficult passage to the eastern border, where they'd be left to find their own way through the no-man's-land of the Black Mountains south to Dawngate Pass.

It took a long time for the Crown Court hall to empty. As Wyl waited to make his own discreet exit, he listened to what the various baronnes and warlords said amongst themselves after the Gerisari and Royenne Errengard and her Icebears were gone.

Servants came to take away the curule chairs, but they left the Gerisari bribe where it was. Many of the departing Dremn courtiers paused to admire the gifts, but none of them so much as touched the raised lid of the chest, save for a Wolverine warlord who fingered the merkusar mail before leaving.

The opinions Wyl overheard among the courtiers all agreed that raiding Milkdales with Helgurdda's rebels was one thing. Fighting to give Trascolm's crown to an outlawed rebel and—with the certainty of a treaty afterwards—desisting from further raids into the royal barony of Milkdales, was quite another. In Dremnar, there was more honor in taking plunder than in trading goods.

For the present, the warlords were pleased they wouldn't be giving up their lucrative raiding. They believed the new Evroza royenne sought time to deal with the unrest brewing in the rest of Trascolm— the Dremn nobles all knew how the noble Tras clans detested Evroza rule and threatened revolt at every opportunity.

Was it the enriching tradition of winter raids into Milkdales that was the obstacle preventing Royenne Errengard from carrying out her kinship-obligated support of Helgurdda's bid for Trascolm's crown? Did canny old Royenne Errengard fear a revolt by her warlords and baronnes as much as the Evroza royenne did hers?

✦

19ᵗʰ Day of the Moon of Ice, 113 G.E.

Kotakei leaned against the sill of the south window in her seventh floor hall. She watched as the snow continued to fall, and coincidentally, also watched the Gerisari delegation. Overnight, the snowfall had become a blizzard. The Gerisari delegation's departure today was out of the question. Their caravan's sumpters and riding horses remained in a makeshift pen next to the argali fold. Prince-Envoy Kreseyn stood at the side of the pen, watching slaves tend to the horses.

Kotakei was impressed that a man as old as the envoy showed no sign of the weariness the rest of his party suffered. He reminded her of Eirgei, an old campaigner hardened by time rather than undone by it— though Prince-Envoy Kreseyn was much older than Eirgei and dressed as a statesman rather than a warlord.

She straightened in surprise when she saw Norren, backed by Martei and Sammei, walking across the lower bailey.

Norren stopped and exchanged the head-nods of princes with Kreseyn, then turned and joined him in watching the Gerisari slaves tend the horses while Martei and Sammei waited a discreet distance from them.

Eirgei and Helgurdda had both brought Gerisari horses into Dremnar with them, and every year, raids into Milk Dales brought in more of the prized beasts—though, disappointingly, always geldings. It was not like Norren had never seen such creatures before. So why was her brother standing in the snowstorm, admiring those tired, dispirited horses?

He was up to something.

She grabbed the palest of her cloaks and threw it over her black-speckled, white-furred Ice Bear ceremonial robe—court dress for as long as the Gerisari remained in Norn Holm. The cloak covered it completely. She drew up its hood and hurried down the stairs.

The unprecedented presence of the Gerisari in Norn Holm still held everyone's attention, even that of her guardsmen. They laughed amongst themselves as someone recounted, yet again, the historic meeting with Grandmother. No one paid attention as Kotakei slipped out of the Heir's Tower.

The snow came down harder, and her cloak blended with it. She had hoped the cloak would give her anonymity, but now suspected it was giving her virtual invisibility, as well.

Anger built in her as she passed through the High Gate where the unmoving sentries silently nodded acknowledgement of her. She circled through the lower bailey to where she might have a better view of Norren's face. Norren's deeds forced her to act like a spy, but in this encounter between Norren and the Gerisari envoy, she doubted anyone's honor, hers or Ice Bear clan's, would emerge intact.

Arguably, if something directly involved her or her future Young Viceroye, she was not actually spying, she was simply being discreet in her own affairs—and as the Crown Princess, anything passing between her future Young Viceroye and a foreign envoy representing a hostile, neighboring country was absolutely her affair.

Particularly when her brother had not spoken a word of his intentions to her, and the two of them had never spoken of the Gerisari at all except in connection with the winter raids into Milk Dales.

The goat fold formed one side of the makeshift pen for the Gerisari horses. The argali goats would not be shorn until spring; their bulk was all she could ask for in concealment. The argali were large, but the gentlest of goats, and when she sat down on the thin ground cover of snow, wrapped and hooded in her cream-colored cloak, the curious argali lay down around her, chewing their cud, and making her just another pale lump amid the falling snow.

The large, drifting snowflakes made details more difficult to see, but she was close enough that she could hear the voices of Norren and the

Gerisari envoy carrying lightly across the pen as they faced in her direction.

"—regret the merkusar mail," Norren was saying, apparently having already dispensed with the formal pleasantries while she slipped in among the argali. "I would advise you to take the chest back with you. There is no sense in wasting merkusar on the pyyk in Ice Bear Lake, because I assure you, that is where it will end up."

"Wasting the gifts of a royenne is not Trascolm's loss, but Dremnar's," Prince Kreseyn said, with apparent unconcern. "Merkusar is only rare on this side of the Black Mountains. In Gerisar, we have whole legions equipped in it, from swords to mail to shields. It is a small loss to us."

Norren nodded sagely, as if he had known that.

She knew he had not—and she doubted the envoy's claim was true.

What was her brother up to?

"Your visit here is not entirely wasted," Norren's voice drifted across the expanse of the pen. "My grandmother is not so robust as she appears. She will be missed when MiPaatet claims her, but with a new royenne will come new opportunities."

"Crown Princess Kotakei favored my mission?"

"The Tras have made themselves obnoxious here in Norn Holm, no matter what my grandmother pretends. Eirgei's loyalty is suspect. He has spent a lifetime fighting us, but now we are supposed to trust him just because he has quarreled with the Evroza?"

"It is more than merely a quarrel," Prince-Envoy Kreseyn said. "The Evroza take their blood-feud very seriously. Look at the price Royenne Ragna set for two heads."

"Perhaps the price was just insufficient for Grandmother to favor the request from Royenne Ragna," Norren said. "I, personally, would welcome a cessation of hostilities with Trascolm and the beginning of a profitable friendship with Gerisar. The constant raiding and warfare is a drain on our treasury and a waste of the lives of our finest minions."

"Very true," Prince Kreseyn said.

"I will become viceroye on the day my sister wears the crown—"

Among the argali, Kotakei's jaw dropped.

"—and that day may come sooner rather than later. When it does, my sister will favor your mission. Three foreigners' lives are a small price to pay for saving those of my own people, particularly when a quarrel with the Evroza is no proof of trustworthiness towards us."

"Three lives? Who is the third?"

"Helgurdda's son, Wylheim."

"Royenne Ragna only wants the heads of Helgurdda and Eirgei," the envoy said. He looked curiously at Norren.

The two were nearly eye to eye, but the envoy was the taller. Kotakei imagined he would have been an imposing sight in his prime.

"I have never heard a son mentioned. He cannot be more than a youngling."

"A youth—Helgurdda claims the boy is the Gerisari slave's get. Whatever his breeding, he has been raised and trained in every crime imaginable by Eirgei. He has been taught to hate the Evroza, and if the ransom Royenne Ragna asks in return for peace should be paid in the future, you can be sure of retribution from the son—the Evroza blood-feud will not end until he is dead, too."

This was far and away an overreaction to Prince Tras's ongoing squabble with Martei! Prince Tras could not have known that making an enemy of Martei made an enemy of Norren, as well—and he would not know how bad an enemy until Norren showed his hand with devastating effect.

Like now.

"That would definitely assure an end to the blood-feud," Prince-Envoy Kreseyn answered, undisturbed by Norren's proposal to execute an underage boy. "And I was charged just to return with heads. Royenne Ragna was adamant that she never wants their feet in Trascolm again."

Norren turned away to look at the horses, giving no sign that he had seen Kotakei when his eyes passed briefly over the argali. "Then we are in accord. You must find other reasons to return as an envoy. I think our rustic court here would benefit from a light Gerisari polish."

"I am delighted that the next royenne of Dremnar will have a viceroye of vision. But until then, I must obey the command of the present royenne to depart in the morning. I fear, however, that some of our mounts will not be fit for travel so soon. I dislike having to beg forbearance from Royenne Errengard to give them time to recover. If I could exchange them for fresh horses more accustomed to the rigors of mountain travel, I would be grateful and honored."

"Yes, that would be wise," Norren said. "My grandmother is impatient and will not allow you to linger merely for the sake of horses. I think I see which horses you are concerned about."

Anyone could see those horses were tired, but perfectly sound!

Now that Prince Kreseyn's announcement of Royenne Sharei's death had made that news public—and the bribe from Royenne Ragna had been delivered—surely the Doromont prince's business was concluded. There was no need for the envoy to depart at a pace faster than his horses could manage.

Much as Kotakei despised Prince Tras, she did not wish him dead—she would never give Ice Bear kith over to the Gerisari for execution if she were royenne! But Norren's confidence disturbed her, and she wondered how he could possibly think he would dictate policy in her place?

She gritted her teeth as her brother negotiated the price of his future favor.

How dared Norren say he spoke for her! At best, a viceroye would only be a royenne's Right Hand, never her mouth. Her vague fear of becoming Norren's puppet now seemed all too real.

She remained sitting among the argali long after Norren and the Gerisari envoy parted company, puzzling over Norren's intentions and how she might thwart them.

CHAPTER 26

HERERES'S MASTER

20th Day of the Moon of Ice, 113 G.E.

In an effort to keep tensions checked, Royenne Errengard had decided to keep Wyl's family away from the Gerisari delegation, forbidding them from attending court, or even leaving Tras Tower for as long as the Gerisari remained in Nornholm. A simple matter, except that for yet another day, the snow had delayed the envoy's departure. The Young Court remained in recess to allow Crown Princess Kotakei and Crown Prince Norren—and the other members of the Young Court—to attend Crown Court and witness the political stir caused by the historic Gerisari visit.

Helgurdda and Eirgei had been with Wyl in Tras Tower all three days that the Gerisari had been in Nornholm, giving him no opportunity to slip away and spy on what happened in Crown Court. With his shield-brother in attendance, though, Wyl expected to learn of anything said in court that concerned his family.

Today, the snow melted steadily where the sun hit it, but the deep drifts in the shadows were scarcely touched. All the same, by late morning, it had become much warmer.

With the skies so clear, Viceroye Frekkei had taken the Gerisari envoy and his companions, along with Crown Princess Kotakei, Crown Prince Norren, and the rest of the Young Court, and had gone hawking outside Nornholm. If the milder weather continued, the Gerisari delegation would leave Nornholm the next morning.

Though it was only afternoon, Wyl lay curled in his garnak beside the smoldering kitchen fire, trying to catch up on sleep lost watching for Evroza assassins by night. The hearthstones were warm, and he drowsed lightly. Though Helgurdda watched over him and Eirgei, she had two entrances to cover, and none of them trusted they were safe so long as there were Gerisari in Nornholm.

Wyl roused to wakefulness, cracked open one eye, and saw Helgurdda sitting in the sunny window nook of the kitchen, lost in her thoughts as she soaked up the heat of what had to be the warmest day since they'd come to Dremnar. The news that Sharei was dead and that Ragna was now the royenne had set off a firestorm of emotion in Helgurdda that was only now dying down. The news had affected Wyl more than he'd expected, leaving him with a surprising sense of loss, surely just a reflection of how strongly the news had affected Helgurdda and Eirgei.

He hoped the Gerisari would be sent away soon, so their lives could return to something like normal.

He roused again when he heard a clatter from the direction of the High Gate.

Helgurdda had her head back, eyes closed in thought. He saw her glance out at the commotion.

Then she gasped. Her entire body went rigid. In the next instant, she flung herself off the windowsill and raced up the stairs.

Wyl leaped up from the hearth, coughing and clutching at his throwing knives.

Eirgei had been taking advantage of the respite from training the royenne's minions to get what looked like desperately-needed sleep on the bench next to Wyl. He, too, startled awake, dagger drawn, unsheathed sabre snatched up from the floor before his eyes were even fully open.

Wyl reached the scullery's courtyard door barely a step ahead of Eirgei.

Across the bailey, near the stables and visible in the distance above the low courtyard walls, Wyl could see the commotion was merely the return of Prince Frekkei's hawking party. He stared across at them, baffled. What about the hunters' return had goaded Helgurdda to fury?

Helgurdda clattered back down the stairs, naked sabre in hand.

Eirgei turned, took in her expression and the blade, and looked again at the distant riders filing into the stableyard flanking the High Gate.

Then he tossed his saber aside and lunged for Helgurdda. He tried to wrestle the sabre from her grip.

She fought her uncle for it with a ferocity Wyl had never seen before, her beautiful face contorted with effort.

Eirgei took her sabre with a couple quick wrenches at her wrist and elbow, and threw it away from her across the kitchen.

When he twisted to throw the sabre, Helgurdda took her chance to break free of him, but Wyl braced his hands on either side of the portal and blocked the doorway to the courtyard.

Helgurdda tugged at Wyl's arm, gripped his garnak's sleeve and shoulder, and flung him aside as if he were a mere child, but he had held long enough for Eirgei to put her into a bear hug from behind.

"Close the door! Do not let her pass!" Eirgei cried, still trying to subdue her.

Wyl scrambled back to his feet from where Helgurdda had thrown him—all the way to the foot of the stairs. He'd had doubts about Helgurdda's ability to defend herself against an assassin, but the fight she gave Eirgei now, all the while preventing Wyl from getting past her to close the door, filled him with reluctant admiration and put those doubts to rest.

But, though Eirgei had taught her—and Wyl—many of his moves and taught them well, Eirgei always had tricks neither of them had ever seen.

Eirgei wrestled Helgurdda to the floor and held her pinned against it, but his every limb strained with the effort.

Wyl edged around them, heading to close the door.

"It is him! The Gerisari envoy is Kreseyn!" Helgurdda's voice rose into a screech of fury more intense than anything Wyl had ever heard from her on a battlefield.

She heaved against Eirgei like a bucking horse, but he kept her pinned against the flagstone floor.

"It is," Eirgei agreed tersely.

Wyl stiffened and halted in his tracks.

Helgurdda continued her furious fight to get free of Eirgei.

"And you will keep—your wits about you," Eirgei grunted, still wrestling. "Challenge him if you must—but let me be your champion! We cannot risk—the rebellion for him—Kreseyn did not kill Hereres!"

Both of them gasped for breath, but Helgurdda still fought and Eirgei still held her down.

"He did his best—break Hereres's spirit—those beatings and brandings," Helgurdda panted.

Wyl didn't think she'd deliberately harm Eirgei, but she was in a rage and savagely attempted to head-butt him. She held nothing back in her fight to break free. "He put a price on Hereres's head—high enough—to tempt a Gerisari prince!"

For a moment, she broke Eirgei's hold and tipped him on his side.

"And I agree he must pay—but in our coin—not his. It is not a co-incidence—that he is the envoy," and with a heave, Eirgei again had her limbs pinned against the floor, more securely than before. "Ragna knows all this and chose to send him—it is a trap for you!"

Wyl watched, frozen in place, wide-eyed with fright for both of them. While Helgurdda held nothing back, Eirgei still took care not to do her serious harm, and that made Helgurdda his equal in the strug-gle. If he missed a hold or a counter-move, Eirgei could die—and with Helgurdda so enraged, she wouldn't realize what she had done until it was too late.

If Ragna had laid a trap for Helgurdda, then why not anticipate Eir-gei's response and lay a trap for Eirgei, as well?

There was little notion of fair play in a blood-feud—even less so when one party to the feud had been outlawed. Anyone who knew his elders would have foreseen Eirgei intervening, would have known he'd insist on being Helgurdda's champion.

Helgurdda stilled, more from exhaustion than reason. Eirgei breathed hard—he'd taught Helgurdda the unarmed infighting moves he'd refused to teach Wyl, and she'd come very near to oversetting him and getting away.

From the doorway, Wyl looked closely at Eirgei, thinking about how deeply his granduncle had slept while they had been dozing by the hearth with his mother on watch, and how Eirgei had yet to catch his breath.

Champion or not, Eirgei was too exhausted from his struggle with Helgurdda to fight a duel for long-overdue justice on her behalf. He'd been Trascolm's finest warlord and minion for over thirty years, but while outlawry had kept his skills keen, the years of hard living that had gone with it had taken their toll on his body—no matter that Eirgei refused to concede to his age.

Helgurdda was still pinned, and the two of them breathlessly argued what even Wyl knew would be a political disaster—they couldn't kill an official envoy under Royenne Errengard's protection.

He eased away from the doorway, past where his mother and granduncle were sprawled deadlocked on the floor, then raced up the stairs to the fourth floor armory, unfastening his garnak as he ran.

Under it were his two surcoats, and unseen under his Icebear sur-coat, he still wore his *byrnney*. He'd been wearing it both for fear of ambush by some friend of Lord Martei's with a jeweled side-dagger, and on principle, because he was Tras and surrounded by Dremn.

He flung his garnak to the floor when he reached the alcove that was their makeshift armory. He quickly cinched the belt with his back-knives around his waist, snatched up his sabre, and pulled its shoulder strap over his head. He ran for the stairs, checking that the sabre's sheath lay where it wouldn't foul the draw on his hidden spine blade.

He flew down the spiraling steps, then down the two straight flights of stairs to the kitchen, horribly conscious of how much time had passed getting himself minimally accoutered for war.

When he reached the bottom of the stairs, Helgurdda and Eirgei were already gone.

✦

Kotakei heard shouting from behind her, but could not make out the reason for the commotion. The stablehands had taken away the hawking party's tired mounts. Without her vantage from horseback, she could not see anything except the knot of minions between her and the Gerisari envoy.

Then she heard a woman's voice, shrill with emotion, and realized that the very encounter Uncle Frekkei had hoped to avoid by taking the Gerisari envoy away to spend the day hawking had happened any-way. She threaded her way through the hawking party towards the cursing, screaming woman.

Helgurdda thrust her way through the crowd of nobles and Folk servants, and everyone near her scrambled to get out of her way. She was in a magnificent fury: a Dremn longsword bared in her hand, blood in her eye, and murder in her heart. Uncle Frekkei and Eirgei each gripped an arm and barely kept her from the elderly envoy's throat.

The Gerisari envoy wore a fur-lined tunic and breeches for hunting rather than his *suhav*. He wore a fur cap over his baldness, and the wisps of long, white hair flowed loosely down his back. At the junction of the fur cap and his hair, he wore a princely, golden coronet in much the same style as those that had been part of the bribe he'd offered for two outlawed heads.

"Honor does not require me to answer a challenge from a condemned criminal," Prince-Envoy Kreseyn was saying in a smug tone that Kotakei could see only infuriated Helgurdda the more.

The crowd of stable attendants shrieked and scattered away from Eirgei, who snarled something. There was a sudden movement in the crowd of Ice Bear minions around Helgurdda, and now it was also Eirgei who they ensured remained separated from the envoy.

"It is only concern for my honor that stays me from accepting Eirgei's challenge," Prince-Envoy Kreseyn said calmly to Prince Frekkei. "But he, too, is a condemned traitor and not worthy of my blade in a duel of honor."

"You are afraid to face me!" Eirgei bellowed. "That is not honor—that is cowardice! I am not outlawed in Dremnar!"

"I am a guest of the Royenne of Dremnar," the envoy countered serenely. "No Icebear will allow your challenge."

That was not quite true—Kotakei knew there were quite a few Ice Bears who would dearly love to see Eirgei in a duel to the death, if only to see the legend in action.

But Uncle was not one of them.

"The law of the land is quite clear," Uncle Frekkei said, raising his voice for all to hear. "Eirgei is no outlaw in Dremnar, but the offense named in the challenge took place in Trascolm and judgment has already been rendered against Helgurdda in that quarrel—and therefore no judicial duel is possible between either of you and the envoy. Kithkin though you are, Helgurdda, you will face outlawry in Dremnar if you break the peace."

Behind Prince Frekkei's broad back, Prince-Envoy Kreseyn smirked condescendingly at Helgurdda, inciting a fresh, captive frenzy from her.

Then, from somewhere in the crowd of spectators, a pair of muddy snowballs flew out and hit the Gerisari envoy squarely in the head, one after the other.

Kotakei drew in a sharp breath.

The snowballs had been mixed with mud and fresh horse dung, and they broke apart on impact, harming nothing but the envoy's dignity as the foul mixture clung to his royal circlet and dripped down his face, soiling his loose and princely hair.

There were gasps and laughter from the crowd—many of Grandmother's courtiers shared her disdain for the Gerisari.

Prince-Envoy Kreseyn slapped his hand to his hunting knife, then

Kotakei saw him check when he saw who he faced, even as his Gerisari companions roared their fury at the insult to him and set hands to their swords.

"I trust you'll agree," a guttural, hill-country voice rang out clearly, like an alto bell, as someone approached from the back of the crowd, "that this offense's been given in Dremnar, and that there's no issue of outlawry for this TolDaanyo-damned, Gerisari coward to hide behind instead of facing *me!*"

The crowd parted, and the cheers and jeers died abruptly as they— and Kotakei—realized who spoke.

All but hidden by the taller adults as he had made his way through the crowd, Prince Tras now stalked to the fore. The larger-than-life presence Kotakei remembered from the first day she had seen him was back, heightened by the sight of a sabre hilt peeping over one shoulder in place of the inoffensive quiver she recalled. She was suddenly conscious of the ragged and faded Tras surcoat he wore over his black Ice Bear surcoat.

As he strode through the crowd, he tore furiously at his blue-black braid, undoing it in angry haste so that his long hair, too, hung loose and princely, an ominous dark cloud surrounding his ghastly, graying face and glittering silver eyes.

That he let his hair down to look a prince as he issued his challenge surprised her—it was the first time she had seen him properly conscious of his rank. Was it to ensure that his right to make such a challenge was taken seriously?

It was melodramatic, but no one laughed, least of all the Gerisari envoy, who had just endured a terrible insult before a score of noble witnesses.

"I am Prince Wylheim, son of Helgurdda by Hereres, and I give you scorn and defiance if you refuse to face TolDaanyo's judgment for your part in Hereres's death. Face my blade or you will be admitting, before these witnesses, that you are guilty of the unlawful imprisonment and abuse of my sire, as well as his murder, by contriving his death at the hands of another."

That last accusation, treachery or backstabbing—the cowardly betrayal of trust, which was reckoned the worst of the Three Dishonors—brought a gasp from the crowd.

After three days in the company of the Gerisari, Kotakei now knew the tale, both what the envoy had said and what he had left unsaid. Hereres had been murdered in Trascolm, where there was no slavery and where he should have been a free man, not even a bondsman, thanks to the decades he'd spent as a slave. But the Evroza royenne had not allowed Hereres his freedom, his right to betrothal, or even his protection under the law of the land—or Helgurdda's right to vengeance.

"Now there will be justice at last, and you will suffer for your crimes. I challenge you not merely for the sake of my sire, but for the sake of the unjust outlawry your deeds brought down on my mother and granduncle!"

It seemed to Kotakei that there was a certain incongruity about the whole affair: the formal words of challenge in the old, traditional style, given in a Folk accent coming from the mouth of a Tras rebel, and accusing a Gerisari prince of despicable acts, as well as complicity in a capital crime.

Prince Tras had obviously taken Lord Geilorren's lessons on the ancient law of the land to heart. He stood motionless with more grimness than was conceivable in a boy who could not possibly have the fourteen years he claimed. His black hair was wild and disheveled, and his head was held arrogantly high.

No one laughed, though the confrontation was at once both romantic and ludicrous.

Dremn—herself among them—had a weakness for melodrama, particularly that offered by a duel. Though the gap in age between the challenger and the challenged could easily be sixty years, she thought they would be evenly matched—the vitality of youth countered by the martial wisdom of a lifetime, even if the elderly envoy had not touched a sword in anger in the last thirty years.

Prince Tras's cry echoed off the walls of the upper bailey as he concluded his challenge. "For all these offenses, only your death will satisfy me."

"Do not be ridiculous," Prince Kreseyn said, which was not at all the traditional acceptance of a challenge. There was nothing weak or wavering in his voice. The hooded eyes in his red and outraged face were full of scornful incredulity. "I do not duel children."

His white hair lifted like smoke around him as Prince-Envoy Kreseyn turned on his heel, dismissively waving for the rest of the hawking party and the gathering crowd to disperse.

This time, Prince Tras did not throw a snowball—he threw a knife.

It flew over the Gerisari envoy's shoulder. The razor-sharp blade clipped a long, filth-dripping lock of white hair and left a bloody slash across the envoy's cheek before clattering against the courtyard wall.

As one, the gathering crowd sucked in its breath.

Prince Tras had gone from one insult to an even deadlier one—an insult with blood drawn—again, before a multitude of witnesses. Now there was no honorable response Prince Kreseyn could make to what the boy had done, other than answer his challenge—or admit the truth of his charges and offer himself to the royenne for her justice.

"I have the right," Prince Tras yelled, as the envoy whipped around, hunting knife again in his hand.

Blood dripped from the envoy's jaw.

The Gerisari noblemen around Prince Kreseyn spread out and drew their hunting swords.

Helgurdda's son reached over his shoulder and with one sure, smooth movement, drew his own blade, a thin, curved Gerisari sabre that perfectly suited his size. He pulled a fighting knife from behind his back with his right hand.

"My age doesn't deny me my right to justice! Refuse me again, and my next strike will make you wish I'd killed you!"

The envoy plucked the long, dung-clotted wisps of severed hair from the front of his hunting tunic with blood-smeared fingers. He looked at Prince Tras with narrowed, calculating eyes. There was no fear in them, only something Kotakei suspected was amusement.

The envoy laughed. "Let me explain something to you, little boy. It is not the custom in Gerisar for a prince of my years to defend my honor with a blade—least of all on trumped up charges over a long-dead slave for whose death I was exonerated of all blame by no less than the Royenne of Trascolm before you were even born!"

Prince Kreseyn's smile crinkled the wrinkles in his cheeks, and there was no mistaking the smugness in his voice. "But never let it be said that a Doromont prince refused a duel of honor. I accept your challenge—Prince Frenses will fight as my champion."

Prince Tras looked stunned.

Kotakei could hardly blame him—who would have expected the envoy to accept his challenge, but refuse to fight?

She looked at the man who stepped out from among the Gerisari in answer to the envoy's call.

He was much younger than the envoy—but still at least twice Prince Tras's claimed age—and dressed as a Gerisari imperial legionnaire in full panoply, equipped for war rather than the hunt.

"I am Prince Frenses," the legionnaire said, "of the Royal Branch of the House of Doromont, Champion of Prince Kreseyn of Doromont, and Spanker of Children Who Meddle in Matters They Do Not Understand."

She heard the murmuring prompted by his reply.

"Coward! You can't do this!" Prince Tras protested, looking from Prince Kreseyn's smug face to that of his champion.

From somewhere in the crowd, someone laughed. It sounded like Norren.

Prince Tras glowered.

The legionnaire continued as if he hadn't been interrupted. "I am not familiar with your graceless, antiquated, and barbarous style of challenge, but in Gerisar, it is customary for the challenged party to choose the weapons."

Prince Frenses turned to Uncle Frekkei, who no longer strained to hold Eirgei back—both looked as stunned as Kotakei felt. "Is that also the custom in these lands?"

At Uncle's somewhat bemused nod, Prince Frenses turned back to his challenger.

Prince Tras was motionless in a half-crouch, holding sabre and knife in a low guard, as if he expected the duel to begin then and there.

"Obviously, this is only one of the many things of which you are ignorant," the Gerisari champion said, "or you would not be so recklessly eager to face me. I am the best—"

"—At talking your challenger to death?" Prince Tras cut him off with a sneer that, in itself, Uncle Frekkei would have considered sufficient grounds for a thrashing, had Norren been so rude in a formal, public challenge. "Don't worry about me, worry about yourself! Let this cowardly prince fight his own battles—I have no quarrel with you!"

"You do now, hedge-gotten slave's get! Someone needs to teach you proper respect for your elders and your betters, and I look forward to being the one to do it."

Prince Tras cocked his head warily towards Prince Kreseyn, eyes still on the champion. "This changes nothing! After I'm through with your fancy boot-licker, I'm coming for you!"

"And obviously you have little experience with mortal combat if you think facing me as the envoy's champion is of no concern," Prince Frenses retorted. "But if Eirgei can be Helgurdda's champion, you can hardly deny an old man a champion, as well. Apologize to Prince Kreseyn on both knees, and I will excuse your offensive behavior as the unwitting folly and rashness of the child you are."

Kotakei gasped. Those were not the words of a man who wanted an apology!

Prince Tras slowly looked the Gerisari up and down, and spit derisively, surprising Kotakei with how convincingly he acted like he was completely unimpressed by the Gerisari's impressively martial appearance.

"Choose how you wish to die—it doesn't matter to me—I'm *not* a child, I'm the Wolf of Milkdales's best pupil!" And Prince Tras put back his head and gave an eerily realistic wolf-howl, reminding her that he had ridden with Eirgei and the rebels all his short life—and that perhaps he was not the stranger to mortal combat the Gerisari champion assumed.

Prince Frenses returned Prince Tras's assessing scrutiny, taking in his two surcoats and naked sabre with obvious amusement before his gaze turned to the watching crowd.

The crowd grew and shifted uneasily. Kotakei could hear some laughing and jeering. She heard catcalls from Norren and some of the Bear Cubs from somewhere in the midst of the crowd and even heard a couple cries of support for Prince Tras from young voices she recognized as those of her little cousins, Elfreida and Lokei.

The Gerisari champion was in an unenviable position. He would look a fool, answering Prince Tras's defiance, no matter what mode of fighting he chose.

"Then I choose to fight with sabres—" Prince Frenses declared, surprising her, and if Prince Tras howled like a wolf, then the Gerisari champion smiled like one, "—on horseback. Know this—I am the flower of Gerisari fighting prowess and a master of horse and blade. If you face me, you will die! I give you one last chance to beg Prince Kreseyn's pardon for your offensive behavior. It adds nothing to my glory to kill a helpless child."

"It's the destiny of flowers to be plucked, whether the flower is a delicate Gerisari blossom like yourself," Prince Tras retorted, "or a thorny Evroza rose."

There was nothing fearful in his response, nor was there anything of a child in it. She felt a shiver run up her spine. The champion would be a fool not to take this challenge seriously.

"Don't be concerned about your glory," Prince Tras added. "Think instead of the pretty tale it will make, how one Doromont prince had no honor left to defend, and another whined about the songs that won't be sung about him!"

Prince Tras deliberately spat and sneered again at the Gerisari champion. "This isn't about glory or pretty songs—this is about justice long overdue! If you champion Prince-Coward Kreseyn, be prepared to die for it—my conscience will rest easy for killing you."

"The state of your conscience is your affair, brat," the Gerisari said, losing his appearance of forbearance. All that showed now was his anger. "It is the state of my honor that concerns me. This duel will end as soon as your blood wets my blade—and that will not take long!"

Kotakei let out the breath she had been holding. She tried to feel relieved—surely he meant he would stop at first blood. That would be the sensible thing, and he would avoid becoming a complete laughingstock for dueling a child.

But there was nothing sensible about the rising hostility between the two, and she doubted this would come to the tidy end Prince Frenses predicted, with Prince Tras spanked and ignominiously sent on his way.

Part of her, the part that could not forget the collusion between Norren and the Gerisari envoy, wished there was some way for the Tras boy to prevail. But this situation reminded her of Norren's description of their mother's death, caught on foot against a monstrous bear. This was just as unequal a match and likely to be as deadly.

"I'm not in a merciful mood," Prince Tras growled, and clearly he knew it was within his rights as challenger to set the stakes for their meeting. "When I take you, I'll kill you. I won't be satisfied until the last of your blood's stained the snow—and then I'll have a look at what runs in the veins of that pathetic excuse for a prince who holds your leash. This won't end until Kreseyn, the Coward of Doromont, is dead!"

"This will end," a harsh, new voice crackled from the crowd behind Kotakei, "when *I* say it does."

Total, stunned silence answered.

Kotakei turned to see Grandmother's slow approach and sank to one knee.

Prince Tras took a knee, not both knees as Ice Bear kith-kin, but the single knee of the closest of kin—or a foreign prince.

Grandmother scowled when he then thrust his sabre down into the stableyard's soft ground in front of him, both hands on the crosspiece of the unadorned, leather-wrapped jegurit hilt, and bowed his head to touch it.

There was something of ritual in it that chilled Kotakei—and she recollected that this was the traditional way a challenger declared his intention to fight to the death, in the way such duels had been fought in Dremnar—and in Trascolm—long before the coming of the Gerisari. It was an old-fashioned gesture, something she might have expected from Eirgei, not a young boy.

That was when the murmuring around her began in earnest.

Kotakei could not believe this was happening, that this confrontation had gone so far with no one to stop it. She looked to where Helgurdda and Eirgei were still held back by Uncle Frekkei and his menney.

Helgurdda had stopped trying to fight free, and she stared at her son in horrified shock.

Eirgei looked furious, but Kotakei was not sure if it was directed at the Gerisari champion or at his grandnephew.

But Grandmother looked unimpressed.

"I will permit this challenge to go forward only because after it, there will be no more of them," Grandmother declared into the sudden silence, as was her right as sovereign.

Though Grandmother was little taller than Prince Tras, the crowd did not tower over her—everyone in the courtyard had rippled down to one knee or two, as their kinship—or foreign rank—required.

"The feuding between my Tras kith and the Evroza—and now the Gerisari—has annoyed and inconvenienced me for the last time. Either this puts an end to it or both of you—my troublesome kith-kin and my unwelcome Gerisari guests—will find yourselves outside the gates in the snow, hunted out of Dremnar by my sons and my menney! This duel will last until first blood or until one of you is at the other's mercy. If it is not resolved by the time the mountains pierce the sun, I will declare the boy the winner of the challenge."

Kotakei and most of those watching glanced up at the sky, gauging the height of the sun against the height of the western Ice Peaks. Dusk came early this late in the year, but there was still an hour or two of light left to fight by.

Grandmother turned to Prince Kreseyn. "The life of an envoy is sacrosanct in Norn Holm, no matter the stink of his empress's reputation in other lands. If the boy defeats your champion, your banishment begins at dawn. You will have a full day's grace to flee Norn Holm before my Ice Bear menney begins its pursuit, but if they hunt you down within Dremnar, they will be at liberty to kill you."

The crowd around Kotakei murmured—that one day's lead might

be lost as soon as the Gerisari party entered the high country, if snow still closed the passes around Norn Holm.

Prince Kreseyn did not trouble to hide his outrage. "I am an envoy! My life is sacrosanct wherever I go! If I am killed, my empress will avenge me with a fury you barbarians have never before seen! She will obliterate Icebear clan—and every clan that tries to stand in her way— until this wretched wasteland will be fit only for carrion birds!"

Kotakei wished she could see Norren, see what effect this unsubtle threat had on his smug scheming.

"Then be sure your champion takes this challenge seriously," Grandmother said, "and if TolDaanyo favors your cause, you will have nothing to fear."

"And when my champion is finished grinding this ill-mannered pup into the mud, what penalty will Eirgei and Helgurdda pay?"

Grandmother turned to consider her kith-kin. "They will lose my favor and be banished from Dremnar under the same conditions. No one will die today for the sake of an old quarrel that should have been settled a over a dozen years ago. My kith will learn not to carry their private disputes into a Crown Court, but they will have to apply that lesson somewhere else. Whatever the outcome of this duel, there will be justice—my justice!—and in Dremnar, no child fights to the death, no matter how willing he is to throw his life away or how foolish his family is to encourage him in it!"

Prince Kreseyn's nostrils flared with contempt, but more of the Ice Bear menney suddenly appeared out of the crowd and surrounded him and his companions.

The old Gerisari envoy looked daggers at Prince Tras, and Prince Tras glared back. No matter that Grandmother had called him a child, there was nothing child-like about him.

Grandmother then turned to regard both of them. "I have had enough of this war of words! I give you half an hour to appear before me south of the Folk village, where the sheep pastures lie. Be there, mounted and properly equipped for a duel. If one of you does not comply, I will accept that as an acknowledgement of defeat. The defeated one will abase himself and apologize to me for disrupting my court, and the penalty will be paid at dawn."

Prince Tras acted as if he had forgotten anyone else besides the Gerisari envoy existed. He still glared at Prince Kreseyn. "After I'm done with your champion, I'll hunt you down no matter where you hide and kill you outright in whatever manner I please. There's no apology possible to excuse the death of my sire except one made in blood—a life for a life!"

Grandmother frowned and tapped her lips with one gnarled finger, but she said nothing more.

Kotakei was relieved when Uncle Frekkei took control of the situation, using his menney as a buffer to separate the Gerisari party from the three Tras, who turned to go back to Tras Tower. The Gerisari party, under heavy Ice Bear escort, withdrew to their guest quarters.

The crowd remained, and she heard the betting begin, making the situation suddenly all too-real to her. Why was Prince Tras so determined to make this a fight to the death? Did he seek his own?

"What odds that the Gerisari champion kills the boy on the first exchange of blows?" she heard someone call out.

"How long will it take for Prince Frenses to prevail, and will the boy still be alive?" came another cry.

"Will Helgurdda's rebellion survive once she and Eirgei are exiled farther away from Trascolm than across the Tor? Who will take my odds?" someone called out.

Dremn loved to gamble and would offer stakes in any contest, though she heard no one wagering on who would win the duel. That they would lay bets against a child's survival and do nothing to appeal to Grandmother to let Eirgei champion his underage grandnephew, or to shift the challenge to a bloodless test of martial skill—or even a game of senet—made Kotakei want to cry for the shame of it.

Not that such an appeal would succeed, now.

She knew Grandmother too well. Any attempt to alter her decision would be curtly dismissed. Once her judgment was rendered, Royenne Errengard would stick to the terms she had set—even if *she* had a change of heart; Grandmother would not overturn her own ruling.

Only Lokei offered odds in Prince Tras's favor as he and Elfreida hurried to her. "How long will it take Prince Wylheim to defeat the Gerisari champion?" Lokei cried and followed that up by bellowing, "How many of our minions will flock to join Eirgei, the Wolf of Milk Dales, thanks to victory going to his best pupil?"

"You are fools," she warned her cousins. "He cannot win."

"TolDaanyo favors him," Elfreida said seriously, the dimples in her cheeks nowhere to be seen as she unfastened the jeweled brooch at the base of her throat and gave it to her brother to wager.

"If Wyl wants to fight, it is a fight he is sure he can win," Lokei said, as he bet on the boy despite the long odds. No one else did. The rest of the crowd bet on the Gerisari champion.

Kotakei rolled her eyes and shook her head. "Unless he has found a way to cheat death, he will not win this duel."

"He *will* win," Lokei declared, not troubling to keep his voice low.

"He'll win an early grave," a Folk woman hissed at them. "This duel will be how TolDaanyo punishes him for pretending to be Folk! The Gerisari champion's going to kill him—whether he wants to or not."

Kotakei was afraid the Folk woman had the right of it.

The Gerisari champion would kill Prince Tras—and make it look accidental.

CHAPTER 27

THE DUEL

"You are a fool, boy," Eirgei growled at Wyl, as they waited for Helgurdda to return from the Menney Tower armory. "A hot-headed fool! You cannot win this fight, not against that legionnaire. I could have told you at a glance, he is no stranger to duels."

"You told me to learn whatever I could from the Young Court, so I did!" Wyl said. "Just a few days ago, before the Gerisari came, I studied the law of the land on justice denied and legal retribution—we are in the right!"

At the time, he'd thought that lesson a shrewd bit of persuasion on Lord Geilorren's part, using that particular text to lure him into making an extra effort to read and transcribe something out of Runic—a practical lesson rather than what Wyl regarded as pointless drills.

"That's how I know I'm the only one of us who can legally pursue vengeance against Prince Kreseyn," he continued. "I'm not afraid—by the law of the land, TolDaanyo favors our cause."

He hoped.

"You should be afraid!" Eirgei retorted. "You would have been hard-pressed to prevail against Prince Kreseyn—but against this legionnaire...."

Eirgei paced the scullery floor, brow furrowed, thinking hard.

Wyl tried to concentrate on inspecting his saddle's billets, looking for wear—or tampering—and wistfully fingered the plain, worn flap.

If only he could believe he'd regained MiPaatet's favor, even temporarily. But he doubted it—if he had, Eirgei would've gone with Helgurdda to help her find a suitable shield for him, giving him a chance to scratch a long-overdue *luck* charm into the leather flap—and reinforce it with blood-magic into a *hex*, in case he was wrong about MiPaatet's forgiveness.

But he'd been under Eirgei's eye from the moment he'd made his challenge, even when he went to fetch Firebrand's tack for inspection. Eirgei hadn't left him alone for one moment.

Eirgei wouldn't regard a spitcrafted charm as a dishonorable cheat: the law of the land didn't forbid the use of magic in a duel. But Eirgei would try to stop him from using it, just because he'd be afraid Wyl would rely on what Eirgei considered superstitious, wishful thinking—and that he'd die in the first exchange of blows because of it.

But it probably didn't matter that Eirgei had been practically breathing down Wyl's neck, preventing him from making a charm. There just hadn't been enough time, not enough to gain the calm concentration needed to make even a simple, spitcrafted *luck* charm and still properly prepare himself for the duel. He'd need more than mere minutes to really *be* calm, not just pretend it.

Still, he wished he'd resorted to blood-magic and scratched a *hex* into the underside of his saddle when he'd had the chance any time in the last six weeks.

"MiPaatet's justice has to prevail," he insisted, as much to himself as to Eirgei.

With or without the aid of a *luck* charm or *hex*, he couldn't regret what he'd done. He'd had no other choice—once more, there was no one else who could avert disaster. Once Helgurdda knew Prince Kreseyn was within her reach, he couldn't trust that madness wouldn't take her and drive her to murder—or that Eirgei wouldn't try to prevent her by murdering Prince Kreseyn first.

If one of them were charged with murder, under the law of the land, Royenne Errengard would be within her rights to have the killer executed and the other banished. Either way, Helgurdda's rebellion would be doomed.

And wasn't this what he'd wanted, a chance to make up for his mistake with the Evroza weather-mage?

This time, he couldn't fail. The consequences were too dire—they'd never make it to Tokar alive, not on the run in winter, hunted by Icebears as well as Evroza assassins.

He could feel his sire's massive bronze troth-ring lying just above his breast bone under his *byrnney*, and with very little effort, he could imagine Hereres calling for the justice he'd never received, in life or death.

Helgurdda had brought herself to give him the troth-ring because she expected him to follow her example and commit himself to avenging Hereres—and what better place to start, than with the man who had kept his sire brutally enslaved and had then persuaded Royenne Sharei to hold the Gerisari embassy to Gerisari law rather than the law of the land?

As an additional insult, after Hereres had been slaughtered, Prince Kreseyn had received a handful of bronze denarreis from Royenne Sharei as payment for his loss of property, denying Helgurdda even a modest blood-price for the loss of her consort. In a final mockery of justice, Royenne Sharei had punished Helgurdda's repeated calls for justice with outlawry.

Now it was up to Wyl to see that his mother and sire finally received their due.

"I can take Prince Frenses on Firebrand," he said, as much to himself as Eirgei.

Eirgei wheeled on him angrily. "Wyl, I am serious! The best war-horse in Trascolm won't make you that Gerisari's equal in strength or reach. Your skills are—maybe!—sufficient to defend yourself, but you know you can't win a battle by fighting defensively."

"I can if I hold out until dusk—Royenne Errengard said so!"

"There are at least two hours before dusk, and your strength will be gone long before that! You've gotten us banished with nowhere left to go except Tokar!"

"Prince Frenses will kill you," Helgurdda said, entering from the courtyard and frowning at the Dremn shield she carried. "I couldn't find a hide shield with even jektrar reinforcement—this one is the best compromise I could find—it's wood bound in jegurit and too heavy for you, Wyl, but you will have to make it work. If he lands a single blow squarely on your *byrnney*, you will do more than just bleed! I know Kreseyn—this Prince Frenses will be under orders to kill you. Kreseyn hated your sire and will be happy to have his champion take your head! Gerisari aren't so tenderhearted about younglings as we or the Dremn are."

"I'm not a youngling," Wyl said sullenly. "I'm the Wolf of Milkdales's best pupil. Prince Frenses won't beat me."

He turned his attention back to his saddle and fingered a worn spot on one stirrup leather where the stirrup would lie when it was pulled down. He was doing his best to focus on what he had to do now, rather than on what he'd be doing soon.

Helgurdda sighed strangely. "If we flee west and cross the Tor on Dremnar's western border, northwest of Moorlands, then head south across the baronies of Smokelands and Rivermist, we can probably make it out of Trascolm and all the way to Tokar. We should be able to raise a menney there on the promise of plundering Crossroads Keep. I'll make the apology—"

At the odd break in her voice, Wyl jerked around, his arms full of Firebrand's unmagical tack.

Helgurdda had been speaking to Eirgei, and she was crying as he had never, ever, seen her do before, emotion surging out of her like blood from a mortal wound.

"—I will not lose all I have left of Hereres! I will not lose my son, my only child, to this folly!"

"What else have I been trained for, if not this?" Wyl demanded, trying to keep up his nerve in the face of their utter lack of confidence in him. Their despair shook him. Despite Eirgei's attempts to discourage him from following in his footsteps, his granduncle had never doubted Wyl's skill before, not even when sending him out alone to spy in Myymor.

"You've been trained, boy," Eirgei said gruffly, "because you came crying to me seven years ago wanting to learn to fight—and when I said I would not teach you, you picked the worst possible rogue to teach you instead. He would have gotten you killed if I hadn't found out and put a stop to it. You were too young, then—and you still are—but I knew you would have asked someone else if I refused you again. You may have become my best pupil, Wyl, but you are not the best fighter I have ever trained. Not yet."

"TolDaanyo will side with me," Wyl said, trying to reassure himself as much as Eirgei. He coughed.

"This is not senet! This is no civilized game played with cones and reeds!" Helgurdda snarled, now angry at him as well as tearful. "This is bronze and blood—and if that Gerisari has his way, it will be your life-blood!"

Their fear infected him, but it was too late now to back down, too late to—what?

Watch Helgurdda swallow the insults of the man who'd owned his sire?

Let Eirgei sacrifice his honor and commit murder, damning himself to Royenne Errengard's justice, and with his execution, saving Helgurdda's life at the cost of all their hopes and this refuge?

There was no action either of his elders could take that wouldn't, at best, end their quest for a Dremn menney and see them doubly outlawed.

Wyl had had no choice—there was no one else who could legally fight for justice thirteen years overdue.

Only the old envoy had been too clever for him, naming a champion to fight in his place when Wyl had been so sure the envoy would take the bait offered, that he'd be eager to take pleasure in personally killing Hereres's son before Helgurdda's eyes.

"I'm not afraid," Wyl repeated, as if it were still true.

"You should be! I have gone too easy on you in training," Eirgei retorted and rubbed his temples. "Your mother is right. We can still keep the rebellion alive from Tokar, maybe even raise an army of mercenaries there. I will make the apology, Niece. There is no need to give Kreseyn the satisfaction of humiliating you."

"There's no need for anyone to apologize," Wyl said, aghast at the idea, at the image of either of them on their knees, humbly begging Prince Kreseyn for anything, least of all forgiveness for seeking justice! "By the law of the land, the only apology the challenged must accept is from the challenger—and I will not apologize!"

Eirgei and Helgurdda exchanged unreadable looks. Eirgei faintly shook his head. Helgurdda turned aside and covered her face with her hands.

"If you're bent on suicide, boy—" Eirgei said abruptly.

Wyl dragged his eyes away from his mother's tears to attend to his granduncle's words.

"—Then there is nothing more to be said. What is done is done. But the only way you can win is if you can draw this Gerisari, this Prince Frenses, into making a foolish mistake, a mistake of overconfidence. But he does not look to be an arrogant fool. You have ensured he will take you seriously."

Eirgei breathed out with frustration. "I am tempted to let you use my merkusar sabre, or even your mother's artisanry blade, but both are too long for you, and you are not strong enough for either to make a difference in this duel—it will only take away your speed and that will be yet another fatal handicap." Eirgei rubbed his face with his palms.

"He must make a mistake—and you cannot. Take the initiative. Control the fight. Make him fight defensively."

Helgurdda hiccupped and wrapped her arms around Wyl in a hug that crushed him against Firebrand's saddle. "And he will only be on the defensive until he learns your strength—or lack of it," she said in his ear. "If Prince Frenses does not make a huge mistake, then your only hope of survival will be Firebrand—use her to keep out of the Gerisari's reach."

She released him then to look out at the sky. She bowed her head, too late to hide a fresh torrent of tears. "And do it for two hours."

✦

It took the whole half hour for the Folk stablehands to get Kotakei and her Young Court remounted on fresh horses for the ride down through the town and out to where the duel was to take place.

Just ahead of them on the road, the Gerisari legionnaire made final adjustments to his panoply as he rode with Prince Kreseyn by his side.

There was no sign of Prince Tras, and Kotakei hoped that meant his elders had done the sensible thing and chosen banishment.

But no, Prince Tras was already at the meeting place, waiting for Prince Frenses and Prince Kreseyn. He was flanked by Helgurdda and Eirgei. His mother was pale, her hair formally unbound—it was her cause he championed. His granduncle looked grim.

Prince Tras was nearly in full panoply—Helgurdda held a shield that was ludicrously overlarge for a boy his size.

He had removed his black Ice Bear kith surcoat, but still wore his rebel one over the *byrnney* Kotakei remembered. He wore no helm, just a twist of white cloth to hold back his gleaming hair—first blood meant the face was a principal target, the one place where blood could be most easily seen.

"Half an hour is not much time to prepare for potentially mortal combat," Tirrengard said, riding beside her. "I know Grandmother decreed it would only be a duel to first blood, but in a fight with edged weapons anything can happen."

"Especially in a duel like this," Kotakei said. "I see not even the Gerisari champion wants to leave open any chance for a freak outcome."

Grandmother arrived, now mounted on her own palfrey—she and her escort of guardsmen loomed above the foot crowd making its way towards them, eager to witness the novelty of a mounted duel. She rode out into the middle of the road, the better to see both duelers. Everyone either went to their knees in the road or bowed low in their saddles.

"The duel will be fought over there, in that field next to the woods, alongside that pasture walled with stone," Grandmother said.

The hay field she pointed to lay open to the sun, and the snow had melted off it. The hemlock forest had been cut well-back from the end of the stone wall on the south side, but it still encroached on the open field on the west side, where snow still lay in drifts under the trees. The trees' lower limbs drooped under their burden of snow and spear-length icicles, posing a potential obstacle for the tall Gerisari. The trees' long afternoon shadows stretched far into the dueling field.

Kotakei saw Helgurdda turn and snarl something at Prince Kreseyn, seemingly oblivious to all else, including Eirgei's grip on her shoulder.

"Oh, I hope Prince Wylheim will come out of this alive!" Tirrengard said.

"So do I," Kotakei said, resigned to being on Prince Tras's side in this. Not only was Prince Kreseyn in secret alliance with her bafflingly treacherous brother, but the envoy had never denied Prince Tras's charges. "Except it will surely take TolDaanyo's intervention—I doubt the legionnaire will settle for mere first blood." She fussed with her riding gloves. "Grandmother did not set a penalty for killing that boy."

Tirrengard shook her head. "Justice must be on Prince Wylheim's side—what could be more repugnant to the Goddess than enslavement? For all that the Gerisari act so superior to us, we simply execute any criminals too terrible to sentence to bondage. If they escape execution, then they are condemned to outlawry and eventually death—but never lifelong servitude. And they call *us* barbarians!"

Kotakei nodded. No matter her personal revulsion for Prince Tras, she had moral as well as personal—even political—reasons for preferring that the victory somehow go to him and not to the Gerisari envoy, Norren's secret ally.

"Let justice be satisfied!" Grandmother shouted the traditional charge to the duelers, "and let TolDaanyo favor the just cause!"

It seemed to Kotakei as if all of Norn Holm had gathered here—most of them safely behind the stone wall—to watch the mismatched challenge. She looked into the crowd and saw it contained the Ice Bear menney, her own Bear Cubs, other clans' guardsmen attendant on various noblewomen from the Crown Court, townspeople, and surely all the Folk from the village.

Helgurdda helped her son settle the last of his panoply. He wore his sabre set for a left shoulder-draw, along with a belt bearing a matched set of long knives crossing horizontally below the small of his back, which provoked some comments from a trio of Ice Bear minions nearby. Helgurdda drew the shield's carry strap over Prince Tras's head so it hung diagonally behind his right shoulder—if he tried to wear it on his arm, Kotakei doubted he could lift it.

Three Ice Bear minions nearby watched and murmured about what they saw—something about left-handedness and fighting sword-to-sword and shield-to-shield.

Thanks to watching her Bear Cubs at their martial training, Kotakei could appreciate the challenge that mismatch might pose to the champion. Prince Tras did not entirely lack advantages—he had to be accustomed to fighting right-handed opponents, while the Gerisari champion likely had not faced many left-handed ones.

Lastly, Prince Tras drew on bronze-reinforced gauntlets long enough to cover the bottom of the bracer on his right forearm—the bracer he had worn on his left arm had somehow come to be in her cousin Lokei's possession. Those gauntlets fit Prince Tras's smaller hands and were reinforced with jegurit mail that glinted gold in places where the brown patina had been scraped away by a blade. He sat easily in the saddle as he drew them on, despite the shield and various sheathed weapons encumbering him—as if fighting a duel were an everyday occurrence for him.

His silver eyes shone uncannily out of his set, grim face, like sunlight reflecting off fractured ice. From the distant expression on his face, he seemed to have no awareness of the swelling mass of spectators. All of his attention was fixed on the Gerisari champion. The intensity of his concentration was palpable.

She heard Lokei yell, "TolDaanyo favors you, Wyl!" from somewhere closer to the dueling field than she was, but Prince Tras gave no sign of having heard.

She swallowed, surprised by how tense she'd become.

"I cannot believe Grandmother has allowed this," Tirrengard said. "Prince Wylheim is too young to risk his life trying to avenge a man who has been dead longer than he has been alive—Eirgei's ruthlessness is legendary, but what of his mother? How can she be so willing to risk her only child, her son by the consort she still mourns? Why does she not stop this?"

If Helgurdda had any fear for her young son, Kotakei couldn't detect it. Helgurdda took one last tug on her son's horse's girth strap. Then she stepped several paces back from Prince Tras and looked him over with an impassive face and the critical eye of a commander—not that of an anxious mother—and nodded.

The two foreign champions rode onto the dueling field.

The Gerisari sat at his ease on a tall, rangy black charger. No surcoat covered the Gerisari's shining, golden jegurit mail, but he wore a flowing, sleeved Gerisari cloak in the Doromont colors of sky-blue bordered by gold. The gold borders glinted like metal, but the fabric still floated like Gerisari silk should. The champion bore a naked jegurit sabre across his saddlebow. He carried no shield, but held a wide shortsword in his gleaming, mail-gauntleted left hand, pommel-up with its blade pointing toward his elbow along the underside of his forearm, its wide guard protecting his fingers. His reins lay untouched over his saddlebow, and his black charger took to the field seemingly of its own volition.

"The Gerisari champion looks princely enough in his panoply," Kotakei said to her cousin, with a grimace.

Prince Tras moved through the crowd towards the open field. His exotic black hair shone blue in the sunlight, and the long hair behind his ears was neatly held by Helgurdda's own gold, flower-shaped hairpin in a princely war-knot at the nape of his neck rather than in his usual braid. He handled his smaller, more fractious warhorse with unconscious poise, his attention entirely given to his opponent and the place where they'd meet.

"I was afraid this duel would be a laughable travesty, but somehow," Kotakei said to Tirrengard, "he does not look like a stripling dressed in his granduncle's panoply: everything—well, except for his shield—but everything else, from his weapons to his horse, is a perfect fit for his stature and build."

"Ah, and in that *byrnney*, Prince Wylheim looks like a dark minion out of one of our clan's ancestral tales. He looks so martial and romantic!" Tirrengard sighed.

Kotakei shook her head. "Name an ancestral tale where the dark minion comes out of a duel alive."

Tirrengard wasn't the only one mesmerized by the Tras boy's appearance. When the crowd parted around him, all eyes followed him as he trailed the Gerisari champion onto the field. By the sound of the comments from beside Kotakei, a pair of oldsters—long-retired from

Ice Bear clan's menney—agreed with Tirrengard, finding something to approve in the youngest generation.

Prince Tras sat calmly, his beautiful face distant and expressionless. His mare gleamed like burnished copper, trembling and rising up on two legs, white foam dripping from her bit. By that, Kotakei suspected Prince Tras was not so calm and confident as he appeared.

The Gerisari looked surprised at Prince Tras's Folk-style panoply and did not trouble to hide his disdain as he led the way out to the center of the field on his snorting black gelding.

"Romantic and traditional his *byrnney* might be," Kotakei pointed out, "but it is no match for modern, Gerisari-forged, jegurit-bronze blades. You have only to see the expressions on the faces of our minions over there by Helgurdda—they know it, too."

Helgurdda's son did not follow his opponent, but rather rode at a walk along the perimeter of the field and the drystone wall, then along the side bounded by forest. He studied the ground and frowned.

She could see how the surface dissolved under his horse's hoofs, leaving a muddy trail behind him. There was no snow left on the open field, but the horses sank fetlock-deep into the dead grass and ooze.

Prince Frenses sat his horse calmly in the middle of the field, like the veteran champion he surely was, and didn't trouble to hide his exasperation as he waited for Prince Tras to finally join him in the center of the field.

If there were formalities to mark the actual start of the duel—as had been observed during the challenge—neither dueler indulged in them.

Without a warning, word, or flourish, Prince Tras began to circle his opponent, testing him with feints. Though the Gerisari tried to trap Prince Tras against the pasture wall, the boy easily maneuvered away without providing his opponent an opening to attack him.

There was a part of the foot crowd not safely behind the pasture wall like Kotakei and her court, and they surged back and forth, heedless of the danger, following the champions as they shifted around the field at a dog-trot.

"That Gerisari acts like he has to feel out Prince Wylheim. I think he is impressed by him," Tirrengard said.

"No," Kotakei said. "I think he wants to give Prince Tras a chance to rethink this duel and lose his nerve."

She heard Norren call out, "When will you fight—or do you plan to keep running away until dusk?"

Lokei yelled, "Plant the flower of Gerisar in the mud!"

CHAPTER 28

IGNOMINIOUS DEFEAT

"Ready for me to kill you, boy?" Prince Frenses grinned down at Wyl.

"Ready for you to try," Wyl retorted, his voice reeking with a disdain he didn't feel—his skin crawled and his stomach churned.

"I suppose it is only fair that I tell you Prince Kreseyn has given me special instructions."

"Surrender now?" he sneered. "Before I mar your pretty face?"

Prince Frenses laughed easily, not the least sign of tension in him. "You will not be allowed to surrender, but I promise to let you keep *your* pretty face when I take your head."

"As if a Gerisari promise is worth more than an Evrozing's spit!"

"You can make this an easy death or a hard one," the Gerisari prince said, unperturbed. "But understand this: you will die. I have my orders. Prince Kreseyn wants to see you scrambling for your life—take my advice and stay away from the wall where your mother stands watching, and you'll live longer."

That rattled Wyl's composure. How could he protect Helgurdda as well as himself? The champion didn't care about the duel. He just meant to use it to get close enough to Helgurdda to kill her! "I won't let you come within a dagger's throw of her!"

"Oh, I will not kill her there, under the Dremn royenne's very nose," the champion laughed. "That is where I will kill *you*—right before Helgurdda's eyes. That ought to bring her out onto the dueling field, do you not agree? Once she attacks me out here, like a mad, mongrel bitch, I can kill her with impunity. It is not your death that matters, you know, it is hers. Prince Kreseyn came for her head, and he always gets what he wants."

"Not this time! Eirgei will see to that—the only head your master will come away with will be yours, once Eirgei finishes with you!"

"That old man? Boy, I am in my prime, and he is long past it, living off the glory of thirty years ago. If he comes on the field, I will take his head, too—in fact, Royenne Ragna will reward me well for it."

"No! This is a duel for justice—TolDaanyo will see to it that I prevail!"

"I knew you were a fool, boy, so perhaps I should not be surprised that you are a superstitious fool, given your barbarously-accented speech. But Folk armor *and* Folk beliefs? Your elders have sent you out to die—the old man probably hopes I will be tired from chasing you around when he tries to kill me for killing that rabid bitch and you, her pitiful, only pup. We came for two heads, but I think it would be a shame to break up your family and leave your head behind."

"I had you figured out, didn't I," Wyl said. "You've already nearly talked me to death. I'm not some pitiful pup! I'm the Wolf of Milkdales's best pupil, and my actions will speak louder than your words!"

✦

With an evil squeal that made Kotakei jerk in surprise, Prince Tras's mare suddenly flagged her coppery tail and exploded into a charge.

"He is insane to attack first!" she exclaimed. Had he heard Norren's goading shout after all?

The Gerisari's horse reared and charged to meet the smaller Tras horse.

A stride away from contact, the little mare slammed to a dead stop in a spray of mud and water, then spun just as the Gerisari's sabre passed through the air where Prince Tras should have been. Instead, the mare's spin presented the shield that was still slung behind Prince Tras's right shoulder by its carry strap.

The sabre blow glanced off it with a loud clang.

"That was not meant for first blood—he tried to kill him!" Kotakei cried indignantly, but a part of her was not surprised. This duel was merely an extension of the Evroza blood-feud, which recognized no boundaries or rules.

"And that wooden shield will not be enough to turn many blows delivered at full strength," Tirrengard said worriedly. "Like that blow would have been, if Prince Wylheim's horse had not swung sideways."

But Prince Tras's spinning move was not strictly defensive. His curved, narrow-bladed sabre was very like Prince Frenses's—just half the width of the straight swords Kotakei's own people favored. As his mare spun back around, full circle, Prince Tras reached out under the Gerisari prince's extended arm and stabbed.

It seemed a risky tactic and revealed a telling handicap she saw no way for Prince Tras to overcome. Though his sabre got past Prince Frenses's guard, it was chillingly obvious that his arm was not strong enough to punch the sabre's point through the links of golden mail protecting the Gerisari's armpit.

He did not seem interested in first blood, either.

Prince Tras reined-back his mare until several strides separated him from his enemy.

The Gerisari champion's horse slid to a stop and started to turn back towards him.

Prince Tras's mare sprang across the gap and shouldered into the taller horse. As the mare rammed into the black gelding, Prince Tras again swooped in under the Gerisari's counter-sword's defensive parry. He struck using all the power of his arm, this time with all the force of his charging horse behind it.

It was a dangerous move. His charge placed his entire body within reach of the Gerisari's weapons, though he landed his blow first.

Prince Frenses immediately seized his opportunity, yet once more, his powerful return stroke missed, clanging against Prince Tras's shield as the boy ducked down flat against his mare's neck so that his shield's boss was the only thing struck.

The powerful, but glancing blow swept Prince Frenses's arm to full extension.

That confirmed Kotakei's suspicion that this duel would not be decided by drawing token first blood.

"Someone has to stop the duel—the Gerisari champion has broken Grandmother's conditions!" Tirrengard cried, looking about her for that *someone*.

"Cousin!" Kotakei snapped. "Look at how those two are so intent on each other. The first to break that focus and obey a call to stand down will die on the other's sword."

The Gerisari horse leaped sideways, taking Prince Frenses again out of Prince Tras's reach without taking Prince Tras out of Prince Frenses's, forcing the boy to duck low under the sweep of the Gerisari champion's blade.

The sabre missed cleanly, and Prince Tras pressed the Doromont prince at the black gelding's right flank. It placed him sabre to sabre with the Gerisari champion, but he crowded too close for Prince Frenses's sabre to touch him, even when he twisted to swing back-wards.

Prince Tras struck from behind the champion's shoulder, repeatedly jabbing his sabre upward under the champion's arm. In that position, he obviously knew he held an advantage because he stuck there like a burr as the Gerisari tried to turn away from him, unable to bring his sabre so close behind himself or put Prince Tras in front of him.

Prince Tras stabbed and stabbed, seeking a chink in the Gerisari's mail with swift, sure strokes. His jegurit blade always struck hard, visi-bly jarring the boy's whole body, yet nothing came of his effort; he was simply not strong enough to penetrate the champion's mail.

The Gerisari made his horse pivot and turn as Prince Tras drew back to strike once more, putting himself a comfortable sabre-length out of reach.

There had been no true sabre-to-sabre exchanges, no real parries. Prince Tras was wise to avoid them—clearly he was not strong enough to match blows with his adversary.

Instead, the battle became a chaotic whirlwind of streaming horse-hair.

The minions of both Gerisar and Trascolm were famous for their horsemanship. If the Gerisari champion had chosen mounted combat for the duel because he reckoned his horsemanship superior, in young Prince Tras, he had met his match.

It even seemed to Kotakei that Prince Tras enjoyed a slight ad-vantage—though each sabreer rode and fought like his mount was a part of him, Prince Tras's mare was more agile, and like her master, surprisingly quick. The Gerisari's gelding was remarkably nimble for its size, but no match for the mare as Prince Tras continued to seek an opening while his mount easily outran the longer-striding, larger horse burdened by a big man in mail.

Bits of horn flew from Prince Tras's *byrnney* as he took ever-more outrageous risks to exploit even the most fleeting apparent vulnerabil-ity.

Nor was his mare above participating in the battle on his behalf.

She closed with the gelding and struck out with a forefoot to its neck, followed by her head snaking out with teeth bared to tear at its flared nostril.

The gelding shied away from her ferocity, and the Gerisari split only air when he chopped down at Prince Tras's head. After that, the gelding took care to keep itself at a distance, just out of reach of the mare—and therefore keeping Prince Frenses out of reach of Prince Tras's sabre—while leaving Prince Tras still within the sweep of the Gerisari's long arm and longer sabre.

Then the two sabreers galloped side-by-side across the field, shield-side against shield-side.

It pitted Prince Tras's battered shield against the Gerisari's counter-sword. Each shifted sideways—the Gerisari used his counter-sword to push against the shield, trying to jam Prince Tras against the stone wall. With more bits of horn flying from his *byrnney*, Prince Tras managed to slip away before he could be trapped.

The Gerisari whirled after him and employed his counter-sword not only as a fast, light shield, but also as a weapon. He reached out with the long hilt's pommel protruding from his fist, and tried to use it and his greater mass to bash Prince Tras out of his saddle.

When Prince Tras ducked flush with the mare's neck, the champion missed him entirely. The Gerisari circled to try again, using the blade's point to stab down over the rim of the wooden shield.

Prince Tras again dodged the blow and kept trying to circle to get sabre-to-sabre with an advantage.

Prince Frenses jabbed his counter-sword backward, attempting to skewer Prince Tras with the length of blade that protruded past his elbow.

Prince Tras was too close to take that blow on his shield. He slid sideways away from the counter-sword, hooking his shield over his saddle as a counterbalance as he left his saddle.

The Gerisari missed cleanly.

Prince Tras quickly recovered to slide back upright in his saddle again. His own answering sabre thrust struck its target, this time under the Doromont prince's left arm, but it did not penetrate the mail.

"I cannot believe they are fighting so ferociously!" Tirrengard exclaimed, dismayed.

"Neither of them will be able to keep this up until dusk," Kotakei agreed.

"This has to be an awkward situation for the Gerisari champion," one of the minions behind them said, "facing a left-handed fighter, no matter how small. I have heard that in the Gerisari legions, left-handed fighters are made to fight with their right hands."

"You cannot wonder that the Evroza would copy their style of fighting. There is a reason why the Gerisari trade empire is so powerful, despite their troubles with the Teboan empire," another remarked.

"But the rest of Trascolm and all of Dremnar fight as individuals," the first man said. "I think a Dremn champion would find it easier to deal with Prince Wylheim's left-handed fighting style than the Gerisari is."

The other man snorted a laugh. "That is only one problem for the Gerisari. He's bigger, stronger, and clearly more experienced, while the only advantage the Tras boy has is being a small, very mobile target! I should have wagered more on the boy's death."

The mare suddenly half-reared, spun around, and cut behind the Gerisari horse's tail. The Doromont prince's mount propped and lashed out with its hind feet, but missed both horse and rider, and nearly unseated Prince Frenses.

Again and again, Prince Tras's darting attacks penetrated Prince Frenses's defenses. He struck each blow with all his might, yet merely left the Gerisari's jegurit mail with dull scratches under either arm. Despite those repeated failures, he continued to initiate the attacks, and Prince Frenses continued to fend them off.

Prince Tras carried out several more exhausting, useless attacks.

Eirgei was right, as usual. The Gerisari's mail might as well be merkusar for all the success Wyl had had in trying to penetrate it. The arcane throb he felt whenever he got close to Prince Frenses made him wonder if the mail's strength had been reinforced with artisanry—quite an arcane feat—or if one of the Gerisari's two blades would never grow dull.

He hoped the artisanry had been wasted on a blade—the Gerisari champion wouldn't need magic to penetrate Wyl's armor. But he was coming to suspect artisanry was why the Gerisari's mail still foiled him. He'd jabbed at least a dozen thrusts at the same link of mail with his jegurit sabre, and it still held.

Worse, the Gerisari had begun laughing at him as every strike failed, rattling his concentration as he tired. The champion now disdained to do more than make a pretense of returning his blows and disengaging.

Not even jegurit mail should have held after Wyl's repeated attacks on a single link with his jegurit sabre—the first attacks Eirgei had ever taught him had been how to ruin good mail. It puzzled him that the link of mail he targeted hadn't brightened under the brutal burnishing, but rather had darkened, making it an increasingly difficult target.

For a moment, after yet another unsuccessful hit on that stubborn link, he thought he saw red, but the link remained intact, and his sabre withdrew unblooded.

On his next strike, he saw the flash of red again—and on his blade's return, he saw deep nicks in the tip of his jegurit sabre—and all became clear.

The mail wasn't jegurit—it was merkusar—it *really was* merkusar! The impenetrable armor had been covered with a thin layer of paint. *That* was why the scratches had dulled the mail's golden sheen rather than brightening it—and why a single link of mail had held so stubbornly against his blows.

He wished he had Eirgei's merkusar sabre, or that his own sabre had an ever-sharp artisanry edge like his mother's—maybe that would have been sufficient to damage a merkusar link. But ordinary jegurit-bronze, no matter how well-crafted and forged, was no match for merkusar.

This was the real reason why Prince Frenses toyed with him, purposefully baiting him into those futile strikes—he knew he was safe from an ordinary, jegurit-bronze blade.

The Gerisari champion knew Wyl's attacks were hopeless.

Kotakei bit her lip as Prince Tras once more put himself on Prince Frenses's right side, pitting him sabre-to-sabre again with his opponent. He now raced beside the Gerisari champion, gobs of mud flying from the horses' hoofs.

He yanked on his shield's strap to shift it toward his left side—Kotakei could see that would allow him to attack while still giving himself a measure of protection.

This time, it was the Gerisari who pivoted his horse around, swinging himself away from Prince Tras's sabre without giving ground.

Prince Tras's sabre darted out, and for the first time, it was aimed not at Prince Frenses's armpit, but at his face.

"The boy grows tired," a man behind Kotakei pointed out. "He has decided to content himself with drawing first blood—that is the only way I see for him to end the duel in his favor."

"Fruitless to continue trying to land a mortal blow," another agreed. "First blood is the only way so weak a fighter can have even the remotest hope of winning."

Prince Frenses leaned far back in his saddle, saving his eyes, and the boy's slash missed, scraping against the mail at the base of the Gerisari's throat.

Prince Frenses returned the slash, but instead of leaning back, the boy countered it, even standing in his stirrups and leaning forward to throw his weight into the parry.

Bronze rang on bronze as Prince Frenses leaned forward, too.

For a long moment, the two blades were in a bind.

In that instant, Prince Tras twisted and surprised Prince Frenses by striking for the first time with a long back-knife in his right hand.

That had to have been the reason he had shifted his shield to the left!

Prince Tras's back-knife streaked upward, yet another strike for Prince Frenses's eyes.

Prince Frenses twisted far around and used his counter-sword, clubbing at the boy's gauntleted wrist with its pommel.

Prince Tras kept his grip on his knife, but in the distraction of the counterattack, the Gerisari prince's sabre escaped the clinch.

It came back at the boy as a powerful slash.

Prince Tras hunched and deflected the blow with the shield on his shoulder.

Then, he stood in his stirrups, trying to whip his long knife into the Gerisari's face while the champion's sabre rebounded away from his shield.

The champion leaned far back again, out of Prince Tras's shorter reach.

Instead of over-extending with either sabre or back-knife, Prince Tras's foot lashed out, striking the champion in the side at the hip with a force she could both see and hear. Prince Tras nearly toppled from his own saddle from the force of his kick, but Prince Frenses did not so much as shift on his horse.

Both of them remained mounted and disengaged completely.

"Despite making such a showing," one of the Ice Bear minions near Kotakei said, "I would not want to be in Prince Wylheim's place. He may be fast and agile and focused—a credit to his granduncle—but in order to strike the Doromont prince, he takes outrageous risks to get past the greater reach of the champion's sabre."

"And all for nothing," agreed another. "The boy simply lacks the strength to contend with the Gerisari champion on equal terms."

Helgurdda's son was still alive for only one reason, Kotakei suddenly understood.

The stronger fighter was not fighting.

For the first time, she became aware that the two duelers snarled words at each other, words unintelligible over the din of the fighting.

"Well, Prince Frenses has not made any mistakes—and by refusing to fight all-out against the boy, it is clear to everyone with the wits to see it that he just plays with the Tras boy," a minion she couldn't see said.

And Prince Frenses was making sure Prince Tras knew it—now that she knew to look for it, she could see his lips moving, remaining on the defensive while trying—with some success—to goad Prince Tras into taking ever-more dangerous risks.

Yet, if the Gerisari held back, it was not to avoid maiming or killing a boy. More than once, Prince Tras was forced to flatten over his mare's neck to duck low enough to avoid a cut he could not turn with his blade or take on his battered, notched shield.

She watched as Prince Tras used any number of clever ploys to successfully come up inside Prince Frenses's superior reach, but always without reward.

Prince Frenses gradually maneuvered Prince Tras back towards the wall along the road. The foot spectators shifted back, away from the circling, shifting, and charging horses.

Prince Tras kept glancing over his shoulder, and Kotakei saw he was looking at something—or someone.

The Gerisari champion determinedly pushed Prince Tras towards the place where Helgurdda stood with Grandmother and Uncle Frekkei, and the boy struggled to slip away, to go back toward the trees.

Both sabreers were visibly tired, Prince Tras more so than the Gerisari—from the moment they had begun, he had steadily carried the fight to the champion, keeping him on the defensive. Prince Tras's horse looked as agile as ever, despite being nearly white with lathered sweat, but Prince Tras himself was gray-faced and panting.

What had started as amused forbearance on the champion's part was now clearly gone—by his actions, Prince Frenses was taking his challenger as seriously any arrogant, overconfident boy could have wished.

There was a flurry of blows.

Those delivered by Prince Frenses again glanced off Prince Tras's shield.

Then the momentum of the battle suddenly shifted.

Prince Frenses flipped the hilt of his counter-sword in his left hand, reversed it, and struck out with it as a second sword, seizing the initiative.

Now it was Prince Tras who was on the defensive, struggling to defend his vastly inferior *byrnney*, desperately trying to prevent Prince Frenses from landing a direct hit on it with either sword or sabre. Prince Tras even resorted to boys' riding tricks like rolling out of the saddle to hide on the other side of his horse, risking the saddle slipping as he survived yet another unequal exchange of blows.

The Gerisari champion was impressive to watch, Kotakei silently conceded.

The combat had gone on far longer than anyone could have expected, long enough that the Gerisari's own tactics now were merely to try to land a solid blow that the Folk armor couldn't withstand.

The only question remaining in her mind about this duel was how badly Prince Tras would be defeated—and if he would survive it. She could hear more wagering on that coming from behind her.

The boy's exhaustion was impossible to hide—he did not try to get in a sly stab now whenever Prince Frenses's own slowing reactions left brief openings in his defenses. All Prince Tras's energy was spent in maneuvering his horse, trying to keep himself from receiving the full force of the powerful strokes his older opponent now rained down on him with both hands. If even one powerful slash or stab made a direct hit on his horn-scaled *byrnney*, he would surely die.

By the grim intensity on Prince Frenses's face, he had long since forgotten he fought a boy and was bent only on destroying his opponent.

"I do not see any way for Prince Wylheim to win this duel," Tirrengard said, in a hushed voice. "It is obvious that he will not last many more exchanges, let alone until dusk."

Kotakei regretfully agreed. "The way I see it, the best outcome now would be if the Gerisari knocks him out of the saddle, leaving him stunned and unable to rise to face him. That would put the boy at his mercy, meeting Grandmother's terms for victory, but leaving him alive and virtually unharmed."

Kotakei stared out into the field.

Helgurdda's son slumped in the saddle. His moves lagged too much to fully block the Gerisari's blades now. His *byrnney* suffered for it, shedding bits of horn with every glancing blow as he twisted and tried to shield himself, evading the direct, full force of each blow, if not the actual hit.

"Prince Wylheim does not look ready to cry for quarter," Tirrengard said.

"Do you think Prince Frenses will give it to him?" Kotakei asked, bitterly.

Norren would win, and more than merely wagers.

The end was near. Everyone knew it—Kotakei could feel the tension around her.

Then, Prince Tras made a weak, awkward swing with his sabre, and when it was parried by the Gerisari's sabre, it twisted in his hand and flew out of his grasp.

For several heartbeats, Prince Tras was virtually disarmed, his sabre dangling from the leather keeper looped around his wrist.

Then he flipped the hilt back into his palm and backed his mare, trying to escape Prince Frenses's follow-up attack.

Prince Frenses pressed his attack harder and faster.

✦

Wyl trembled with exhaustion.

More than ever, he wished he'd had a chance to make a *hex* or even just a spitcrafted *luck* charm.

Eirgei was right. He was no match for the Gerisari in strength or reach, and was merely his equal in horsemanship. The longer the combat went on, the more Prince Frenses's greater endurance and years of experience made a difference.

Firebrand was the only reason he'd stayed alive as long as he had— fighting a duel against a grown man on a Gerisari horse was familiar to her from all the mounted training bouts he'd fought over the years against Eirgei.

But soon Firebrand's training wouldn't be enough—before much longer, Wyl wouldn't be able to raise his sabre to attack or defend himself—and that was when Prince Frenses would go for the kill.

He had yet to trick the champion into an error of confidence as Eirgei had advised him.

There had been mistakes made, but he had been the one who'd made them. When Prince Frenses had briefly disarmed him, he'd been lucky to survive it—the man still amused himself with Wyl, cat to his fading mouse.

The only choice he had left was whether to die fighting now, or wait until he could no longer stay in the saddle when he tried to block the champion's still-powerful blows. Once out of the saddle and on the ground, he'd be slaughtered.

✦

Near Kotakei, one of the pair of graying veteran minions avidly watching the duel commented, "I do not know whether to be relieved or sorry when the Gerisari champion kills the boy, and the Tras are banished."

"Even then," his companion replied, "it will be the boy's performance everyone will talk about, not the Gerisari's. The champion will be humiliated."

"Much good that will do a dead boy."

With Prince Tras dead, the other Tras banished, and Norren's secret ally exonerated, the reality of Kotakei's own situation suddenly turned frightening. What would happen if the Gerisari won? If the rebel Tras were banished, the Gerisari envoy could hardly be driven from Norn Holm and Dremnar. Prince-Envoy Kreseyn would be free to remain in Norn Holm, free to assist Norren with his schemes until the passes were clear enough for safe travel, which might not be until spring!

She had seen enough of Prince Kreseyn's character today to dread what Norren might learn from him.

The Gerisari champion pushed his horse against Prince Tras's mare, and this time, Kotakei could see it was Prince Tras who was handicapped—he was too close to dodge away and too tired to shift his shield high enough to fend off the Gerisari's powerful, overhead blow.

There was something of desperation in the way Prince Tras parried with his sabre, deflecting the blow. Even had he been fresh, his strength could never have been the equal of an adult's—and now his defensive moves were growing weaker and weaker.

Prince Frenses pushed his horse against the mare, against her right side—the side Prince Tras's heavy shield no longer adequately protected—and swept a high, backhanded blow meant to behead.

The boy could not raise his shield to counter it, so he did the only thing he could—he whirled left and intercepted the blow with his own sabre in a feeble parry.

The parry faltered, but it redirected the blow.

Prince Frenses had put so much force behind it that when his arm was deflected backwards at full extension, he nearly slashed his own horse's rump.

Once again, the force of the parry twisted the sabre out of Prince Tras's hand, only this time, it flew free.

The sabre cartwheeled halfway to the trees at the back of the trampled hay field.

Prince Frenses's horse swung its haunches away from its rider's blow and turned into the mare, and as it did, the Gerisari champion recklessly reversed his stroke and swept his arm forward in an attempt to behead Prince Tras from behind.

Somehow the boy sensed his danger. He flattened himself impossibly low over his mare's neck and twisted enough that the shield covered him.

The champion's stroke skidded off the shield's dented boss, and he was forced to rein sharply to the left or let his missed slash sink into his own horse's neck instead.

Kotakei could see that Prince Tras had slipped completely off his horse's back and now clung to its side with one foot in a stirrup, his shield hooked over the saddle's cantle, and one hand clutching the flying mane as he sent the mare racing after his sabre, now lying in the churned-up mud across the field.

As the mare ran, he righted himself back into the saddle and wrestled with his heavy, battered shield, shifting it to the right, freeing his left hand to reach down for the sabre.

Helgurdda's son was not conceding the fight, even disarmed. He was fighting like an outlaw with no hope for quarter or mercy. No matter that Grandmother had decreed the duel was *not* to be a fight to the death, he clearly did not believe it.

After seeing that last blow from Prince Frenses, still with all his power behind it and meant to behead, Kotakei doubted anyone watching believed it, either.

Prince Frenses brought his horse back around to the right and swung his sabre again, then realized Prince Tras was no longer beside him. He looked about, then caught sight of the boy, already halfway across the field, heading to where his sabre had fallen. The legionnaire let out an angry roar and gave chase.

Prince Tras reached his fallen sabre. He halted his mare and stretched down for it, clinging to the side of his horse to take it from the ground rather than try to dismount and risk being caught afoot when Prince Frenses caught up with him.

The heavy shield shifted suddenly, sliding back to his left side, and pitched him awkwardly into the mud.

The mare shied half-heartedly and moved a couple steps, dragging her rider with his foot caught in a stirrup, then halted, head low and sides heaving.

The duel was over.

Prince Tras turned his head, and his eyes widened at the sight of Prince Frenses lumbering towards him on his own exhausted horse. The boy flung his other leg up and thrashed with his free foot, trying to kick the other one loose. As he did, the wicked war spur strapped to his boot raked the mare's ribs.

His mare squealed and bolted into the trees, dragging Prince Tras bouncing and skidding through the mud alongside her like a broken doll.

The mare's sudden burst of energy took the Gerisari by surprise. For several long moments, Prince Frenses stared in clear disbelief, then he turned his mount, and spurred hard in pursuit.

But his horse was nearly blown, and though it galloped laboriously after Prince Tras, Prince Frenses remained more than a dozen strides behind the flying mare still dragging her rider.

Kotakei wondered if the Gerisari recognized, as she did, that the fight was over. When he caught up with Prince Tras, he would definitely be at his mercy. And when that happened, what did he intend to do about it?

Did he intend to humiliate and spank a boy—or finish an opponent who had humiliated *him?*

The Gerisari checked his horse's headlong charge into the trees. Kotakei heard him swear as branch-loads of snow cascaded down onto his head and neck. He was forced to slow and duck branches while the panicked mare he chased crashed heedlessly under low tree limbs and through icicles, dumping snow, breaking brush and shrubs, and disappearing among the hemlocks.

The Gerisari followed, and for too many of Kotakei's long, bated breaths, nothing could be seen.

Then, the mare came galloping back out of the trees, no longer dragging her rider, clods of muddy snow flying up from her hoofs.

Through the trees, Kotakei could now see Prince Frenses bent over his horse's neck, not empty-handed to lift an injured boy, but with his sabre poised to thrust as he wove between the tall hemlock trees. If the champion had any qualms about fighting a boy—or killing one—he had forgotten them, no matter Grandmother's instructions to the contrary.

Strain as she might, Kotakei could not see where Prince Tras had fallen, though his mare's trail out of the woods was plain in the snow lingering in the shade of the dense hemlocks.

Prince Frenses leaned down, ducking tree limbs, back-tracking the mare's trail.

There was a brown lump at the base of a large hemlock, barely visible from where she watched.

The Gerisari saw it, too, and sent his horse trotting deeper into the trees towards it, leaning forward with his sabre ready to thrust.

A branch-load of snow fell from overhead and struck the Gerisari's back.

Somehow, the snow became Prince Tras in his snow-and-mud-caked *byrnney*.

He came down with knives in both hands and his right arm around the Gerisari's neck. His left knife-hand swept down over his victim's shoulder.

Prince Frenses bowed under the unexpected impact on his head and neck, and convulsively brought up his arm and the long pommel of his counter-sword to protect his throat.

Prince Tras's knee smashed into the back of the champion's elbow, sending his counter-sword flying from his hand.

The champion lost his balance and fell out of the saddle. He hit the ground heavily, the boy riding him down and trapping the man's right arm and sabre under his heavy, mailed body.

Prince Tras, who had twisted to avoid the Gerisari coming down on *him*, recovered from the jolt of hitting the ground with astonishing speed. He scrambled up onto his knees in the trampled snow.

The champion twisted and started to lunge up at him, his now-empty left hand streaking for Prince Tras's throat.

The boy's left hand, held low, swept around from behind his back. He chopped upward under the champion's jaw, leading with the pommel of his back-knife.

The Gerisari's clawing fingers hooked the *byrnney's* collar.

The back-knife's pommel smashed against the point of the champion's chin from below.

Kotakei heard Prince Frenses's teeth snap together, audible even across the field. The Gerisari's body spasmed, then went limp.

On his knees straddling Prince Frenses, Prince Tras lost his balance when his opponent collapsed, but caught himself, then dropped a knife to wrench the champion's head back by his dark hair, panting and baring his teeth savagely as he exposed the Gerisari champion's throat above the high, leather-lined collar of his mail.

CHAPTER 29

EIRGEI'S MASTER

Wyl stared down at the unconscious Gerisari lying helpless and at his mercy. He remembered vividly the expression of brutal delight on Prince Frenses's face when his sabre had flown across the field, leaving him virtually disarmed and defenseless.

There'd been killing force behind the champion's follow-up swing: the champion had intended to part Wyl's head from his neck.

Since their duel had become a mortal combat by the champion's own actions, ruthless good sense told Wyl to kill Prince Frenses now—which was nothing more than the champion deserved.

Yet, never during their battle had he envisioned executing a helpless enemy in cold blood—if he did, would he ever escape the memory of it?

What difference could one more memory possibly make?

He shuddered and coughed.

By the terms of Royenne Errengard's sanction, the duel was over. According to her decree, if he let Prince Frenses live, all the Gerisari would be banished from Dremnar, never to be seen again.

Not even in his dreams, covered in blood and reeking of death.

He hadn't received an offer of mercy from Prince Frenses and—after the disaster he had caused with his own misplaced mercy towards the weather-mage—there was still the matter of the oath he'd sworn on his honor to never again show mercy to an enemy.

But if he kept that oath, Royenne Errengard would outlaw him.

Being banished and hunted was not the same as being abandoned in a safe haven for his own good, which meant his family would flee with him. He'd lose everything he'd hoped to gain by challenging Prince Kreseyn—they'd still end up dead or in Tokar.

How could he cling to what was left of his honor and keep his oath when it would put his family at risk?

If mercy for the cold-blooded Gerisari champion was another of his soft-hearted mistakes, then so be it. His word—the oath he'd sworn the day Lanney died—was not worth the price of keeping it.

End this duel on Royenne Errengard's terms, and their position in Nornholm would be more secure than ever. Ultimately, sparing this life was the right choice for his family.

But he was equally sure this was another enemy he'd regret letting live. He coughed.

He took the dead weight of the champion's head by the hair, tilted it back, and with his practiced right hand, sliced into the champion's right cheek, drawing blood with each loop and line.

Now, with both first blood and his enemy helpless in his hands, he had more than satisfied the terms Royenne Errengard had decreed for winning the duel.

✦

Kotakei gasped, her eyes widening as the boy's right hand moved, the golden edge of the brown blade flashing in the dying rays of the sun.

"Hold!" bellowed Uncle Frekkei, faster than Kotakei to realize Prince Tras's intention—the death-blow he had promised in his challenge.

The boy's knife jerked back, leaving the champion's right cheek scratched and bloody.

"He is at your mercy," Uncle shouted, "and in Dremnar, we do not allow children to get blood on their hands! You have won, boy."

Prince Tras blinked, breathing hard where he knelt. He stared at her uncle.

Uncle Frekkei started running towards him.

Prince Tras staggered up and off the Gerisari, the direction of his hostility shifting, as if Uncle were a new threat. Uncle checked and halted, but the boy lost none of his wariness.

Did he expect the unconscious champion to spring to his feet and continue the fight? Or that Uncle Frekkei would draw a weapon?

Or did the boy intend to defy Uncle and kill the downed Gerisari?

Silence hung over the challenge field.

As kith-kin to Ice Bear clan, Prince Tras should have counted as the crowd favorite over the Gerisari. Yet, though he had accomplished the impossible, there were only a few sporadic cheers from the watching crowd. Most of the members of the Young Court, who should have been his partisans, stayed silent.

Kotakei was among the silent ones, dazed with relief that Prince-Envoy Kreseyn would be sent away from Norn Holm—away from her brother. She was too stunned by the impossible outcome of a duel that had been going so badly to feel anything other than shock.

How many of the other spectators were also speechless simply because they, too, were surprised by the abrupt, unexpected reversal that ended the duel?

She looked around.

Mostly, she saw mute astonishment. Only on a few faces did she see anger—and those were the faces of Norren's favorite young minions. Rather than cheering Prince Tras—Ice Bear kith-kin—for an impossible victory over a Gerisari champion, Norren's friends openly showed disgust and hatred.

But Prince Tras was not entirely without acclaim.

"Two moons shy of thirteen years old, and he has already defeated a Gerisari champion in his first duel!" Kotakei heard the Wolf of Milk Dales crow.

From the man Uncle Frekkei had described to her as close-mouthed and taciturn to a fault, this was an unusual display of emotion.

It had to mean Eirgei had not been so confident as he had pretended—like everyone else, he, too, had expected his grandnephew—his *twelve-year-old* grandnephew!—to die.

She searched out Helgurdda's face in the crowd, but saw her hair first—she had her bowed face in her hands, her shoulders bobbing.

Helgurdda's son finally realized that Uncle Frekkei would not come nearer, that the duel was over. He looked dazed as he wiped his knife on the back of his leg, smearing it with mud rather than cleaning it. There was plenty of mud on his face and in a liberal coating over the rest of him. He began coughing.

He wobbled backwards from the unconscious Gerisari champion—filthy, exhausted, but unscathed. He limped a little way farther into the trees to stoop and pick up his notched and battered shield. He propped it against a tree trunk. It dripped with mud.

So that was what had drawn Prince Frenses under Prince Tras's perch and into his ambush!

Kotakei took a sharp breath. Helgurdda's son had not been dragged—he'd used his oversized shield as a sled. The unexpected end had not come by accident.

Prince Tras leaned over and wiped mud from his face with the twist of once-white handkerchief that had been holding his hair out of his eyes. Freed, the dripping wet curtain of hair blocked her view of his face, but she could see by the way his shoulders heaved that he still panted hard—he leaned heavily against the tree as he turned his back to the crowd and bent over, hands on knees, to catch his breath.

Eirgei gloated with his delight in the outcome of the duel. "He may not look like much now, *heh*, but give him three more years, and a man's strength and reach—*heh, heh!* He is by far the best I have ever trained. There is no adult in the world I could make his equal in just seven years!"

Eirgei looked at Norren and the openly-disgruntled young minions with him and glowered evilly at them. "The day will come when Prince Wylheim will not be at a disadvantage like he was today, and he will not need to resort to tricks to defeat his opponent—best you decide now whether you want to be his friend or his enemy."

Then, Eirgei vaulted the pasture wall with the ease of a young man and strode through the woods to his grandnephew.

"In another three years, when he comes of age," Eirgei called loudly over his shoulder as he tousled the boy's wet, mud-streaked hair, "I will have met my master in the arts of war."

Looking at Prince Tras, bent-over, hands on his knees, dripping mud and barely able to stand, that boast seemed laughable.

But this was the Wolf of Milk Dales, who—as Uncle Raldorrei had complained privately—rarely praised those he taught. Eirgei, she understood now, was not a man given to idle boasts.

He tightened his fingers in his grandnephew's sopping hair and lightly shook him until the boy looked up and focused on him.

"By then, he should be able to make a blade hit point-first when he throws it away!" But he grinned and gave Prince Tras's head a rub, followed by a pat on his back.

"Prince Frenses should die for trying to kill my son—and Prince Kreseyn should, too!" Helgurdda cried out. "He tried to contrive my son's death the same way he had Hereres killed—again, with another's hand on the blade. Ragna wanted two heads—I say send the Gerisari delegation back with exactly that—the heads of Prince Kreseyn and Prince Frenses, the would-be child-murderers!"

"I have set the forfeits for this duel," Grandmother said. "An Ice Bear keeps her word. If the Gerisari linger in Dremnar, my menney will be within their rights to take their heads. But the duel is over. TolDaanyo has answered and rendered His judgment. There is nothing more to be said. The only further satisfaction I can offer you, Helgurdda, is to watch Prince Kreseyn and his party flee Norn Holm in the morning."

"We leave now!" declared Prince-Envoy Kreseyn. "My empress will hear of this!"

"Very well," said Grandmother, not the least perturbed. "The sooner, the better."

That caught Eirgei's attention.

He must have seen something in his niece's face, even from across the field, because he turned away from his grandnephew and stared back at her. "Helgurdda! Wait! Do not risk throwing away what the boy has won!"

Eirgei said something to Prince Tras, who was still bent over, tousled his hair once more, then turned and jogged back to Helgurdda, who looked at Prince Kreseyn with such hatred, Kotakei didn't wonder at Eirgei's hurry.

One of the Gerisari noblemen directed four slaves to collect Prince Frenses, who still lay unconscious in the snow. The slaves used the fallen champion's sleeved cloak as a crude litter to take him from the field.

All around Kotakei, Ice Bears murmured, both impressed and disturbed.

Ordinarily, MiPaatet was an aloof goddess, sparing in Her attention to human appeals. Her Brother, TolDaanyo, was not one whose attention men courted. Kotakei wondered if anyone else saw the unequal duel's outcome as an omen.

Why had the Horned Hunter felt compelled to take a hand in Prince Tras's impossible victory—what dire future did the Goddess foresee to warrant such open interest in a stripling boy?

Because if TolDaanyo had acted to spare the boy's life now, Kotakei feared it was only to sacrifice it in the future.

✦

Wyl stayed braced against the tree, panting—not to get his breath, but to keep his gorge down. Winning the duel against the Gerisari champion felt little different from receiving one of Eirgei's armed thrashings, except that he was still conscious—and the Gerisari truly had intended to kill him, which Eirgei never would do.

His last desperate ploy—that insane impulse to throw away his sabre and deal with the champion the way he would an assassin—had come to him just as he'd become incapable of holding onto his sabre any longer. He'd slipped the leather keeper and had taken the next opportunity to fling it away. He hadn't dared give Prince Frenses time to think about how his sabre had come free in the first place. If he hadn't succeeded in tricking the Gerisari champion into thinking the loss of his sabre—and the subsequent chain of misfortunes—had all been accidental, the champion would have suspected a trick.

Without utter surprise—and armed only with his knives—Wyl would have been slain.

For a moment, as he'd fallen onto his shield and jabbed his war spur into Firebrand's unsuspecting side to send her bolting into the woods, he'd been tempted to take refuge in a tree and stay there until sunset, refusing to fight.

But how much more humiliating an ending to his first duel could there have been, short of getting himself killed?

And the outcome would still have been banishment—a shameful refusal to fight wouldn't have satisfied the terms for victory. He would have had to live with the knowledge that he'd failed once again, that he'd become responsible for yet another exile—and a worse one than coming to Dremnar had turned out to be.

He'd imagined himself facing Eirgei, knowing he'd discredited him by reneging on his champion's duty to fight, that he'd rightly be deemed a coward, as well—a public slap in the face to his honor-bound granduncle. Just the thought of doing that to him had made Wyl desperate.

There was no honor in using his ambush skills against an enemy, but there were no rules forbidding any tactics in a duel, save the royenne's declaration that this was supposed to have been a fight to first blood—which Prince Frenses had violated in the first exchange of blows.

Pitting his stealth against Prince Frenses's strength by setting an ambush for him had seemed as wretched a tactic as everything else he'd tried. There was only one explanation for its success—TolDaanyo had troubled to take a hand in the outcome of the duel. How else could he still be alive without so much as a *luck* charm to aid him? One cough would have betrayed his ambush in the trees, ruining his fragile hope.

He felt like a fraud, hearing Eirgei credit him with defeating the Gerisari champion rather than giving that credit to TolDaanyo.

He couldn't pretend that what lay between him and Prince Kreseyn was over. Prince Kreseyn was not the kind of man who'd accept being thwarted in achieving his goal—the heads of Wyl's mother and grand-uncle. By publicly humiliating both Prince Kreseyn and his champion, Wyl had made two deadly and implacable enemies.

He could hear Eirgei still praising him.

He wanted to bask in the warmth of it, but quickly came to his senses—this victory had won *him* nothing. He had learned more than Runic and the law of the land from the Young Court. He'd also learned something of royal politics.

It didn't matter if Eirgei's claim were true, that another three years of training could somehow make him Eirgei's master in the arts of war.

Wyl wasn't destined to be Helgurdda's viceroye, not her warleader, not even the warlord of her menney, either.

He was certain of it now.

As Helgurdda's only child, his destiny was to become a treaty con-sort—but unlike Helgurdda's future Icebear consort, who would seal an alliance between kith-kin, Wyl would be Helgurdda's stake in des-perate political gambles during the treacherous early years of her reign, a sacrifice to forestall open war with her enemies until she had allies in Trascolm who were stronger than her enemies.

It meant that once he was sixteen, he would face betrothal after be-trothal to undermine enemy alliances within Trascolm. By the time Helgurdda needed someone as Eirgei's successor, he'd either be un-worthy—his skills long-squandered by disuse—or he'd be long-dead at the hands of the hostile kin of his last betrothed enemy.

He felt sick.

He'd spend the rest of what would likely be a short life in nomadic exile, always surrounded by people who hated Helgurdda—and him.

But until she took another consort and bore an heir to establish her own dynasty—a girl-child who would need Wyl as her future Prince-Viceroye—those treacherously false alliances forged through him would be all Helgurdda would have to keep her hold over Trascolm's great noble clans.

He shuddered, coughed, and felt a helpless giddiness.

He coughed hard and lost his battle with the inevitable. He puked until his stomach felt like it was inside out. He shook so badly with exhaustion and nerves, he could barely stand.

Only after he spit and straightened did he notice how quiet it was.

The dueling field was empty.

His audience had likely grown bored while he remained in the deep shadows and trees, so they had gone to watch the banishment of the Gerisari.

He was alone, and relief flooded through him.

His family was safe. Despite the presence of the Gerisari legionnaires watching the duel, he'd seen Helgurdda and Eirgei surrounded by watchful Icebear minions. He'd also seen Lokei make himself and Firebrand safe from Martei and a mob of scowling young minions by cleverly leading the mare into the protective presence of Viceroye Frekkei.

Wyl's frantic heart stopped pounding in his ears, and now he could breathe a little easier, though he still couldn't stop coughing.

Snow crunched behind him.

He wasn't alone in the woods.

He spun around, and his wrenched knee tried again to buckle under him. He staggered and put his back to the trunk of the big hemlock.

But it was only Lord Geilorren.

His tutor leaned against a tree, a short but unthreatening distance away. There was a look of sympathetic concern on his face under the neatly-trimmed, blond-and-gray-streaked beard.

"So how fares the champion of the moment, now that the moment has passed and the crowd has moved on to other thrills, like jeering the Gerisar envoy out of Norn Holm?"

Wyl stiffened, then realized the sarcasm wasn't meant for him.

"The Gerisari came for two heads." His voice came out weak and rasping. He paused to steady it. "So Royenne Errengard ought to send two back—Prince Kreseyn's and his champion's. This blood-feud will never be over now, not so long as Prince Kreseyn lives."

"I know sending Prince Kreseyn back to Milk Dales is not much of a penalty," his tutor commiserated.

Wyl glared at him and his unwanted sympathy, and coughed again.

"A humiliating exit from Norn Holm," Lord Geilorren said, "might be a novel and degrading experience for such a proud prince, but I suspect it will not satisfy your mother as a fitting vengeance for your sire."

Wyl silently agreed.

"You can hardly stay on your feet," Lord Geilorren said. "Let me help you. It is a long walk back to Norn Holm in the state you're in."

Was it so obvious he was done in? That alarmed him.

It didn't help that Lord Geilorren was right—with Firebrand well on her way back to Nornholm under royal escort, it would be a very long, uphill walk with a twisted knee.

Wyl eyed his tutor warily, struggling to think clearly through the thickening fog of exhaustion.

There were only three people left in the world he could trust— Eirgei, Helgurdda, and Lokei.

Why did Lord Geilorren keep trying to befriend a Tras? What could possibly attract the tutor to him like this? He had to want something of Wyl, either a word in Helgurdda's ear or—

"The whole world is not bent on your destruction, Prince Wylheim. You need to learn who your friends are and learn to trust them enough to take their help when they offer it. I am not just your tutor," Lord Geilorren said, as he approached. "I count myself as one of your friends. You can trust me."

Wyl instinctively pulled a boot-knife.

That was a mistake—its trembling made it clear he was too exhausted to pose a threat to anyone, even so poor a foe as the tutor.

He coughed and felt woozy.

It didn't help that Lord Geilorren was right. Wyl did need allies in the Young Court very badly.

The tutor walked towards him, wearing an expression of benign concern until he saw the knife in Wyl's hand and wisely halted his advance.

"You have a courageous heart, but you do not seem to realize it is still inside a boy's body. If you will let me, I can carry you back to Norn Holm, and we will get there in time to see the Gerisari envoy sent on his way."

Wyl shuddered at the offer, but those words made him think— though Lord Geilorren was no minion, if he truly was an enemy and meant him harm, the tutor could have taken him while he had been bent over with his back turned, helplessly emptying his stomach.

He was so tired.

It tempted him, what Lord Geilorren offered.

What would it be like to give himself over to someone like the tutor, to rely on someone else to keep him safe?

Lord Geilorren was a scholar, not a warrior. He had a peaceful existence.

What wouldn't Wyl give for that?

Yet trusting Lord Geilorren would mean deliberately violating habits built up over the course of his short, uncertain lifetime—and his instincts screamed, *no!*

"No, I can walk," Wyl said at last, trying to hide his reluctance, but the words came out in a wistful voice.

He coughed and covered the weakness with a glare at his tutor. He hoped he could walk the distance to Nornholm. He'd look a fool, falling flat on his face in the road. "I just need to catch my breath."

And look for his sabre.

Maybe then he'd feel safer—and how pathetic was that? Just how big a weapon would he need to feel safe in the presence of an old Dremn lord—one unarmed, unarmored, and with no stake in the Evroza blood-feud?

Wyl was a hypocrite for accusing Prince Kreseyn of cowardice.

In the weeks he'd known Lord Geilorren, the tutor had shown him only goodwill and concern. But, no matter that the tutor was no minion and was past his prime, Lord Geilorren was still bigger and stronger than Wyl. Pathetic or not, Wyl couldn't help but be afraid of him. In the state he was in now, dead on his feet, Lord Geilorren wouldn't need minion training to take him and make him even deader.

If Wyl could tell the truth—and he couldn't—there was very little in the world that didn't frighten him. All his life he'd been afraid. Just something unusual, out of place, or unexpected was enough to reduce him to feeling like a terrified youngling.

Wyl was the coward, not the crafty Gerisari envoy.

And that wasn't going to change today.

He sheathed his knife, pushed off the trunk of the tree, and started limping towards where he'd thrown his sabre. He was unsteady, but still on his feet—and a careful distance from his tutor.

Halfway there, a coughing fit took him. His head swam and felt peculiarly light. His heart pounded erratically. By the time he reached his sabre, he couldn't seem to catch his breath.

He bent to pick up his sabre and somehow ended up on his knees.

He shakily ran the blade between his fingers, stripping it of muck, then wiped it on his sleeve and reached behind his shoulder to sheathe it.

It took him several focused attempts before he succeeded.

He took a determined breath, cut short by a cough, and started rising to his feet.

When he did, blackness rose with him, as abruptly as wine sloshing from a cup.

EPILOGUE

Wyl struggled out of the darkness and became aware that he was caught up in a firm grip.

He writhed to escape it, but it was a feeble effort—he was too exhausted to free himself.

He was still on the dueling field—half the hay field, now churned into a sea of mud, stretched out in front of him.

The aged, bearded face of the Young Court's royal tutor looked down on him. His blood-shot blue eyes were calm, as if he had hauled pupils off dueling fields many times in the past.

Wyl's memory rushed back. With an inward wince, he recalled how Lord Geilorren had come upon him after the duel, heroically puking his guts out. He remembered the tutor making some cutting remarks about the crowd rushing back to Nornholm, eager to watch the Gerisari be banished.

Save for the tutor, no one else had stayed behind.

He remembered more words, not what the tutor had said, but how he'd said them—like the kind of nonsense Wyl would have used to calm and reassure a badly-spooked horse. How odd that the tutor's words had had a similar effect on him.

No one had ever spoken to him like that before. No one, except this tutor, who Wyl had known in Dremnar's Young Court for all of two moons and had never had reason to trust.

Or distrust—except that Wyl distrusted everyone.

He coughed and tried to twist free again.

"It is all right," Lord Geilorren said softly in his aristocrat's diction, his lips next to Wyl's ear. He kept repeating it in a soothing voice while supporting Wyl under his knees and shoulders. The tutor didn't seem to care about the mud coating what remained of Wyl's *byrnney*.

Nor did he seem to care that, with his hands full holding Wyl, he was totally defenseless.

Wyl's fingertips grazed the boot cuff at his thigh, and under it, the knife hidden there. He yanked it out and whipped it up under the tutor's chin.

"Put me down!"

His voice came out wavering and breathless. He felt dizzy. The hard-fought duel had utterly drained him.

"There is no need to fight me," Lord Geilorren said in his soothing voice as he walked on, careful of his footing in the mud—and making no attempt to comply with Wyl's demand. "You should know by now that you have nothing to fear from me. We are alone here and if I had meant you any harm, I have had the time and opportunity to do it while you were unconscious and helpless."

Wyl's knife hand sagged.

That was true—and contrary to everything in his experience back in Trascolm.

He remembered going back onto the field to retrieve his sabre after the duel. He remembered struggling to sheath it and nothing more.

Obviously, he'd collapsed, and as Lord Geilorren had said, he'd lain defenseless in the mud. Despite the fact that Wyl was Tras and his people were the traditional enemies of the Dremn, Lord Geilorren was clearly not an enemy. Not cutting a Tras's throat while he had the chance was sufficient to show a Dremn's goodwill. Nor did the tutor bear the least resemblance to the motherless rogues whose company Wyl had grown up among.

"But perhaps you would prefer go to back to Tras Tower rather than watch the Gerisari envoy be banished?" Lord Geilorren asked, as if there were no knife at his throat. "I know you well enough to doubt you want anyone to see you like this." Lord Geilorren shifted his arm under Wyl's shoulders and gently smoothed Wyl's hair out of one eye and away from his muddy cheek.

The gesture was uncannily like one of Wyl's mother's rare caresses.

It took Wyl off-guard, and he flinched into the tutor's chest. He wasn't accustomed to allowing others within an arm's reach of him, let alone allowing someone to wrap their arms around him.

Lord Geilorren did not take his recoil amiss. "I know a postern gate in the lower bailey that will take us to the High Gate and back into the palace without attracting attention. I promise I will get you safely home.”

Home? That crumbling tower Royenne Errengard had given his family as living quarters?

Wyl’s eyes fluttered shut, and he forced them back open. He slumped down into his tutor’s arms, letting his knife hand rest harmlessly on what remained of the scales covering his belly.

He involuntarily shuddered and coughed, and tried to catch his breath. He couldn’t remember when he’d ever been carried like this. He’d made it a point of honor to ensure none of the rebels treated him like a baby.

He was the Wolf of Milkdales’s best pupil, the rebels’ best and most daring spy. He was a veteran of a disastrous, magic-warped battle and had survived the massacre that had cost him an old friend and forced his family to flee into exile. He’d more than proven he didn’t need childish coddling.

But his family wasn’t here at the dueling field. He and the royal tutor were alone. What did he have to prove to Lord Geilorren?

Nothing.

How odd that felt, not having a point to prove to someone.

What if he *could* just lay back and let himself be held in an adult’s stronger arms? How would it feel to feel safe?

Maybe it would feel like when Prince Lokei had wanted to be his shield-brother—but without the guilt of being judged unworthy by TolDaanyo and having to keep it secret from Lokei that their sacred brotherhood had been rejected.

It might feel like how he felt, now.

Whatever he was feeling, it wasn’t fear.

He’d never experienced anything like this before, not even in the company of his mother or granduncle.

How was it possible to feel this way when Lord Geilorren was Dremn and nothing more to Wyl than the Young Court’s royal tutor?

Could he trust that feeling of safety?

There was a certain reckless thrill to it—trusting the tutor would require a new and different sort of bravery.

He smiled tentatively up at Lord Geilorren, and *willed* himself to trust him, the same way he had with Lokei, when Lokei had proposed they become shield-brothers.

He *wanted* to feel safe and dared slide his knife back into his boot.

Something came undone inside him, unraveling along with his

strength.

He was just too tired to be afraid of an old Dremn lord.

His breath sighed out, and he collapsed inward with it. His head lolled back against Lord Geilorren's arm. His eyes drooped shut and refused to open.

He felt boneless and distant from his own body.

He gave up and plunged back into darkness.

✦✦✦

The story continues in
Legend of the Spider-Prince #2
ROGUE

ABOUT MARGO ANDER

I loved fairy tales as a child, but could never get enough of them until I learned to read for myself. I spent my formative years with my nose in a book or playing dungeon master for my sisters long before there were actual games requiring one. Our Barbies fought Klingons, conquered the galaxy—and always had room on their spaceship for horses.

I am a horsewoman, an archer, a fencer, a former military officer, and a member of the Society for Creative Anachronism—all useful skills and experiences for a fantasy novelist. I am currently holding down a day job in Mississippi, USA, where I live with my husband and two daughters, and am presently down to one horse, one cat, and one dog—and way too many books.

Visit me on the web at **www.margoander.com**

My Facebook page is at **www.facebook.com/AuthorMargoAnder**

I have a blog, **margoander.wordpress.com**, where I review books I like by other indie authors.

I have another blog, **marguerot.wordpress.com**, where I blog about writing.